HOW TO BE A STUPID GIRL IN LAGOS

BIBIKE
1996

THERE WERE MANY easy ways to be a stupid girl in Lagos. We were not stupid girls. We were bright with borrowed wisdom. We never paid full fare to drivers of yellow city cabs before we arrived at the final stop. We did not wear any kind of visible jewelry walking around busy streets like Balogun. When we went to Tejuosho market and a stranger shouted, "Hey. Fine girl. Stop, see your money for ground," we never stopped to look.

When many of the ECOMOG soldiers were returning from peacekeeping in Liberia, flush with UN dollars, we were still protected prepubescent girls, yet we knew to avoid the one we called Uncle Timo, the one who gave all the little girls Mills & Boon paperbacks wrapped in old newspapers.

MY TWIN SISTER and I were almost stupid girls once, and this is how it begins, with Ariyike and me lost on our way home from school. I am holding on to her out of habit; she is pulling away, walking up to and talking to every stranger we meet, asking over and over, "Uncle, please, where can we get a bus to Fadeyi?"

We are walking home from secondary school. Today is the first time we have been allowed to come home by ourselves. Our younger brothers, Andrew and Peter, attend Holy Child Academy, the primary school that shares a fence with the military cemetery where all the agbalumo trees grow. They don't need to be picked up. The church bus drops them off every day at half past four.

I am thinking of school and today's government studies class and *gerrymandering*, how I like the way that word sounds, well calculated and important, like *meandering*, only with purpose. Everything is better with purpose.

I am also thinking of Father, who likes to say our government studies teacher is verbose:

"Mr. Agbo fancies himself a university lecturer, he is always going off tangent, completely missing the point."

And of Mother, who likes to say: "We pay a lot of money for you girls to go to that school." Or: "You girls should listen to Mr. Agbo. He is a brilliant man."

We have walked for almost twenty minutes, and now we make our first stop, to buy roast plantains and groundnuts from the woman who is selling them under a 7 Up canopy. She is amused when we ask if she has any cold drinks for sale.

"Can you see any fridge here?" she asks. "Will I keep the drinks in my brassiere?" We are waiting for our plantains when Ariyike stops a stranger on a motorcycle. He is a tall man wearing combat shorts and a black T-shirt that says GOT MILK? in bold white print. They take a few steps together, her listening, him pointing. When she is done, she comes back under the canopy. I clench my right fist and put it under her chin.

"Here, take this microphone. Announce to all the world that we are two girls who don't know the way home," I say.

The woman selling plantains laughs. She says Ariyike is being stupid, walking up to strange men. She tells us that just last week three girls got kidnapped in Mushin. They were found dismembered in a roadside heap.

Ariyike looks at me like she is about to say something but changes her mind.

"So, what did that motorcycle man say?" I ask.

"He says we should come with him, he'd take us home," she says.

"Really?" I ask.

"No. He said keep walking straight down, the buses are waiting under the pedestrian bridge," she says.

Our plantains are soon ready. The woman gives us extra groundnuts.

"Pray for me o," she says. "I want fine ibeji twins like you two."

Ariyike assures her that we will pray every day. She is the friendly one. The *friendlier* one. My sister talks to strangers because she likes people, she likes to hear their stories, she likes to make people feel comfortable, welcome. I do not think that I am mean, I just let her be the nice and welcoming one. We work better that way.

I learned when I was a little girl that people always lie. I am not sure everyone means to lie. It is just that they have in their hearts ideas of who they should be, and they are trying to convince themselves that they are who they insist on being. It is tiring. I learn a lot more about people, about who they are and what they care about, by observing in quiet.

There are many buses and hundreds of people waiting at the bus stop. There are many young men hanging at the sides of the buses shouting their destinations—"Maryland," "CMS," "Obalende." There is no bus going to Fadeyi. We stand next to a row of older women with woven baskets and trays in front of them selling all types of things, fruits, vegetables, tiny toys.

I watch a young woman haggle with almost every seller. Finally, she buys smoked fish, okra, tomatoes, habaneros, and red bell peppers. She will go home to her tiny, sufficient apartment with one soot-stained kerosene stove in a corner and make food just enough for herself and eat less than half of it and fall asleep on her bed and be glad to be alone and unbothered.

The first bus going to Fadeyi is a danfo, a 1988 Volkswagen bus. Its wooden, cushionless seats are filled with people before we get a chance to go in. We are part of the small crowd of people who fail to make it in. We murmur one to another, we hope more buses come quickly. Two curly-haired girls come to stand next to the group. They hold out cracked plastic bowls and begin singing in Yoruba.

"Brother, God bless you.

Sister, God bless you.

Give me money and I pray for you.

A setup,

A trap,

May God prevent its occurrence."

The woman who bought her dinner now drops five naira in one bowl, then five naira in the other. I plan to give them money, but they do not come close to us, and no one else gives them money, so they move away, singing to other adults.

There is a group of kids from the public school talking in a corner. The beggar children attempt to avoid them as they go past. One of the kids tugs at the wrapper of the older girl as she walks past him. She does not notice. After walking a couple of steps, her wrapper unravels. It's then I see that she isn't wearing any underwear. She drops her bowl and wraps the cloth back around herself in a quick second. She walks on without looking back. I make Ariyike turn around to look but it is too late for her to see anything. The public school kids laugh and laugh. Stupid children laughing out loud with their torn rubber sandals and dirty shirts and books in black shopping bags and yellowing teeth and rusty fake gold earrings and matted braids. Stupid children.

When we were in primary school at St. Catherine's, there

was another set of identical twins. They were short, bow-legged boys who got into fights with everyone. We hated that because they were also Yoruba twins, we had the same traditional names. Ariyike and I therefore became "Girl Taiwo" and "Girl Kehinde." The most annoying people were the ones who called me "Girl Kenny." Kenny is a totally different name, it is not short for Kehinde no matter how hard Yoruba people try. These public school kids make me think of Boy Kehinde and Boy Taiwo. I wonder what they are like now. Still stupid, I bet.

Once we got to secondary school, we insisted on being called by our middle names, and even though Ariyike and Bibike have the exact same meaning and everywhere we go people still ask, "Who is Kehinde, who is Taiwo?" I like our new names.

Ariyike was born first, so she is Taiwo. Our grandmother, Father's mother, says that Kehinde is the elder twin because Orisa ibeji, the god of twin births, is Kehinde. He was the one who sent his younger one to be born first to confirm by loud crying that the world was fit for him.

Father's mother believes all these things with her whole heart. Mother says her stories are tales of demons. She says if we listen to her too closely, we invite evil beings into our destinies and we will end up poor and alone.

I think everything is a story unless you live in it. I like the idea of a god who knows what it's like to be a twin. To have no memory of ever being alone. To be happy you are different from your twin but also to be sad about it. To know almost everything about your twin and sometimes want to

stop knowing so much. To know you were born with everything you will ever need for love but to be afraid that this
one person is too important. Or that this person will never
be enough. To pray to a god like that, all I would ever have
to say is Help me.

There are many more people at the bus stop now. We are
all standing so close to one another. Ariyike and I have our
backpacks turned to the front of us, protecting them like little babies. We have eaten all our plantains and groundnuts.
She tells me she is going to look for drinking water to buy,
but just as she is about to leave, a molue bus arrives, its rusty
croaking like an old man's cough. I call out her name but
there are already seven people between us. I push through
and get in the bus, hoping I can save her a seat; the bus is
already filled up with many standing people, holding on to
the metal poles. I find a seat in the back of the bus and shout
for my sister as loud as I can. She finds me and sits on my
thighs. The public school kids are sitting close to us, three
on a single seat. I have no idea how they plan to sit like that
for so long.

Across from me is a lady I did not see at the bus stop. I
wonder how long she has been on the bus. She looks like she
just got out of university, or maybe she still is in university.
She is wearing jeans, and only university girls wear jeans
outside the house. Her shoulder-length auburn braids with
burnt ends are tucked behind her ears, kajal eyeliner spilling
under her eyes, cream foundation drying in uneven patches,
and she is talking to a beautiful bearded man with sad brown
eyes seated next to her. He is wearing brown corduroy pants

and a black-and-white checkered shirt. He has a black brief-case and a white lab coat. Their voices are raised loud enough to hear each other over the noise of cars honking through traffic, of bus tires grinding to abrupt stops on cold concrete and the voices of others conversing around them.

"Did I tell you my horse got stolen?" she asks.

"No."

"Yeah, it did. I still ride, though, whenever I visit the village."

"I have only ridden that one time." He laughs and shakes his head as though this is something no one else can believe.

"Remember that day my mother came to your house?" she says after a short pause.

This time his reply is hesitant, quiet. "Yeah," he says.

"When she came to drag me away? How she was saying, I have warned you about this boy, you can't be here, you have to leave."

She is laughing as she says it. And it's a laugh I know, one most women I know have. Mother has it, too. Laughter you use when nothing is funny, but you are lighthearted and resilient and eager to show it.

"Have you seen anyone else lately? Anita? Banke? Emmanuel?" she asks with leftover laughter in her mouth.

The conversation on his side is no longer loud or discernible. There is no way to be sure why he now mumbles. Maybe it's been a long day and he is tired and wants to ride the bus in peace. Maybe he has never liked her or maybe she just reminded him of the hurts he has also covered up with laughter, and muscles, and gorgeous facial hair.

"Banke is married, she has like six kids or something," she says.

"Really," he exclaims. "Banke. Married! I definitely did not see that coming."

There is more laughter, more exclaiming, more naming names, more asking what are they up to now.

"So, are you seeing anyone?" she asks, deliberate, flippant.

"No, I am just focusing on leaving this stupid country. Ties just make things difficult," he says.

If she says anything after this, I do not hear it. The bus conductor announces the next stop and several people shuffle and respond. When the doors open, she grabs the black briefcase and lab coat that I had assumed were his, he has a doctor's face. She gets out of the bus, shouting, Excuse me, excuse me, at all the people in her way. One of the public school kids now sits where she was sitting. There is quiet and there is noise.

She will walk to her apartment, where she lives with her older sister and her sister's husband, and wonder if the universe was helped by her vulnerability, if she will get any closer to living in her dreams because she laid bare her desires to a man like that. She will wish for a second encounter with him. One where the best decisions of her years are on display. Like he walks into the hospital where she is a pharmacist or the church where she sings solos on Sundays. Or they meet in the parking lot of a supermarket the weekend after salaries are paid so he can witness all the imported foreign things she can now afford to buy on her own.

I hope she finds someone new.

I wish her love without this shared lament of people who remain in a failing city when others who are not stupid have left. I wish her love that makes her less ashamed, love that is ignorant of the specifics of her failed dreams and unaware of the details of her lost youth. I hope she finds a loving gaze that will not see how her face has fallen and where her arms have swollen or how her family has lost all they took great pride in.

WE GOT HOME a little after five p.m. that day, bubbling with the ignorant excitement of young children who'd completed their first adult task. It did not occur to us to wonder why our schedules had changed or whether this was a permanent kind of change. We did not yet have the kind of familiarity with misfortune that cultivated a sense of foreboding. We could only assume that Father was too busy to come pick us up and Mother was beginning to understand that we were grown enough to navigate Lagos streets on our own.

WE ATE OUR dinner in a hurry and, while we ate, Andrew and Peter watched cartoons and argued with each other in the living room. As soon as we were done with dinner, Father and Mother called us into their room for a talk. I was absolute in my certainty that they were about to announce we were expecting a new sibling.

This was the first time we had been allowed in our parents' room. It was, until this day, an odd place, with regular fluorescent lamps for the daytime and a tiny blue bulb turned on at night. The lights were like secret codes for access—white light meant it was okay to knock, to ask to be let in; the night-light meant to keep away.

But on this day—the day things were beginning to fall apart, the day we were too stupid to notice—we swelled with the confident pride of new initiates. The room smelled like Cussons baby powder and Mother's favorite perfume, Elizabeth Arden's Red Door.

I sat on the rug in the center of the room. It was yellow, brown, blue, and black, stripe-patterned and soft. It made me think of Joseph and his coat of many colors. My sister lay on the brown leather armchair opposite their bed, folding herself in it like a bush baby, one foot swinging down the side of the chair.

Mother and Father sat next to each other on the king-size bed.

It was Mother who spoke first:

"You are big girls now, so behave yourselves. Something really bad has happened to this family and—"

"We will be all right, though. This is nothing for you both to worry about," Father interrupted.

"I am not telling them to worry," Mother said. "We agreed to tell them, so we can handle this as a family."

"A few weeks ago, your mother got into some trouble at work and she was let go," Father said. "None of it is her fault. We will get through this, I promise you girls."

Mother was with the Ministry of Petroleum for ten years. In the last two years, she worked as one of the three personal assistants to the minister of petroleum. Her boss, the Honorable Minister Dakuku, had been fired by the military president, and a new minister of petroleum was appointed in his place. It was this new minister who, rather unexpectedly, considering that civil servants existed, under the national laws and in the valid assumptions of many, in a labor-protected space where the worst thing that could happen was a transfer to a remote village, fired all those staff he considered close associates of the former minister.

The ex-minister's falling-out with the military president was over approval given to an American company for oil drilling in the Niger Delta. It was not until the agreements were signed and money was paid that the president became aware that the Americans were in fact an Israeli company incorporated in the United States. The military president was a great friend of Yasser Arafat, apparently, and an avid defender of his politics. He wanted nothing to do with the American company once these facts were revealed.

Father explained these facts to us in short, straight-to-the-point sentences.

"The ex-minister is in hiding. Some say he is in America."

"Many people were also let go. It was not only your mother."

As much as he tried, he did not help me understand how anything that happened was our mother's fault. Until that day I'd thought her job as an assistant was limited to serving the minister and his guests tea and smelling nice as she did this. Even though I was confused, I was not surprised. In Lagos bad things happened all the time.

My sister's dangling foot tapped the leg of the armchair over and over, a little loud, but no one told her to stop doing that. Father reached over and patted me on the center of my head, ta, ta, ta, harmonizing with the tidi, tidi, tidi my sister was making with her foot against the wooden chair leg. He patted me on the head several times, until it started to hurt. I started trying to think of something to say, something reassuring, sensing that Father had planned a more confident rendering of this tale, but he now sat quiet and absentminded, forgetting the words he planned to say or why he was convinced they would help.

I MAKE A pillow fort for Andrew and Peter under our dining table. I have modified a simple nighttime ritual. Every night, I sit on a stool in the boys' room. I tell my younger brothers stories before bed.

Today, Mother and Father are locked in their room yelling at each other again. So we sit in our dining room fort, talking and laughing. The dining room is right next to our parents' bedroom, there is only a thin wall between us, we are close enough to know when the first punch lands, close enough to scream if it continues. Peter sits next to me, his elbows are on the floor, his round face is nestled in the curve of both palms. His hair smells like Blue Band margarine. Sometimes after eating, he wipes his hands on the living room curtains, other times he wipes them on his hair when he thinks no one is looking. His face is oily, shining like a lamp in a dark room.

"Can you tell us a story?" he asks me. "You do not have to make it up. It can be one of Father's or Mother's stories, but nothing with a tortoise or a monkey in it."

"Should it have a song?" I ask.

"Yes," my brothers answer at the same time.

"But only if you really want to," Andrew adds quickly. He is the older brother, he does not want to appear too interested in childish stories.

"Way back before the rebellion, when animals and people could talk to and understand one another, a woman buys two hens on her way home from the market. They cost only half a penny each and so she buys them even though she really does not need any more hens. The woman soon gets tired of carrying her basket on her head and holding hens in both hands, so she throws one of them away, right into the forest, and thinks nothing of it. And a few months later when she is walking down the same road after a market day, she sees her hen walking along the path. Only this time, the hen has several chicks walking in a straight line behind her."

"How did she know it was hers?" Peter asks.

"Because, back then when you bought poultry, you cut a tiny piece off the edge of your wrapper and tied it around the legs of your hen. The rope was still there," I reply.

"People still do that today," Andrew says.

"The woman is excited," I say. "She chases after the hen, but the hen refuses to be caught. It scratches her a couple of times and then runs to the palace of the king.

"The hen gets to talk to the king, but decides to sing instead. She tells her story, the hen does, with singing. How the woman bought her for half a penny and threw her in the forest and how the lord of the forest fed her with corn husks and water from a well. The hen says she is now a mother of many children: her first son is called the Warrior Prevails, the second is called Finger of the Truth—"

"How many children did she have?" Andrew asks.

"What did the king decide?" Peter asks.

"The song says they were six or three," I reply. "I don't really know, *meta* and *mefa* sound the same, especially in a song."

We are singing the story's song, "Iya Elediye eyen ye kuye," whispering the words now because Mother is crying in the bedroom. Loud crying and hiccupping. And Father is shouting at her to stop.

"The king said the woman could take the first chick with her, and the hen was free to go back to the forest with the rest of her children."

"And that is how it ends?" says Andrew. "You should have just told us the one about the tortoise and the hyena."

Peter laughs because Andrew said *hyena*, he is laughing and laughing, and then Andrew and I also start laughing. Peter's giggle is laughter at its best, light and loud, floating around then resting on you, making you woozy and hopeful. Andrew already has a man's laugh.

Something breaks in our parents' room. We stop laughing to listen. Everything is quiet, Mother is no longer crying, and Father is saying nothing. Then Father comes out of the room. We watch his feet walk past the dining table, along the hallway, and down the stairs. We listen to the sounds he makes in the kitchen. A clank of metal, a swish, water splashing on a face. We watch him walk back to the room. There is a tumbler filled with cold water in his hand.

When he opens the door to their room, we hear Mother whisper, "Thank you, dear."

It is hot here in our fort. Peter is sitting close to me with his knees folded to his chin. He is sweating, his forehead covered in shiny droplets of sweat.

"Tell us about that time you saw them burn a robber in Fashoro," Andrew says to me. "Or about that time armed robbers came to the beer parlor and shot a man's ear off."

"I was going to buy pepper in Fashoro when I saw a boy running with a small generator on his head. Suddenly, one woman started running after him shouting, *Ole ole ole*, another woman came out of her shop and joined the other woman shouting. Then I saw the tailor who made your Easter suits come out of his shop. He started running after the boy. It was now that the stupid boy decided to drop the generator and run as fast as he could. The tailor was almost losing him, so he bent down and picked a giant stone and threw it at the boy. It landed right in the middle of his back. The boy fell down flat. Plenty of people now surrounded him. Iya Togo even came and said, Is this not Gbenga, the one who stole my pot of beans while it was still on the fire?"

"Was it Brother Gbenga?" Peter asks.

"No jare, did we not still see Brother Gbenga yesterday?" Andrew replies.

I am listening for sounds from our parents' room, but I hear nothing now.

"Then many other people came and started accusing the boy of stealing from them," I say. "He was crying, saying he was not the one, but your tailor kept slapping him. Then somebody brought a tire and put it on the boy's neck. He was screaming and begging. Someone else opened the tank of the generator and poured out the petrol. They poured it on his face and on the tire and then they set it on fire. He got up and started running but that just made the fire worse, then he fell on the floor and someone took a big brick and smashed it on his head."

"Did he die for real?" Peter asks me. He is yawning, so at first I think he asks did he die for *free*.

"Of course he did. He died, and several vultures came to eat his eyes," Andrew says.

"Don't listen to him, Peter. Nothing like that happened," I reply.

"What do you think happened to him?" Peter asks again.

"He went to heaven," I tell him. Someone must tell him about these things. "He went to a special heaven where only dead children go. And God gave him a room full of jean jackets that never get dirty and candy that gets sweeter while in your mouth—"

"And video games?"

"Yes, Peter, and video games, and TVs as wide as the walls of this house."

WHEN ANDREW AND Peter finally go to their room, I go to our room.

Ariyike is awake and listening to the sounds from our parents' room. I sit next to her on her bed and tell her this same story even though she has heard it all before. I tell her everything from the beginning—how the first time I saw the boy, I smiled at him. I told him I liked his FUBU shirt. He winked at me and walked away. And the end—that I saw the thief's mother run to where his dead body was still burning, take off her cloth wrapper, wrap it around his body to try to carry his body home, and fail. All she did was separate burnt clothing from skin, skin from bones. She stood there crying, "My daughter. My daughter. I warned you not to dress like a boy. Now see what you have done to yourself."

I told Ariyike that all the women who stood there earlier, accusing him of stealing food, laundry drying on the line, generators and coolers, came to the mother, pulling her away from the body, crying with her. That one of them gave her another wrapper to wear but she rejected it. Instead she stood there in her little green slip, crying and screaming, saying that they had stripped her naked in the streets and she would now be naked for the rest of her life.

I told Ariyike all the things I saw and heard, and she was as quiet as a mouse until I was done.

"He was just a stupid girl, Bibi, just a stupid girl," she said.

Then she put her arms around me and cried with me, and this was how I knew that she felt all the things that I felt, and we did not sleep at all that night because we were the same sad the same angry the same afraid.

NEW CHURCH

ARIYIKE

1998–1999

WE WERE SITTING at the back of the house, peeling the skin off black-eyed beans we had soaked in water for hours. The water was dark and particulate, black eyes and brown skins slid off the beans, away from our grasp, floating around the kitchen bowl. The skins reminded me of those newly hatched little tadpoles swimming in the drains out in the street. We could hear Jennifer Lopez playing from speakers in the neighbor's house. My sister was singing along, quietly because she did not want the neighbor to hear her enjoying it and turn it off.

"Jesus is coming soon, Bibike," I said.

"Okay," she said and continued singing.

"You can't be singing these types of songs. Do you want to be left behind?"

She was ignoring me. She continued singing along. She grabbed a handful of beans and swirled it quickly several times in the bowl, troubling the water until it moved around and around on its own, dark and misty, like a dirty whirlpool.

"I'm serious," I said. "Jesus is coming really soon. Like before the end of this year."

"Okay. You know this how?" she said.

"I saw it. No. Pastor David told us. But he prayed our eyes open and I saw, too."

My twin sister, Bibike, started laughing at me. She kissed her teeth, letting out a short but loud sound. She laughed hard, shaking her head, cackling. She is the one everyone calls quiet, so all the noise she was making was a surprise.

"Stop laughing at me. You are being annoying and rude," I said.

She did not stop. Her laughter made me think of water in the canal and how we loved to go there when we were younger. The canal water was usually calm and still. I hated it when it was like that. I used to throw rocks in the water just to disturb it. First, I'd cause a small ripple, which would create a larger one, and then another ripple, and then it was no longer calm undisturbed water but a series of unending circles. That's how laughter poured out of her, in waves and ripples. When I thought she was done, she only paused to laugh even harder.

"Are you done laughing?" I asked.

"Are you done saying stupid things?" she answered.

"Have you finished?" I asked again.

She did not answer. She just wiped her eyes with the back of her dress.

"These are the last days," I continued. "Everything the Bible talked about so far has happened. Wars, pestilences, rebellions. The only thing left is the Rapture. God told Pastor David that it's happening really soon."

"Ariyike, even if that is true, God won't tell anyone. Especially not Pastor David."

"Why won't he?" I said.

"Because it will be unfair." She got up as she said this, pouring the beans out from the bowl and into a large sieve, washing them under running water, splashing everywhere, on her dress, running down her legs, settling around her feet in a small puddle. "He will have to tell everyone or tell no one at all. God should be fair. Treat everyone the same. Like sunlight—"

"You're getting drenched," I said, interrupting her.

"I know. I will change before Mother gets back."

MOTHER HAD A new job. She was teaching business studies, shorthand writing, and typing at Oguntade Secondary. It was a private school, two streets away from us. She was offered a discount to enroll two children, but she didn't take it. We were enrolled in the neighborhood public school. She complained about her job every day.

"These children are so terrifyingly lazy."

"This proprietor is the most miserly man I have ever met. He is making us pay for tissue paper in the teachers' lounge, can you imagine it?"

"The parents want you to give their children marks they haven't earned; not me, let the other teachers cater to these nincompoops."

Mother was unsuited for this position. I felt sorry for her students. She was taking out her disappointments on them, I was sure. I hoped they knew that when she called them stupid or insolent, it was not because they were exceptionally incompetent. She just did not expect to be herding other people's children at this stage in her life.

Bibike and I were making moimoi. Mother sold moimoi wrapped in clear plastic bags to kids at her school during lunch. Lately we also had moimoi for lunch every day. We half joked to Mother as we cooked, "Can we eat something else? Peas will soon start growing from our ears o."

But her reply was: "You'd better be grateful you have any food to eat." She said this like it was the most normal thing to say to your own children.

Since she'd lost her job, Mother had been different, always angry, always tired, always looking for something to criticize us over. The boys, though, could do nothing wrong. One Friday, Andrew stayed out late. He was playing football at the stadium. Mother did not even notice he was not home. Or if she did, she said nothing. Bibike and I would never have tried something like that.

Father noticed everything but said nothing. It was harder for him, I assumed, because when Mother lost her job, he lost his inside connections and could no longer get printing contracts from the government. Father had never had a regular job. This was why he was our favorite parent; he had the time to do things with us. Before Mother lost her job and we all became poor, Father drove us to school every day. The first car I remember was a yellow '88 Mitsubishi Galant, but then he had it repainted to a brash red-wine color, because people in Lagos always thought it was a cab. They sold that car when Bibike and I were in primary 6, to buy a white Volkswagen Jetta. I loved that Jetta so much. Father washed it by himself every single day and it always had a fresh clean smell like a baby's bathwater.

Ever since selling the Jetta, Father had been home all the time. He had no connections, no car, and nothing to do. He spent most of his time indoors reading old newspapers, using a blue pen to mark them up. Other times, he was outside the house, "spending time with friends," "making money moves," "cultivating new business relationships."

"They are nothing but a bunch of time wasters," Mother said once, the day after Father's new group of friends visited him at home for the first time. "Time wasters. Roaming about looking for whom to devour."

We were all in the living room when she said it. She was standing by the dining table folding laundry. Father was sitting in his armchair, Andrew and Peter sat on the floor, Bibike and I lay on the purple couch. I could feel my face swelling with anger. Bibike was patting me on my back, calming me down without words. How could Mother think it was okay to talk about Father like that—and in front of him? All he was doing was trying. Trying to make something happen.

She would have continued like that, going on and on, if I

hadn't jumped off the couch and started singing, out of nowhere, the reggae dancehall song "Murder She Wrote." Peter
joined in singing, and soon we were dancing, swaying this
way and that, flinging imaginary dreadlocks right, left, and
right again. Andrew was providing the beat and shouting, in
his imitation Jamaican accent, "Mderation Man," over and
over, and Mother was saying, "Stop making noise," but no
one was listening anymore to anything she had to say. She
walked away, into our room, with a pile of folded clothes to
put in our chest of drawers. Then Father said, "Stop making
that racket. I want to watch the news.

Afterward, Mother spoke to Bibike and me yet again
about the dangers of worldly music, that it was the devil's
mascot, leading young girls to bad things, like boys and
drugs, and how we had to be better examples for our brothers. And in this moment, I wanted worldly music more than
I ever had. Nothing Mother was saying was new. I had
heard it all in church already

I listened to Mother repentant now. I started crying not
because of what she was saying but because I was afraid. I
was afraid of failing God. My pastor, David Shamonka, the
reason I knew Jesus was coming soon, had been in university
studying medicine when God called him to win souls. He
left medical school, he left his parents and siblings, he left
everything to start his ministry. If God called me like he did
him, what is worldly music that I couldn't give it up?

I hoped that God could tell that my heart wanted him
more than it wanted worldly music, or anything else. I could
sense that the world was changing, that big things were

about to happen. Of course, I could not say for certain that it was the end of the world, the Rapture or the Second Coming or anything like Pastor David said—Bibike's mocking made it hard for me to believe everything he said—but I felt something.

On some days, right after I said my night prayer, when I focused hard enough, I could hear the voice of God in the evening breeze. It sounded like an old man speaking softly in the distance. I did not know, in the way Pastor David apparently did, how to decipher what the voice was saying. But I believed that someday I, too, would understand His voice. I think I love Pastor David.

Once, before Mother lost her job, a street magician visited Fadeyi. All of us children paid five naira per head to watch his act. I watched the magician swallow a whole python alive, only to vomit it up five minutes later. It was an unforgettable sight. Pastor David reminded me of that magician. The difference was that he was teaching me, teaching all of us his congregants, how to do all the same glorious things he did.

I had first met Pastor David six months after Father sold the car. It happened in my school principal's office. I was there that day because Mrs. Modele the math teacher had reported me for copying my test answers from Bibike. I was walking up the stairs past the courtyard when I saw him approaching. He was smiling directly at my face. I pretended not to notice him looking, but I walked even more slowly, waiting to see where he was headed.

When I got to the principal's office, after stopping to

drink water in the teachers' lounge, he was already there. Before the principal could say anything, he was sitting and saying, "Please attend to your student, sir. I can wait."

Then the principal, determined to embarrass me, started bringing up unrelated stuff, eye makeup, short skirts, and the pack of Benson & Hedges from months ago.

Pastor David seemed to fight back an amused, puzzled look, and when the principal was done, he said: "If you don't mind, can I pray for this little girl?"

Then the principal said, "Of course, she needs it. I don't think it will help. This one is already a lost cause."

Then Pastor David held my right hand gently and said, "Loving God Abba Father, reveal Your love to her," and then I felt like my brain was expanding and my heart heating up at the same time.

I later learned he had come to ask to use the assembly grounds for midweek church services, and so I started to attend his services. I was hoping to be friends, but joining the church made me see how big he was, and how small I am. Whenever he caught my eye from the pulpit during services each Sunday, I wondered if he could tell how much I loved him.

We exchanged gifts. Just before Christmas, it was the annual love feast, and Pastor David picked my name out of the Christmas partner names bucket, right in the middle of service, and everyone cheered. He gave me a bracelet and a note that was just a long list of Bible verses selected "For the Godly Woman You Are Becoming, My Darling."

We exchanged even more notes after that. Mine were

my meditations on the Bible verses I studied each day. I was trying to read the entire Bible in a year. His notes were more mercurial. Once, he wrote several lines describing the hills in Jos when he'd visited for an evangelical outreach. Other times, it was lyrics to worship songs, in full, name of songwriter included. At the bottom of one note he wrote:

Everything softens when I worship.

HE LOVES TO sing. He cannot sing. Singing, he sounds like a bush baby crying for his lamp and lantern. He says that people who are not broken by God will be broken by life. I do not know what that means but I think it means tears. Cry when you sing worship songs.

He loves Lagos. He once said that people who haven't visited Lagos have yet to meet their country. He said that Lagos is a mini–Nigeria, only much better. I thought then that maybe he was talking to me alone, trying to make me feel not so bad for knowing only Lagos. Someday soon, I will travel. I want to see the Mambila Plateau.

My sister, Bibike, is less yielded than I am. She comes with me to church sometimes, especially Thanksgiving Sunday, when rice is served. First time she came, Pastor David didn't know it wasn't me; I was folding prayer clothes behind the altar curtain, she was talking to someone from the choir. They were standing in front of the altar. He said, "Madam dancer, I saw you digging it during praise and worship, keep it up." She laughed her laugh and said thank you. I was angry at her for smiling at him, so I walked into their midst and said, "Pastor, hi, this is my twin, Bibike, the One Who Doesn't Believe in Jesus."

And so that day, the day Mother was speaking to us about comportment, abstaining from all that sex music, the importance of respect, self-respect, and respecting others—I was crying and pretending to listen. I was really wondering, wondering whether maybe this house, Lagos, maybe even the world, was melting away and I was the only one who could remember how things used to be.

I wanted to answer her with the thoughts I was thinking, but I could not form a complete sentence. My thoughts were choking me, draining me. I wanted to ask how she could have no faith in Father. But I could not say what I wanted to say. She was stern and angry, pitiful. She looked old to me, like one of those women who sold tomatoes at Sabo night market.

Yet, after that occasion, whenever Father's friends came by she was well dressed, commanding, funny. Mother was funny when she wanted to be, she would speak in the military president's voice, making solemn announcements: Fellow Nigerians, I Am Announcing the Suspension of Milk Subsidy with Immediate Effect.

I saw that Father enjoyed her new attitude. He stayed home longer, started going out only in the evenings. He was talking about starting a business of his own, being an entrepreneur. One of his friends had recently been deported from Germany. It was this friend, Mr. Gary, who had all these big ideas about what they could do for money. They were becoming motivational speakers for hire. Gary had the interesting accent, my father had the looks, together they booked deals in colleges and universities, speaking to graduating students about the job market. But their partnership lasted less than a year, ending things quickly. They argued about splitting profits and separated. Then Father became a recruitment consultant. After that failed to work out, he started a business magazine with some other friends.

"What's this?" Mother asked him when he brought home the galley copy.

"What does it look like?"

"Like another stupid way you're wasting my money."

"I am a businessman. This is what I do," he said.

"You are a lazy man," she replied. "Get a job."

When *Business Insights* magazine failed—they kept at it far longer than they should have—Father's group of friends disbanded. They had run out of courage and enthusiasm, each person moving on to independent pursuits. Father was keen to start something new. He wanted to convert the lower part of our home into a business-services support center. With a couple of computers and printers, some old photocopiers, the business would provide services to other businesses in the neighborhood, ones still dependent on traditional typewriters.

"I would rather convert it to a flat and rent it out," Mother replied when he told her his idea. "The Soweres next door paid two years' rent in advance; how much can a business center bring in?"

We were sitting at dinner while they argued. Peter was

making a mess: okra soup spilled from his plate, forming a tiny puddle on the table. He was putting his fingers in it, handwriting *shit fuck* on the walls. They did not notice.

Bibike and I had visited the Soweres the day before. Their daughter, Titi, was a year older than we were. Her parents were home early from work. I was impressed by how basic and transactional their conversation that afternoon was.

"Did you put on the water-pumping machine?" Titi's mother had asked.

"Do we still have yellow garri?" Titi's father asked.

"What time will you be back tomorrow?" Titi asked.

It was nothing like our house. In our home, everything was at stake. Nothing was inconsequential. Even the way you said good morning could set them off. The house we lived in was a wedding gift from Mother's father. Whenever they argued about Father's idea, Mother said, "I will do what I like with my father's house," and Father said, "Do what you like, endanger our children because of your being stubborn."

After a few months, the arguments were no longer as loud as they had been. Father was resigned, quiet. Mother was eating less and less, drinking schnapps and agbo, laughing even when nothing was funny. We entertained ourselves by dressing up with Mother's makeup and hanging out in filling station tuck shops. I am great at meeting new people; Bibike just went everywhere I did. We made plans to run away, to leave the country. Move to Ghana, make our own money, get our brothers, Andrew and Peter, into better schools. Bibike was to sing in a live band. I would work as a waitress in the bar.

We even met a man who promised to get us ECOWAS travel booklets. We wouldn't need visas to travel anywhere in West Africa. It was such a simple plan, really. He just wanted to take pictures of us in swimsuits, which was silly because we had already told him we did not know how to swim.

Mother announced one day at dinner that the school where she was teaching was closing in the middle of the school year. She said the owner had sold the property it was built on. The new owner was tearing down the school to build an apartment complex.

It was March of '98, and Mother was without a job again. We, *all* of us, went to visit Mother's boss, the proprietor of Oguntade school. He hadn't paid Mother any salary for the last three months before the school closed, and it was her idea to take the whole family to his house.

"I know that man made millions when he sold the school. Yet he refuses to pay me my arrears. If my pleas have not moved him, let him look into the eyes of the children he is starving," she said before we left our house. And so, the six of us got in a bus and went to his house.

It did not work.

"I will pay you as soon as I get the money, madam," the proprietor had said. "I cannot turn myself to money for you. My children are also hungry."

"So, will you now consider trying out my idea?" Father asked.

We were sitting in the back, the very last row of the danfo bus, when they were talking about this. Mother was whispering. The quietness made her voice sound like she was about to cry.

"It's not like I have a choice," Mother answered.

LATER THAT MONTH, our parents asked me what I thought of their business plans. I promised to work in the business center as often as possible. They had taken to including Bibike and me in every discussion about the family's finances. We did not give any opinions, we just listened and tried to look sad. Father's plan was all we had left. Money for the business center came from selling our parents' wedding bands and Nestlé PLC shares, the only other thing (apart from the house) Mother had inherited from her deceased parents. The money bought two used photocopiers, one desktop computer, one scanner, one laminator, and one printer. Father was excited to finally get his chance. He promised his business would bring in, every other day, what Mother had made in a month as a teacher.

The trouble with his new business started early. Our photocopy machines were temperamental and unreliable. They made faint and unreadable copies, they leaked ink all over the place, they consumed way too much electricity and even more petrol whenever there were power cuts. Our patrons were infrequent and often needed services rendered on credit.

It was during this season of hopelessness, when we were learning to wait for whatever money was to be made from the business center, to know whether there would be food to eat the next day, that an old work colleague, visiting the neighborhood and seeing Mother manning the typesetting business, had advised her, face contorting with the exaggerated sympathy usually reserved for victims of hit and run accidents, to attend Pastor David's church.

My sista! Please attend this meeting. You will receive a breakthrough. Your life will change.

I was so happy when Father and Mother told me they had heard wonderful things about my Pastor David and were going to see for themselves. They attended a Wednesday miracle night the week after. Bibike and I stayed home with our brothers. Later that night at dinner, they spoke of all they had seen and heard. Stories of people who had been worse off than they could ever dream of being who experienced great change through the church. There was the illiterate taxi driver who found favor with an expatriate and became his personal assistant, earning a salary in dollars. And the man who won the visa lottery after he was prayed for and who was leaving for America soon. And another, a man once so poor he sewed boxer shorts out of his wife's old wrappers, who, after prayers at church, won a government tender and made so much money, he bought three brand-new cars in one day.

It was the very best day of my life. Even though I wished they had joined because they loved Jesus, I was happy that the rest of my family had finally come to the New Church. We were desperate for better things, feverish with expectation that church was the missing link.

Andrew and Peter missed our old church, All Saints Anglican Cathedral. They were chubby, round-faced boys who had been doted on by most of the elderly congregants of the old church. Andrew had been nicknamed the King Himself, for his portrayal of King Herod at the Christmas play in '94, and Peter delighted everyone with his recital of the First Psalm in English and Yoruba. It was something they did every year after that, until we left: Andrew was always the lead in church plays; Peter always recited long Bible passages from memory.

My mother still struggled with being poor and needy. The women of the New Church discomfited her for this reason. They were, in many ways, unlike the women who attended the old church. Women from our old church, like my mother, had been raised as privileged Lagos girls, attended competitive all girls' schools like Anglican Girls or Queens College, lived in London for a year, perhaps taking Cambridge A levels, or perfecting their typing and shorthand skills, then returned to steady careers and marriages. Most of the New Church women usually had little or no education. They came to Lagos from their villages for the first time as adults, courtesy of born-in-the-village husbands who had found work here. They were very dependent on these husbands and other male relatives in a way that our mother found annoying in the beginning, but later began to envy.

Whenever they gathered together for prayer meetings in our business center, they generally had the same kind of conversations. Gossip, grievances, and barely concealed guile masking as prayer requests. "I asked my husband for money for food shopping and he did not give me." "My brother in Germany has forgotten the family." "My neighbor needs to come to the Lord. Her husband won't stop beating her till she becomes a praying wife." When they were around, Mother made a show of being a model Christian woman. Behind their backs, though, Mother mocked and mimicked these women. Bibike and I were glad to have Mother's attention again, and so we laughed aloud each time she did. We were fakers, but we were happy.

Pastor David's church was growing. The New Church moved out of the public school into a new, purpose-built church building. For the first time, there was a separate youth church, called the Burning Citadel, and it was one of the first youth churches in Lagos to attempt being simultaneously cool and godly. Sunday services were called "hangout sessions" and midweek services were called "meet-up gigs." There was an effusive worship band with electric guitars and large drums, which made Ron Kenoly and Don Moen songs sound super cool. The band took the music from "Malaika," made famous by Miriam Makeba, and turned it into a song of Christian dedication. We sang, "My lifetime, I give Jesus my lifetime," with contrite hearts. I no longer saw Pastor David and I did not care that much. I had Jesus, I had my family.

Father found himself a new group of henchmen, similarly smooth-talking, broke men with big dreams and loud voices. They congregated almost daily in our business center. The business was getting better at this time, and Mother had even expanded it to include wholesale office materials and beverages.

They were like Father's earlier group of men. Loud, noisy dreamers. These dreamers, though, said bless you instead of good morning, and "I am a winner" when you asked, "How is your day going, sir?"

One of Father's closest friends was a young man named Pastor Samuel. He was one of the assistant pastors and was always in a suit no matter how hot the weather. He came to the house, to our business center, almost every day. He always bought a bottle of Coke, first wiping the rim clean with a white handkerchief he kept in his shirt pocket. Then he told stories of all the business deals he was about to strike. The stories he told Father were rivaled only by the ones he told as testimonies in church. He spoke of connections with military administrators in various states of the republic. One Sunday, Pastor Samuel presented to the church a "sacrificial thanksgiving seed" of an imported fourteen-seater bus. He announced that he was thanking God for connecting him with the highest-ranking military men in the state. We were so happy for Pastor Sam's newest blessings. Especially because, like oil on Aaron's head, they were sure to trickle down to us.

Most days when Pastor Samuel visited Father at home, he paid special attention to us girls, dashing Bibike and me money. He was nice and friendly. He sat with us and talked with us, wanting to know what books we were reading, what music we liked, whether we had boyfriends. Mother hated the attention Pastor Samuel gave us and one day, after she walked in on him giving Bibike a foot massage, asked us to never speak to him again unless it was in church. Father agreed with her and began sending us upstairs whenever Pastor Samuel came to visit.

When the military president died in June of '98, things fell apart all over the nation. The chaos was particularly intense in Lagos. As commercial capital of the republic, the unexpected changes in political leadership led to panicked trading activity among the ruling class. People were hoarding food—rice, garri, yams. Gas stations shut down. Electronics stores moved their goods into more secure warehouses, fearing a riot.

IT WAS DURING this time that Pastor Sam approached Father about a deal. He told Father that one of his connections, a top admiral in the navy, was in possession of a shipment containing foreign currency that the deceased military president had been taking out of the country. The admiral needed money to transfer ownership of the shipping containers to someone outside the military. The reasoning was a new government in the impending democracy would most likely investigate all past military personnel for corrupt practices.

The money, ten million naira, was the admiral's share of the container's worth, and he insisted on getting cash upfront. Pastor Samuel came to Father because he did not have that type of money. He offered to pay Father back the ten million plus 50 percent of the shipment. With such looming promise of profits, Father was convinced to secure a high-interest loan on our family home for the value of the proposed bribe. The home was conservatively valued at almost double that amount at this time; it was sitting on acreage that could support two other buildings. But being confident that once the shipment cleared and the money was shared, the mortgage would be paid in full, Father signed the loan papers. Mother noticed that the visits of Pastor Samuel were more frequent in this period, and the men's discussions intense. She asked Father several times what they were up to. "God has remembered us, dear. Something big is on the way," was all he said.

She responded by being even more protective of Bibike and me, keeping us indoors as much as she could. Father was a changed man this season. He woke up with songs of praise every day: "Isn't He good, isn't He good, hasn't He done all He said He would, faithful and true to me and you, isn't He good?"

His enthusiasm was easy to catch. Even Mother, who was usually cautious about his schemes, finally caught it, this exhilaration of faith. We the children were beyond excited. Every night, we sat in our fort and talked to one another about what would happen when the money Father was expecting arrived.

"Father will buy me a BMX bicycle," Andrew said.

"Me, I want a Game Boy," Peter replied.

Bibike and I dreamed of buying brand-new clothes from Collectibles, jeans from Wrangler, clogs, and Lycra skirts. We were going to be again what we used to be, and did not know until we no longer were, the prettiest, best-dressed girls in the neighborhood.

It would have been easier for Mother to handle if she had been aware of any of the particulars of the deal. Father said nothing to her about it until the day after he had handed over the money to Pastor Samuel. He waited all day for Pastor Samuel to bring over the bill of lading. Next, he went looking for Pastor Samuel in the New Church. Pastor David had no idea where Pastor Samuel was. In fact, no one could find him. It was almost as though he had never existed. The only proof was the Volkswagen bus the church had repainted blue and on which it had written EVANGE-LISM in block letters on both sides.

I supposed this was another way that the New Church differed from the old one. The older churches taught of a God who was responsible for everything, both good and bad. Believers were encouraged to accept their fate with good cheer, trusting the God who would deliver if He chose to. The God of the New Church was a good God, but he was only good, and He was good all the time. He took credit for everything pleasant and the blame for evil was shared between the devil and his cohort of doubting Christians. Evil of any kind, from an injured toe to lung cancer, happened only to the unbelieving or those with feeble faith.

This was the way the New Church handled our heart-break. First, they christened it the work of the devil, asking us to pray harder than ever—expecting the Holy Spirit to bring Pastor Samuel back. Later, we were denounced as agents of Satan, concocting a scandal to bring disgrace to the church.

In my heart, I knew it was just a temporary trial. Like Job, we were being tested of God. I gave myself to prayer and reading the Bible. I encouraged my brothers and sister as they wept themselves sore. God had not forgotten us. He would deliver us in His own time.

That Friday night, after we got the "last and final warning" from Fountain Mortgage Bank's lawyer posted on the front door, Mother woke me up in the middle of the night and asked me to help with tidying the boys' room. She gave me two hundred naira right then, so I asked her no questions, I put the money in my pillowcase and followed her to their room. We stood in front of the blue chest of drawers at the foot of the bed, saying nothing as we rolled up Andrew's socks one into the other and tied Peter's in knots. It was a little glimpse of the type of mother she once was, the type of mother who was careful to do the little things you asked from her. She folded Andrew's underwear into tiny squares, and Peter's she rolled into short scrolls.

We folded T-shirts, singlets, and trousers, and then we hung up all their church clothes in the wardrobe. My brothers slept soundly next to each other on a queen-size bed beneath a white mosquito net suspended with twine from nails in the ceiling. There was a ceiling fan that no longer worked. The windows of the room were wide open, letting in a misty draft. Peter coughed but didn't wake up, Mother looked like she wanted to go to him, but then she turned around and asked me to shut the windows.

I woke up late the next morning. It was nine thirty, and I was really angry with myself for accepting Mother's bribe and ruining my sleep. I had woken up late and missed the first part of Cadbury's breakfast television. It was a once-a-week, two-hour program on the Lagos state-owned television channel showing premium American television. They had, in the month before, begun showing *Family Matters*

and *A Different World*. Cadbury's breakfast television was
the only interesting thing available to watch on Saturday—
the rest of the day's television stations devoted themselves to
live soccer matches and replays.

I loved Carl Winslow. He was the perfect father. He even
looked like a father was supposed to look: balding, round-
faced, and old. For a few necessary minutes every Saturday, I
would watch *Family Matters* and pretend he was mine. But on
this Saturday, the television was turned off. Father sat quietly
in his armchair, his *Dake Annotated Reference Bible* between
his thighs. There was no one else in the sitting room. Bibike
was still asleep and the boys were sitting on the kitchen floor,
whispering. The note, a sheet torn off a reporter's notebook
and placed slightly underneath the television, said:

> *My dear children,*
>
> *I have gone to New York.*
> *There is nothing left here for me anymore.*
> *Peter, if God blesses me, I will send for you.*
>
> *Love,*
> *Your mother.*

In the end, our mother was just the first to leave. My family unraveled rapidly, in messy loose knots, hastening away
from one another, shamefaced and lonesome, injured solitary animals in a happy world.

HOW TO BUILD A
CHICKEN COOP

ANDREW

2000

WE ARE BUILDING a chicken coop.

My brother, Peter, and I came up with this plan just last weekend. Already we have started working it out. We have no hens yet, but we know that Nonso's mother's hen always has eggs. When Nonso is over here trying his best to make our sister Ariyike smile, we will walk into their compound all majestic and what, go all the way to the poultry at the back, take as many eggs as we want, hope they hatch.

We have wood, gravel, and leftover roofing sheets from the time the local government built a shed with a roof for the transformers down the road because electricity shocks killed some boy's father during the last flood.

We have old wood, nails, and sawdust, and we will find old plastic bowls no one uses anymore.

All of Grandmother's things are old. She still has those green Pyrex dishes, teacups, saucers. They are older than all of us grandchildren. She still wears the aso oke wrappers she wore when Sister Kehinde and Sister Taiwo were baptized. We will not use any of Grandmother's things. She has given us the space at the back of the house for the chicken coop, and that's just enough.

We do not need a hammer. That's what stones are for.

We are digging the hole already. It's ankle deep and is wide enough for us to stand back-to-back in it. Already we have a heap of sand-dirt. Grandmother says that chicken coops do not need a foundation. We both insist that they do. So we promise that we will spread the sand-dirt all over the back of the yard instead of leaving an unsightly heap.

We do not have a phone. We are thinking of ways to get one.

We are alone at home. Grandmother is out shopping. Our sisters are at work. We are big boys, eleven and nine, old enough to be by ourselves staying out of trouble.

We have walked all over the carpenters' shed in the next street, picking as many old wood nails as we can find. We are sitting at the back of the house, straightening bent nails with a big stone. Sometimes we think we hear the gates opening, someone coming, but there is no one else here.

The boys next door are playing table soccer in their back-yard. We cannot hear the sound of bottle caps falling off the table or large suit buttons pushed into a goalpost made of paper. It is their happiness we can hear, the sounds of boys our age cheering and screaming. It sounds like it is coming from a galaxy far away.

Last Saturday, we walked for fifty minutes till we got to Rita Lori Hotel in Ikeja. There was a wedding reception. We had two black shopping bags. We were going to pick up as many bottle caps as we could find, start our own league. I was going to take all the Coca-Cola covers; all the Fanta and Sprite covers were to be Peter's. If we got more than enough to split evenly this way, we were going to scratch the covers till the names disappeared and write our player numbers with red ink.

There was no guard at the gate, so we walked in. We searched for covers but there were none. We were too late; the hall had been cleaned up. We went outside to the dumpster behind the hotel. The guard was there smoking cigarettes. He offered them to us. I refused, and he chased us away.

When our hens are grown, they will lay eggs of their own. Then we will sell them for money. We will buy a crate of soda, and drink as often as we like. We will have our own teams and players.

Peter is unhappy with this work. He is focused on the nail in front of him, squinting like the sun is in his eyes even though we are in the shade of the cashew tree, straightening nails as he is supposed to, bottom first then the top, over and over. There is an interesting melody in this repeated banging, easy to get swept up in, gbam gbam gbam, shake your head, gbam gbam gbam, from side to side.

He is sitting with his legs crossed under him like he is in a mosque about to pray.

"Andrew? Are you hungry?" he asks. Looking up at me.

He is just like Mother, staring and squinting like that. I do not mention that. Instead I say, "Let us go and search for something to eat."

We leave our pile of nails there and go looking for our friend. His name is Solomon, but everyone calls him If You See My Mama. He is a good dancer. He dances all the time. Anytime there's loud music. Especially when there's a ready audience, like people gathered at the beer parlor or at Rosetta's snooker joint. People sometimes give him money. Most give him food.

I can do what he does, dance galala like Daddy Showkey, but I have no plans to dance for food. To dance for food, you have to be able both to dance and to eat anything. I don't like stew without pepper. I cannot stand vegetable soup with crayfish in it. Peter can't eat eggs or beans.

Solomon lives with his mother in the house where the TV repairman Uncle George lives. There is a pile of broken televisions on the veranda outside their house. There is a big one with a brown wood-paneled back, the TV like a long rectangle lying on its side. Sometimes, the littler kids sit in it and pretend to be newscasters reading the evening news.

I am Frank Olize
And I am Abike Dabiri
This is NTA Newsline

Today there is no one sitting inside the TV. We go into the house and find Solomon's mother's room. It is the third on the left. The one with a charismatic renewal sticker on the door.

It says HONORING MARY, NEVER WORSHIPPING. I have no idea what it means.

Solomon is inside. He opens the door only when he hears my voice.

"Andy dudu." He calls me by the nickname I hate. His room smells like freshly cooked egusi soup, so I let it go.

"If You See My Mama," I sing out loud.

"Tell am say I dey for Lagos," he replies.

"I no get trouble." Peter supplies this last part. Solomon and I laugh at him because he still makes *r* sound like *w*.

"Sit down," Solomon says as he laughs. "I wan turn garri. You go chop?"

"What type of soup do you have?" I ask.

"Egusi," he says.

"Nice," Peter says.

Peter and I sit on the floor. There is a curtain with little blue fish and yellow bubbles demarcating the bed from the rest of the room. Solomon kneels by the bed and pulls out a tiny stove and an old Mobil tin gallon out from under it. He opens the door and places the stove and keg outside. As he pours kerosene into the stove, I tell him what we are up to.

"We are building a chicken coop."

"Since when?" he asks.

"A few days now," I reply.

"For sell or for choppin?"

"Both," I say.

"For selling," Peter says.

Solomon comes back into the room, picking up a kettle and a box of matches. There is a covered plastic drum at the foot of the bed. He opens it, puts a cup in it, and fills the kettle with water.

"This is the perfect time for chicken business," he says to us. "It will be almost Christmas by the time the chickens are big, then you can sell them for even more money because of Christmas rush."

We did not think it would take that long to raise chickens.

"Let me tell you where you can get maize for free." Solomon puts the kettle to boil and comes to sit on a stool next to us.

"What for?" Peter asks.

"Where?" I ask at the same time.

"For feeding your chickens na." He looks at Peter like a fly is on his nose. He turns to me and asks, "You know where the bakery is?"

"Not really." This time I am not ashamed of not knowing. Solomon has lived here since he was five years old. Father brought us here this year to live with his mother, our grandmother. We do not know where our father lives now.

"It is bit far. I don't know how to describe it. There is the borehole with three huge water tanks right next to it," Solomon says.

"Our sisters will know," Peter says.

"Every morning when my mother goes to buy bread for sale from the bakery," Solomon continues, "there's always fresh maize in a calabash. She says people leave it there as offerings to spirits."

We will take maize offered to spirits for our hens.

When Solomon is done, he brings the food in two bowls, one for garri, the other for soup. He sets it right in the middle of the room. Peter and I sit next to each other, Solomon sits on the opposite side facing us. I have a feeling that I have been here before. That all this has happened already, and I am just now remembering it.

"You better don't touch my meat," Solomon says to Peter.

"Sorry. It was a mistake," Peter says, and the feeling is now stronger than it has ever been. I force myself to eat but I can no longer do it. I am searching inside my brain to know what I remember, what happens after this. There's nothing. My mouth is bitter, my stomach feels like I drank cement mix.

Solomon says something to me, but I don't hear it. Peter laughs and replies.

"—he say he wan free money."

They finish the food, but we do not get up. We are talking in this room, a multipurpose room where I can see everything Solomon's mother has got—plates, pots, and pans poking out of old moving boxes, a pile of old clothes in a brown leather box with a broken handle. There is a black-and-white TV with a wire antenna on top of it.

We are sitting on a scratchy faded green rug with spots of candle wax all over it.

We are talking about new music. We all agree not to like musicians who start their choruses with names of girls. ("Sade" by Remedies is a stupid song; "Omode Meta n Sere" is the greatest song of all time.) I am thinking about Mother and Father. Mother hates worldly music. Father hates it but smiles anytime our sister Bibike sings.

As we sit here talking, a short man I do not know walks in. He does not knock, he just pushes the door open like that.

"Welcome," Solomon says to him as he motions for us to get up, leave.

"Sit down and continue your enjoyment." The man speaks to us, smiling a wide white smile that brightens his face. His lips look too wide for such a small face. The man has dark blotched skin. His face is a perfect round shape. His eyes are swollen and red. He looks like Raphael the Teenage Mutant Ninja Turtle without the green. The man sits on the bed behind us and starts taking off his clothes. Solomon springs up.

"We are leaving. My friends have to be home before their grandma comes back."

"They don't have to leave. Okay. Take this money. Let the small one stay. The two of you go and buy something to eat—" The man is still talking. I get up. I pull Peter onto his feet. The man is still smiling, softer now, hopeful even. He is sweaty even though he has taken off everything but his undershorts. I do not know what he sees in my face but he stops smiling immediately. His transformation is instant, almost funny.

"Get out of here, foolish children. Shut the door," he screams. "And Solomon, you better not come back till your mother comes home this night."

We rush down the hallway, to the veranda of TVs and into the streets. Peter is humming. We are walking slower now, still saying nothing. Peter stops in front of a dusty Datsun that looks like it's been there for ten years and starts to write on the windscreen, "Wash me please."

We walk in silence until we get to our home. The boys next door are still playing a game. We can also hear some girls singing.

"Let's go see Stanley." Solomon does not wait for me to respond. He walks to their house, opening the gate.

Peter and I look at each other, then we go in with him. Their house looks just like ours—cracked plaster walls, a moldy well to the left at the entrance, a veranda made with red brick paving stones.

At the back of the house, the boys are playing table soccer in one corner. Stanley is winning. Their table is huge. They have taped a linoleum rug over the wooden top. The bottle covers just glide over it. Peter and I will never be able to make a table like that on our own. I must become friends with Stanley.

A group of girls are in dance formation. They have strips of aso oke tied across their chests. Longer ones cover their waists down to their knees. Girls are magic beings. They have to be not to die from itching, wearing scratchy aso oke next to their bare skin like that. They are singing in Yoruba:

We are here
We are here again

The eagle is the king of birds
The lion is the king of forest animals
We are greater than these by far
We are singers, dancers too

I am watching them but pretending not to do so. Soon they start to argue. One girl, the shortest, the one with blue stars drawn on her legs, wants the group to roar like a lion at the end of the first verse. Many disagree with her. As she talks, explaining her point, she keeps untying and retying her waist wrapper. It is a very womanly move and it makes me feel like my stomach is punching itself. It also makes me think of Mother. Mother once made us crowns out of her old gold aso oke. Peter and I hated it. We wanted store-bought crowns, like the other kids in the play.

As I watch the girls dance, I start to feel the feeling again. This time it is a different, more sure feeling. I am certain all of this has happened before. I have seen this before—little girls singing, dancing, smiling, one in the middle stopping occasionally to stare at me, saying nothing, just smiling. I feel like all I need to do is focus my brain and I will remember what I am remembering.

I notice a lizard running across the yard, it runs over my feet and then goes up the wall separating our house and Stanley's. Once it gets to the middle of the wall it stops, still except for bobbing its little red head every few seconds. I have seen this before. Even this red-orange lizard crawling over the wall, nodding.

The girl looks at me again. This time I smile back. I blow

a kiss. She spreads out five fingers, points them at me. "Your mother," she screams.

Girls are crazy.

There is a concrete slab in the center of this backyard. It is a long rectangle that extends almost to the end of the east wall. It's as if someone intended to cover the ground completely but ran out of concrete too early. The girls are dancing on one side of the slab. On the other, Stanley's mother has spread out yellow maize and red guinea corn to dry on a raffia mat.

Some white pigeons circle around above. The girls love birds, they wave at them singing the leke leke song, *Leke leke, give me white fingers, won't you?*

Sometimes the birds swoop down as fast as lightning. They pick bread crumbs or a smooth pebble or chicken feed. A couple of pigeons hover close to our heads then fly away. They want the maize, but they won't land because we are here. There are too many of us.

One of the boys notices the pigeons and says something. The rest of them stop playing to look at the birds. Then someone says, "I have an idea. Let's make a bird trap." Another says, "I know how to build one." They begin to argue about what is needed when Peter invites them to our house.

"We live next door. We have extra wood and nails. We are building a chicken coop," he says.

They want to see what we are up to. They want pieces of wood to make a trap. And so we walk away, a small crowd of boys in two lines. If the girls notice us leaving, they don't show it.

As we walk into our house, I see it the way they see it. Our moldy well has a pile of broken plastic buckets next to it. Our laundry is drying on the walls of the perimeter.

Solomon laughs when we get to the hole we have dug.

"Just look at this." He is laughing. It is the second time he has spoken since we left his house.

"You don't need this big hole, don't you know?" a skinny tall boy says to me. He is wearing a white shirt. His dreadlocks are long and dusty. "You just need four small holes for your four-by-twos, then you pour in a little concrete and it stays."

"We were going to fill the hole with stones," Peter says.

He sounds like he is annoyed and impatient. He must be unhappy with me. This is our house, I should not just stand there like a fool while these boys laugh at us.

"Which is easier? Stones or concrete? Where will we get concrete from?" Peter continues. It is hard for him to say concrete, so he is making everything worse.

"Okay. Do you want to help with the bird trap, then, or are you still digging your nonsense hole?"

"Just shut up. With your scanty hair like an abandoned mop."

Now everyone is laughing at tall-skinny-dreadlock guy. Peter just walks away, into the house. Not even glorying in delivering the perfect insult.

A gentle wind stirs in the cashew tree in the middle of our yard. It is becoming evening, the warm humidity is being replaced by the cool breeze. When the boys stop laughing to begin sorting through nails and wood pieces, I continue standing where I am, watching the wind make the leaves dance. I notice a lizard, I think it is the same one that was in Stanley's yard, dash up the tree.

The boys have gathered wood pieces of different sizes. Some the length of a walking stick, others short as a pencil. Skinny-dreadlock guy sits under the cashew tree and gathers all the materials to himself. He starts to arrange them in a pyramid-like pile. When he figures out the arrangement of sticks that makes up a perfect pile he splits them up in pairs, giving one pair to each boy.

"Take. Look for stone. Knack these two together," he says.

Peter comes out of the house but doesn't speak to me. He walks right to skinny-dreadlock guy and sits next to him. I do not know what he says to him, but he looks like he is apologizing.

When Peter was younger, he was so slim (even slimmer than dreadlock guy), his head was huge, his legs were super short. I called him Mr. Big Head Small Body because he looked like those cartoons in the Sunday paper. He hated it, but I couldn't stop. The more he protested, the more I enjoyed teasing him. One day, Father showed him a picture of a lion in a calendar and said: "That's who you are, son, a lion. A son of a lion is a lion."

A son of a foolish man who loses all his money to fraudsters is what? A son of a poor man whose wife leaves him is what? A son of a man who runs away, leaving his children with his mother, is what?

Father should see Peter now. He is no longer tiny. He is

tall, almost as tall as I am. His head is bigger and harder. No one can tell him nothing.

I watch the two of them talking. Then skinny-dreadlock guy picks up three sticks, he sets them in position, he makes a shape like a small letter *t*. He starts to nail them together. Peter reaches out to steady the longer piece underneath. The nail goes through both pieces of wood and into the thin skin between Peter's thumb and his forefinger.

"Oh my God."

"Sorry. Sorry. I'm so sorry."

We are all scrambling. The nail, the *t*-shaped sticks, are stuck in Peter's hand, like they are sprouting. We surround him. We hold him down and pull it out. There wasn't blood before. Now there is a lot of it. There is a lot of blood. Someone wipes it with his shirt. Another grabs a fistful of sand, pours it over the wound. The blood stops rushing out. Someone tells Peter to shake his hand. As he shakes it sand and blood fall to the ground at his feet.

I see the lizard fall off the tree, race over to be next to Peter, lap droplets of blood as they fall to the ground. I look in its eyes and see myself the way it sees me. I am dark and dusty like a school blackboard, my head is bigger than the rest of my body, my hands are tiny, plastered to my side. The lizard stops to look at me. He is nodding again and again. I think the lizard is laughing at me. I am sure of it.

I AM SOMETHING

PETER

2000

I LIKED TO think that no matter what happened, my older brother, Andrew, and I would always be close. This was exactly the kind of thing I worried about, growing older, being on my own, my sisters leading happy, glamorous lives, my brother busy and distant.

Many times, it felt like Andrew and I were only one argument away from being enemies. Other times, we were the best brothers in all of Lagos. I made it my business to try, to make sure we always were getting along, fun and happy. We were best friends only because I did everything he said to do, and I did not mind every time he ignored me to go play with Solomon, Babu, and Eric. Each time he said something mean, I tolerated it, pretending the pain was from something else, like a stomachache from food I did not enjoy, beans or something like that. I stored the hurt for a while in my belly, then I found a place to let it out. Other times, he was the nicest brother, taking care of me.

"I am something," Andrew said that day, to distract me from the pain he was inflicting as he was massaging mentholated balm all over my swollen palm. "I am tall in the morning, short in the evening, even shorter at night. What am I?"

"You are an old man," I said, after thinking about the riddle for a little while.

When he said that was the wrong answer, I did not argue. I watched him pour boiling hot water into the bowl we use for washing up before meals. He pulled out an old towel he had tucked in the back of his trousers and sat on the floor before me.

"The answer is a candle. I am a candle," Andrew said.

A CANDLE IS long, an old man was tall now shrunken, I wanted to say but did not. I grabbed the handle of the chair I sat on with my left hand, steadying myself as he pressed the heat of the rag against my wound. I did not cry out. I did not want Grandmother waking up and looking too closely at my hand. Better for her to sleep, I thought. Better for us that she sleeps as long as she wants to because then when she wakes, it will be easier to talk to her about money for Panadol painkillers.

Andrew leaned in with the full weight of his grip, applying pressure to my swollen palm. As he did, bloody pus oozed out in a slow and steady drip.

"Sorry," he said.

"I am something," I said, interrupting his pity. "I am light as a feather, yet the strongest man in the world can't hold on to me for more than ten minutes. What am I?"

"You are water," Andrew said. "Am I right?"

"No. Not really."

"What is the right answer?"

"It's air. Actually. Breathing air. No one can hold his breath for up to ten minutes."

The air around us was humid and difficult to endure without murmuring. My scalp was wet and sweat was going down my face, even into my ears. My shirt was soaked with sweat, but I could not take it off until Andrew was done cleaning my palm. It was early evening, and we were boiling a half yam for our night meal. I could hear the slices boiling in the pot a few feet away from us because Andrew used the wrong pot cover, so the heat was escaping, and floating bubbles were bursting and spilling all over the stove. That was just one more thing for Grandmother to be angry with us about when she woke up.

It was as if she considered us two children instead of four. Our sisters were one person, the girls, and Andrew and I were one person, the boys. Whatever he did, I was equally responsible for and there was nothing I could do to escape it.

Once, Andrew had dropped his undershorts in the hallway when he was taking his house clothes out back to wash. He did not notice them quickly enough. Grandmother found them and lifted them with a broken plastic hanger, waving them around like a flagpole.

"Do you see what I have to live with?" she asked, screaming

in Yoruba at no one in particular as she walked around the house. "Dirty smelling children. Underwear smelling like the penises of dead male goats, in the middle of the house where I get up each morning to pray to my creator."

"God, is this not too much for a little old woman? When did I become the palm nut in the middle of the street that even little boys are stepping on me so mercilessly?"

For days, she continued like that. She did not allow any of us to retrieve the underwear from the place she had mounted it, in the center of the living room right next to the pile of Father's university textbooks. Andrew waited until she left one evening to sing with a funeral procession for one of the commercial bus drivers in the neighborhood who had been killed in an accident with a delivery truck. He waited until the voices singing "Jesus, the Way, the Truth, and the Life, whosoever comes to Him shall never die" were a distant hollow, then he picked up his underwear and threw it in the trash along with the plastic hanger.

"This woman is pushing me to the wall. I am going to deal with her very soon," he said that day to me, his eyes cloudy with not-shed tears.

Andrew was not massaging my arm fast enough to stop the cramping in my back. My face felt hotter and hotter, so I asked him to stop.

"Do you feel better yet?" he asked.

"Yes," I answered. "I am just hungry."

Andrew stood up off the floor. He had the bowl and the towel with him. I let go of the chair and wiped my face with the back of my hand.

"The food should be ready now," he said. He was looking in the direction of the kitchen, nodding toward it. "Do you need my help to get up?"

I did not. I was dehydrated, hot, and my throat ached, but I did not need his help. But Andrew must have misheard me, I thought, for he reached out his hand and pulled me up out of the chair. I stood up, my legs burning and my steps shaky, taking off my shirt and walking into the house in nothing but my undershorts.

The palm oil came out in thick droplets as Andrew shook the bottle over the plated yams. The heat of the yams melted the droplets immediately on contact till there was a small puddle of oil around the yams. Andrew sprinkled a small pinch of salt over the plate.

"My neck does not feel so good," I said.

"Just eat this. Then I will go out to buy you Panadol Extra," Andrew said.

"Just Panadol. Panadol Extra is for adults only," I said.

"Panadol Extra is for stubborn pain. Children can have stubborn pain, too, you know," Andrew said.

He had made the yams soft, just how I liked to eat them. I squished them with my fingers into the body of oil, watching steaming white yam take on the red of palm oil. I took a little piece of yam then molded it into a tiny ball and put it in my mouth. This is how I knew how sick I had become, because Andrew did not complain about the mess I was making.

Back when I was younger, back when we had Father and Mother, Andrew twisted my shortest finger so hard it came close to snapping because I was playing with our food. Mother screamed at him for hours after that and she stopped serving us in the same bowls, even though Father told her that it was perfectly normal for brothers to fight over such things. *Rough play does not kill boys, it makes them stronger,* Father said to Mother. *You should have seen what my cousins and I got into growing up.*

That was before they were gone, before it became so hard to remember what they looked like. Sometimes when I watched Nigerian movies, I looked out for ones with actors and actresses that were around my parents' age. I did not remember them and so I imagined. It was easy to imagine Mother in a thick coat shivering in the London cold, her makeup bright and irreverent like Gloria Anozie in that movie. It was easier to imagine Father with a group of men arguing politics, his beard uncombed, short and thick like Sam Dede in any of his movies. I wondered about my ability to identify them in a crowd of people. I suspected that I would have been unable to pick them out, unable to remember any distinguishing fact about either of them.

"Peter?" Andrew said my name. I opened my eyes.

"Yes? I am not sleeping," I said.

"I am going to get you medicine now," he said.

"Okay. Thank you," I said.

He went into Grandmother's room, where she was still asleep, and brought out one of her old duvets, covering my feet with them.

"I found some money," he said. "I will be back right away."

When he was gone, the house began making those empty-house sounds, the ones you hear only because everything else is quiet—water dropping from wet clothes recently hung on the line, a fly sizzling after contact with the metal body of the kerosene lantern, the curtains dancing in the breeze, the wooden doors shifting on loose metal hinges.

In the early evening quiet, our tiny house felt like a large expanse of forest with sounds from unseen sources I had to decipher to keep from being frightened and overwhelmed. In my little corner of the forest, I was like a squirrel in a hollow hole in a tall tree, all the outside sound first filtered, then condensed and magnified. I had to try to guess, to know and explain to myself what each sound was, to keep from being afraid of it.

When you're the youngest in the family, everyone tries to protect you. They lie to you, they cover for you. You learn to do your own investigating. You have to be both persistent and invisible. Sometimes it seemed like there was a duvet of silence over all the important stuff about our family. There was no one willing to lift it up for me, to let me see for myself what it was all about.

When we first moved to Grandmother's house, it took me three months to figure out that Father was not just job searching in Abuja.

When we walked around the streets, I liked to walk behind Andrew. He had no idea I was being slow on purpose. I hid it well. I stopped to pick up stones or write on dirty cars or hurl stuff at stray cats. But what I was really doing was waiting for Andrew to go ahead of me, so I could walk behind him, keeping him in my sights.

If he walked away from me, at least I would have seen him leaving. I wouldn't have been left to wonder if someone had snatched him and made him a houseboy. Or if he stepped on a charm and dissolved into liquid or picked up money off the floor and became a tuber of yam.

Andrew returned with the painkillers and a small bag of roasted groundnuts with the skins still on. He smashed the pills into a stony powder then stirred it into a thick mix, adding about two teaspoons of water. It tasted like drops from the stalk of the bitter leaf dipped into classroom chalk. When I was done swallowing the medicine, he sat next to me eating his groundnuts.

"Here," he said. "Take some." He was stretching out a fistful of nuts to me.

"Take that away from me. My mouth is too bitter." I said. "I may never eat again."

"Do you know what I was thinking when I was walking home just now?" Andrew asked.

"No, I do not," I said.

"I was thinking about porridge," he said.

"What type of porridge?" I asked.

"Any type," he said. "I think porridge is the worst food in the world."

"Because it looks like poop?" I asked.

"Nope," Andrew said. He did not laugh, so I wondered if he knew I was joking. "Only beans porridge looks like poop. Asaro does not."

"Tell me what you were thinking," I said.

"I was thinking about stories. The stories about porridge I know. In at least three of them, terrible things happen to people after eating porridge," Andrew said.

"Are they real life or just ordinary stories?" I said.

"It's in the Bible, okay?" he said. "That makes it real."

"Are all the stories in the Bible?" I asked.

"Just the one about a boy who had worked all day hunting for meat for his family and when he came home he was tired, but his brother was making porridge for lunch, so he was excited—"

"What type of porridge?" I asked.

"I have no idea, maybe the type you make with grains, milk, and cheese. What is terrible is how much the older brother lost because he agreed to pay what his younger brother asked for the porridge."

"What should he have done?" I asked.

"He should have just waited till his brother was done and served himself. Worst thing that will happen, they fight like men," Andrew said.

"Hmmm," I said.

"Do you remember that story of the tortoise dying because he ate the medicine the Babalowo made for his wife, Yarinbo?" he asked.

"I do," I said.

"Another tragic porridge story," Andrew said.

"That was medicine, not porridge," I said, laughing a little.

"It was porridge. Irresistible porridge. That is why it was so tempting to the tortoise," he said. "When I get married, I am never letting any woman send me on stupid errands. A person can meet their death just like that, no warning given."

Our front gate opened, then banged shut. From the antiseptic smell slowly filling the air, I could tell it was Sister Bibike coming home from the hospital where she worked as a cleaner.

"My favorite tortoise story is when Tortoise goes to heaven," I said to Andrew.

"Really?" he asked. "You know that it ends with him being thrown down back to earth, right?"

"Yes, I do," I said. "But before all that, there was a feast and he ate till he was full and bursting, and the angels waited on him."

Our sister hovered over me for a few seconds, her large work bag dangling from her shoulders like a third limb. She placed the back of her palm, clammy from the humid evening, on the right side of my neck.

"You have a serious fever," she said, her voice filled with the forced calm of a nurse.

"I just gave him Panadol. He is getting better," Andrew said.

"Look. Andrew, come over here. Look at this. Look at your brother's face," our sister said.

The two of them bent over me, the smell of chewed groundnuts mingling with the smell of medical disinfectant.

It was like being in the rain with an umbrella too feeble for the wind. It took too much effort to hold on, there was sense in letting go, giving in to the wind.

"My back. It hurts. Bad." I screamed as I gave in to the wind. It was liberating, comforting.

"Mama!" our sister shouted toward the direction of Grandmother's room, where she still was asleep. "Andrew, run down the street to Aminat's house, see if Alhaji Sule is home so he can drive us to the hospital."

My brother stood stunned for a second then moved away from his spot above me.

"Hurry," she said. "And if he isn't home, ask Aminat to lend us five hundred naira. We have to go to a hospital far away from here where no one knows us. So we can run away if the bills are too expensive."

I heard the gate shut with the loud precision of a gunshot. Andrew was out before the import of our sister's words hit him. Grandmother was helping to lift me up, and I felt like I was sinking into the floor no matter how hard they tried to lift me.

In the corner of my eye, I saw an old tortoise, his shell cracked in several places, smiling a tired smile.

"How are you feeling?" I asked in a voice I did not recognize for its cheer.

"Better now that you are here," the old tortoise said.

We studied each other in silence for several minutes.

"Was it worth it? Falling from the sky? The anger from your friends? Your imperfect shell?" I asked.

"Have you had food from heaven?" he asked. "Have you

had everything, every kind of food you ever imagined spread out before you, an expanse as wide as the sea?"

"There would have been enough for all of you to share, you should have just waited," I said.

"No, there wasn't. Don't you get it?" the old tortoise asked. "That was the moral of the story, that there was not enough for all of us."

"And you had it all. And you were punished for that," I said.

"But I survived," the old tortoise said. "I am still here. Where are all the others?"

The hospital was the teaching hospital affiliated with Lagos State University. The children's ward smelled like a buka—like fried meat, heat from woodstoves, and jollof rice. There were more guardians and parents than there were sick children. They hovered over them like musical mobiles attached to the cribs of babies, soothing their restlessness and cajoling food and drink into tight lips.

By my side, what was left of my family smoothed into something firm, thorough and lasting, like starched clothes dried in the open sun.

It began with my grandmother, who said to the doctors who were urging her to leave my side, "I am going nowhere, I have heard you people kill poor children, so you can give their organs to rich people."

My sister Ariyike, who read from the Bible over and over again till the rhythm of her recitals became the rhythm of my dreams:

"You will not allow your Holy One see corruption.

You will protect my soul from Hades.

Therefore, my heart is glad.

My glory rejoices."

My back settled into the stiff sweetness of the hospital mattress. Unlike on the woven mat Andrew and I slept on at home, I rested in the hospital. I felt my muscles relax, become compliant as I lay down.

It was my sister Bibike who explained to me:

"You are getting fluids as well as antibiotics. They expect to be able to save your entire arm."

It was my brother who said to me, "You are going to be a footballer anyway, you do not need two hands to score goals like Yekini."

When you are the youngest child in a Lagos family, you are the custodian of the most precious unacknowledged hopes. Every sentence to you is a prayer, every sentence about you is an expression of possibility, everything you hear is love. I did not know this at first. Around the time I was learning to use my left hand to draw superheroes, I learned to listen for those hopes like words from a new language.

The boy on the bed next to me had a clean-shaven head and a full body cast. His mother, a plump woman with two bluish green tribal marks underneath each eye, made a contraption from a metal hanger to scratch his body with. As she scratched underneath his feet, she reported all that was going on in their family.

"Fadeke lost her tooth yesterday. And she nearly swallowed it. Thank God your daddy was with her, he caught it right in time."

She passed along to us his uneaten meal, long-grain rice sitting on a bed of tomato and carrot stew, pieces of fried beef and cow skin in a second bowl.

"I am something," Andrew said. "If you do not have strong teeth, you cannot eat me. What am I?"

He dipped his hand into the bowl, picking up both pieces of cow skin at the same time. This was how I knew everything was going to be all right: my brother was eating food meant for me, and I was laughing with him.

2

HOW TO WEAR
MOM'S JEANS

BIBIKE

2002

THERE WAS A black leather portmanteau filled with Mother's things sitting under the bed our grandmother slept in. The first time my twin sister, Ariyike, saw it, she pulled it out by its patchy leather handle and it snagged on a loose nail, making a small rip along its side. She was in the middle of cleaning up Grandmother's room and so she was sitting there in the center of the floor, her broom and dustpan at her side, staring at old photographs, when Grandmother and I came back from working at the hospital.

Ariyike had examined the portmanteau's contents, memorizing them without trying—one wedding dress, two ankle-length dinner dresses, two pairs of boot-cut jeans, one pair of black kitten heels, one shoebox filled with jewelry, forty-five photographs with Father in them.

"Did you know Mother and Father honeymooned in Spain?" she'd asked me that first time.

"They did not. They went to Tel Aviv," I said.

She did not argue with me, but she should have, because she was half right; they had gone to the Spanish border, had taken pictures standing at the foot of the Rock of Gibraltar.

"We should sell her jewelry," she said instead. "We should sell everything, even the portmanteau."

I laughed because surely she intended it as a joke. The portmanteau was old, torn and falling apart, no one wanted it. Besides, it once belonged to Justice Silver, Mother's granduncle. He gave it to her when she was about our age and traveling to Lancaster for A levels.

"You should not laugh," she'd said. "Let us take this stuff to Tejuosho market. We can sell it to those Mallams, get some money for new clothes."

She was sitting there, holding out the shoebox, a silver necklace tangled in the middle hanging from the end. I took the shoebox from her, pushed the tangled necklace inside a heart-shaped emerald pendant, and shoved the shoebox back in the portmanteau.

"It is not ours to sell," I had said.

My sister did not like that I said this. And she was right. She should have insisted. We needed money. We always needed money. Grandmother was still getting used to having four children depending on her. She still went on complaining about how much food we ate, how much soap was left after we showered, how much noise we made. Sometimes she forgot how she spent her money, so she accused us of stealing it, then made us empty our luggage and purses searching for it. Once, a few months after we arrived to live with her here, after she had searched us and found none of her missing things, she made us walk with her around the neighborhood, from the man who sold chewing gum and candy in a tuck shop, to the woman hawking bread and beans, to the old man mending plastic buckets with pieces of scrap plastic. She made us stop at every shop, showing our faces to them, telling all the owners to never sell us anything because if we ever had any money, it was money we must have stolen from her. We walked past Uche, the jollof rice seller, and even though my belly was filled with water and tumbling with anger, I wanted the jollof rice so much in that moment that I would have stolen to buy it. By the time we had walked to the houses nearest the canal, houses so close together that you could stand at any point on the street and tell which mothers had started dinner and which ones hadn't, I realized that we were to blame for the shame we had experienced. It was indeed my own legs walking behind her, wasn't it? My own head, bowing shamefaced.

Ariyike and I decided that day to start earning our own money. First, we started to sell sachet water we had kept in plastic buckets filled with ice overnight, but too many kids here already did that. We had to walk as far as the tollgate and wait until there was serious traffic to make good sales. We did this together, my sister and I, for a few months until one of grandmother's co-workers at the hospital died and I decided to take the job. Ariyike continued to sell water in traffic.

I worked mostly in the children's wing of the orthopedic department. Most of the time, all I did was empty trash bins and wastebaskets in doctors' offices. The favorite part of my day was running errands for doctors and nurses. Most of them were nice; they let me keep the change.

Sometimes the older cleaners did not show up and it fell on me to clean the toilets. It was on one of these days that I met and befriended Aminat. The supervisor had found me sitting beneath the stairs in radiology and said, "This girl again. Don't you have something to do?"

I had just come back from walking thirty minutes to and fro, buying lunch for some doctors. I could have told him that, but then he would have laughed, telling me that was "extracurricular." Instead I said nothing, pointing in the direction of the nearest toilets, and walked away.

The men's toilet smelled like boiling hot piss mixed with something superconcentrated, like hair dye or shoe polish. The cleaning bucket was in a corner by the washbasin but there was no mop or scrubbing brush. I made a makeshift bowl by breaking the top half off a plastic bottle I found in the trash. Afterward, I mixed some cleaning detergent with disinfectant and water then took to sprinkling it over and over around the bathroom. I sprinkled all around the steel pipes jutting out of the wall where the urinals were once erect. I sprinkled inside the doorless stalls, on the mirrorless walls. Unlike in the women's bathrooms, there was running water. I walked into every stall, flushing toilets repeatedly. I had spent what I considered enough time in there and was getting ready to leave when a woman walked in and shut the door behind her. I watched her lean against the door, sighing loudly as she pulled out a sanitary pad from a large red purse shaped like an envelope. It was the cheap kind of pad, not the flat type with wings, but one of the thicker ones, the ones that look like a long lump of cotton wool. She was a tiny woman. Her long box braids were waist length. They made slow, somber movements across her face as she pulled down her skirt to tuck the pad in. She was wearing one of those tight Lycra skirts with mid-thigh slits, so I had to wonder why a young lady would use such older-woman pads. She looked like the kind of person who would choose Always every day.

She did not care that I was watching her. I was not even pretending to be cleaning at this point. She stuck the pad onto her underwear then took out a Wet n Wild lipstick from her purse. She pressed it onto the pad, making a bold red stain. She drew a couple more poorly structured stains then pulled up her underwear. It was then she looked up at me and asked with that inventive mix of Yoruba and pidgin that took me months to get accustomed to, "Watch me like TV. You no get work to do?"

I realized then that there was no real way she was as old as I had assumed she was. She was only a little older than Ariyike and me, probably—eighteen, maybe twenty. It was the way she carried herself upright in the world that had thrown me off, like she knew things no one else did, like she had plans and she was thoroughly convinced of their brilliance. Her makeup of course contributed to it: she had shaved off her eyebrows and drawn thin straight lines with red pencil, and her lips shone with bright red lipstick. Her eyes were lined with the darkest shade of black possible and contrasted with her light brown skin; she looked like she had been punched several times.

The door opened and, once she was satisfied with who it was, Aminat moved out of the way to let him in. It was one of the technicians who handled X-rays. His colleagues called him Four Fiber because he held on to copies of X-rays until patients gave him at least four twenty-naira notes.

He motioned to leave as soon as he saw me, but Aminat caught him by the arm, pulling him to her. I was so happy to have spent enough time pretending to clean the toilets that I left immediately, kicking my cleaning bucket back into the corner. I walked into the nearest office and picked up their trash bin, waiting for a full minute before walking back to the toilet door, stopping to listen. I heard the sound of struggling, her braided twists smacking the small of her back as she tried to wriggle out of his grasp.

"I do not believe you," he was saying to her.

"Why will I lie about this. I have been looking forward to spending the weekend with you. Don't you believe me?" she asked.

"Show me, then, show me," he said.

"Someone might be coming. Calm down."

He pulled down her underwear, not listening to her protest. When he found the stained pad, he said he was sorry he did not believe her. He watched her as she pulled on her underwear and adjusted her skirt, then put his hand in the inner pockets of his coat, giving her all the money he could pull out.

He was sorry that he had given the girl a real reason to end the relationship with him. A relationship that had cost him a lot of money to begin and maintain. He was ashamed of how excited he became after those few moments of struggle, deflated by the possibility that all that potential had gone to waste.

He would be sad for a few weeks because Aminat will no longer have anything to do with him, then he would learn to accept it. One day, six months later, a tiny light-skinned girl who had been in the hospital for days taking care of a little brother in a hit-and-run would take the lab technician up on his offer for a hot lunch and a cold shower in his apartment. He would wait until she was fed and clean and initiate a struggle. It would be everything he imagined, then he would find another girl and do it again and again and again.

AFTER HE WALKED out of the toilets, Aminat waited a few seconds. Then she walked out after him. I was outside, right by the door, making a show of taking a broom to the cobwebs on the hallway ceilings when Aminat walked up to me.

"Here, take your share," she said, tapping me on my shoulder. She had two twenty-naira notes in her hand. She was trying to shove them down my bra.

"Stop it. I don't want that," I said.

"Why? Are you planning to broadcast on me?" she asked.

"Yes, I am. That is exactly my job here. Administrator of periods, chief commissioner of sanitary pads."

She laughed a loud hearty laugh and walked away from me, taking her money with her. I watched her go, wondering if she was walking home with the lipstick-stained pad still between her legs.

The next time I saw her, she was standing by herself in the sidelines watching our neighborhood boys play Saturday soccer. It was then I realized that I had probably seen her so many times before, but that there had been nothing about her that interested me back then. She was several inches shorter than we were. Ariyike and I tended to befriend tall girls because we do not enjoy towering over people, like their mothers. Aminat had her hair in two braided buns that Saturday. The buns were inelegantly knotted, as though she was trying really hard to look like a messy little girl.

She looked in my direction but made no attempt to acknowledge me. There were a couple of other girls with her. Maimuna, who was newly pretty, was getting a lot of attention because Agbani Darego had won Miss World. Thanks to Agbani, every tall skinny girl with skin like a dusty blackboard would forever think they were better than everybody else. Thank you, Agbani. Then Adanna, who always told the most ridiculous stories, like the time she claimed she knew someone who ate boiled yams and palm oil that she found at the T junction and now coughed up naira notes at night. Why aren't you rich, Adanna? Where the naira notes?

They all had on the same type of jeans, low waisted, light blue with horizontal white stripes around the hips.

They were talking, waving to the boys and calling the referee names. I was about to walk away when one of the boys kicked the ball in my direction. It was rolling out of the area, so I stopped it with my feet. Another boy ran up to me to get it, his feet dusty and bare. He said thank you with a shy smile, then walked away. A few minutes later, another boy threw the ball, and another came to get it. By the third time it happened, I started to suspect it was deliberate. Aminat and her friends were leaving. None of the players had paid much attention to them.

As she walked away, she came close to me and whispered in my ear:

"Next time put on some jeans," she said. "The boys have been making all kinds of excuses to look up your skirt."

I ran home like I was seven and a boy kissed me at playtime, my ears warm from embarrassment. Andrew was home by himself building giant kites from old calendars. I ran into Grandmother's room, pulling out the portmanteau.

My mother's jeans were too short for me and too tight around the hip. They made my legs look as long as the road to Oyo. I hated them. But we had only two thousand naira saved—actually, it was a thousand six fifty because Ariyike had taken three hundred and fifty to buy us Vanilla Ice deodorant spray.

When she returned from selling water, her bucket still half full, she found me sitting outside in Mother's jeans, watching the evening make way for nighttime.

"Why are you wearing that?" she asked.

And so I told her the whole story.

"You should keep away from those girls," she said. "I have heard many bad things."

"Do we have enough money for jeans?" I replied.

She sat on the floor next to me, taking off her top and then tucking it under both arms, covering her breasts.

"We can if we have to," she said.

"Look at this, what do you think?" I laid our mother's jeans on the floor between us. "I'm thinking of cutting it short right here, just under my knees."

She leaned back into the wall, wiping her face with her shirt. "You do not need my permission to do anything" she said. "I am not your mother."

A short distance away, Ibrahim the muezzin sang in his clear loud voice the call for evening prayers. There was no real mosque in the area, so the Muslims brought their mats from home and spread out in the corner of the football field that faced east.

Grandmother was making a soup dinner, but we called Andrew and Peter. Together we had bread and akara that Ariyike had bought on her way back from selling water. We sat there, the four of us, chewing and listening to the fading sounds of the neighborhood as it settled into nighttime.

In the morning, my sister woke me up before we headed out and gave me a list of all the things we needed money for, along with all the money we had saved. She did not have to. I knew what we needed and what we had. But I was thinking about more, I was thinking that most of the money was mine, anyway. Ariyike made barely sixty naira a day from water and always spent it before she got home.

We needed a new kerosene stove, lightbulbs for the living room lamp, sugar, rice, beans, smoked fish, dry okra, palm oil. Grandmother rarely did anything for us in those days, and we had learned to stop asking. She still accused us of stealing from her sometimes, and so we kept away, spending most of our time outdoors and in the bedroom that we all shared.

The next time I saw Aminat, she had a pimple the size of a bean on the side of her face. She spoke like her mouth was filled with warm water.

"Nice jeans, where you buy it?"

"A shop close by," I said.

"Your boyfriend won't like it?" She said it like a question. "You want many new toasters, showing off your hot legs—"

That was the way she acted. If the last time, she had made me feel like a toddler, now she was making me feel older, sophisticated, the kind of girl who had a jealous boyfriend.

"Who cares what anyone thinks." I laughed.

We had started off at the hospital and were walking toward her house. Her father was crippled in both legs and moved about on a wheelchair that had an exposed battery attached to it. She was telling me about her ex who was so jealous, and I could not tell if it was the technician or some other fellow, but I had never known another girl our age with an ex, so I listened to her stories about the time he ripped her blouse open in a restaurant because she was talking to some other man. By the time we got to her house, I felt like a stranger in my body. I spent a lot of time thinking about Aminat, how she was just a girl like me, we lived in the same neighborhood, but she was from another world. She made me think I could create a world for myself, but I was hesitant. I did not know how many worlds could fit into ours and not explode when they came in contact.

I had planned to stop at the entrance of her house, but by the time we arrived I just had to go inside. There are two types of ambitious families, I think. Some are so enamored with connections, they can live in the dingiest house in a nice neighborhood; others are more concerned with being considered wealthy, so they build the nicest house in a poor neighborhood.

Aminat's father was the second type. His house, a four-bedroom bungalow, had a white Mercedes 300 class in the driveway. There were numerous, similar-sized posters of Indian actresses on the walls of the hallway that ran from the front of the house to the back. Alongside them, in a strange kinship with them, was a wood-framed black-and-white photograph of a woman who had to be Aminat's mom. She was sitting, back straight, both hands clasped before her and resting on her thighs, looking into the camera with Aminat's same resolve. Her headscarf was loose around her neck, both ends falling forward in front of her chest, as though it had been a last-minute addition to her self-assured pose.

Their television stood over a sturdy bookcase overflowing with old books. From my position in the hallway, I could see those unmistakable James Hadley Chase covers.

"Those are all my father's," she said, "please don't touch anything."

In her room, she had several suitcases around her bed.

The wall was bare and without character, and her mattress was on the floor like she was resident in a dorm room, just moved in and already waiting for the end of the semester. She rummaged through a couple of suitcases and brought out baggy T-shirts with no sleeves, the kind all of us had been crazy about the year before, and long khakis with several pockets.

"You can have these if you want," she said.

I had laughed when she said that, thinking it was a joke, but she was serious. In a quick moment, I pretended my laughter was joy at the unexpected largesse of it. Andrew was already almost as tall as we were at this time, and because I knew he would be glad for those clothes, I laughed again and smiled with real gratitude for the unisex style of American rappers of the nineties.

It was harder to be her friend after that, for in that moment I had seen what she had, the bounty of it, all types of clothes slipping out of boxes, her bedroom untidy in the way only the rooms of girls with too many things could be. We had stood there laughing, sister-friends, with the same concerns and goals, and then she had looked at me and handed me clothes that she would never wear again. This was the summary of her estimation of me, I concluded, *Poor Bibike, she is desperate enough to be grateful for anything.* After, we remained friends for the sake of habit. There was no easy way to begin to avoid her in the neighborhood, no polite way to ignore the carefree persistence with which she ingratiated herself into my life.

My sister, Ariyike, hated that the "corrupting" influence

of this friendship. My brothers did not mind, all they cared was that Aminat's house had cable and someday they could visit with me—they really wanted to watch episodes of *Captain Planet*. I always said no to them tagging along.

They did not understand that being Aminat's friend was like taking a bus to a different part of town. She showed me a different Lagos, a happy Lagos. Aminat had grown up the richest girl in a poor neighborhood. She was used to a certain type of authority, her own brand of soft worship. I did not want to fawn over her, not over her beauty and not over the nice stuff she had access to. When she got CK One perfume as her birthday gift from her father a few weeks after we became friendly, even though I was impressed about the reach of her father's influence—a friend of the family had brought it all the way from New York just in time for her nineteenth—I still did not fawn. For her birthday party, I again reached inside Mother's portmanteau, modifying one of her old dinner dresses into a minidress, to my sister's chagrin. I told anyone who asked that it was vintage, and therefore priceless. They all laughed at my lack of shame. At the party, the red looked fluorescent on my skin in the dark lights of a nightclub. When two different boys tried to touch my thighs, I knew there was something about the dress. I was beautiful in my mother's dress, and sometimes beauty was just as powerful as wealth.

I met Alhaji Sule, Aminat's father, months after we became friends. It was after I had already gone to her house several times, attended her birthday party, taught her how to make moimoi to impress a new boyfriend. On this first day, her father rolled up in his wheelchair, sitting beside us as we watched dancehall music videos on Channel O. Aminat changed the channel to CNN immediately and motioned, her fingers slow, wary, pointing to her bedroom, asking me to leave the room with her.

"You girls should spend more time reading than watching all that junk," he said as he pulled himself out of the wheelchair to sit next to us on the sofa. He was a tall, broad-shouldered man; even beneath his jalabia, you could see the dips and curves of defined biceps.

He spoke with the cultured precision of the educated northerner, his vowel sounds not exaggerated, his *th*s smooth, his *r*s elucidated. As soon as began to explain the severity of America's actions in Afghanistan, Aminat walked away with the dismissive rudeness only children could exhibit to parents regardless of who was watching. I sat there polite and smiling, listening until the news report ended and he lifted himself back into his chair and rolled over to the bookshelf/TV stand, picking up three books.

After he had set himself as close as possible to me on the sofa, he handed me the three books, one Danielle Steele, one John Grisham, one James Hadley Chase.

"One for passion, one for wit, and one for cunning, I will leave you to figure out what is what," he said, and I laughed with him in spite of myself.

He was emboldened, it appeared, by my unforced laugh and the quiet of Aminat's room. He moved closer to me, cupping my chin and whispering, his breath warming my face. He smelled like dabino and sugarcane.

"You have a pure smile," he said. "It's golden."

I did not feel the disgust I would have expected to feel, but instead, a sense of relief, of superiority, that continued to accrete as he slid his hands down my dress, tugging on a nipple.

It was the way he spoke and looked at me, both shy and hopeful like a boy but also like a medicated puppy, the way he was polishing his words and making an effort to sustain a loud conversation when all I was saying was *yes sir* that stripped me of every kind of envy I had felt for Aminat. Instead, I realized how tenuous her position was, how vulnerable her life really was. Her Lagos was just as sad as mine.

"I have many Nigerian paperbacks as well," he was saying. "Do you know Anezi Okoro? He writes the best stories about what it means to be around your age."

I was wearing my mother's dress, the one I wore to Aminat's party, that neck-too-wide dress, that hand-stitched-hem dress. Aminat's father moved from one nipple to the next, watching my face for a reaction. His fingers were dry and cold, and if I had been as present in that afternoon as I should have been, his grip on my nipples would have hurt.

"I suppose you may not like Okoro as much as I do. He writes about teenage boys. But perhaps you will enjoy Nengi Koin's *Time Changes Yesterday?*"

He was slower and gentler and warming my belly, so I pulled his hand out in one deft move.

Aminat was on her bed, both ears covered with headphones, hands holding a bright yellow Discman. It was a recent purchase, and I performed, for the first time with delight, the friendly responsibility of admiring it and congratulating her.

My world had shifted and collided with Aminat's, and I could not tell my sister what had happened. I spent way too long thinking about how to frame it, so as to understand my reaction to it. Why did Alhaji Sule touch me like me that? He wanted to. Why did I sit there quiet like nothing was happening?

I was a parentless teenage girl living with my grandmother in the slums of Lagos. Beauty was a gift, but what was I to do with it? It was fortunate to be beautiful and desired. It made people smile at me. I was used to strangers wishing me well. But what is a girl's beauty, but a man's promise of reward? What was my beauty but a proclamation of potential, an illusion of choice?

All women are owned by someone, some are owned by many; a beautiful girl's only advantage is that she may get to choose her owner. If beauty was a gift, it was not a gift to me, I could not eat my own beauty, I could not improve my life by beauty alone. I was born beautiful, I was a beautiful baby. It did not change my life. I was a beautiful girl. Still, my life was ordinary. But a beautiful woman was another type of thing. I had waited too long to choose my owner, dillydallying in my ignorance, and so someone chose me. What was I to do about that?

THE LAST TIME I saw Alhaji Sule, Aminat's father, I was standing on a bed in a hotel in Sabo. He was sitting in his wheelchair, his head beneath my dress. The hotel building stood adjacent to the All Saints Girls Secondary School. Every time his beard tickled my outer lips, instead of laughing, I looked outside my upstairs window and watched girls in blue checkered dresses, worn with matching blue berets, playing, reading, and writing.

It was like any other ordinary day in Lagos. My sister, Ariyike, thinking I was on my way to work, had tucked in my purse a short list of things to buy. My brothers, also not caring where the money was coming from, asked me to buy the two Westlife audio CDs everyone had been talking about.

"I promise to take care of you, my little angel," Alhaji Sule had said that day, reaching up under my dress and pulling down my underwear. "You are too beautiful to be walking around in your mom's jeans."

Alhaji Sule kissed the back of my neck as he wrapped his arms around me, and his body was like mine, pudgy and soft, his skin unlike mine, wrinkly, tough and warm like a fake leather bag left in the sun too long.

I searched inside me for something to stop me, for a reason to say *no*. I found nothing. There was nothing to stop me.

HOW TO RECEIVE FROM GOD

ARIYIKE

2004

"When you sell cold water on the streets of Lagos, you meet different types of people. Mess with the wrong thirsty bastard, your day can be ruined just like that.

"You learn to separate them into people in cars and people in buses. If you sell water mostly to people in cars, you will have a good day. If you sell to people in buses, there are two things involved.

"You will sell water to women or to men. If the bus patrons are women, you are safe. But if they are men, there are two things involved. It is either that they are old men, or they are young men. If your male bus patrons are forty and older you are safe. If they are younger men, then there are two things involved. It is either that they are ass men or boobs men. If they are ass men, you are safe—"

"I don't think you can say *ass* on a live radio show," Bibike interrupted. "Or *boobs* for that matter."

We were practicing for my audition to be an on-air presenter for a radio comedy show. In the weeks before, I had been writing several original jokes for my audition. Unsure of which way to lean, I had run through many tactics, trying to find my own distinctive style. I had started with the obvious—things of concern to young girls my age, like makeup, lace shrugs, and long belts that hang loose around your hips.

My first jokes had been drawn from my life. They had included one about buying two used skirts for two hundred naira after waking up at five a.m. on a Friday to get to the Katangwa secondhand clothes market the day all the used clothes from America arrived. But then we got home and could not wash off the telltale smell of imported used clothes: cheap fabric softener and naphthalene mothballs.

The final version of the joke was not that funny, to be honest. Besides, like my sister Bibike said, it just made me seem poor and desperate. So I had decided to go for sexy jokes. To tell a joke with a punch line about jiggling breasts, bonus points being that I could perform the jiggling.

Then my sister again, wet blanket that she was, pointed out that there was a limit to all the things I could say on air. As if I did not know that. As if we did not know that the unacknowledged goal was to seduce the interview panel.

"If you sell water on the streets," I continued, ignoring her, "young men wait until the bus is driving off. They do this so you can run after them. They love to watch breasts bounce."

•

ON THE DAY of the scheduled interview, when I finally made it to the little flat at the back of the Karamorose restaurant on Victoria Island, I was aghast to find at least thirty other girls auditioning for the same role.

It was easy to feel immediately drained and defeated and, in that moment, I did, especially after I noticed that most of the girls auditioning spoke English with accents polished, it seemed to me, by international travel and private schools. Their sentences, as they spoke in loud whispers to one another, were cheery and bright, their diphthongs cleaner, glossier than mine.

I did not know anyone at the radio station, Chill FM. My referral had been DJ Angro, a friend of a friend, one of the few boys who in recent times had made it out of our neighborhood. He was trying to give a fellow ghetto girl a leg up in this world. I had met him only once at this time. He was short and stocky, loud and enthusiastic, with prominent round eyes always red with wine or something stronger. He wore his "hair" in a hairless shine, a clean skin cut that aged him and contrasted with the baggy jeans and baseball jerseys he always wore to affect a well-traveled-young-person aesthetic.

I liked the Chill FM offices. I liked the idea that I had made it to such an opportunity. DJ Angro had been calm and reassuring when he told me what to do at the audition.

"Dress sexy, be confident, smell nice, and if you are offered something to drink, ask for water first," he said. "If they insist, ask for something foreign and healthy, like green tea."

The job entailed everything I dreamed, a chance for the restoration of all we had lost. A sufficient salary working four shifts a week on air, four shifts off air. A furnished apartment in the gated Victoria Island neighborhood, for me to arrive early or sleep off late shifts. The job also included an allowance for clothes, for hair, for makeup. A glamour crew to help with celebrity interviews and public appearances, a driver to take me around the city.

DJ Angro had said his bosses were Lebanese and so they were more interested in natural talent, unlike other owners of FM stations around Lagos who had become somewhat notorious for being more impressed by pedigree. I laughed as he told me many stories about talentless kids from wealthy families—offspring of diplomats and politicians, who, eager for jobs on the radio, had been humiliated during Chill FM auditions. Many people wanted to be on radio: it required less skill than movies or music, with about the same access to celebrity.

I wanted the job so badly that it made me physically ill with longing. Not just because I wanted to make people laugh, but because radio stations were one of the few places in Lagos that did not care that I had dropped out of school at fourteen and barely made five credits in the GCE Bibike and I had written the year before. They were interested only in talent. The only other available profession with such lax entry-level requirements was stripping.

As I waited to be interviewed, I sat on a chaise in the

waiting area, watching a girl in a bright yellow midriff top sip water so delicately that it looked as if she was taking invisible sips, and I felt like I was about to scream. Whoever these women were, they were born to be stars. They were confident. They smelled like mothers who baked meat pies and made the sign of the cross over them when they sneezed, and fathers who had other kids' fathers drive them around.

A girl in a TM Lewin shirt with a boy's haircut, her hair wet and slick like she had just showered, sat next to me. She smelled like old cigarette smoke and hair gel. She reached into a side pocket of her jeans and pulled out a new pack of Orbit gum, offering me one. I smiled gratefully at the kindness of her gesture; I was beginning to worry about how my mouth smelled after sitting quietly for over an hour.

"The wrapping is still on," I said.

"I know. I was not really offering. You were just to say no thank you," she said, laughing. She unwrapped the pack, took two sticks of gum out of the first row, and tucked the pack back into her pocket.

As she chewed the gum with her mouth closed, her mouth twitching only a little at the corner, I wondered if the humming I could hear was coming from her or someone else. I was upset but smiling to keep from crying. For the purposes of this job, I was pretending to be twenty-one instead of my actual eighteen years, but next to this girl, I felt fourteen. I felt both alien and plain. It was as though I had accidentally sat at a T junction with my knees spread apart and everyone could see my lies and inexperience.

She was doing nothing but sit there, chewing gum soundlessly, and I was unraveling.

"You have the widest face I have ever seen on a not fat person," I said to her suddenly, without thinking. My voice carried above the whispers; three other girls turned in our direction then immediately looked away.

"Your cheeks are huge, you look like you have whole lemons stuck under there," I continued.

She stared at me, still calm, with only her widened eyes revealing that she had been surprised. But I was not even sure whether she was amused or annoyed.

"Well, not everyone needs to be pretty, being cultured is often enough," she replied.

There were other girls in that room, but it seemed in that moment that it was just the two of us. I knew then that I did not mind not getting the job, as long as she, this girl with the boy's haircut, was not the one to take it from me. I did not understand the rage I was feeling nor the discomfort I felt watching her get out of the chair to work the room, flamboyantly on display, a magician, mesmerizing anyone watching.

She introduced herself over and over as Erica. She gave everyone rich, wordy, flattering compliments.

"Your hair is so beautiful. It looks like it smells like fresh oranges," she said to one.

"Your eyebrows! Such a perfect arc. I am coming home with you for makeup classes," she said to another.

She acted like she was the hostess and all of us were guests at her home, like that wide waiting room with the leather bar stools and earthen sculptures of Yoruba goddesses and antique mirrors was hers, like she had seen the world, made her money, and gathered us here together to bask in her joy.

I immediately made it my business to be outside every small group she was in, to work the room in the opposite direction to her, from the girls gathered closest to the elevator to the girls gathered nearest the director's office.

What I'd really wanted was to run away, to go home, to tell my sister that of course she was right, jobs like that were reserved for a certain type of girl, to admit that the false courage I had conjured to get me to the interview had evaporated and I was without cover.

Instead, I steadied my heart, told myself that it was as good a time as any to become someone else. No one knows me here, I'd thought, no one knows I am a nobody.

The girl Erica was a somebody, she had lived in Senegal, then France, then had gone to college in Florida. Her degree was in art appreciation and history. The person I decided to become temporarily, as a perfect counter to her cultured charm, was Keke, former child model and aspiring actress.

It rained that day. I remember because some of the girls who came in later had water in their weave and Keke was there to console them with loud exaggerated sighs.

"Your hair, your makeup, you must have spent so much time getting dressed," I said.

All my life until that day, I thought the effort it took to be mean without reason could poison me, that I would never be happy or comfortable with myself acting that way. What I discovered instead was how empowered I felt, talking to the other girls like that. A well-calculated snide remark said with a smile, a small laugh that made another uncomfortable. I even tried something I had seen on a TV show, saying *darling* at the end of every sentence, rolling that middle *r*, caressing it like a long-lost friend. All I could think of, apart from the desire to not lose to Erica, was my sister, Bibike, waiting at home for me to come back with good news.

When it was my turn to interview, I went in as Keke. I walked into that interview room pulling my stomach in, all the way into my belly button, and pushing my chest out. I was smiling so wide I could taste the humid air.

In the middle of rendering a highly edited version of my education and work history, the lead interviewer, a large man sitting at the center of the group, interrupted me.

"Tell me something interesting. If you could change something about your life, what'd it be?" he asked.

His voice, one I had heard too many times over the airwaves, startled me. It was difficult to imagine that this large, dimpled man, beautiful in a way that was almost feminine, was the possessor of the sexy baritone of nighttime radio. I had expected that Dexter, the British Nigerian who had revolutionized Nigerian radio, would be on the interview panel, but I had not expected my physical reaction to his dimpled smile.

"To be clear," he continued, "I am not talking about physical attributes, especially because they are outside your control."

"Dexter, is it okay I call you Dexter?" I asked.

"Yes. Shoot," Dexter said.

"If I could change anything, I'd choose to not be a twin. Even though I love being a twin, and appreciate the intense connection I have with her, sometimes I wish I wasn't a twin. It's been difficult learning independence." I said of all these things without thinking, still smiling.

I had resisted by instinct the urge to talk about our parents leaving, about the unending challenges we had faced raising our brothers in a cesspit of a neighborhood, raising ourselves. I had been honest yet circumspect; if Bibike had known what I'd said, it's possible she might have laughed. She also would have insisted that it was a great way to be evasive, introducing new information.

But no, I had not been trying to evade. I was realizing for the first time my tendency to think always in terms of "us" instead of "me." The shoes I wore were ours, the clothes ours, the parents who left without saying goodbye, ours.

When we finally ended the interview and I freed my face from the burden of a smile, the sun was setting in the street below. To avoid the other girls milling around the elevators, exchanging numbers to keep up with who gets called back, I took the stairs to the floor below, then stopped to stare at a Ben Enwonwu painting in the hallway.

I FELT A man's shadow fall over the painting like the shade of a tree. He reached over and touched the painting's edges, wiping off a speck of dust I had not noticed until he touched it.

"We keep our replicas clean around here," he said.

The woman in the portrait was bare chested, her breasts, rendered without nipples, were lopsided and uneven, her eyebrows thin and shaped like a half moon, like Beyoncé in her "Check On It" video.

"In the original, the woman is wearing a long-sleeved cardigan or something," he said. "The original is called *Portrait of a Girl*."

"Are the eyes in both pictures the same?"

I frowned as I listened to him. His deeper dimple broadened when he talked, making his face look lopsided, his smile artificial and forced. Perhaps it was just to me, I thought. Maybe to most other people, he was just a good-looking man with the face of a baby.

"I don't usually do this," he said, interrupting me. "I promise you. Do you mind coming with me? I'd very much like to show you something."

"I guess I can spare a few minutes," I said.

I walked behind him down the hall, toward a narrow stairwell. On this new floor, we walked past three locked doors, stopping at the fourth. He opened it with a key card. It was the first time I had seen one used, and I immediately felt smaller and more vulnerable. The room was a similar size to the type the interview had been held in; this one, however, had been furnished like a studio efficiency. Through a balcony overlooking the busy street below, I watched several of the girls just ending their interviews get into their cars and drive themselves away.

"What do you think about this?" Dexter said. He pointed

at a sculpted head in the corner of the room. "I had this made as soon as I could afford it."

"Oh, that's you," I said, laughing at the absurdity of it.

Dexter was no longer smiling. He was watching me, his eyes squinting with either concern for my sanity or anger at my effrontery.

"It is very accurate," I said.

DEXTER EXCUSED HIMSELF, disappearing behind a closed door. I had not realized until then that the room had a smaller connected room. Outside, I saw Erica wave to someone before taking a sip from a bottle of water in her hand. Another girl stopped beside her and they began to talk.

When Dexter reemerged, he saw what I was looking at. "One of those two girls is our new OAP," he said.

In the street below, a third girl walked up to them. I watched as Erica hugged each girl and then walked away.

"Which of them is it?" I asked.

"The one who walked away," Dexter said.

When I said nothing, he continued.

"It was an easy decision really, she was head and shoulders better, the most qualified."

In that moment, I remembered the chapter in the Bible, the one the night before Jesus was crucified, when Judas walked up to kiss him right at the time that the soldiers came to get him.

JESUS, WHO HAD always known who would betray him, seemed to me strangely hurt by the fact that Judas kissed him. I had always found that part of the story hard to believe. It seemed to me an exaggeration, included for dramatic effect, something to be easily memorized and repeated by children all over the world in Easter plays.

Judas, are you betraying the Son of Man with a kiss?

I stepped away from the window and sat on the armchair by the side of the bed. Dexter sat next to me and helped take my shoes off.

"Is there anything you can do about that?" I asked him, surprised by how shaky my voice sounded.

I HAD OVERESTIMATED this invitation to Dexter's privacy. Maybe it was an underestimation of how male desire worked, maybe none of it was true, maybe Dexter had choreographed several moments like this in the past. There had once been another girl, it seemed to me easily possible, and she had wanted a job almost as much as Dexter had wanted her.

"There is nothing I can do, Keke," he said. And as he spoke, my heartbeat sped up like a car losing control on a racetrack. "I do not want to lie to you. It is done."

Dexter reached down to my lap and stroked the top of my thigh, right above my knee. It was a slow, oddly calming motion, and we sat there in quiet for a few minutes.

"Are you really sure?" I asked. "Is this what you brought me down here to tell me?"

I WAS CRYING freely, crying ugly, the tears and snot and shoulders shuddering type of crying.

Dexter continued stroking my thigh, murmuring in what he assumed were calming whispers.

"Don't cry, baby girl. I promise you things will work out just fine," he said. "I'm here for you. Let me help you. Everyone starts from somewhere, this is just the intermission, not the end."

The room had gotten quiet and uncomfortable. The street sounds had lessened and the dark of night was beginning to cover us all.

"Do you know that all three Gospels report the kiss of Judas but give different versions of how Jesus dealt with it?" I asked him, even though I knew he did not understand the parallels my mind was drawing or my tendency to exaggerate my hurts.

"Well, I am not sure I ever paid attention to that," he said.

"Only Luke records, 'Are you betraying the Son of Man with a kiss,'" I said.

"What do the others write?" he asked.

"Matthew says something that can be read as completely opposite to Luke. According to Matthew's gospel, Jesus said to Judas, 'Friend, why have you come?' It may seem that in Luke's version Jesus was surprised about the kiss, but in Matthew, he was surprised that Judas actually went through with the betrayal," I continued.

Dexter was patient, if still a little stunned by the direction our conversation had taken.

"Maybe both recordings are accurate. Maybe each disciple just wrote what they were absolutely certain happened.

Maybe we are to read them all to get the full picture instead of looking for inconsistencies," he said.

"I guess so."

"Are you going to be all right?" he asked.

"I just don't understand all of this, why I am here, why you told me Erica got the job," I said.

"I was hoping to spend some more time with you," he said. "Getting to know you, figuring you out. Your interview was an act, it seemed. I was curious about the real you."

I do not remember exactly why, but I started laughing at this point. Maybe it was the audacity of it all. Maybe it was my inner mind confronting the utter folly of my permutations. Of course, Dexter wanted me, that part was obvious. I had imagined some negotiation, a quid pro quo, while he had planned to rely solely on seduction.

"Keke, are you okay?" he asked.

"I am fine. I promise you I am not losing my mind right now."

Dexter shuffled around the room. I wondered if it was strange that I was still sitting in the chair I had been in since I followed him up the stairwell into this room. I shut my eyes and listened to what he was up to. He seemed to be walking the length and breadth of the room without direction, like someone in one those Nollywood movies, demonstrating their mulling over an idea.

"Have you ever listened to my Sunday morning show?" he asked eventually.

"*How to Receive from God*? Yes, I have," I said.

"Do you know it has been sponsored by Pastor David of New Citizens' Church for the past year?" he asked.

There was no way for Dexter to know of my history with Pastor David or my family's experiences with his church.

"I did not know that," I said instead.

"Would you like to take over that show?" he asked.

"Really? How would that work?"

"Well, I will have to convince the station to hire you as off-air staff," he said. "You can help set up the studio, edit interviews, follow up with advertisers, but on Sundays, you would do the church show."

"Why? Why are you offering me this?" I asked.

He came over to where I was sitting and settled into the other chair, shifting his weight now and again to better fit the chair and extend his hand to clasp mine. I watched him do all of this but said nothing, waiting for his reply.

"You need this. And I like you. I want to help you," he said.

"I am not a fan of Pentecostalism. I am not sure I want to be a part of this," I said.

"Let me help you. This is the only way I can help you. And you will be good at it. Just now, you taught me Scripture without trying," he said.

If the church was coming again into my life as an answer, it was okay for me to be weary, but it was stupid for me to say no. Dexter was right. I needed a job. My whole family needed it.

"I will do it. Thank you so much, I am sorry for

overthinking it." I turned, facing him so that our faces were right in front of each other. He was smiling at me.

"You are most definitely welcome," he said.

Still smiling at me, he clasped both of his hands around my neck, pulling my face closer to him. He kissed me. At first, it was a gentle kiss. His lips against mine felt weak and beggarly. Just when I was about to pull away, irritated by his hesitation, he got out of the chair, pulling me up with him.

"Is this okay? Can I continue?" he asked.

I looked at his face, still smiling his dimpled smile, and down at his jeans, his unbuckled belt, and his bare feet. His hands followed my eyes, his face contorted in a small groan. The smile never left his eyes. He placed my hand on the bulge of him.

"I am ready for you, can't you see?" he said.

I was about to begin another bout of hysterical laughter when he lifted me and in three quick steps placed me on the single bed. As he stood at the foot, hurriedly stepping out of his jeans, I wondered about the bed, about how many other desperate dreaming girls like me had inevitably ended up on it, despite their initial hesitation.

Dexter got up on the bed, kneeling and crouching over me so that, in the moment, I was overwhelmed by his calm confidence, by the sheer size of him, the smell of him, the width of him. I surprised myself by thinking about our father in that moment. I was thinking that since the day my father left, I had yet to smell this stench of maleness up close, this sweat and lust and cologne.

"Hey, Keke. Stay with me. Why are you so quiet?" he asked.

"I don't know what to do," I said.

"Do you know what you want me to do?" he asked.

"Not really," I said.

A strange calm had fallen upon us. I told myself to stop wondering how much was planned, or whether or not I could trust him to keep his word to me. It was possible, after all, that even the Gospel show was a hoax, a part of this seduction plan.

"Do you like what I am doing?" He was kissing my breasts all over, rapid wet kisses that did nothing for me.

"You should maybe kiss my nipples," I said. "Slowly. Please."

Somehow in the middle of my clumsiness and his eagerness, we found a way to move right. We had not turned on any lamps in this room, so the dark of night had engulfed us. I could see nothing but the brightness of his eyes. It felt like I was remembering a past life, like I had stored up a peculiar specificity of desire for that moment with Dexter. I was filled to the full measure of it and in every place he kissed me slowly, more desire poured until I could not recognize the words pouring out of my own mouth, their need or their satiation.

WE HAVE TO TALK ABOUT GIRLS

ANDREW

2005

I WAS A Ju-boy that year. My school father was Ricky, the sanitation prefect. Ricky had six other school sons from all three junior classes. Each of us had been assigned specific duties. I washed and ironed all Ricky's clothes. Every day after lunch, right before siesta, I went to his room to check in his laundry basket for whatever clothes were there. I returned them handwashed, ironed, and folded in twenty-four hours or less.

Ju-boys. This was what we called the younger boys in junior classes 1 to 3. Ju-boys were identifiable by their uniforms, white shirts worn over blue shorts instead of the full-length trousers all boys in the senior classes wore. The Ju-boys were the nobodies.

•

ORDINARY BOYS. THIS was what we called the older boys in senior classes 1 to 2. The ordinary boys were almost nobodies or nearly somebodies, it depended on how you considered their situation. Ordinary boys were greater than Ju-boys but less than the ordinary men. Ju-boys ran every conceivable errand for ordinary boys, but they were not assigned to serve them.

The ordinary men were the senior boys in class 3 who were not appointed prefects. The prefects were the senior boys in class 3 who ruled Odogolu secondary school.

All ordinary men and prefects had Ju-boys assigned to serve them each year. On the first day of the new term, the head prefect posted a list of Ju-boys and their school fathers on the dormitory's central notice board. It was normal to see boys, their faces fat, full, and fresh from the joys of vacation, burst out weeping after learning they had been assigned to serve someone with a reputation for cruelty.

We called them our school fathers. A school father was the ordinary man or prefect a ju-boy was assigned to. A school son was the Ju-boy assigned to a school father.

I WAS ONE of the luckier Ju-boys. It would have been beyond me to oversee Ricky's food, water, or bedding, because most of the time you had to spend your own money doing things for your school father. I would have been terrible at cuddling or singing him to sleep like my school brother Teddy, the round-faced boy with a girl's voice, who had all the nighttime duties. Fortunately, all I needed was soap, and I had lots of that. My sisters sent us to boarding school with more than a dozen bars of soap; they wanted Peter and me to have more than enough for ourselves and to give away.

Our school was a mixed boarding school. This meant we had girls all around us. There were so many girls, there were even more girls than boys. In our school, girls did everything differently. They served nobody. They had a different set of rules. Girls had their own prefects, called aunties. Our prefects could not punish them. When they got in trouble, they were made to write book reports or apology letters. They did not have to do chores around the school grounds like clearing the lawns or trimming shrubs. They had their own hostels with running water flowing inside their washrooms.

We had chapel with girls. We had classes with girls. We had meals with girls. All the places you would think we needed focus and concentration, girls waddled in, pretty in their purple-and-yellow checkered dresses and white socks with tiny bows.

We were obsessed with girls. All of us were. Ju-boys had games where we wrote down names of girls on pieces of paper, which we then all drew from and dared one another to go ask out. We never did. We were Ju-boys; we knew our place.

Senior boys were obsessed with sex. They all were.

As a matter of fact, I was not even supposed to be a junior boy. When Sister Ariyike got her job and decided we had to go back to school, on account of my age, I was going to be in senior class 1 and Peter in junior class 2. But we had been out of school so long, I had not taken the junior secondary certificate examination. The school principal was only following administrative policy by requiring me to enroll in junior class 3.

"It can't be helped," he said to our sister. "I have been a principal for almost eight years. If there was something I could do, surely, I will do it for you. Especially because it's you."

Sister Ariyike was some kind of celebrity in those days because of her radio job. Everyone, strangers included, was nice to her. Once in a supermarket, an older man recognized her voice and paid for all the stuff we had in our shopping basket. Our sister did not even have to pretend to be interested in dating him or take his business card. He just said, "I am so proud of the work you do, praising God every day with your pretty voice," and walked away.

A bagger is what you were called if you could not handle your school father's business as well as all your chores and schoolwork without falling apart. A bloody bagger is what you were called if your incompetence was so glaringly bad that your school father had to report you to other prefects for reprimand.

Community murder is what a bloody bagger got. A small crowd of ordinary men and prefects made a circle around the erring Ju-boy, shouting punishments.

"Bloody bagger. Roll in the dirt."

"Dirty stinky bloody bagger. Now let me see you do five hundred frog jumps."

Ordinary men and prefects were fully grown men,

unlike the rest of us. They shaved every day, they walked around smelling like cologne and Irish Spring bath soap. When they slapped your face or the center of your back, you wondered how it was possible that something that hurt so bad was not fatal.

There was a hard-won peace between ordinary men and ordinary boys. This was on account of soccer. Before Friday evening soccer became a regular thing at Odogolu Secondary, clashes between ordinary men and ordinary boys were said to have been so frequent, the school sick bay had to get a second full-time nurse in charge of deep wounds.

They brawled about everything; everything escalated easily into fracas. A tussle between a small-for-his-age ordinary man and a bigger-than-normal ordinary boy over seats on the school bus trip to the village market resulted in the Great Destruction of 2003. This was before we arrived, so everything we heard about it was hearsay. There are many versions of the story. The most consistent facts are that the ordinary man tried to take a seat in the bus the ordinary boy had reserved for his girlfriend. The ordinary boy refused to give up the seat. The smaller but older ordinary man, who had a reputation for wild anger—he was overcompensating for what he lacked in height—slashed the ordinary boy's cheek with a razor. The bleeding boy punched the man, knocking him out. Other ordinary men attacked the bleeding boy in a bid to subdue him. The bleeding boy's classmates and friends tried to help him. Soon no one cared how it had started, it was ordinary men vs. ordinary boys. According to the legend, the resulting free-for-all lasted hours.

It is, however, unquestioned that the police descended upon the school with antiriot gear, batons, and tear gas. They arrested at least twenty students that day. There was a noticeboard at the entrance of the teachers' lounge with the names as well as passport photographs of all thirteen boys expelled from school after the incident. We were in awe of all of them. We called them the League of Extraordinary Gentlemen.

Every Saturday, my school father, Ricky, assembled us all, the seven of us school sons, in a straight line at the foot of his single bed in the prefects' dorm.

They were only six boys in the room, which loomed large, imposing because I shared a room of the same size with about sixty other junior boys. Our walls did not have the same fresh coat of paint nor the full-length posters of Aaliyah and TLC, of Britney Spears. We did not have a wall dedicated to bras, thongs, and whatever else the prefects could produce as proof of conquest.

Every Saturday, Ricky assigned us tasks for the week.

"Andrew, make my whites sparkle, my trousers sharp."

"Temirin, I need warm water for my bath. Warm, not room temperature."

"Tarfa, I am the sanitation prefect, not the garbage truck handler. Polish my fucking shoes."

After the tasks were assigned, Ricky asked about our classes. We were required to show him results from any tests and any written reprimands from teachers or, worse, other prefects.

He certainly could have gotten away with not caring

about any aspect of our lives, but Ricky liked the idea that he was fathering us. He enjoyed the neatness of that description. A couple of prefects would walk over to his bed and say something like, "Ricky, your Ju-boys are having a blast. See how freely they are speaking with you."

When anyone said this, most of the time, right in the middle of him calling one of us a fucking bastard of a bagger for failing a mathematics test, Ricky looked up at his colleagues and smiled in his wide, clueless way.

"My guy, someone has to raise these bastards."

He called all of us bastards. It hurt me more than most on account of Father leaving me for God knows where, but I learned to hide it. Ricky could smell weakness and despair like a hungry leopard.

ON ONE OF those Saturday mornings when we were gathered together in the prefects' dorm room, I looked out the window behind Ricky's bed and noticed a senior girl walking up the courtyard. While Ricky berated someone for something that meant nothing, I nodded intermittently, faking attentiveness. I was watching the senior girl hide behind a tree; she seemed to be waiting for someone. She was crouching behind a stack of recently cut branches, her back to the dorm. From the distance, it appeared as if she had been trying to hold on to something for balance with one hand, and with the other was spreading a crumpled old newspaper so she could sit.

It took me too long to realize that she had actually been hiding behind the tree, unwrapping the newspaper as soundlessly as possible, so she could shit without anyone no-ticing. By the time I screamed, she had already begun fling-ing freshly released poop into the prefects' dorm through the open windows.

"Stupid muthafuckers, smelling bastards, mad men will fuck your mother's pussy raw," she was screaming, marching toward Ricky's window.

"I curse all of you demons," she said. "Every single one of you spreading lies about me. You will fail your final exams. No universities will accept you. You will die in roadside ac-cidents. No one will claim your rotten bodies."

As though collectively released from a spell, most of the dorm emptied out, running toward the screaming female is-suing death curses. We were terrified of the death curse. One of the prefects, the only one brave enough, grabbed her, at-tempting to restrain her by twisting her hands behind her in a lock. She fought him off successfully, slapping him all over his face with the leftover poop pebbles, wiping her hands on his shirt. A small crowd of laughing boys had gathered. No one tried to do anything, learning quickly the folly of inter-rupting this strange display of rage. It was easy to imagine what had happened. The senior girl had learned that one or more of the ordinary men and prefects had bragged about sleeping with her. It could have been even more vulgar; they might have included an aborted pregnancy or claimed she was a lesbian.

They were monsters, all of them, ordinary men and boys, iron sharpening iron to destruction. It would be a mistake to try to infer a logic or science to their taunts. They were just boys being teenage boys, drunk on power and lust, unguided and free.

ON THE MORNING of the day the girl, Nadia, the girl whom we really have to talk about, first spoke to me, I had burned Father Ricky's school uniform trousers while ironing them. Instead of owning up to the accident, I had pulled someone else's trousers off the clothesline, ironed those ones, and given them to him. Just when I had begun thinking I'd got away with the switch, Father Ricky found me on the class line in the assembly hall and began whipping me with his leather belt.

"You useless Ju-boy. What did you do with my trousers? Can you see what I look like in this trash? They don't fuckin fit right!" He was screaming and whipping and screaming and whipping.

The other boys in line made no attempts to hide their laughter. The boy nearest to me laughed so loudly, Ricky paused the whipping to shut him up.

"Shut up, you fuckin bastard. Am I now a fuckin clown to you fuckin Ju-boys?"

I could not bear to look at the girls. It would have been too much to turn around and see their disgust, or worse, their pity. When his rage was spent, he walked away. He wore those replacements till the end of the year. For the next week, welts the shape of his leather belt lined my face, neck, and arms like stripes on a flag. I considered it a fair trade.

We were in class, later that day. It was the end of English

period. We were waiting for the social studies teacher to arrive. Nadia walked to where I sat by myself at the back of the class and asked to see my stripes.

"No," I said. I folded my arms across my chest to create a distance between us, realizing too late that it only made my stripes evident to her.

"You think you always have to act so tough, don't you?" she said, as she tried to unfold my arms.

"I am tough. I do not have to pretend," I said.

She was standing before me, wearing ankle socks, so when I looked away from her face because it made me feel warm, I was staring instead at her legs, bare and long like prize yams.

"You should report him to the principal. He will get in trouble," she said.

"I hear you," I said.

I did not want to talk about it anymore. Nadia did not understand that things in our school worked differently for boys. She could not see the thing that was right under her nose; no girl would ever have been whipped like that. So could she be expected to understand how particularly different things were for me? I was not like the other Ju-boys. I was older, I was taller, I was meaner, and I was convinced that I could have beaten Ricky to a stupor if I had been allowed to fight back.

NADIA WAS THE most beautiful junior girl. It was not because her skin was brown and clear like still water, or because her eyes were huge and bright like a mirror, or that her hair was reddish brown without dyes. Nadia had breasts, full, round, grown woman breasts.

The story the junior boys told about Nadia was that she was full of herself. The story the junior girls told of Nadia was that she was the uglier sister. It was said that her older sister, who graduated the year before I enrolled, was even more beautiful, but I could not imagine a more beautiful girl.

I had seen Nadia's father walk around the school with her a couple of times. He was an older Anglican reverend, an albino who had married one of his parishioners later in life. This is one of the reasons Nadia had such pale beautiful skin; she was almost an albino, but she wasn't.

The walls of our classroom were without paint. Nadia reached over my head and sketched a sumo wrestler on the wall, writing below it this caption: ANDREW IS THE MI-CHELIN MAN.

"That is a terrible drawing. It looks like an amoeba," I said.

She laughed a loud, hearty laugh, and just like that, my arms stopped hurting.

We were both facing the wall, backs turned to the blackboard, when our social studies teacher walked into the class.

"The two of you standing at the back. Husband and wife," she screamed, startling us. "Come to the front. Now tell the whole class what is so funny."

We spent the rest of that class in a corner, standing next to each other, heads bowed in the perfunctory performance of shame. The teacher interrupted her class to mock us. Other times, she asked us pointed questions, trying to show us as ignorant.

"Which deposed king was allowed to return from exile when the British annexed Lagos?" she asked.

"King Kosoko," Nadia said.

"What year did this take place?" she asked me.

I did not know. I was bad with dates. I was terrible with all things involving the remembering and reorganizing of numbers.

"In 1840," I said.

"Wrong as expected. It was 1861. Keep playing with the beautiful girls instead of facing your studies. I am sure you can get a job as her driver when she marries a rich man," the teacher said.

Everyone in our class laughed out loud. My ears burned. I imagined running into the crowd of them with Ricky's two-pronged whip, slashing this way and that all over their smiling faces.

It was exactly the kind of day that made me wish I could go back home, but Nadia saved me. She was the kind of girl to make you smile on the worst day of your life. For a long time after that, we sat next to each other at the back of the class, never getting in trouble but barely participating. She was always smiling, always happy, shiny and bright in the way a few girls are, like a pink lollipop.

THERE IS A little Valentine's Day card with petals of a dried rose I still have somewhere in the house. It says:

*To Andrew, who will grow up to be badder than
Tuface and Shaggy combined.
Never forget me.*

The card does not tell the story of Nadia. Her face was round and pleasant from having a father who stopped by every other weekend to visit her, who loaded her with cookies, fruits, noodles in a care package. Her family had built her up with good fruitful words like:

"You are God's example to the world of godliness."

"You are the salt of the earth."

"You are the light of the world."

Her father visited her regularly without fail. Even in the bad weeks, those last two weeks when all the students had run out of provisions and no parents were visiting because it was almost time for the school term to end.

THE DAY NADIA asked me to meet her in the shade of the trees beside the girls' dorm to exchange Valentine's Day gifts, I showered twice. The first time, I thought I was ready to leave but then Father Ricky appeared in my dorm room, handing over to me his brown pair of boots to shine because he wanted to look good for his own Valentine's Day plans.

The second time, after I was done polishing and shining those shoes, I got dressed in the boys' bathroom and ran all the way to the girls' dorm, where Nadia waited. When I stepped outside, I could see several girls emerging from their dormitories with gift bags and identical white teddy bears with tiny red hearts. I held the single rose and the single bar of Kit Kat I had purchased with two weeks' allowance and ran to her.

My feet were fast and fluid and free. It felt like I was floating in the air. Nadia was there waiting. She was my dream, sitting on an abandoned granite heap, sipping from a can of Sprite and looking in the direction of the boys' dorm as though she wondered whether I was coming.

When I got to her side, I called Nadia the most beautiful girl in the world. Even though her hair was braided back in S-shaped cornrows and I could see the shine of her scalp, she was beautiful.

I TOLD NADIA that her mouth was the warmest mouth in the world, that inside it was soft and cozy like a nest, that I was settling in there. I said she smelled like lilies in the springtime field, and she laughed because she knew I had never smelled lilies or seen them spring. She made words fill my mouth and I poured them out and over her, without thinking.

We heard the last bell for the night ring, but we did not leave for our dorm room. Every time I tried to pull away, she asked for five more minutes.

"Kiss me again," she said.

I kissed her again.

"Consider the lilies of the field, how they grow," she said.

"What?" I asked.

"Consider the lilies of the field, how they grow; they toil not, neither do they spin. It's from the Bible, words of Jesus, one of my father's favorite scriptures," she said.

•

EVERY TIME SHE spoke of her father, I tried to change the subject. She did not like her father. He pressured her to be the perfect Christian girl. He was stern, demanding, and overprotective. He was brutal in his discipline. His regular visits were really inspections, as he looked over her class notes, her clothes, nails, hairdo. Her hatred of him was like black soot over her shiny soul, like a scar on her face, swallowing up her beauty.

"Do you know what my father will do if he finds out I have a boyfriend?" she asked me once.

I had almost smiled, because it appeared to me that she had formalized our relationship.

"What?" I asked instead. "Who is telling him anything, anyway?"

"He will beat me worse than Ricky beat you, a lot worse, then burn my feet with fire so I imagine the terrors of hell anytime I am tempted to fornicate," she said.

Even though I was thinking about the terrors of hell and her father's words, I let my hands travel down to her breasts and she did not stop me. Instead, she wrapped her hands around my neck and drew me closer to her. The school was as quiet as a cemetery when we finally decided to pull away and head back to our dorms.

Nadia stood at the top of the heap, buttoning her shirt, muttering the words to "Lucky" by Britney Spears. She was facing me and therefore did not see in good enough time to run away the bright flashlight and the two people who walked toward us.

"The two of you, stop right there," screamed one.

"Ju-boy and junior girl, I can see who you are. Run and get expelled," the other screamed.

They kept their flashlights in our faces, blinding us. I could hear Nadia's heart beating wildly. She tried to hold my hand, but I let the grip wane; I did not want to give the teachers who had just caught us together after our bedtime more to be angry about.

"We are really sorry," Nadia said. "We just slept off. We did not hear the lights-out bell ring."

One of the men laughed a loud laugh that reverberated in the emptiness around us.

"So what were you doing before you slept off?" the other man asked.

"We were just talking. About classwork. That is all. I swear to God," I said.

The man who asked me a question slapped me so hard I fell forward. That was how I was sure that he was not a student. It was one of the teachers; his palm was as large as my entire head.

Nadia began to cry. I sat back on the heap rubbing my face. The men stood at our sides, shouting at us, calling us disgusting perverts, telling us how we had to stand before the whole school and be punished for our crimes. It was hard to tell how long we stayed there, the night getting colder around us, when the man closest to Nadia, the man who had slapped me, pulled her to him, hugging her like a father would.

"It is okay. Stop crying. It will be okay, come with me," he said.

I tried to turn my neck to watch as they walked a little distance away from me, but the man standing before me screamed vile words at me.

"No looking. You will wish you were dead when we are done with you tonight, stupid boy," he screamed.

"Please, sir, I cannot do that, sir," I heard Nadia plead in the distance.

"Well, I am not going to force you. No one wants you to scream and bring the whole school here," the man replied.

"Please stop this. I beg you in the name of God," I heard Nadia say.

She soon began gagging and choking. Every time it sounded like she was about to stop, it started over again. I turned to look in spite of myself. Nadia was on her knees before the man, and he was leaning over her and moving his hips back and forth. Nadia was pulling her head away and he was pushing her head back onto him.

The contents of my stomach rushed out of my mouth with the speed of running water. It was a lumpy mess of chocolate and bread and sardines. In that instant, the man by my side forgot to shine his torch in my face. Instead, he pointed it downward, checking to see if any of my vomit had spilled on his shoes. As my eyes traveled to those shoes, I realized that they were the same ones I had cleaned and shined earlier. I stilled my stomach, but another rush of vomit exploded all over the place.

It was past midnight. The clouds over us had merged into one big lump of gray, covering the moon. The air was dry and there was nothing to be heard but Nadia's gagging and my retching. The smell traveled far. The smell of that night, vomit and shoe polish and fear, surrounded the school.

Ricky, my school father, hunched over. I flinched because I had assumed he was about to hit me again.

"Run and don't look back," he said instead. I ran. My legs ran before my head could convince them to stay. The smell of sorrow stayed with me. I took my shirt off and wiped my mouth as I ran. I was crying like a little boy. I turned around as soon as I could hide in the cover of the night. The shape of two bodies huddled over one lying-down girl swelled over the granite heap like the orange of a large traffic cone. Then their hold broke. I watched her try and fail to pull herself up. Her legs were kicking up granite dust, writhing weakly like an injured snake.

"Andrew, please, please, help me."

I turned toward the path. I continued running. The door to my dorm seemed like a faraway mirage, like a gateway to another world.

Everyone was asleep like it was any other night. I ran on. I found my brother half asleep in his own bed. He made space for me and asked no questions, even though we were both in trouble if we got caught sharing a bed. I could not sleep. Around me, several cone shadows danced. My ears were ringing from being slapped so hard. My mouth tasted of blood and granite. Then my heart began to rise to meet the shadows, to demand they cease their dancing and move away from my brother's bed. But it was a shadow of fathers. My father and Nadia's father and Ricky were all dancing in the room. I opened my mouth, but no sound poured out. I had forgotten how to talk to fathers. The dancing fathers stared me down, and the angrier I was, the better they danced. I shooed them away with my hands, but they did not leave. They danced and laughed and danced some more, and no matter what I did, no matter how angry I got, the fathers did not stop dancing and I could not bring my mouth to say the words, "Go away, fathers."

HOW TO BE THE TEACHER'S PET

PETER

2006

SHE WAS HIRED to teach you English and elocution because your last teacher, Mr. Atogun, had died after being attacked by a horde of bees in the yam farm he kept behind the school fence. You all attended his burial service. Seventeen government buses had taken all students living in the boarding house to Atanda cemetery that Saturday in November. You treated that bus ride to the cemetery like any other school trip to the city, singing Tuface songs out loud in the bus, shouting hoarse cusswords at people driving past in fancy cars, the better the cars, the nastier your insults. When a taxicab driver drove close enough to the bus, you yelled with all the other boys, "Oko ashawo"—husband to prostitutes—"watch where you are going."

The Monday morning after the burial, Miss Abigail was there in your junior secondary class, teaching English language and literature. She was dressed like those women in old English textbooks, her natural hair pulled up high over her head, her blouse wide with big, fluffy sleeves, her skirt—well, she always wore skirts.

You were not happy at the quickness with which there was a replacement teacher. You imagined that for a couple of weeks at the minimum, you would spend your English and literature class periods sleeping, eating, and talking with friends.

There was nothing lazy about wanting free, unregulated time in a Lagos boarding school. Every single moment of your waking life was regulated by the bell—which was technically just a rusty wheel from an abandoned lorry—hanging in the center of your school. At six a.m. and every thirty minutes after until your nine p.m. bedtime, some person unlucky enough to be appointed timekeeping prefect rang the bell, telling you all it was time to do something else.

Catching all the junior boys, and some of the junior girls, giving her tired, annoyed looks that first day in your class, Miss Abigail assumed you all were upset to see her because you all missed your old teacher. She decided to begin your class that morning by saying prayers for the safe repose of Mr. Atogun's departed soul. Unfortunately for her, she called on—with no clue of how bad an idea it was—Adebayo, the tallest boy in your class and the most incorrigible class clown, to say this prayer.

Adebayo began in his best attempt at invoking reverence,

his voice hoarse from early puberty, projecting as far as he could:

"Dear Lord, we are nothing but stories written in pencil by your hand. When you bring your giant eraser in the sky, you wipe us away, no one will remember us.

Do not wipe us away, Lord.

Do not erase us, Daddy Jesus.

Do not remove us, Jehovah.

Do not delete us, Almighty God—"

The class erupted first in giggles and then, as he continued praying in that manner, outright laughter. You all laughed with glee at his audacity. You, Peter, laughed especially because Miss Abigail stood there before the blackboard, her eyes wide with shock, her lips thin from restrained anger.

The new teacher allowed him to go on like that for at least five minutes, then interrupted him with her calm, "In Jesus's name we pray. Amen."

Later, Miss Abigail, after you had become the teacher's pet, would tell you she knew that Adebayo was making a mockery of prayer. "I have been a teacher for a long time," she said to you. "I can tell who the mischievous children are just by watching how the class reacts to them."

The rumors began spreading a few weeks after Miss Abigail joined the school. First, it was said that by being a stickler for rules, promoting to higher classes only those students who had a 60 percent average, she had made enemies in her former school, the all-girls school in the city. They said this was her last chance to teach in a government school.

Later, it was modified to include a story where she had quit because the teacher she loved had jilted her without warning, marrying some other lady. She discovered his deceit by stumbling upon his village wedding photos while cleaning up after him in his off-campus apartment.

You did not often believe things just because of the number of times you heard them repeated. You needed to see with your own eyes, this cruelty, this naivete. This was why you watched her closely, any chance you got. You sometimes saw Miss Abigail talking to herself as she walked the path to her apartment in staff housing. Sometimes she held in her hands a pile of books. Other times it was a grocery bag filled with fresh fruits. Once you watched her eat a bunch of tangerines. She peeled the skin off each one and then, instead of littering the path like anyone else would have, she wrapped the skins in a white handkerchief, tucking them back into her grocery bag.

Miss Abigail had a way of talking about the world that made her different from all your other teachers. Before she became your teacher, English literature class was the one place where you struggled to stay awake. You had no interest in dead or almost dead white men writing about springtime and snow. You definitely had no interest in memorizing lines from Shakespearean plays so that, like Mr. Atogun, you could say things like "Yet, to say the truth, reason and love keep little company together nowadays," laughing at your own little joke.

She was hired to teach English literature from books

written by the English, but she taught you about the fall of Rhodesia, the fight for black freedom in South Africa, and black dignity in America.

She was asked to teach poetry, but all she did was ask her students questions like, "If you are in prison or separated from your family because you have to flee an oppressive government, will you write poetry? Is writing or reading poetry an appropriate response to pain?"

You all laughed. You all said you would not have time for poetry, but for forgetting your sorrow or remembering the good in the past or imagining a better future. But you were beginning to understand what she meant. Poems are tears of the soul. You had never imagined that poems could help a person survive. Then you read "Nightfall in Soweto" by Oswald Mtshali, then you read "Letter to Martha" by Dennis Brutus. Then you read.

After you first arrived at your grandmother's house, after Father left you one evening with nothing but clothes in your backpack, telling you he was going after a job lead in Abuja, you spent the first few weeks waiting with patience for his return. You sat on the veranda looking out into the street from the moment you woke up. You were there early enough that it was before the women hawking bread and beans began their rounds and before tricycles overcrowded with schoolchildren hobbled down the street. You were still there when nighttime arrived, when the entire neighborhood began to shut down in a dependable rhythm. First, the giant lights of the gas station went out, then the generators of the beer parlor got turned off, and finally the small ki-osk owners turned off their candle and kerosene lamps and locked up their stalls.

MOST OF THE time your grandmother left you alone with your watching. Sometimes she even let you sleep out there on the veranda without waking you. She never said anything about it to you. You were not even sure she noticed or even cared. Then one day, when she thought you were sleeping, you heard her crying. She was standing over you, covering your feet with a blanket, mumbling to herself, *Ibanuje ka ori agba ko odo ki la fe se ti omode.*

"Sadness inverts the old person's head, what won't it do to a little boy?"

It was the first time you heard anyone use the Yoruba noun for "sadness"—*ibanuje.* You had no idea what the word meant; your literal interpretation made you think of a dis-ease, of a rotting of the insides. That frightened you, because you wondered whether maybe you were sick and dying, which was why your grandmother had left you alone to sit and mope.

THEN YOU ASKED your sister what the meaning of *iba-nuje* was and she said "sadness," adding, when she saw your confusion at her interpretation, "It's just classic Yoruba overstatement."

The first time Miss Abigail had your class read "Night-fall in Soweto," you thought immediately about those nights.

You knew nothing of the world outside Lagos. You did not know that the world outside Lagos was just as hard for many people. You would never have imagined that it was sometimes even harder.

Surely, there were kids like you all over the world with missing parents who also could not go to the police station and say, "Excuse me, sir, policeman. Can you please find my mother or my father? I am not greedy; either of them will be enough."

The television shows you watched at home with your brother and sisters only showed loud and happy families, kids with parents who drove them to school and read bedtime stories. Where were all the shows for children like you? The ones who went to bed screaming, or the ones without beds.

You realized then from reading those poems that every language in the world must have a word like *ibanuje*, a word for "afraid" and a word for "sad" and a word for "tears." You did not tell Miss Abigail, but the more you read the *sufferhead* poetry she gave your class, the less alone you began to feel.

Miss Abigail said, one day in the middle of class, that she was up at night reading your original poem, turned in as part of your midterms. She said that her heart broke and fixed itself, that you are pure of heart and full of empathy.

"We want to hear this pure poem," some junior boy said.

What choice did she have? She made you read it out loud to them all. She must have imagined that you liked that type of attention. Or that you were glowing with pride at her praise.

Rain
There is such a thing as too much rain.
It is too much rain if we grow nothing.
It is too much rain if it hides our pain.

What does one do with heads that turn to mash?
And hearts that flee in fright?
It is too much rain because we grow nothing.
We grow nothing because there is too much rain.

When she asked you to read it again, slower this time, for the benefit of the members of your class, those ones you called backbenchers, the boys and girls who sat all the way at the back committed to nothing but disorderliness, you acted like you did not hear her. You sat back in your seat, putting your head on the desk. You thought about your disobedience later and decided it was a pretty harmless way to make the point that you were not soft. You were under no compulsion to keep standing there reading, looking like the teacher's pet, but then, after class was over, you began thinking about the look of pain or confusion she had on her face as you ignored her. You decided to be better to her.

Miss Abigail arrived for her next class with copies of the class list and announced a surprise quiz, a thing she had never done, not even in the week the state inspector visited your school and all the other teachers had chosen to have surprise quizzes so that they were not nervous and shaken when the inspector stopped by to listen to their classes.

On her way out after the test, she called on you and another student to carry the test papers behind her. You did it in a hurry. You picked up all the papers so there were none for the other student to carry, so that he went back to his seat. You were the picture of efficiency. You wanted her to think of you with kindness when she read the incorrect answers you had written out.

When Adebayo shouted as you walked out of the class, "Peter, the teacher's pet," you laughed and said to Miss Abigail, "I am sorry about that, Ma. I think he is just jealous."

Later, after you have become the teacher's pet, Miss Abigail will tell you that you broke her heart that day you refused to read your poem the second time. That you embarrassed her.

You talked about Miss Abigail to anyone who would listen. All your brother, Andrew, who did not have any classes with Miss Abigail because he was two classes ahead of you, said was, "Peter, just begin falling asleep in her class and she will leave you the fuck alone."

You talked to Fat Fred, the boy who sat next to you in class who just laughed and said, *Miss Abigail doesn't want you, I heard she had to leave her old school because she was teaching the junior girls lesbianism.* Your friend Irene just said you had a crush on her and it was beyond disgusting.

Miss Abigail never acted like there was something special between you when other teachers where around. When her best friend, Miss Ufot, the math teacher who was also the soccer coach, was around, Miss Abigail acted like you did not exist. Sometimes, Miss Ufot stopped by as your teacher began her lessons, her smile wide as she listened in to Miss Abigail's teaching.When Miss Abigail stopped you one evening as you walked out of the dining hall to ask if you had eaten dinner and if you liked what was served, you said, "I'm sure you have seen the trash we are served. I would have to be a goat to enjoy that."

Miss Abigail shook her head, laughing. She reached into her purse and held out a fifty-naira note.

"Okay. Go buy bread with this. Things will get better. Cheer up," she said. She did not ever get angry with you.

Later, after you have become the teacher's pet, Miss Abigail will tell you that your anger frightens her. When she tells you this, you just shrug and say nothing. In your heart, you say to yourself, that is just what boys without mothers do.

Almost every night, you dreamed about your mother, only it was not your mother but your older sister Ariyike, only she was not loving you, she was asking if you remembered to hang your towel out to dry. Sometimes she was sitting at the edge of your bed, shouting at you to put some lotion on.

"Peter, look how scaly and ashy your elbows are," she said in those dreams.

You answered, "Auntie mi, I cannot see my own elbows."

The day you became the teacher's pet, Mr. Ahmed, the Islamic teacher, who was the new head guardian of the junior boys' dormitory, led all the boys in your class to clear out weeds from the soccer field. It was a Saturday morning, and all students had to do weekend chores. You walked at the very end of that procession, rehearsing over and over how you could explain to Mr. Ahmed that weeding was one of the few chores you could no longer do because your right hand had no grip. In the past, Mr. Atogun had let you be in charge of taking attendance and giving boys water to drink.

All your rehearsing did not matter because Mr. Ahmed insisted that you grab a hoe like the other boys. When you did not do that, he asked one of the boys to get two branches from the guava tree. The boy bought three. When Mr. Ahmed began to whip you, some of the boys began to scream.

"Please, sir, don't beat him. He has sickle cell disease," one said, lying.

"Sir, he is suffering from beriberi, he is not strong," Adebayo, the class clown, said jesting.

"Sir, he has fainted three times this term already, please leave him alone," a different boy said.

Mr. Ahmed didn't listen, even though your face had swollen from crying and the fresh bark of the tree branch had left numerous green stains all over your limbs and on your clothes.

It was Miss Abigail who ran all the way from the other side of the school, who lifted you up in her arms as though you were a feather pillow, who walked away without saying anything.

When she put you down with the same gentleness with which she had lifted you, it was on the front lawn of her staff quarters, and you had stopped crying. You sat in the arm-chair closest to the door. She went into her kitchen, making a large mug of warm cocoa. She brought it to where you were sitting, with a red straw inside it so you did not have to lift it up.

There was no TV in her living room, but her battery-operated radio was tuned to a station playing country songs.

"Do you want to talk to the principal about what happened?" she asked right after an advert for insecticide ended and Kelly Clarkson's soft voice began singing "Because of You."

"It is fine. I'm okay," you said.

She walked back into the kitchen and even though you wanted to tell her to turn off the radio because you were about to begin crying again, you said nothing. Miss Abigail was doing dishes and humming along with the radio and you did not want to ruin it for her.

"Teachers like Mr. Ahmed do not belong in government schools, I can tell you that right now." She walked into the living room, her hands dripping with water.

"That man did not even study a proper subject in the university, that is, if where he went can even be called a university. He studied Arabic and Islamic studies."

You had no idea why she said it like it was a bad thing. To you, Arabic seemed like the right subject for an Islamic studies teacher.

"Can you imagine that, Arabic studies? Yet he is probably going to become principal ten years before someone like me can even be considered. Do you know why?" She stood in the center of her living room, towering over you like a statue.

You did not know anything about how teachers in government schools were promoted. What you knew was that her question did not need an answer as much as she needed reassurance that it was okay for her to continue. You nodded, giving her permission to continue unburdening.

"Federal character is destroying civil service. Let me tell you right now. Federal character is destroying us all. Every time promotion comes, the government must make sure an equal number of people are promoted from all the states. Can you imagine anything more bonkers? People like Ahmed, who come from states with few teachers, always get promoted. Do you know I have a master's degree? I have a master's degree from OAU, and Ahmed, with his National Diploma, is two levels above me."

She walked away from you as she spoke, back to her kitchen, stopping at the doorway to pat her hands against the lace curtain. She did this several times absentmindedly.

"That is why he is impudent. He is so arrogant. He doesn't care what anyone does. Even our principal is afraid of him. Ahmed could become principal within the next two years—even state inspector."

The radio stops playing music. The announcer reads out the next program; *Storytime* for early readers. The story is titled "Pot of Gold." Miss Abigail walks away from the curtain with dry hands, she sits next to you, her cold hand rests on your knees.

You have heard many versions of this story, it is the story

of a rude little girl who demands a pot of gold from the ancient forest spirit.

"Once upon a time, there lived a poor orphan girl in the village of Iperu." The radio announcer reads quickly in a deep voice, it sounds like a waterfall. This story, in the version your sister Bibike told you, begins when the poor orphan girl helps an old stranger do some chores in the stranger's home. In that house, a wood shack up a hill, the orphan girl is asked to pick a fair price for her labor from a hidden room filled with great treasure of all types—gold necklaces, diamond rings, colorful waist beads. The orphan girl picks the thing she needs the most, a clay pot. However, when she gets home, the clay pot cracks, hatches, and becomes an unending stream of gold.

The rude little girl, from the richest family in Iperu, hears the story and runs up the hill to the old stranger's home, demanding her own pot of gold. The strangers leads her to the hidden room. She is also asked to pick whatever she wants. She picks a gold necklace. When she gets home it becomes a hive of bees and the bees sting her to death.

As the radio announcer reads his version of this story, you think about the orphan girl, about what she wanted and what she got instead.

Miss Abigail sat in the chair next to you, and you could smell the citrus scent of her dish soap.

"Huhh! I know this story," she said.

"I don't like this story." You did not even know you had said it out loud.

"Yeah! It's a problematic tale, like most of our traditional stories," she said.

You could smell something else, something dry and dusty like old shoes.

"Give me my own pot of gold, I want the biggest pot you have," the radio announcer continued in his loud voice. The two of you sat in silence, listening as the rude girl met an unfortunate end.

"Do you want something to eat?" she asked.

"I really hate this story," you said.

A smile spread across Miss Abigail's face. "Oh, Peter. You're so smart. You are thinking that there is nothing wrong with wanting good things, right? A little greed is in fact a good thing." She laughed. "Don't worry, you can ignore it, it's folklore, not doctrine."

"What about what she wanted?" you asked.

"Who?"

"The orphan girl, what about what she really wanted?"

Miss Abigail looked at you from the corners of her eyes like she had words to say but did not want them to leave her mouth. She pursed her lips together and nodded slowly but said nothing.

You were thinking about the orphan girl who got a pot of gold from an ancient spirit. "I bet she would have asked for something else, if the spirit had asked her what she wanted. I bet she would have asked for her parents back, or a new family, not money, not gold. Why will a spirit give an orphan girl money?" you said.

Miss Abigail turned her face to you with sad eyes.

"I think the spirit just gave her what he had," she said.

"Yeah. That's it. When you are like me, people give you what they have, and you are supposed to be grateful, say thank you, sir, thank you, madam. This is going to be my whole life, isn't it, being thankful for things other children don't have to be? The spirit should have asked what she wanted and she would have said, Can I have my parents back, even for one day, and then even if that did not happen, if that was beyond the spirit's ability, at least the story would be about family, not gold. What type of orphan cares about gold?"

Miss Abigail placed one slim finger on your face and wiped underneath your eye. She did it quickly and quietly like she needed to make sure the tears did not fall all the way down. This made you cry harder, fuller, and freer. Soon you were wailing and hiccupping, she was cradling your head in her breasts and rocking you back and forth, back and forth.

This was how you became the teacher's pet, by talking about what you wanted. By reading poems, by writing your own poetry. It was not the life you would have had if your mother had not left you, but it was a soft and quiet life. As much as you hated school, with the hundreds of boys living in small rooms, the loud bells, numerous activities, unending chores, Miss Abigail made it bearable, even pleasurable for you to be there. She was constant and available, always there when you needed her to be.

Even those times when you did not know you needed her, she showed up swiftly for you, like that Saturday when all the junior boys stood in line for the visiting barber, who charged twenty naira a cut to make you all look like wrinkly grandfathers. Just when it was almost your turn, she appeared before you in line, interrupting the order of things, asking the barber what sterilization process he used for his clippers. She did not leave him alone until he poured some methylated spirit on the clippers' teeth and lit it on fire for five seconds with a cigarette lighter.

"See, now it is safe," the barber said to your teacher. "Nothing survives fire."

HOW TO LOSE YOUR LAGOS LOVER

BIBIKE

2006

WE MET BEFORE I was ready. It was the year I turned twenty. All the signs were already there. The earth was instructing me to prepare my heart for a solitary life. But I am not a good listener. I was not watching for signs. My mouth was instead wide open like a crocodile's, begging for more.

His face was like the Benin moat; firm, brown, and wide like it was built to keep strangers out. He had a big mouth filled with crowded teeth struggling for space, like a deep ditch overflowing with water. There may be other ways to describe the fullness of his lips, the hollow of his cheeks, the four equal parts his bulging forehead split into when he frowned, but even now I can only think of the cultivated inaccessibility of it all.

His face really was unapproachable, believe me. It was like the run-down house in our neighborhood where the boys who worked in long-distance transit buses gathered to smoke weed at the end of the day. His eyes were small and always red. When he looked at me, he made me want to apologize for all the wrong I ever did.

But the first time I saw him, I was not looking at his face. I saw only his legs. It was a Saturday at the start of the rainy season. I had hurried out of the house without my umbrella. The winds were bellowing before I arrived at the bus shelter, but I could not go home and come back in time for the bus. He saw me before I saw him. I felt the warmth of a gaze at the back of my neck, but when I turned in his direction all I could see were those legs. I was wearing a happy dress and the wind was battling with it, I was gathering the tulle with my hands, tucking the skirts between my legs. His legs were thick and long, majestic, like the trunk of a leadwood tree. He must have noticed me staring at them, for he moved them with swiftness to my side, covering me beneath the shade of his umbrella. It was already raining. It really was only a light drizzle, but the drains around us were blocked with refuse, so soon my feet were soaked with murky water. He was looking at me, saying nothing, as I watched the water ruin my work shoes and caress his ankles.

All those people waiting for the Rapid Transit Bus, sheltered under raincoats, umbrellas, polyethenebags, all their noise, all their muttering—about the morning crowd, about the clogged drain, at the lateness of the bus, about the unnecessary earliness of the Lagos rains—was nothing but the incidental music to my destiny.

I waited until the fifth time I saw him to speak with him. When I did, it was to ask him if he lived alone.

His name was Constantine, like the emperor, but I called him Aba for the city where he was born. He did not speak often of Aba, except to say, "A man must go where the money is. Aba will be there when I get back."

His mother was a fisherperson. She was getting older so no longer went out to sea, but her boats did, and once a month she sent him a basket of fish smoked in her coal oven.

I never saw him shave, but he was always groomed in that way few Nigerian men are, clean and only a little prickly with stubble. He would kiss me all over and my toes would twist with need. When he slid into me, my mouth erupted in a tangy sweetness. He was from the river and so everything about him was full and wide, his nose wide like the ocean, his navel full as the deep blue sea.

HE WORKED AT the wharf. He took the Rapid Transit Bus to Apapa every day, like I did. He did not believe in destiny, God, or the internet, but when I bent my elbows and knees, when I lengthened my torso and stretched like a yogi in compass mode, he believed in me.

I was becoming a grown-up madam of a woman. It was happening like my grandmother once said, "A girl becomes a woman when she finds a man she would do anything for."

I had found a man. I had taken a loverman for myself. My loverman did not laugh when I tickled. He did not cry when he was spent. He shuddered, like a possessed man at the command of the exorcist, like he was expelling whatsoever joy was trying to lay a hold on him.

My Aba was exacting and exhausting, like all my favorite sad songs, so I rolled around when he asked and played him over and over. I played him like I was a little girl again, sitting at home singing myself sore.

Back then, before our mother disappeared like smoke, before I had any real reason to weep, I would sing sad songs and cry so hard until I was sick with a high fever. My mother never could figure out how I got so sick sitting at home all by myself. But I knew what I was doing. I was sick with longing. I was sick with the curse of sensation, with all the world's sadness seeking and finding a resting place in my bones and in my marrow. One day, I was just a little girl who sometimes got out her seat in the neighborhood bar to dance, even if no one else was dancing. Then the next day, I was in love, I was a woman.

Did the world end when I lay on top of him? I think it did. The first time my hands traveled down his hips and I found the place where he had taken two bullets to protect his post from smugglers at the border, I placed my fingers on scars the size of a coin and asked Eledua to make the world kinder to men.

Did the world become nothing but a treasure trove when he kissed the back of my thighs? I expect that it did. I had formed a habit; a time-tasking habit of listing all the kinds of happinesses a grown-up in-love woman could feel. Every time I found a type I did not know by taste or a level I had not yet ascended, I shared it with my Aba and he showed me how to get there by myself.

WHAT IS THE morning? How did Oluwa mi make my morning like ten thousand mornings and my nighttime like one unending night? One day, as I was walking to my business place, my bunch of keys in one hand, my letter opener in the other, I watched a woman who had my Aba's face printed on the white T-shirt that she wore cross over to my side of the street. I stopped to let her walk ahead of me. The back of her T-shirt said

GONE BUT NOT FORGOTTEN
FEBRUARY 27, 1972–May 22, 2005.

She was one of those bony, shrunken women, and as she said her good-mornings and how have you been to other pedestrians, her thin voice scratched my ears. I walked discreetly behind her for a couple of miles, wondering about the least intrusive way to ask about the shirt she wore. When she arrived at her destination, a store where she sold all types of phones, cell phones and landlines, I waited a few minutes then walked in, acting like a customer in search of a new phone.

She smelled like her store, like sawdust, mothballs, and sunlight. When she replied to my greetings, her smile was weak and brief, her lower lip quivering after it ended. I complained about her prices, but she did not argue. One section of her store was dedicated to phone covers. I walked to that section, picking a case that was both phone case and wallet, neon pink and blue, altogether garish.

I turned to her. "How much will you accept for this case?"

We were no longer alone. A man had walked in, wearing the bright yellow branded T-shirt of the telecommunications company most people in Lagos used. He had placed at the top of one of her display cases a large expanding file folder, and they were looking through a small pile of forms, receipts, and price lists.

"Excuse me?" I said to her again.

"What do you want?" she asked me.

"I want to know how much this is," I said, holding out the ugly phone cover.

"Do you want to buy that?" she asked.

"Why will you not just tell me how much it is?" I asked.

"Please can you help me drive this woman away," she said, turning to the man with her. "I do not know what she wants, she has been here almost an hour, she has nothing to buy."

Time had run away from me like butter running from a hot spoon.

"I'm sorry for wasting your time, I just wanted to ask you a question. Please, who is that man on your shirt? He looks like my boyfriend," I said very quickly, not giving the man in yellow a chance to throw me out.

The storekeeper laughed for a long time. It was a sad laugh. When she spoke again, it was still to the man in yellow.

"You remember my brother Constantine, the one we hired your company bus for, to take his body to bury in Aba last October?" she asked.

"Yes. The customs officer. The one who died in Yobe," the man answered.

"Please, he did not die. What is die? My brother was killed. He was shot right here by smugglers." She slapped the right side of her pelvic bone hard, pointing out where our Constantine was shot.

Ta ta ta.

The fat around her hip sounded soft, tender, firm like the sound a cut of meat makes when a meat seller slaps it on his table in the market to convince you of its freshness. She did not hit me, but I felt on my own hips the intense force of her raging.

"This useless government killed him with that stupid job and their useless hospitals with no doctors. Is that how a grown man dies, just like that?" she asked.

It was like I was standing outside my own body, watching it fall from the world's tallest building.

The man in the yellow shirt walked to the other side of the display case. He placed one arm around the angry shopkeeper.

"Sister, please leave this place. You have upset her so much," he said to me.

I walked away, even though I had several questions with no one to answer them. I wanted to show her the pictures on my phone. The one with us in the mall, taken by a stranger, the one where we are holding hands going down the escalator. The one with us in his bedroom, the one where he had my blue bra around his head like oversize headphones. The one I took myself, where he was shirtless in his kitchen, frying plantains.

I wanted to show her his teeth marks on my thigh, fresh from that morning. I wanted to show her his seed still caught in the spaces between my own teeth. I could imagine her surprise, or anger, her mouth stretching taut then erupting, flowing with cursewords. I wanted her to feel this same disorientation I was feeling, like my face was filled with air and I was floating about without arms.

I wanted to tell her about all the names my Aba called me—Nkem, Ifunaya, Obidia. I wanted to talk about all the stuff my Aba taught me. Sometimes, when he sat next to me on the bus to Apapa, he would point out all the cars he would have detained for further checking at his duty post at the border.

"Kehinde, look, that red '88 Honda Accord, why is it getting stopped?" he would ask.

"Too old to be legally imported," I would say quickly, without even looking at the car. "Personal cars have to be fifteen years old or less."

Other times, it wasn't so easy. I did not have the discernment to notice unevenly balanced vehicles suggesting contraband hidden in their undercarriages or number plates much older than the car, suggesting stolen plates. Constantine was a patient teacher, saying everything with a smile.

My sister got her period first, weeks before I did. Our

grandmother called her into her room the day she got her first period, and they had a long talk. When I asked Ariyike what they talked about she refused to tell me.

"Don't worry, it was just her normal Yoruba spiritual nonsense, she will tell you herself when your time comes."

Six weeks later it was my turn to get the talk from Grandmother. She told us we were twins, therefore the elect of gods. We were to be careful not to get pregnant as teenagers; there is nothing sadder than a young mother of twins, she said. More important, she warned me to be careful when I chose my sexual partners.

"Before you have sex, remember you are Ibeji, you are a disruption that is tolerated only because you are good. We are Ibeji, the benevolent spirits, we bring fortune and good luck. But we are spirits, never forget that. So be careful of malevolent spirits. Do not befriend Anjonu. Abiku and Ibeji will wage war on their family, Ibeji and Emere will pollute the earth, Ibeji and Atunwaye will destroy each other."

If Constantine had indeed died a full year before I met him in Lagos, did that not make him Atunwaye, one who returns to the earth? Was he now Akuudaaya, one who creates for himself a second life after an abrupt end? I had many questions without answers, big questions pregnant with smaller questions. There was no one I could trust to give me the answers I needed, especially not my grandmother.

What do men want? What do they want from the earth? What do they want from love? I think all men want to live like trees. I think they want to be rooted in the earth, growing indeterminately, first as tall as they want and after that, as wide as their frames can carry. I think men want to die with their leaves green but their trunks hollow. They all want a slow, painless, gentle, suffocating death—not this sorrow, this terror, this fear.

I wandered around the city until it was dark. I had planned to say to my Aba when I saw him again, "You know how they say everyone has a second somewhere in the world? I think I met your second today. Although, I did not technically meet him, I saw a picture of him."

This is what I was going to say. When I arrived at his apartment, he was standing at his front door, a large suitcase packed, like he was ready for a trip and was just waiting to say goodbye.

"My mother has sent for me," he said. He did not give me a chance to ask questions.

I looked at his face, his hooded eyes swollen and dry, and I was surprised to find them completely without sadness. He looked resigned, even bored. Instead of all I planned to say, this is what I said:

"Constantine, who is your mother but me? Where are you thinking of going without me?"

I took the suitcase from him, walking into the kitchen. Everything in the kitchen was gone. From the gas stove and the oven mittens hanging above them, to the stack of washed dinner plates drying on the stainless-steel dish rack we had purchased together at the Lagos city mall.

I kicked off my shoes, running into the bedroom. The first time I visited him in this apartment, he asked me to be quiet because his neighbors in the next apartment just had a baby. I had tiptoed theatrically around the house and when that did not make him laugh, I coated my face with cornstarch baby powder and began to mime.

We were in the bedroom. He was sitting on the bed, both feet to the ground. My mime began with this—I believe I began with the basics—getting out of a box, eating invisible food, winning a tug-of-war. He sat there still staring, still saying nothing. Next, I stood with all the weight of my body on my right leg. With my left hand, I mimed knocking on and leaning against a door, waiting for whoever was home to come open up.

"Why don't you just come sit next to me?" my Aba said eventually.

I sat next to him and let him ease me out of my clothes. I was nervous and shaking that first time. This was the time before I knew I loved him and before the time I learned that the taste of him was smooth and filling, like coconut water. To distract myself, that first time, I thought about Saint Genesius of Rome, the mime who converted to the Christian faith as he mimed what he had planned as a mockery of the ritual of baptism.

I thought about the way his mind must have had to rearrange itself to accept a new reality. How was it so easy for him to believe that a voice from heaven had spoken to him, reporting his record of sins, washing them with water, declaring him forgiven?

Often, as Constantine wrapped himself around my naked back, I wondered if records were being kept about my sins, and if there were records, how detailed were they? I wondered if there was, somewhere, a long list of all the times I licked his legs, or all the times after the first time and before the next, when I was by myself at home yet feeling aftershocks of how he made my body move.

ON THE DAY I lost him, the room had been emptied before I arrived. The bed was gone, the covers, the sheets, the area rug, all gone. His wardrobe stood emptied of everything but a pair of black shoes, four shirts, and two full sets of his customs officer's uniforms.

I walked out of the bedroom. He was standing at the door where I had left him, a suitcase in his hands as though I had not just taken it out of them.

"I am going to Aba" was all he said. "I have just spoken to my mother, she needs to see me now."

The part of me that loved him beyond words, that is my mouth, fell before him, kissing his feet. He did not move, even as I reached up to his knees, kissing and pleading with him to stay. The part of me that would miss him for all time, that is, my hands, rose up to his waist, pulling down his belted jeans. What I found was the quiet of the ocean in the morning, slithering and slim like a baby fish. He did not move away, so I filled myself with him in every way that I could. I filled my heart, I filled my tongue, I filled my womb. I took my calabash to the ocean, but the longing had arrived by boat.

··

SOMETHING HAPPENED ON THE WAY TO LOVE

ARIYIKE

2010

A YEAR AFTER I began co-hosting the Christian-themed radio show at Chill FM 97.5 Lagos, we included a segment where we had famous Christians—pastors and their wives, mostly—telling our listeners their love stories. We called this segment "Letting God Write Your Love Story." Most of the time, it was the same regurgitated boringness: the couple always met in church or in a university campus fellowship. The Lord Jesus told the man that the woman, usually a one-of-a-kind beauty and from a wealthier family, was to be his wife. The woman, usually much younger, and lacking in any personal, distinctive ambition, prayed to God and received her own sign that the rising gospel star was her husband.

I hated doing those interviews. I wanted more than

anything to ask those pastors about their ex-girlfriends, about how many women had refused their advances, about their failures at love. I would have given anything to ask these stunning wives if they truly were attracted to these plain men, if they loved having husbands who were never at home. Ask them what it's like to fuck a man who believes he hears the voice of God.

I am not a fan of love stories in general. I find the entire subject absurd and contradictory. By the time you decide to make a relationship into a story, the love part is already ending. My favorite books and movies have always been those dealing with anything but love. I remember seeing the movie *Dogville* with my twin sister and our brothers. I LOVED IT. They slept through it. My sister, Bibike, hated the blunt bleakness of it.

"If I want to think about misery and injustice, I just look outside my window," she said right after the movie ended. "You know I like my movies entertaining; next time, rent a happy movie like *Drumline* or *Love Don't Cost a Thing*."

I loved *Dogville*. Even now, I consider it one of the best movies of all time. I loved the sense of compounding evil evoked throughout the movie and the fact that the towns-people got worse, instead of better. They were exactly like I have come to realize most people truly are, completely evil and irredeemable.

I THINK PEOPLE who, like my sister, say they can only be entertained by happy love stories are selfish and hypocrit-ical. They want to pretend that only happy stories are real stories. They want to hear a great big love story. It is not, I think, that they care that Mr. So So and Miss Do Do have arrived at happiness and are on the way to love. No, they are taking notes for their own journey. They are inspecting their own lives, comparing it with the stories they hear. They are wondering, when they meet an old couple married forty years, whether their own loves or lives will last that long. It is also that they are unwilling to confront the reality of the world we are all creating together. We all are both heroes and villains, both lovelorn and callous.

"These people are our bread and butter," my boss, Dexter, always said to me. "Do not antagonize them."

And he was right, as usual. Our loyal listeners, the ones who had made us so popular, were church people and, like people who only watched romantic comedies and read romance novels, they had come to expect a specific brand of sanguinity from our show.

The month before Dexter announced plans to leave Chill FM to start the first-of-its-kind sports radio station in Lagos, he had introduced his fiancée—a tall, mixed-race European named Cindy—to all of us at the office. Cindy and Erica, the other on-air personality hired the same day I was, became fast friends. Sometimes they stood right outside the sound booth whilst Dexter and I recorded our show, *How to Receive from God*, sipping from tall foam cups and smiling wide smiles at each other.

It was also the month Dexter and I resumed fucking everywhere we could—in the staff bathroom, in the service elevator, in the rarely used staff director's personal kitchen. It was a mix of the knowledge that he was on the brink of becoming truly phenomenal in the industry and the idea that I had the ability to hurt someone as beautiful and carefree as Cindy that I found so addictive and intoxicating.

It was also the month when I learned in a staff meeting, instead of from Dexter, that our show was ending because the New Church had decided to invest in a church satellite TV station instead. The station was cutting the whole religious programming schedule, and I was to be without a job. Stunned, I looked around the meeting room, from Dexter, whose face was without fear or remorse, to Erica, who made no attempt to hide her grin. No one was looking at me.

It was, therefore, the month I decided to go see Pastor David Shamonka again for myself, even though it had been almost ten years since we had last spoken.

BANKOLE, MY FATHER, had left us suddenly that October, ten years before. He had called my twin sister and me into the bedroom, after the boys were worn out and asleep, asking us to take care of our brothers.

I called a taxi at the crack of dawn, took it all the way to the New Church to see Pastor David. Pastor David was not as easy to see as he had been ten years before. It took me seven tries calling his office to be passed on to the assistant who wasn't too frightened to ask him if he wanted to see me. A few hours later, I received a call back from another assistant, telling me that Pastor would see me if I could make it to the Nigerian capital, Abuja, for the Full Gospel Business Crusade.

It was the month before Cindy found out Dexter and I had been fucking. She had found a voice note he had sent to me, a voice note that was nothing but sounds of us climaxing that he had recorded surreptitiously. Dexter, of course, insisted that the voice note was recent, but the recording old, and that it was born from nostalgia and nothing else. Even though his Cindy believed him totally, with the typical gullibility of a woman in love, she still was heartbroken that Dexter could be engaged to her and still miss me.

It was the month I surprised Dexter by continuing our situation even after he told me he had asked Cindy to be his wife. I did not care about her feelings, and I told him so easily because it was absolutely normal for us to talk about stuff like that. Back then, I had yet to grasp how little men, no matter how old, know about women. Most men have no idea how female resentment works. I was not sorry she found out the way she did. I enjoyed it. I wanted his Cindy to hate me. I was not even trying to hide it. Dexter, bright as the morning sun, never understood that.

More and more after that, I let Dexter kiss between my legs even though I did not enjoy it. He would lick and spit and nibble until I was irritated enough to smack him in the face. I never told him to stop. Instead, I would close my eyes and imagine those same lips that were licking me instead kissing Cindy's pale face, and my heart would quicken with joy. I did not realize then why I did what I did.

If a person has never had agbalumo, no matter how hard you try to explain the unique balance of sweet and sour to them, they cannot comprehend the reality of the "African star apple." Even for those familiar with agbalumo, very few are skillful enough to determine just by looking at the outside flesh which ones will taste good. The key, I think, is to focus on knowing several irrebuttable distinguishing features of great agbalumo.

I wish I could tell what makes good girls go bad. I wish I could identify, before becoming entangled, which people are traps and which are true friends. Maybe I am the kind of woman who will never have any real friends because I am always aiming for more, always seeking increase.

I cannot give anyone the experience of living my life, of knowing how I felt. I am still trying to understand these things myself. It is obvious to me now that back then, when I was desperate and needy, even though I was many years and several income streams removed from that girl who hawked water in traffic, running after cars while young men made fun of my bouncing breasts, I was nothing in my own eyes.

Yes, I was so small in my own eyes that the idea that the same penis I buried deep inside me could be in the pert mouth of part-Italian, part-German, part-Nigerian Cindy made me feel bigger, brighter, and better than anything else I had ever done at that point. Even earning my first one million naira did not compare. I told myself that Dexter, by sleeping with Cindy and me at the same time, made us equal. I told myself that Dexter, by risking hurting Cindy to continue fucking me, made me better than her.

AS TEENAGERS, MY twin sister and I dressed the same way every day, continuing the tradition our mother had started when we were little girls. We wore the same jeans, same tops, and dragged around the same little purses popular with the girls in our neighborhood. We had to be matching, always. The first morning after we bought our first pair of jeans, we put them on and took a walk around the neighborhood. I was so uncomfortable at first. I felt vulnerable and on display immediately. The tightness of those jeans, combined with the shortness of the tops we wore over them, made me feel like everyone around us was watching our booties jiggle. My sister, who always thought everyone was trying to sleep with us, enjoyed the attention, as though she was glad, finally, to be proved right.

I kept the jeans, even though I hated them. It was easier, more comfortable, to sell water in traffic wearing jeans. I ran faster in them, and when men in cars stretched out their hands to smack my butt, I was comforted by the barrier of jeans between us, that they did not feel the texture or soft of me.

Before the radio station, I got a full-time clerk job at a beauty supply store. I spent the day giving women suggestions on the right hair extensions and makeup for their skin tone. Sometimes, my sister visited me at work. She made the day brighter; the customers stayed longer, bought more weaves, left bigger tips after listening to our team efforts at marketing.

One evening while Bibike visited, a tall, middle-aged man came to the shop. Having a man dressed so formally, as though he were on his way back from his job as a bank manager, was such a surprise. We sometimes had a few men come in to buy stuff as gifts for lovers and wives, but this man was different. He wore the darkest black shoes I had ever seen. He smelled like old wood and rich-man tobacco. He had a BMW saloon car parked right in front of the entrance. He picked up several Kanekalon hair extension bundles in black and came up to the counter to pay. He left a significant tip, then asked me to walk with him to his car. Even though it was stupid to be interested in a customer who was obviously committed to someone else, I still allowed myself to dream. I made several excuses for him. It was possible he was single, I reasoned. Maybe he was shopping for a family member or an acquaintance, I let myself think.

"That's a lot of hair, who is it for?" I asked as he got into his car, sitting behind the wheel.

"My wife and my two daughters," he said. "They are getting braids done. They are traveling abroad for holiday and want something that will not need to be redone until they get back to Lagos."

"Okay. I hope they like it," I said, turning around to leave.

This man, Lucky—I remember his name like it was yesterday—smiled and called me back.

"Wait, please, I want to talk to you," he said.

I turned back to him, standing as close as possible to the driver's window.

"You and your sister are such beautiful girls, can the both of you come visit me at home next week?" he asked.

"Why? Where do you live?" I asked.

"I live in Fola Agoro, it's close to Shomolu," he said. With one finger, he rubbed his left eye as though something had gotten inside it. "I will pay you thirty thousand naira each."

"Thirty thousand naira for what?" I asked.

"See, my wife is traveling. I don't want to be alone. I have never been with twins at the same time. The house will be empty, we can have so much fun together." He was frowning as he said this, angry, it seemed, at my bewildered questioning.

I AUDITIONED FOR and got the presenting job at Chill FM a few months after this, and quitting that sales clerk job was one of the best days of my life. It was even more satisfying than getting the new job. But that day, and all the days of my life, are colored by incidents such as the day with Mr. Lucky. I do not expect that I will ever be able to forget that feeling, like an old rag, dirty and dispensable. I did not tell my sister what the man had said, but after that day I stopped dressing up identical to her. If she got braids, I was sure to wear a weave. When she wore bright colors, I wore dark.

And so, that Saturday morning, the day I saw Pastor David again, I walked into the conference hall of the Ibeto Hotel in Abuja dressed in my best corporate skirt suit and black peep-toe high heels. I walked out of the elevator into the nearest women's bathroom. Standing in front of the mirror, I willed myself to speak with Pastor David again. Several groups of women walked in and out of that bathroom and I stood there, saying nothing to anyone. The floor was white and shiny, as were the tiled walls. Everywhere I turned, my reflection—a put-together businesswoman in a gray suit—stared at me. She made me want to run away.

I was unprepared for the nervous energy stirring inside me. Within the conference room, a crowd of mostly younger men in dark-colored suits stood with arms raised or outstretched, singing worship songs The only women I could see were ushers and greeters scattered across the room. I grew even more nervous. My scalp was sweaty. The air-conditioning was failing to contain the dampness and heat. I walked around for a little while until I found a place to sit, an empty seat a few rows away from the makeshift podium set up in the conference hall. Just as I was relaxing into the chair, a fat man in a bright orange suit, his high compact belly straining the buttons of his jacket, walked up from behind me, asking me to get out of his reserved spot.

Pastor David walked in right as I was standing up out of the chair. Before I turned to look at the stage, I could feel him. It was as though a gust of wind blew into the room, over all of our heads. People screamed. Some cried. Everyone was clapping, even me. It took him several minutes to hush us up, and then he began to sing. His voice threw me. It was still as hoarse as I remembered but it was skillful now, tempered by better musical equipment. He sounded more than tolerable. His voice was pleasant. Arresting.

He moved from worship song to worship song with such passion and ease that when he was done, almost no one was left standing. We all were on our knees singing, praising God. "There is no one like you God, our Father."

Finally, Pastor Shamonka began his message on the

Cave of Adullam. He read from the Amplified version the story of future King David seeking refuge from King Saul.

"In the first book of Samuel, chapter twenty-two, we are told David escaped to Adullam. Just like some of you. You have escaped your town and village. You are in Abuja hiding. Trying to make money so you can go home with pride. Or maybe, like David, you are hiding from the enemy of your destiny. Like David, some of you have left your father and mother. Like David, you have the promise of God in your life, but life has forced you into hiding.

"Book of Samuel, chapter twenty-two, verse two, says, 'Everyone who was suffering hardship, and everyone who was in debt, and everyone who was discontented gathered to him; and he became captain over them. There were about four hundred men with him.'

"Can you see what happened here? That is the difference between you and David. That is why David won and you are losing. David did not stop winning souls. David did not stop building his army. He did not stop leading.

"But I have come in the glory of God Most High to raise up the new mighty men of David!" he screamed into the crowd.

"I am here to raise up glorious men. Men who will not give up or turn backwards. Men who have been brought up to fight.

"You will fight for your money. You will fight for your job. Fight for your business. And when the enemy comes against you like a flood, you will raise up a standard against them. Somebody scream, 'I am a standard!'"

As the audience screamed, Pastor David took two steps off the podium. For a moment my heart stopped beating. I thought he was walking my way. He began to touch the foreheads of all the people in the front row, and as he did, he screamed into the microphone.

"You are the standard. You are the best man for the job. You are anointed for victory. Success is your birthright."

One woman in a yellow blazer over a black skirt began to scream. She was loud and unrestrained, as though she were in pain. Another man shook like a vibrating phone. People were falling on their faces, this way and that. My hands began shaking on their own accord. Waves after waves of something like electricity ran from my wrists to my fingers. Before long, I was praying like everyone else at that meeting. I was crying and weeping, I was praying with all my heart. I was pleading with God in Yoruba and English and asking him to help my family. I was not asking to be rich, a standard, a mighty man, or whatever. No, none of that was for me. I just wanted to have enough.

That service ended about three hours after I arrived, and it was not enough time to calm my nerves. When Pastor got off the stage, I realized to my dismay that I was on a long queue of people waiting to speak with him. Up close and away from the bright yellow lights of the stage, I noticed that his hair had begun to gray at the edges. His cheeks were full, round and wrinkly, and his eyes had a yellow tint to them, a yellow that contrasted with the deep dark circles around his eyes. He yawned at least three times in the minutes I waited in line.

During my wait, I chatted with a man next to me about the Word we had heard and the blessing we had received. The man had a large shipping envelope of papers with him, related to his manufacturing business.

"I just need Pastor to bless this," the man said, showing me the contents of his envelope. "I don't even need prayer. If he can just touch this. I know my business will revive."

The man was going on and on, and because I was being polite, standing there and listening to him, I realized too late that Pastor had decided to stop his one-on-one meetings. He was headed out of the venue. Without thinking, I ran after him and his entourage, screaming, "Daddy, Pastor, Daddy Pastor, I am here to see you, sir."

Immediately, the men around him linked arms, making a human fence around him.

I persisted with my screaming. I screamed even louder.

"Daddy, its Keke from Chill FM, we have a meeting for today. Daddy Pastor, sir, I just need five minutes."

Pastor David turned to his right when I said this. He did not turn around to look at me, he spoke inaudibly with the man closest to his right. Then he walked away. The man Pastor David had spoken to walked up to me with a wide smile.

"Good evening, Sister Keke. It is okay, Pastor says to bring you with us to the hotel."

"You have grown into the most beautiful woman in the world. And I am not even the man I was ten years ago," Pastor David Shamonka was saying to me later that night in a voice hoarse from all that preaching. We were sitting next to each other in the L-shaped sitting area of his penthouse suite. "I think I am better in many ways. I am richer, of course. But I know I am no longer young and hip."

I told him he had never really been young or hip. He laughed gently at this.

"You are loved by many people," I added quickly, keeping the mood light.

"People will love anything under a spotlight," he said. "Especially troubled people."

I did not agree with him. "Well, they must like what they see."

"I am just God's conduit. If I die today, someone else will take my place. Blessed be the name of the Lord," he said.

"Blessed be the name of the Lord."

"You are the reason I never married," he said then, with a small sigh.

I laughed without thinking. The large power inverter next to the mini fridge hummed loudly. It was an awkward and foolish laugh, and immediately I tried to remedy it.

"I'm sorry. I didn't mean to laugh," I said.

"Are you courting anyone right now?" he asked a few quiet moments after.

"Courting? I think so. I don't know," I said.

"I thought about you every day back then. You were so young, and the ministry was so young, and I did not handle many things very well," he said.

He had gotten out of his chair as he spoke. He picked out a candy bar and two bottles of water from the mini fridge, handing the candy and one bottle of water to me before sitting back down.

"When did you realize I was the one working at Chill FM?" I asked after taking a bite of the candy.

"I knew right from the start. Who do you think told Dexter to hire you? You do not know this, but I saw you arriving for the interview. I had planned to sit on the panel, but I left when I saw you in the lobby," he said.

I laughed again, this bout longer than the last.

"Please do not cancel the show," I said finally. "Andrew, my younger brother, I'm not sure if you remember him. He is about to start university, and I am his sponsor. I need this job."

"We are starting our own satellite station, my dear. The radio programming was canceled months ago, did you just now hear of it?" It was the impatience in his words that wounded me.

"Have you heard about our new station?" he continued. "It will be called New Hearts TV. We will be broadcasting from South Africa and Lagos. We have spent millions of dollars on it. We will change this world. I promise you."

"Amen," I said.

I felt a gust of wind blow through the room and all over me. I realized that I was sitting on the floor, with no recollection of when I got out of the chair. I wondered if I had fainted from shock but did not realize it. How and why can it be so easy to fall again into poverty, after having come so close? I had paid my dues. I was always on time, working as hard as a donkey. I built a solid reputation as a Christian radio presenter, supported controversial public topics like anti-gay legislation and the criminalization of adultery. No reputable radio station was willing to hire me. It was hard to believe I was being cast away so easily.

"What is your boyfriend like?" Pastor David asked. He was a little bent over, looking down at me and smiling, the kind of bright smile a father might force to comfort his daughter.

"Which boyfriend? I never said I had a boyfriend."

"There's someone in your life, you said. You don't have to tell me who he is." He was frowning as he said this. "He should be taking care of you. You shouldn't be here begging for your job if he is doing his job well." He took a long gulp from my half-filled bottle of water, then set it down before me.

"Well, I have nobody to help me. I'm all my brothers have right now," I said.

"You are so wrong. You have God and you have me," he said. Water dripped down the side of his mouth and, without thinking, I reached out to wipe his face.

"Amen. Daddy, I believe. Blessed be the name of the Lord."

His phone rang at that moment and he reached to the top of the coffee table to pick it up. He did not leave the sitting area. Instinctively, realizing it was what he expected, I got up off the floor next to him and walked toward the door, giving him space for his call. I considered leaving at that point; it was obvious already that my job was gone and Pastor had other plans. I imagined the look on my brothers' faces when

I told them. Andrew had been so excited to begin studying at the University of Lagos, he had taken entrance exams and practice O levels before getting to his final year of secondary school. We were beyond surprised when he was admitted to study public administration. Finally, it seemed, good things were happening to us. We were lifting off, ascending, and we were doing it together as a team.

Pastor David's call lasted longer than I expected. I stood quiet as a statue for at least thirty minutes, then I walked briskly past him and into the bathroom. I was just seeking a place to be quiet for myself. Every time Pastor David laughed during that call, it felt like he was laughing at me. I sat fully dressed inside the bathtub and began to think up a plan.

In the bathroom was a second door connected to the suite's bedroom. Opening the door as quietly as I could, I went into Pastor David's bedroom. I spent time looking at his briefcase, his computer, his international passport. I picked up the phone and, in my most businesslike voice, ordered room service.

When the meal arrived, he was still on the phone. As the bellboy opened the door, I realized that two assistants stood outside. They were the ones I had seen at the start of the service, but not the two who had driven the pastor back here. His life was organized and opulent in ways beyond my imagining.

I ate most of the dinner and was beginning to contemplate taking a shower and changing into a bathrobe just to scandalize him into ending the call when he in fact ended the call and came into the bedroom.

"Did you order the catfish pepper soup? It is usually really good," he said, opening up the covered plates on the cart.

"I haven't had any food all day," I replied, embarrassed that every plate was empty.

He laughed. "That is okay," he said.

Pastor David turned on the TV in the bedroom as he sat on the bed. If he thought the moment with both of us in this hotel bedroom was awkward, weird, or un-Christian, he did not show it.

"You can come work for me," he said suddenly. The TV was on some news station, but he was not looking at it. He was taking off his shoes, then his socks. He rolled both socks into one ball then picked up both shoes and socks, placing them in a shoebox in the corner of the room.

"What kind of job do you have in mind?" I asked.

"Our director of programs will be able to find something for you at New Hearts TV."

"That would be wonderful, Pastor," I said.

"Don't thank me yet," he said. "It probably will pay a lot less than you are used to. But the reward is the Kingdom."

"Hallelujah," I said.

"Can you call the desk and ask why we do not have TBN or CBN? Also, ask the assistants at the door to go get me my dinner," he said.

As I made the phone call in the living room, I heard the shower turn on in the bathroom. I was surprised to hear him call me some minutes later.

"Can I come in?" I asked.

"Yes," he said.

He was inside the wide tub with the curtain drawn all the way around, but I still could see the clear, full outline of him.

"Taiwo, did you call reception?" he asked.

"Yes, Pastor," I answered.

"What did they say?" he asked.

"They described how to set up TBN or Daystar here on this TV. They have a second network that is programmable," I said.

"Great," he said. "Let me know when the food comes."

"I have to leave now," I said. "It's getting too late."

"What? Don't leave." He flung the shower curtain to the side, water droplets splashing around. Pastor David stood in the shower, naked and wet, his penis erect and as long as a schoolboy's wood ruler. "Please don't leave yet."

I stayed until morning that day, like he asked. I stayed because I was hoping to negotiate a better life for myself. I stayed not because I was still the girl who had had fan girl crushes on this man as a teenager but because something had happened to me in all these years. I did not believe in love, in marital love, in righteous men or justice.

I did want to plant myself like a parasite at the side of Pastor David for as long as I could. I wanted the penthouse, the designer suits, the poorly paid people making my life easier, I admit it. I knew what he was doing by asking the girl he used to know to stay over. I knew he was trusting her—me—to be quiet and discreet.

I was falling asleep on the living room sofa when the assistants returned with Pastor David's dinner. They did not acknowledge my presence. The food tray was rolled in on the branded hotel cart even though it was obvious the meal had come from outside. There were gold-rimmed tureens of fish, gizdodo, and brown rice. A small serving of coleslaw and eggs.

One after the other, both assistants served portions onto gorgeous china, then took full spoons out of the tureens' remnants, making a show of chewing and swallowing and drinking the water.

I walked into the bathroom. It was misty from Pastor David's bath. I looked at my reflection again, wondering if it was not too late to leave. Surely there was something else I could do. I had some money saved, I could start a business. I got in the shower instead and washed all of my crevices with hotel soap.

When I was done, the food-serving assistants were gone and Pastor was on another conference call. I went into the bedroom, still naked under the bathrobe, and willed myself to sleep. It must have been almost morning when Pastor David made it to bed. I looked up and he was kneeling between my legs. My legs were spread apart and raised, my heels balanced on both of his shoulders.

"It is okay, you can go back to sleep," he said in a hoarse whisper. "I'm wearing a condom."

I did not go back to sleep, even though I pretended to be asleep. Instinctively, I realized that my nonparticipation was important to him. I realized he had come prepared and had waited it out. It hurt more than I expected. Everything hurt. He dug his fingernails in my ankle flesh, digging and pinching, harder and harder with each thrust. The first time I thought he was done, he had only paused to reach for the television remote, making TBN louder in the background. The second time he paused, he pulled out a soft penis, smacking hard at my vagina and inner thighs over and over until he was hard again. He was, all this time, singing along to the worship music filling the room.

It was a small surprise to me that I could make my body so still that nothing moved as he shook me—not my hips, not my breasts, not my hair.

"I'm sorry for shushing you," he said after he was done. He was lying next to me and whispering again in my ear. "I did not want to make any sounds my assistants could hear."

"I understand," I said.

"I am going to find your mother and father," he said, still whispering. "I am going to ask their permission to make you my wife."

Good luck to you and good luck to me, I thought to myself.

··

STACY'S BOYS

ANDREW

2011

ON THE DAY she came back for us, I ran away. I ran as fast as I could down the street, away from their scent. I noticed him first, he had a sweet, sharp scent cutting through the stale air of Grandmother's house. It was his hair I smelled, some loud citrus-based baby shampoo, announcing their arrival, announcing their strangeness, overpowering the smell of Grandmother's garden egg soup boiling on the stove.

Not even the stench of my brother Peter's soccer cleats, fresh from the field and sitting at the entrance to our room, or the rotting garlic cloves Sister Bibike had hung over all the house, on the doorposts and pinned to pillars to drive away bad spirits, could muddy his scent.

I saw him first, the back of him. His hair was brown, thick and curly. An alphabet onesie with a hood attached covered half his face. He looked less like a baby, more like a short, fat wrestler eager to jump into the ring. He was making those loud baby noises, saying gu gu gu ga ga over and over. As soon as he saw me, he turned so fast he slid halfway down to the floor of our grandmother's living room before his mother, my mother, caught him in her arms.

My mother saw me in the same moment I saw her. She said nothing at first. She just looked at me, from the top of my head to the shoes on my feet, and smiled a small smile.

It was Grandmother who spoke to me, disintegrating the peace.

"Andrew, leave your shoes outside," she said in Yoruba. I looked at her, surprised to find that her eyes were teary, even though she sounded joyful, even energized.

My mother cradled her baby in one hand. With the other, she searched around in a large handbag shaped like a boat. She found it, a little yellow pacifier. She unscrewed the cover and put it in his mouth. The baby went gu gu gu ga ga ga again then slumped in the nook of her arm like a half-filled bag of rice.

"His name is Zion," she said to me. "His father is an American soldier." She was still smiling that smile, wiping drool off her new baby's face.

"Where are your sisters?" she asked. Talking to me like it was nothing, like she had a right to be here, like everything was normal and fine.

"Did they go out? Grandma said they don't work on Saturdays," she asked.

Before I found the words to answer, Grandmother rescued me again.

"Andrew, there is rice in the pot. Go have some, take some garden egg soup with it," she said.

It was a short distance to the kitchen. Twelve steps end to end. I made it to the pot in six.

"THE RICE MUST be cold. Let me turn on the stove to heat it up," I said.

I took the pot from its position on the wooden kitchen shelf and was about to place it on the stove. Instead, I put it down, back onto the kitchen shelf, and I just ran. I ran out of the kitchen, through the back door, into the street.

Grandmother did not try to call me back. If she had, it is unlikely that I would have listened. My feet were swift and sweaty. The insides of my shoes felt like I had been wading around in a flood. As I ran, I caught glimpses of my reflection in car windows and the glass doors of storefronts. I was running like a thief being chased by an angry mob.

When I turned into the street with the many potholes, I realized where I was running to. I could see various men, some with faces stained with engine oil and car grime, washing their shirtless bodies at the sides of the street. A couple of men were washing their motorcycles with water collected from puddles. I walked the row of small houses, shacks really, on the corner, houses built with reclaimed wood from the old civil defense corps training ground. The house I was looking for was painted blue. The paint was the wrong kind for wood, so the color was faded, cracked, and peeling. There was mildew growing in the spaces between the boards. I stopped a few feet away from her door, trying to convince myself to turn back home. She came out of her house right at that moment, startling me. She was wearing a short white dress, and in her right hand was a small transparent bucket filled with black-eyed beans and sliced pepper, tomatoes, and onions.

Just as I was getting ready to leave, she saw me.

"Andy dudu. Were you about to pass through my street without visiting me? What is this type of life you're living?" Her voice was louder than necessary. Some of the car mechanics turned to look at us, then, immediately dismissing us, they continued washing their bodies and motorcycles.

"Good evening, Stacy. I don't want to disturb you. I can see you are busy." I was walking toward her as I spoke.

"Come over here. I have been looking for you," she said.

When I got to where she stood, she hugged me. Her body was both soft and firm, like a good-quality mattress. She handed over her bucket and continued walking. I walked beside her. Her pace was slow and leisurely. It was hard at first for me not to run ahead.

"Where were you going?" she asked.

"Nowhere. I was just taking a walk. What are you making, moimoi or akara?" I replied.

"Moimoi," she said.

Stacy and her mother had come to the neighborhood around the same time we moved in with Grandmother. She was only a little older than me but she was never really a girl, even back then. My friends and I used to play soccer on this street. We dug large stones from the ground, marking out our goalposts. Stacy was always quiet, not trying to join in like the other girls. She just stood there, watching us. I always played midfield. Peter was always goalkeeper, even after he nearly died from tetanus infection. Stacy watched us every day, saying nothing until the day her mother left and didn't return and she walked to Tamuno, the oldest of us, and asked him to give her fifty naira for a chance to look at her breasts.

For most of us boys in the area, Stacy's was the first adult female body we saw naked. We did not think much of it. We played football and went to Stacy's house and took turns watching her bathe.

When any boy tried to touch her, and there always was one foolish enough, the rest of us beat him up and dared him to tell his parents what happened. I think we liked to believe we were taking care of Stacy. We helped her eat, go to school, buy clothes. In return, she taught us what no one else would teach us about girls.

"If I go with you all the way to grind these beans, does that mean I get to eat some?" I asked.

"Of course, even if you didn't help, you are always welcome," she said.

"Are you going to work later tonight?" I asked.

"No, I am not, my boyfriend is coming to visit tonight," she said.

Stacy worked as a dancer/bartender in one of the adult clubs on Victoria Island. Her boyfriend, an older man in his thirties, was someone she'd met at her workplace. Whenever he visited, driving his white Toyota Camry through the puddles and mud, Stacy always paid boys in the neighborhood money for the "protection" of her boyfriend and his car. Of course, if any damage happened to the car, it wouldn't have been by any outsider. Stacy was just cunning in that way.

As we got closer to the mill, Stacy sang gently under her breath. It was one of those Igbo hymns, but she made it sound like something Mariah Carey would sing. I wondered then if anything ever stunned or disappointed her. She still had the same peace from when we were kids, when she'd run up all the way to the goalposts just to stand in silence for two hours.

"Do you think he loves you?" I asked.

"Who?" she answered.

"Your boyfriend," I said.

"I think so, but I do not really think about things like that," she said.

"What do you think about?" I asked.

"The important stuff. How to get money, how to be happy," she said.

It was Stacy who explained to me what a period was. Once, while I was watching her get dressed, she pulled out a face towel, folding it into four parts and tucking it into her underwear. After she explained everything about periods, I began stealing Always pads from my sisters and bringing them to her.

"So? Does Andy dudu have a girlfriend?" Stacy asked just as we arrived at the mill.

"Why do you keep calling me Andy dudu? I am not even that dark skinned," I said.

Stacy took the bucket from me, handing it over to the

girl manning the mill. The mill girl had one of those faces whose age you could not really guess. She was either a young-looking sixteen-year-old or an older-looking twelve-year-old. The mill was old and loud, but we stood right next to it. Stacy watched the girl's every movement even as she talked to me.

"Andy, are you angry with me? Don't be angry with me. We just call you Andy dudu because everyone else in your house, your sisters, Peter, even your grandma, is yellow like pawpaw," Stacy said. "But truth be told, eh, you are the most good-looking one. Auntie, isn't he good-looking?" She nudged the milling girl as she spoke, screaming all the sentences without pausing.

"Yes, he is. Tall, dark, handsome, like Desmond Elliot," the milling lady replied.

The first time I saw Stacy naked, I remember thinking she looked quite ordinary, like a little baby, spotless skin all fresh and shiny. I did not understand the excitement all the other boys had from the experience. It was a strangely painful feeling, like scoring a goal and having it unfairly disqualified by the referee. Then, one day, I saw her walking home and she was wearing a pair of those low-ride jeans and pulling them up every time they rode down to her hips and revealed her butt crack. When she turned around once and saw that I was watching her, she smiled a wide, bright white smile that was almost a laugh. And just like that, I understood what it was all about. After that, whenever it was my turn to watch her, I always tried to make her laugh or at least smile.

"I look like my mother. She has the dark skin. It's my

father who is, how did you say it again? Yellow like pawpaw, even though everyone knows pawpaws are orange, not yellow," I said.

"Hold still." Stacy placed the bowl of pureed beans in my hand and shut the lid. "I'm sorry if I offended you," she said. "It is just a funny nickname. You're funny, you always make me laugh. I thought you liked it."

I stopped for a moment, allowing her to walk ahead of me. A car was passing by and there was no room for us to walk side by side anymore.

"It's okay. Not such a big deal," I said.

I did not think she understood, but she was trying to. She laughed out loud for no reason. She walked ahead of me until we got to her house. I walked in right behind her. It was dark inside. Standing in the darkness while she fumbled around for matches and a candle, I imagined what would happen if her boyfriend arrived and I was still here. I daydreamed that he would go crazy with jealousy and start a fight. Then all of us, the boys in the neighborhood, would gather together to beat him senseless, then send him away.

There was one full-size mattress on the floor and one bean bag in the corner. I sat on the mattress. Stacy brought out some blankets and covered my legs with them. It was always too cold in her house. Once, I asked her if she cared that people knew what she did for money. "The people who love me are more than those who hate me," she said. "But I try to be the kind of person who is hard to hate."

As she poured the pureed beans into small tins and set them in a pot filled with boiling water, I lay on my back and looked up at the ceiling and thought about Stacy living here alone for so long. Maybe that was why she had us come here. Maybe that was why she did not pick just one for so long. Did she need all of us to feel less lonely? Was a prostitute just another type of lonely girl?

When she was done, she came to lie right next to me. Her breath was warm. She smelled like smoke and kerosene.

"I heard your Mother is back," she said. "Is it really her?"

"Yes, it is. She came this morning," I said.

"If you are worried about what happens next, you should not be. If her absence could not kill you, then her presence cannot kill you. Look here, you and me, we are like the barracks. Like Fela sang, 'Soldier go, soldier come, barracks remains,'" she said.

I put my left hand in her right, then I squeezed gently. We locked hands for a few minutes and then we let each other go. Just like we did when we were younger, our hands went beneath the blankets. I shuffled my way out of my boxers and jeans; her waistband made a *smack* sound as she pulled it down. I waited until the air smelled different and the force with which she moved rocked the little mattress and then I began rubbing myself. Remembering that she always finished first, I rubbed valiantly, trying to get to the end before her. I worked in vain. She went to the kitchen to tend to her moimoi and I remained on that bed. The room was cold and I was going so fast that my heart was racing, beating so loudly that I could hear it in my own ears. The blanket alone was failing to keep me warm; my legs were tingly and it felt as if I were about to lose feeling in them.

Stacy was moving about in her tiny kitchen. This made it so much harder to keep my focus. Just when I was about to give up, she started singing again. Her voice lifted, pulled, reinvigorated me. I worked faster, thinking that if she realized what her singing *Follow the ladder the heaven* did to me, she'd laugh and I would never stop feeling ashamed.

I pulled the first thing I could grab from a pile of clothes in the corner. It was a black-and-yellow headscarf. I wiped my hands all over it and sat up, my back to the wall.

"I will wash this and bring it back," I said when she came into the room.

"I know," she said. "You always do what you say."

When I left Stacy's house in the morning, I saw that there was a basket of fruit sitting on her doorstep.

I considered going back in to wake Stacy to tell her what I had seen. It was six a.m. on a Monday and people were opening their stores or homes, sweeping out dirt and debris, all evidence of a weekend of carelessness. I picked up the basket and walked away with it. I imagined that someone was watching me walk away. I imagined that the someone watching was cheering me on.

It took me almost thirty minutes to walk back home. I was slow, absentminded, hesitant to see my mother again. When I got home, there was nothing but three soft limes in the basket. I threw them in our trash can.

THE NEXT MORNING, two days after Mother arrived, I woke to the sound of loud arguing. My sisters were in the living room, and our mother was there with her baby, and they were talking all at once, over one another. I borrowed one of Peter's jalabias, got dressed, and walked into the living room. I was startled immediately by how ordinary it all seemed. As though we had been this family forever.

Sometimes, Mother would pause right in the middle of what she was saying to take a sip of water. As she did, I just stared at her. Her fingers seemed crooked, the skin on them wrinkly and hyperpigmented. My sister Ariyike, the one who was marrying Pastor David Shamonka, the one all the commotion was about, had a giant number 2 pencil in her hand that she waved this way and that as she spoke. The pencil was bright yellow and thick, making a wisp through the air as she waved it. Their voices over one another sounded both pleasant and weary, traveling through the air and landing in my ears. It seemed to me that whatever they were arguing about, the point had been made long ago and they were persisting just for the privilege of hearing one another, over and over, like the pleasant hook of a catchy song.

IT WAS FOR this reason that I sat down but said nothing.

"We all know that man is too old for you," our mother said.

"Age is just a number, madam," Ariyike replied.

"You are too young to be married, you have done nothing, gone nowhere," my sister Bibike said.

"I have done enough and I will do more," my sister Ariyike replied.

"We all know you do not love that man," our mother said.

"He loves me. That is enough for both of us," my sister Ariyike said.

"You are too pretty to end up with someone like that," my sister Bibike said.

They went on and on like that for a while. Sometimes, for a couple of minutes, Sister Ariyike pretended to be engrossed in the list she was making. She smiled as she scribbled in her notepad, looking up only when asked a direct question. She did not appear to be offended by their questions. It made me think of the types of argument strangers had in public places about soccer, how passionate people got and yet how no one fretted because it was all jocular, harmless fun. Soon enough, they were talking about dresses, decoration, colors, about the numbers of guests coming to the wedding. Did our mother have anyone from her extended family she wanted to invite? Would there be a camera crew? Had Ariyike met any of Pastor David's exes?

When our mother first came back, it was hard for me to believe our family could fit together again like an old jacket after a little mending. I would have been quite sure, once, that this jovial teasing was fraudulent—there was a suspicious ease in it, a hollow sweetness in their kindness to one another. However, as I watched them that morning planning for a wedding, I thought about Stacy and my heart ached because I realized how lucky she would have felt to have her mother back to argue with, to laugh with, to lie to.

THE BEAUTIFUL PEOPLE AND THE BELOVED COUNTRY

PETER

2011

My mother, who had appeared again in our lives easily and without warning, like a pimple on my forehead, asked me that Saturday morning to go to Tejuosho market with her. My grandmother, placated by gifts she had received—packed foods from Walmart and shiny fabric from Mother's stopover in Dubai—assured me that it was okay to go.

When her encouragement was not enough to make me decide, our grandmother tried tears. She made a production of weeping and wailing, accusing me of ingratitude.

"Peter, you have only one mother, for God's sake. You are too young to be this unforgiving. Can't you just be grateful she's here with us now and be thankful to God she is alive and well?"

I was nineteen. Old enough to keep a grudge until I decided for myself it was time to let go. Tall enough to look down into the center of Mother's head where the repeated doses of blond dye had thinned her hair into near baldness.

My mother, who stood there staring with hope-filled eyes, looked up at me and patted my right shoulder.

"My dear, please come with me. I will leave Zion with your grandmother. It will be just the two of us," she said. "I just need to buy some sandals and ankara fabric to take back home with me. You can get whatever you want."

My mother picked up her handbag, flinging it over her shoulder as she pleaded, wrapping her blond hair in a thick green scarf and exchanging her fluffy pink slippers for flat sandals.

"Have you decided? Are you coming along? Are you gonna wear those?" she asked.

She motioned with a flick of her wrist in the direction of the half-a-size-too-big shoes she had bought me, black-and-white sneakers I would not have dreamed of wearing around our neighborhood. It would have been nothing more than an advertisement to thieves or an invitation for a violent beating from jealous boys.

"I am not wearing those," I said. I slipped into the tried and trusted rubber slide sandals I wore everywhere those days. My toenails were dirty and chipped, but I pretended not to care about what I looked like. Our mother looked at me, her eyes narrowing with hurt by what appeared to her to be my rejection of her gift.

"I will wear them. I promise," I said without thinking.

"I will wear them when I have someplace nice to go, not to the market."

She said nothing. I was not sure if my reply satisfied her. She walked out of the living room, through the veranda, out to the gate. She said nothing as we walked down the street to the closest junction hoping to find a vacant taxicab.

When we arrived at the end of our street, Mother stopped by the last of the small goods kiosks. There was a bench in the street next to the kiosk, and Mother sat on this bench. I stood next to her. We waited.

It was Emmanuel's mother's kiosk. She was the young widow who took over her late husband's business selling fried yams and potatoes in the night market. After her husband died, her friends had encouraged her to start taking new lovers in the city to help pay her bills. It was said around the neighborhood that she went out with one man her friend introduced her to and the very next day, her mouth began to swell up like a balloon. Within a week, her gums had turned black and all of her teeth had fallen out. Grandmother was the only person I knew who acted like any of it was normal and expected.

"Mama Emmanuel knows that her late husband was a very jealous man. What did she expect?" she said.

Mother ordered some fried yams and peppered snails. She waited for Emmanuel's mother to finish wrapping them up then she handed the pack over to me. "There's something I want to tell you, son," she said. "Something I've not yet told your sisters or your brother. Can I tell you? Then you can let me know what you think. Is that okay?"

"I think so," I said.

"Peter? Think so?" she asked.

"I don't know what else to say," I said.

"You can try to say something definite," she said.

As she talked, she flagged down a private car. The driver stopped, and Mother got closer to the car, leaning over the front passenger's seat with the exaggerated giddiness of a teenager as she asked for a ride to the nearest bus stop. Her voice was bright and calming, with just a hint of her American-influenced accent. I did not hear what the driver said but I watched her move away to let the car drive off.

"That man wasn't nice. What happened to all the okadas around here?" she asked.

"The government banned all commercial motorcycles," I said.

"How do you all get around, then?" she said.

"We walk everywhere," I said.

"Of course. No wonder you are all so skinny," she said.

I almost said something about hunger, but I did not. I unwrapped the fried yams and began to eat.

"What do we do now?" I asked.

"We walk. We walk to the bus stop," she said.

We walked for several minutes, saying nothing to each other. I focused on eating the yams as quickly as I could, hoping none of the neighborhood girls I liked passed by. We walked past many people. None of them paid too much attention to us. We walked past Maisuya, who appeared to be on his way to the bus stop as well, but he was slower, a thick roll of newspapers tucked under one arm, a working transistor radio hanging from a rope on his shoulder.

"Peter," he called out in jovial tone. "Peter the goal-keeper, the magnet, Sanu," he said.

"My customer, good evening. How's the Amariya? How's work?" I replied.

There was no need to introduce Mother to him. I did not want to have to explain her absence or be asked to relay greetings when she left again.

"Fine, everyone is fine," he said as he stopped to fiddle with his batteries. It seemed to me as though he was just giving us time to create distance. I did not like that even this neighbor, who knew me only through my fame as the one-handed goalkeeper, could sense how uncomfortable walking down the street with Mother was making me.

"So, I can talk to you about it?" she asked. Again.

"Yes. Go ahead," I said.

She reached into her handbag and pulled out a smaller clutch made of some type of velvety red material. She handed me a folded photo.

"I was in a detention center for eighteen months," she said. "Those are the friends I made there."

In the picture were four women, all dark and slim like my mother. They wore oversize men's clothes and brown boots.

"I was arrested for being an illegal alien. They got me six months after my visa expired. It took eighteen months for my asylum application to be granted."

Ori-ona, the mentally ill woman who claimed to talk to God, was screaming close to a bus parked in front of the beauty-supply store. She was dressed in her usual attire, two woven poly sacks formerly used by farmers to pack red beans, repurposed into a knee-length dress. Her head was clean shaven, her face glowing with a bright shiny oil. Apart from the odd choice of attire, she looked quite clean, almost ordinary, like any other woman in the neighborhood.

"I am the voice of one crying in the wilderness," she shouted as we walked past. "Prepare the way of the Lord."

"Who is that?" Mother asked.

"No one really knows. We call her Ori-ona," I answered.

"Ori-ona? Because she always knows where to go?" Mother asked.

"Well, it has been said that she hears directly from God," I said.

"Who said?" she asked.

"Everyone around here. People take her warnings seriously."

"Well," Mother said, "I guess that makes sense. God can use anyone, even babies."

A few months before Mother returned, the government had hired a construction crew to strengthen the pedestrian footbridge above the highway. Ori-ona made her camp inches away from the construction workers' tent. No one paid her any mind. Every morning she was awake before the sun was up, screaming till she was sore, "Repent, the kingdom of God is at hand. Repent, the kingdom of God is here."

She went on like this until one day a part of the footbridge being repaired collapsed. Just like that, without warning, one of the pillars cracked, killing more than fifty people. All of the construction workers died in the rubble. The government arrested the head of the foreign-owned construction firm

who had won the contract. Nurses from the Lagos psychi-
atric hospital removed Ori-ona from her spot in the street.

We did not see Ori-ona in the neighborhood for months
after that. Then, one day, she was back. Just like that. No
one could tell why she was released from the hospital or how
she found her way back to her old spot on our street.

I did not tell Mother about any of this. There was no need
to. I did not care if she believed it or not. It did not matter.
There are stories you can appreciate or understand only by
living in a particular place at a particular time. Ori-ona is
necessary for us here. In the middle of the worst type of tragedy, we got strange comfort from the idea that it was possible
someone somewhere had been trying to warn us, to prevent
it. This is how we know that we are not completely forgotten.

Mother and I walked for a few more minutes until we
arrived at the bus stop. We got on a danfo bus going to Yaba,
sitting next to each other in one of the two rows of passenger seats in the middle.

The moment we got into the bus, I noticed a middle-aged
woman outside in iro and buba running and heaving toward
our vehicle. She held two large covered plastic bowls, one in
each hand. They seemed full and bubbling with liquid. As
she ran, she stopped several times to catch her breath.

"Look at that yeye woman," the bus driver said to a male
passenger in the front. "When I married her, she was slim,
fine lepa shandy, now just look at her, like Agege bread
someone threw in the river."

The passenger laughed. We watched the woman hurry to
the bus. She was the driver's wife, bringing him his lunch.

Several passengers grumbled as the driver got out of his seat to meet with her.

"Sorry, just give me five minutes to quickly eat this food," he said to the grumbling passengers.

They sat in the waiting area attached to the bus shelter. We sat in the bus and counted the minutes until it was time to leave. He was softer, kinder, in front of her. I watched as she tended to him, how he spoke with her; he was so different talking to her. I could see that she excited him and I wondered why he had sounded so ashamed of her a few moments earlier. Why, in spite of how obviously fond of her he was, did he disparage her to a bus filled with strangers? Maybe this is what love is for some people. It requires them to do nothing, only receive.

My mother was also watching them, saying nothing to me. I appreciated the silence, the way she permitted me the illusion of thinking. Many people feel pressured to fill silences with words, to give more information, or to ask you to convince them that what they have spoken to you is still on your mind. I do not like forced discussions.

I was not thinking about her time in the detention center, not at first. I was thinking about Father, wondering how much he knew, wondering if learning what had happened to her was what broke him. Why did he leave like that? Why did she, who went to prison in another continent, come back first?

The bus driver returned to us. He had a cassette player. He made a show of turning off the radio station, slotting in his own tape. The first song began with the distinct mumbling we all associated back then with Craig David.

When the chorus began, half the bus, as if on cue, sang along to lyrics about taking a girl for a drink on Tuesday.

The bus driver screamed at the entire bus like a principal to a restive group of schoolchildren.

"All of you settle down! Don't make so much noise before the police stop us for no gotdamn reason."

My mother was laughing gently. She paused as I turned to look at her.

"This song is at least ten years old, isn't it?" she asked.

"I guess so," I said.

"How is it still so popular here?" Mother asked.

"Because it is not America, we don't get the songs as soon as they are released," I replied.

"I know what you mean," Mother said in a low voice. "Prison is a terrible place, you miss so much of the outside world, music, news, fashion."

After Craig David, we heard Shaggy and Sisqó and Des'ree. People all around us were smiling and humming along. There was a kind of peaceful silence happening inside me because the bus was noisy and hot. It was almost as if I could no longer sense what was going on amid the music, the arguing, people chewing food, the lady in the seat in front of me loosening her shoulder-length box braids with the cap of a Bic pen.

I was thinking about this woman, my mother, disappearing one day like smoke, gone for almost ten years, and then reappearing just like that, expecting everything to be okay.

There was nothing for me to do but watch her. What were her expectations? Love? Respect? Compassion? What did she suppose would happen after all this time? Whatever she expected, I was glad to disappoint her. As I listened to her talk, I was even more determined to make the fantasy she had built crumble before her.

She was so happy and satisfied with her life's choices. That was what I found most surprising about it all. In my mind, I had imagined her always sad, tired, frail, barely alive without us. I imagined her showing up, falling at our knees, crying like actresses in Nollywood movies, begging to be reinstated in our lives, promising to never leave us again. Instead, Grandmother was treating her like a tourist, making the best meals, asking us to show her around the city as though it were no longer the same Lagos she had been born in.

I was thinking of the story Sister Bibike often told my brother and me when we were younger. The story of the woman who threw her hens away because it was too hard to take care of them. When she found that one of the hens had produced seven healthy chicks by itself in the forest, she wanted it back. She demanded the return of the hen and its chicks even after throwing it away without remorse. I remember that story because of the song we sang. I remember that story because I always thought the king who asked the hen to go free but to give the woman one of its chicks was a wicked king. Now I realize that the king, kinder, fairer than I could ever be, was also very wise. No matter what your mother does, this is Lagos. Society will never let you cast her away. Especially when she wants you back.

"Peter, look, when did they build that there?" my mother

asked, pointing out the window at a new estate the state government had set up for civil servants.

"Who knows?" I answered. "We all just woke up one day and it was there."

If Mother had a problem with my tone, she did not show it.

The bus stopped, and two people got out. One person, a tall man carrying a small loaf of bread, got on.

"We should come here tomorrow and go in, see what it looks like," Mother said.

"If you want to, I am sure they will let us in. It's definitely open for everyone, not just people who live there," I said.

Mother said nothing to me after that. I was beginning to feel bad. It is difficult to fight with someone who will not fight you back. The bus arrived at the final stop, the railway tracks adjacent to Yaba market. At the entrance of the market, a group of teenagers, boys and girls around my age and younger, called out to my mother.

"Auntie, we do fine braids."

"Auntie, come and make your nails."

"Auntie, I will fix for you fine eyelashes."

"Things are so different around here," Mother exclaimed. "I cannot believe that in this same Lagos, boys are making hair in the market."

We turned away from the group, walking through the wide gates to the first row of shops. There were two sets of traders in the market. The first were those with shops and goods inside them. These were the minority. Most of the traders were those with mobile stores. Some had their wares in large steel bowls balanced on their heads, others had wheelbarrows filled with stuff for sale. Traders selling the same type of stuff were grouped together in the market. In a Lagos market, there is no reason or means for individual distinction.

The first group of traders were mostly women selling stuff for newborns and babies. Mother stopped in front of a shop. She grabbed at a large yellow bath towel hanging on a nook above the store's entrance. She shook it off the nook, then, squeezing and gripping, asked if it was made in Nigeria.

"And how much is this?" she asked, after the trader told her it was imported from Turkey.

"Three hundred naira," the woman said.

"Three hundred naira? How much is that in dollars?" Mother asked. She had turned to me as she said this, but she was not really talking to me. She was talking to the trader. I said nothing. She continued making a show of inspecting the towel closely. When she found what she was searching for, a loose thread, she picked at it.

"Look at this. This looks like it is made in Nigeria, such poor quality," she said.

"It is a great towel. How much do you want to pay, my sweet auntie?" the woman asked. The trader's voice had a very determined joviality to it. I immediately envied it. I wanted to also be able to talk to the most infuriating people like I couldn't see through their nonsense, and didn't care.

"One hundred naira," Mother said.

She paid two hundred and ninety naira for that bath towel. She seemed pleased with it even though we had just spent a fraction of an hour haggling for a mere ten naira in savings. I said nothing about that. I figured it was best to save my irritation with her for the big stuff. I think families who spend a lot of time arguing about the small stuff do it because they do not have the courage to talk about the big things.

I had learned from my sister Bibike to ask myself: Peter, what is the true source of your anger? Peter, what are you really afraid of? I am angry because I know she will never truly be sorry. I am afraid I will forgive her, trust her, and give her the opportunity to hurt me again. No, I am afraid that I would be unable to forgive her even if I wanted to. I am afraid I am the kind of boy who hates his mother.

After buying the yellow towel, we walked casually around the market, stopping in shops for Mother to try on several sandals and buy none. "I am sorry this is taking so long, Peter. I need to buy a few pairs of sandals to give the neighbors as gifts when I go back home," she explained to me. "But these are not comfortable, no one will wear this."

In a tiny shop at the end of the shoe section, we found a man sitting on a little stool. He rose up when he saw us come in. We could immediately tell that the man had only one good leg; the other one was limp from the knee down. It dragged behind him as he walked.

"In America," Mother said to me, but loudly enough for the man to hear as well, "he would not have to work, the government would pay him over a thousand dollars a month just because of his condition."

The man said nothing.

I said nothing.

"Do you not believe me?" Mother asked. "I know another African who got one hand cut off during the war in Liberia. He has his own house and car, everything from government money."

"Which shoes will you like to take a look at?" the man asked instead.

Mother pointed to a pink pair on the topmost part of the display shelves. The man picked up a long stick I hadn't previously noticed. It had several bent nails attached to its head. With the stick, he hooked the ankle portion of the sandals, pulling them down in one deft move.

The sandals were replicas, one of the many made in Aba as designer dupes. Mother bought several of them from the store owner. She haggled a little more and paid much less than he had asked for. As we walked out, several owners of neighboring stores called out, telling us they had real African leather sandals, handmade. Mother ignored them all as she walked away. I followed. We went back the way we came.

Once we were outside the market gates, Mother asked where we could go get something to eat.

"There is a Mr. Biggs in a plaza close to this place," I answered.

"Really? Do they have meat pies?" she asked.

"They better," I said.

This time, she realized it was a joke and laughed with me. There was something sad and vulnerable in that brief laughter.

"We should go to Chinatown before you leave," I said, feeling the need to say something.

"There's a Chinatown? Here in Lagos?" she asked.

"Yes, there is," I answered. "They have loads of great stuff for sale. Cheap, too."

"I'd love to get some orange chicken and Szechuan dumplings," she said.

"You will have to wait till you get back to America to eat that. There's no restaurant there. Just shopping," I said.

Mother looked down at her watch, then into the wide windows of a perfume shop. There was a sign announcing 50 percent discount on Perry Ellis perfumes.

"Do you think all those perfumes are real?" she asked me.

"Not sure. Probably not. At least expired and repackaged. You know how things are in Lagos," I said.

We arrived at the Mr. Biggs. A security officer wearing a black-and-white shirt and black pants greeted us with exaggerated warmth.

"Madam the madam. Beautiful madam. Is this your brother or your son? You are too young to have such a big man o," he said.

"You should see his older sisters then," Mother said, laughing. This time, her laugh was relaxed, genuine. She reached out to him and dropped in his hand all the change she had received from the shoe seller.

"He must make a ton of money every day, lucky guy," I said.

After we ordered our food, we sat in a booth and watched soccer replays on the big screen.

"Do you get to watch soccer in America?' I asked.

"No. Not really," she said. "American football is way

more interesting," she added quickly. "Basketball is really big there as well."

What was this place, this America she now called home? Who were these people? I wanted there and then, in the market, to scream at her, to ask how she could go to prison just for the chance to live in another country? What kind of country demanded that people make such sacrifices?

I took a loud gulp of my Coca-Cola. Two girls in the booth next to us turned around and laughed loudly at me.

"Mom, I do not want to go to America with you," I said.

"Why?" she asked.

"No reason. I just want to get into Unilag. Like Andrew. Maybe study medicine," I said.

"Andrew is coming along. He is coming with us," she said.

"Has he told you that?" I asked.

One of the girls in the close-by booth turned around and caught my eye. She shook her head slowly. This I interpreted to mean, *You, crazy ungrateful boy.* I said nothing more after that. Mother said nothing as well. We continued to chew and sip in quiet.

The television in the corner began playing church music. My mother pushed her uneaten coleslaw and chicken toward me. All the booths in the restaurant were filled. Another girl joined the girls at the table nearest to us. They were singing along with the songs on the television.

"Is there sugar in this?" Mother asked, pointing to her coleslaw. "I don't like how it tastes."

I shrugged and said nothing. I was looking at the girl

who had just joined the next booth. She had brought a book with her and was trying to read while her friends talked to and over her. The book was open on the table, next to a glass of orange juice. She had placed her dark brown wallet on the thicker side of the book, to hold the pages in place. There was something so calming about watching her read peacefully in all that chaos, and for a moment I wished I was like one of those guys in American sitcoms who could walk up to a strange girl.

"I had no idea," Mother said, her voice startling in its loudness now. "I had no idea your father would leave. I would have stayed if I knew he would do that. Do you believe me?"

I looked around. No one was watching or listening to our conversation. Outwardly, we were just like everyone else here, eating, enjoying our air-conditioned respite from the Lagos heat.

THE BOYS IN the neighborhood who called us abandoned bastards when we argued had been around when Mother arrived a few nights ago. They had helped with getting her boxes out of the taxi. They did not leave until she had handed out several packs of sneakers and Kit Kat bars as thank-you gifts.

"Are you listening to me?" Mother continued, her voice quieter this time. "Peter, I did not know I'd spend all that time in jail either. No one makes plans for suffering."

Above the headboard in the room Grandmother slept in hung a framed picture of Mother and Father at their wedding. Once, when someone shut the front door so hard the walls shook, the frame fell to the floor. Grandmother picked up every shred of glass, patching it all together with clear tape. Two weeks later, I picked up that frame, ran all the way to two streets away, and threw it in a dumpster. For weeks after that, Grandmother shouted and ranted about that picture, but I said nothing. I still haven't told anyone it was me.

"I was set up," Mother said. "I worked as a nanny for a Nigerian doctor and his wife. They were to pay me after six months. I planned to come back within a year. But they called immigration on me instead of paying. You have no idea what I have been through." She was whispering now. "Please just forgive me."

The girl at the next table was still reading. Her neck had been bent, so I had not seen her face. One of her friends raised a piece of sausage on a fork to her lips, forcing her to eat it. As she did, I caught a small glimpse of her. She had been crying, her eyes a dull red, the skin around her nose as brown as a bad tomato. Was she crying about characters in a book?

"But you got your papers years ago. You only came back because Pastor David sent you money. You are here for the wedding," I said.

Mother opened her mouth wide, but no sounds came out. Her mouth was like a fat letter *O*.

A bulb in one of the lanterns hanging from the ceiling flickered, blinking for few seconds. Then it turned off. Our booth and the one next to us went dark. The girl who was reading a book shut it, then placed it under her arm. She opened a case, taking out her glasses. They were tortoise-shell, cat-eye glasses, with a pink tint to the plastic frame. It occurred to me then that she hadn't said anything the entire time she had been there but somehow, she seemed to me like the solid center in her group of friends.

"Pastor David just paid for the tickets," my mother said. "I am here because I want to be."

"We are happy you made it. We all are," I said.

"We will be so happy in America. You'll get a great education, become anything you want to be. You don't even have to be a doctor to get rich," she said.

"We are happy here. I'm not cut out to live in a strange country," I said.

The girls were leaving. I watched the girl with the book finish her orange juice in one long gulp. The other girls reapplied lip gloss and dabbed saliva-stained fingers across one another's eyebrows.

"Do you sometimes wonder what would have happened if you didn't leave us?" I asked. My heart was filling with a strange sadness, watching that girl walk away.

"Every single fucking day," Mother answered.

"You made the wrong choice, and I want to make the right choice for my life," I said.

"Things will be so much easier for you. You will have papers already, I did not, you will have someone to care for you, I did not," she said.

"Can't I just come visit? You know, for Christmas or something?" I asked.

Mother laughed. It was a hearty, sustained laugh. She wiped the corner of her eye when she was done.

"Yes, you can visit, but I promise you, you will not ever want to come back to Lagos as soon as you arrive. This is America we are talking about," she said when she was done laughing.

A man in a green shirt pulled a stepladder into the middle of the room. Around us, church music rang from the television and speakers. If anyone but me minded Don Moen singing God is good, no one said anything. The man with the ladder stood on the second topmost rung and stretched to remove the blown bulb. The bulb cackled and came to life at that moment, stunning him.

The man on the ladder lost his balance and struggled with steadying himself. I got up immediately, as did another young man, from a booth behind me. We stood on opposite sides of the ladder, steadying it.

Once the bulb change was complete, I signaled to Mother that it was time to leave.

The streets were busier now. The sun had gone down, it was early evening. Many people getting off the buses that brought them from jobs on the island were stopping to buy stuff before getting on other buses to take them farther into the mainland.

"Do you think we can get a taxi this time?" Mother asked.

"This is rush hour, the prices will be astronomical," I answered.

"Astronomical," she repeated, laughing again. "Americans will love you. They love black men who use big words."

"If you could do it all again, would you?" I asked.

"Do what?" my mother asked.

A young girl hawking a tray of sliced pineapples and pawpaws wrapped in clear shopping bags walked up to us. "Fine auntie, please buy my fruits so I can go home. My stepmother will beat me if I don't sell them all. It's night. Please, my auntie," the girl was saying.

"Everything. Leave Lagos for America," I replied.

Mother stopped to talk with the girl who had the fruit tray. She bought most of the sliced pineapple on the tray. She let the girl keep the change.

"Now go home and get some sleep," Mother said to her.

"In America, that little darling would be taken away from her parents. Given to people who know better than to let a girl that young roam these dangerous streets selling stuff," she said to me as we watched the girl go away.

I did not really expect her to answer my question about regrets. Just like I needed to ask, she needed to not answer. She did not seem to remember who she was before she ran to America in hopes for a better life. I did not know anything but the mother she used to be. That comparing and contrasting was my burden. I did not pay the price that she did, so America was not at all beautiful to me. What is the value of a thing but the price a buyer pays for it? How can I expect someone who went to prison for a chance to live in a country not to be excited when she got that chance? I did not really hate my mother, I did not even hate America. How can you hate something you do not know? America will always be, to me, the country that stole my mother and sent back something unrecognizable in her place. I will not call that country beautiful, or its people beloved.

The bus we rode home filled with passengers in less than five minutes. When the driver tried to start the engine, it sputtered and coughed several times but failed to start. As if on cue, with no words spoken, I and every other male on the bus got out and began to push. We were seven men trotting behind a bus. As I pushed, I noticed the girl with the fruit tray emerge from behind one of the shops in the market. Her tray was full again and she was looking around the crowd like a trained scout.

I smiled to myself as she ran to a tall, light-skinned woman dressed in a black skirt suit, a lawyer's white bib hanging around her neck.

"Fine auntie, please buy my fruits, so I can go home. It's night. Please." The girl was shouting. Her voice sounded like she had been crying.

The tall lady said something I could not hear and handed the girl some money, taking none of her fruit.

The bus sputtered and came to life. One after the other, all us men ran after the moving bus, jumping in, finding our seats.

4

THIS OLD HOUSE

BIBIKE

2012

IN THE HOUSE where my daughter, Abike, is born, my grandmother, her great-grandmother, sits with my daughter in her arms. My grandmother's legs are stretched out straight before her. Her back is curved in a perfect half circle, bent like the handle of a teacup. She is singing the oriki to my daughter.

> *Abike for whom kings have gathered.*
> *Abike, her skin shines bright as palm oil.*
> *We ask her for meat, she gives the herd.*
> *We ask her for light, she brings the sun down.*

Sometimes my grandmother lifts my daughter's feet to her mouth, gently biting off her overgrown toenails. I tell her I have a baby kit with steady-grip nail clippers and a soft hairbrush and even a nasal aspirator. My grandmother laughs at me.

"Abike is my mother returned to the land again. I will not let you offend her with this imported nonsense," she says.

There is something about a new baby that makes older people think of all those who have passed. Each day of my fourteen-day postpartum hibernation, and many days after that, Grandmother tells me a new story about her own childhood.

"When I was a young girl, maybe just seven or eight years old, my father killed an elephant when he was out hunting by himself in Idanre Forest. Of course, no one believed him because he could not carry it back to the village.

"Then he went to Oshamolu, the native healer, and asked for a transporting spell for two beings. Oshamolu told him he could only transport two live beings at once or two dead beings, so he could not transport a dead elephant and a living hunter.

"My father then went to Father James, the white priest in town, to ask him if he could raise him from the dead, since the priests were always talking about Jesus, who raised people from the dead."

I cannot tell which parts of her story are exaggerated and which ones are real, but I love them so much that I record everything. I have a little voice recorder that records all of her stories and songs. When Abike is grown, I want her to hear it all from my grandmother's mouth. I want to cover my daughter with Grandmother's Yoruba, in the pure softness of her Ondo dialect, baptizing her with every sentence sounding like birdsong when she speaks.

The first thing you see when you walk into my grandmother's living room is the large brown rattan dual reclining daybed with white cushions. It is the kind of set you'd find on a patio in a different country; in Lagos, we keep our expensive furniture indoors. We—my twin sister, Ariyike, and I—got the set for our grandmother after she hurt herself in the kitchen. Now Grandmother spends most of her time sitting in the living room, watching television. A young woman, a daughter of an old friend, comes over three times a week to help with cooking and cleaning.

In this house we grew up in, sometimes I sit next to my grandmother in her recliner, listening to Ariyike preach the gospel of Jesus Christ on national television. It is all still surreal to me, how easily my sister slipped into this role of pastor's wife, women's leader, television minister. Everywhere I go in Lagos, her face is on posters and billboards, right next to Pastor David's, welcoming people to church. In these pictures, she is smiling. She seems comfortable and happy. It is almost as though she has prepared her whole life for this role. How is it possible that I missed that? We are twins, identical. I once believed we were exactly the same. I did not even know she really believed in Jesus.

Often, Grandmother watches Ariyike on television with me, shaking her head as she does this, complaining loud and clear.

"I really wish your Taiwo did not join those people," she says.

"It is a job like any other," I'd answer.

"No, it is not. Cooking is a job. Nursing is a job. Typing is a job. This thing, this telling people what God thinks they should do, is not a job. I have said it many times. I will say it again, but I am just an old lady and no one listens to me anymore."

Grandmother herself was a Christian once. She has told me many stories over and over. As a young girl, she was even baptized in the church. At her catechism, her name was changed from Olanike to Stella Maris. This happened in the fifties, when fewer Yoruba were going to the Catholic church. The Roman Catholics taught in English and sometimes Spanish, but the Anglican churches already had Bibles and hymnbooks in Yoruba. Grandmother went to school during the day and worked in the priest's quarters at night. She insists she was just a hard worker. She insists that she wasn't particularly clever or literary and was always nervous around new people, but that soon enough, all that reading and writing in English paid off and she was hired by A. G. Leventis in Lagos. I do not agree with her assessment of herself. She is the most intelligent person I know.

When my grandmother talks about growing up in the village, her voice is bland and steady, completely devoid of nostalgia. She does not speak ill of her village or speak of her youth with longing or wanting. Whenever I try to ask more questions about her life after she left the village for Lagos, about the grandfather I never met, she evades with Yoruba proverbs like:

"No one has to show a squirrel the way to the stream."

"No one sits by the river and argues about soap suds."

It is easy to get tired of proverbs. They contain a certain specificity of wisdom, a peculiar scale of right and wrong. Sometimes that scale is ineffective in the modern world. I am learning to create my own values. If, for example, I consider it sensible to sit by the river and argue about soap suds—which I think means that trivialities aren't worth discussing—I will very well do that.

I hope to be the kind of mother who answers all the questions my daughter has. I hope when she tries to talk with me about important stuff, she doesn't always feel like she is prying a periwinkle out of its shell.

"Let me tell you why I stopped going to church," Grandmother says to me one day, with no prior warning.

I am in the kitchen doing dishes when she wakes up from her nap. Immediately, I wipe my hands, walking to the living room, where she is seated. Abike, my baby girl, is asleep in a cot in the corner.

"Kehinde, are you hearing me?" she asks before she says anything else.

"Yes. I am here, Maami," I answer.

"Are you going anywhere today?" Grandmother asks.

"No." I said. "I will go out on Friday. I am taking Abike to get vaccinated."

GRANDMOTHER RESPONDS WITH her often repeated suspicions about vaccinations. She knows she is old, but she has seen things and the government is poisoning children with all those injections.

•

SHE SAYS SHE had a dream about her old priest and in spite of it all, it was a great dream, she was a girl again, that is, until she woke up and her legs were disappointingly wrinkly, long and skinny.

I laugh when she says this, disagreeing with her. I tell her that she has hot legs, full, fresh, and fair, that any young girl with sense would envy them. She says the world is a weird and cruel place and only the wise survive. I respond by agreeing with her and praying to Olodumare for the blessings of a wise head. It is part of the family lexicon to acknowledge with prayers Grandmother's opinion of the world. We know all the right ways to respond to her.

Her last day in church was when the priest told the story of Sodom and Gomorrah and said that God destroyed the cities because of panshaga. I laugh every time she says *panshaga* because it is the umbrella Yoruba word for sex between unmarried people, and it is funny as heck to say out loud. Grandmother interrupts my laughing to correct me. She thinks I am laughing at the idea that she was fighting for the right of young people to fornicate. Only the priests fornicated in those days, she tells me. As a young girl, she was more terrified of her parents' curse than anything a priest said.

"I went home that day and read the book of Genesis by myself. You should remember, we only had paraffin lamps and paraffin was too expensive to be using for that type of stuff," she says.

I laugh again. Abike rouses at the sound of my laughter. I pick her up.

"Do you realize that in the same chapter where angels destroy the cities, the daughters of Lot are forced to sleep with their own father and have children by him?" she asks.

"Yes, I know that, Maami," I answer.

"Why did God not destroy them and their children? Did they not do worse than the people in those cities?" Grandmother asks.

"Well, I have heard that Sodom was destroyed because of homosexuality specifically," I answer.

It is my grandmother's turn to laugh.

"Thank God those priests never said that type of stuff, the village people would have stoned them for that type of hypocrisy," she said.

"So what do you think the reason was?" I ask her when she is done laughing. Abike is waking up again. My daughter is drawn to laughter like edible termites are drawn to bright lights.

"Well, in the earlier chapters, God himself tells Abraham that the outcry against the cities is so much. It seems obvious that it was an unjust city and the people were always doing wrong to people who could do nothing but call on God." She picks up the remote and turns on the television. "Anyway, those priests said I was being heretic when I said that the next time in church, so I said goodbye to their nonsense and I have never been in a church again," she says.

"I think that you actually have to believe that the Bible is true to come to those conclusions in the first place, Maami,"

I say after a few minutes. "It is full of all these types of incompatibilities."

"That is why I believe it," Grandmother says. "It is lies that are neat and straightforward."

I imagine what opportunities would have opened up for a woman like my grandmother if she had lived a different life. I imagine her with a robe and a wig, a Justice of the Supreme Court or a professor in a university. I will never know why she did not pursue more education or get married.

"Make sure you get a priest to pray Viaticum when I am dying," Grandmother says, interrupting my thinking. *Viaticum* sticks out of her Yoruba like a strange word from an alien language.

"Maami, you will be with us for a very long time, stop that type of talk," I say.

"Amen," she says.

I pause the video player and begin singing the Yoruba prayer made famous by a local musician.

> *Mommy o, e ma pe laye.*
> *Mommy o, e ma jeun omo.*
> *Eni ba ni ko ni ri be*
> *A fo lo ju.*

> *My mother, you will live long*
> My mother, you will eat food from your children
> Anyone who refutes this
> Will go blind.

She laughs and laughs. Abike wakes up and laughs along.

In this house my grandmother built, there is a framed picture of my father at his second wedding. A young woman I have never met, her face as round as a full moon, is in a white sleeveless dress at his side, smiling directly at the camera. There is a second picture, of her twin boys on their first birthday, their heads still too big for their frames, their faces oily with party food. I wonder about the trip these pictures have made to this house.

A photographer, invited to a wedding, a birthday party, stands in the background seeking a perfect shot. Later, the couple, the parents, look at a screen then select from several shots which ones to order prints for. Next, they order copies, then mail those copies to friends and family, then they order more copies. Did my father and his new wife even stop to wonder if those photographs hurt more than they helped?

When she received them, Grandmother had her young helper buy wooden frames and hang the pictures right in the living room. When I look at those pictures, I wonder how she does not see them as a cruel testament to her abandonment, this smiling, happy, procreating photographed face.

THE MORNING MY father came back, his mother, my grandmother, had stubbed her toe on the edge of her recliner. Immediately, she clicked her fingers, circling them around her head over and over, saying in Yoruba, "My head turns all evil away. Evil will be far from me."

Later that afternoon, he was standing in the doorway

wearing all white, like the Eyo masquerade. He had the same wide, happy face in the wedding picture. He was as tall as he has always been, but it shocked me seeing him again, big-boned and happy. I was reminded instantly of how it felt as a little girl, to sit on his broad shoulders and touch the ceilings of rooms. I hoped that the boys, my brothers, Andrew and Peter, still had a chance to grow into this height and manliness despite the years of poor nutrition and hardship. I imagined them standing next to him and feeling like poor copies of a glorious original.

Grandmother screamed a long noiseless scream when she saw him. Father lay prostrate before her on the floor in the customary Yoruba greeting. I heard her inhale then hold her breath for the longest time, exhaling only after he got up off the floor.

"Why did you not send a message to let me know you were coming, Bankole?" she asked, hugging him. "We would have cleaned up, we would have made you something special to eat."

My father responded with a surprising glibness. He said he was in Lagos for a meeting that ended earlier than expected. It was a last-minute decision to stop by. Only his business partner, who was in the car outside waiting, knew he was here visiting her.

When I left the room to give them some privacy, he had not yet acknowledged my presence or my daughter's. He had taken a seat on one half of Grandmother's recliner and begun whispering to her. The turned-off television displayed their distorted reflection. From the entrance of my room, I watched him whisper. He was cuddling Grandmother with one hand. With the other, he made several frantic hand gestures.

I smelled his eager, brash male cologne. It was an interesting aquatic, synthetic smell that reminded me of resident doctors at the hospital where I worked as a teenager. There was a specific brand of ambition I had unknowingly come to attach to that smell. I did not know why, but at that moment, I was overwhelmed and terrified.

A few moments later, another man walked into the living room without knocking.

"Maami, this is the business partner I told you about," my father said, introducing the stranger to my grandmother.

"Feel free to take a look around," Father said to the visiting man.

I said nothing. I stood at the door to my room and silently hoped the man would come that way. He did not. He walked straight through the living room to the backyard.

"We are more interested in the space itself, to be honest," the male visitor said to Father. "This structure is rather old."

It was then obvious to me that this visit was not accidental. If Grandmother could tell, she did not show it. She clasped my father's hands in one hand and held them up to her face over and over again.

"Bankole, so this is your hand, Bankole, is it really you?" she repeated again and again. "Is it really you? Have you been eating well? Have you been getting enough sleep?" She placed the back of her hand on his face and neck like one would do to feel for the temperature of a sick child.

My father responded with exaggerated warmth. He kissed her forehead. He apologized that it had been so long since his last visit. He promised to bring his little boys to visit next week. His wife was pregnant again, did she know that? The doctor tells him it is another boy, isn't it all so wonderful?

The visitor looked uncomfortable with the display. He stood right by the door, running his hands along the wall above the door frame. When Grandmother embraced her son in another full hug, asking a new set of similar questions, the stranger made a loud throat-clearing sound. When that failed to get the expected attention, he knocked on the walls with his knuckles several times in quick succession.

"I am sorry," he said to me, because I was staring him down. "I just want to be sure this wall is still solid."

Father took full advantage of the opportunity to disentangle himself from Grandmother's arms. He stepped away from her, standing next to the visitor, tapping the wall with a closed fist.

"Ah! What are you talking about? This is a solid structure," he says. "Come outside, let me show you some exposed brick."

They stood together for a few minutes. The visitor insisted the walls sounded a little hollow. Father countered by pointing out they stood next to a well, that the sound he heard was a small echo from the depth of the well. As they strolled to the gate, they remarked how clean the yard was, everything swept and washed and in the right place. It was only after the gate shut and the car drove off that Grandmother moved from the middle of the living room, sitting again on her recliner.

Grandmother was restless after they left. She spent the rest of the day staring at the walls. Her face was blank, and even when she replied to a direct question, she seemed absent and confused. She would sometimes begin to ask a question or make a statement, then, in the middle of what she was saying, she would stop and apologize, telling me or whoever else she was speaking with to forget about it.

When she slept, I watched her for a couple of hours. The rise and fall of her chest was out of rhythm. She was shivering, even though the room was warm and she was wrapped in a blanket. Rapt, I did not notice when the young lady who helped with cleaning walked in.

The young lady bent low to the ground next to me, watching Grandmother for a few minutes. Getting up, she signaled to me to walk with her to the kitchen. I walked behind her to the kitchen. Her sleek black hair was secure in a tight bun. She had several raised red spots at the back of her neck.

"Sister mi, is everything all right with Grandma? Why does she cry?" she asked.

"Crying? She has not been crying," I answered.

"Yes, she has," she said, "her face is wet with tears."

I did not tell her that Grandmother had been asleep for more than two hours and that it meant she must have been crying in her sleep. Instead I asked if she could watch

Grandmother alone for a little while. *There's an errand I have to run*, I said. *There's a prescription for Grandmother's knees I need to pick up from the hospital before her doctor leaves.* She whispered a soft yes. Then she surprised me by hugging me. She was small and wiry. The hug was tight and short. I was calmed and appreciative.

But the calm did not last long. My daughter dropped her pacifier the moment I placed her in her car seat. She began to scream in uncharacteristic despair. Unexpected tears filled my eyes as I searched all over the back seat for the pacifier. I did not find it; it seemed to have been swallowed up by some dark part of my Honda Civic.

WE MADE MY daughter on a Tuesday morning in the living room of my grandmother's house. I had returned to the house three days after taking Grandmother to the hospital for knee replacement surgery, to pick up a change of clothes and a "spicy" meal. Tunde, my boyfriend, a sergeant in the army whom I met in the weekend classes I was taking at Lagos State University, had driven me because I was too sleep deprived to drive myself. Tunde, who had driven the entire way with one hand on the wheel, the other on my thigh, regaling me with pointless Lagos celebrity gossip, was the perfect antidote to all that stress. I remember thinking while we were fucking how intoxicating it felt to do something so teenager-like, many years after I stopped being a teenager myself. I remember instructing myself to do it more often, to be more relaxed and carefree.

It was in the spirit of being carefree and enjoying a cherished independence that I rejected Tunde's pregnancy-inspired marriage proposal, choosing to remain with Grandmother to raise my daughter. I was going to school. I had started my own beauty supply store. I bought a car. Every other Saturday, I took my grandmother and daughter to see the newest movies.

Why was it so easy now for all that to vanish? What chance did Grandmother have against her only child, who had decided he wanted the house for himself? It did not occur to me, as I drove all the way to see Tunde, that he was not at home. He lived in the junior barracks in Sabo, and sometimes overzealous orderlies refused to let guests in if they were not on the circulated list.

The oddest thing about all that worrying is that, although I knew in the back of my mind that I had just seen the man who left us more than fifteen years before, my mind had yet to fully comprehend it. Ariyike, my sister, brought that to the fore when I called her from Tunde's apartment.

"Bibike! What did you say? You saw our father?" she screamed. "When? Where? Today?"

Tunde's apartment was dimly lit. It smelled like cigarettes and beef stew. I placed the receiver down to open the windows, my sister still going on and on. She knew our father was still alive. The Lord had promised to preserve him. She knew a family reconciliation was imminent. That was what happened when you trusted in the Lord and made him your restorer.

"He brought some investor to look at the house. I think he means to sell it. He really upset Maami," I said finally, interrupting her.

"That old house? Someone wants to buy that thing? How much can he even get?" My sister laughed a little.

"I am not going to let him do this," I said. I was angry at my sister for laughing. She was not laughing at me, but it felt that way. I was angry that she was so far removed from all this and she did not need the house in the same way I did.

"Well, he is her only child, and she is so old she is barely functioning. That house is technically his," she said.

"So he should be allowed to disrupt her peace?" I asked.

"Don't get in the middle, Bibike, try to get on Father's good side, you need a man in your life, after all," she replied.

If Tunde's apartment had been anything like Grandmother's house, after ending the call with my twin sister, I would have at that moment gone into the backyard and walked up to the guava tree. I would have grabbed the thickest branches my arms could reach and shaken them so hard, daring them to break off. Instead, I paced the length of his living room, my fingers interlocked and cradling the back of my neck.

"I am not going to let him do this, Tunde," I said. "I swear on my grandmother's head that I will not let him do this."

There were many options open to me, Tunde observed. He was supportive and available to help, he reminded me. He could take us to the State High Courts, for example, and then Grandmother and I could swear to an oath before a judge that she did not want to move, and she wanted me to stay with her. It was all very easy and straightforward the way he explained it.

In the past, I had fought with Tunde for the way he took charge of everything, treating my whole life like a problem needing his intervention. I realized then that my daughter, Abike, was lucky to have that in her father, someone so comfortable with responsibility that he'd take on more without being asked.

WE WERE LONGER than we needed to be getting home. Tunde had asked for a few minutes to shower before going back with us, but showering required clothes coming off and he did not know how to take off his clothes around me without dancing and making a production out of it all.

It was half past eight when all three of us got back to Grandmother's house. The night was dark and humid, and so even though I could not make out the faces of most of the small crowd gathered around my house, I could smell them. It was the smell of a poorly ventilated molue bus stuck in traffic for hours. The crowd was bustling, noisy. Our living room was the nucleus of this diseased cell.

My grandmother was spread out on her daybed, her body straight like a ruler, covered with a long linen cloth. I knew she was gone before anyone said anything. Her body was lying so straight and stiff, stripped of all that mesmerizing unease she carried with her. Grandmother's body was always moving; even when she was still, her finger would twitch for no reason. You would be in another room and hear her bones crack as she stretched.

This old house, the house my grandmother died in, was built in a hurry. That explains the reappearing wall cracks and the fact that the door spaces have always been just a little too wide for regular doors. It had two different sets of builders. The first, a set of German contractors who were in Lagos to help the Nigerian federal government get ready for some international sports or arts festival. The year was 1976 and the Nigerian federal government was building five thousand houses in a hurry to accommodate visitors for this arts/sports festival being held in Lagos. This festival was an ambitious, hurried project, and by the time all the dancers, boaters, singers, thinkers, and artistes had begun to arrive from all over the world, this old house was one of the few hundred yet to be completed.

When my grandmother bought it, the house was halfway completed and abandoned. She finished up one room, the main bedroom, and moved in with her son. She spent the next five years fixing it up little by little, room by room. This is why some rooms have white ceilings while others have gray. Some rooms have those eighties' interlocking rubber tiles, and others have laminate flooring. The one bathroom has had several incarnations. At first, it was nothing but a latrine with a hole in the middle. After Bankole got out of school, he added a water closet, bathtub, and tiled the walls. When Grandmother fell in the kitchen and had surgery on her knees, my sister, Ariyike, had someone take out the old bathtub to install a walk-in cubicle with a custom-made chair. The new bath has a wide swinging door that smells like burning rubber when you take a hot shower.

It was in this new bathroom that I hid to weep. My chest had exploded into several million burning pieces.

A NEIGHBOR I do not know knocked on the door.

"Please do not cry," she said, "Maami has lived well, now she's gone to rest."

The crowd swelled around me like a sick stomach, bloated and moaning, talking in loud whispers to one another, repeating the same questions over and over like an unending chorus.

"Maami die? What happened?"

"Her son came here?"

"What did he do when he came?"

"They say he pushed her."

"No, I heard he shook her like a tray of picking beans."

"Where has he gone now?"

"Who knows where he is?"

"Who will go searching?"

My Tunde with his eager baritone uncharacteristically somber-herded the crowd away from the center toward the gate. The skin was broken, and the pus flowed freely. Our neighbors were weeping loudly and with abandon as they went home. Just like that, the spectacle of the strange death was over, and the mourning began.

In this house my grandmother built, on a short stool in the corner of her room, she has her ere ibeji shrine. There are three small wooden effigies at the center of the shrine. Their bodies are short, about four inches high. They have elongated skulls, exaggerated faces. The oldest one, the one who Grandmother washed, bathed, and sang to regularly, is female. She is dressed in a white dress, doll-sized bangles in each hand. She is Grandmother's twin, who died when they were toddlers, when Grandmother was too young to realize that there were two of them. The other two are identical, Grandmother's first children, dead within months of each other before their first birthday.

The older Yoruba believed that identical twins shared a soul before birth, that the length of their lives was nothing but a conscious uncoupling of souls. When one twin died young, they believed the living twin was in danger of dying as well.

I picked the effigies up, one after the other, wiping them with the hem of my dress. I wished Grandmother had talked to me about them. She did not practice many rituals of Yoruba traditional belief but these effigies she loved. These she bathed and dressed in hand-sewn clothes. I realized then that it was more about grieving than religion. These figures were a testament to her loss.

Tunde walked into the room as I was cleaning. It was his first time in there. If he was startled by the shrine, he did not show it.

"I have called your sister and sent emails to Peter and Andrew. An ambulance is coming to take her away," he said.

The young woman who helped with Grandmother came in with my daughter in her hands.

"Auntie, Abike won't stop crying. I don't know what to do," she said.

They were looking to me for direction, reassurance, something. I did not have it to give.

"WHAT HAPPENED HERE?" I asked her.

"Am I not dreaming?" I asked him.

They had the same look of pity when they looked at me.

The house had emptied out, leaving only a couple of people, one woman who had worked with Grandmother and another woman, the mother of the young help. They were eating puff-puffs and drinking juice out of wineglasses. I had no idea where the food came from.

"Come with me," Tunde said to me.

We walked out of the house and got in my car.

"What do you want to do?" he asked.

"I don't know," I answered.

"DO YOU THINK he may have sold the house already?" he asked.

I had not thought about it again. It was strange how little I cared about this old house now. It was Grandmother I wanted to be around, the mellow person she became in the last five years.

I missed her already. How everything my daughter did made her laugh so hard. How she hoarded the Maltesers that Andrew brought the last time he visited. How she took to wearing sneakers for the first time in her life because Peter gave her Nikes for Christmas.

"You can come live with me," Tunde said. "You know I want nothing more."

"That barracks is no place for a child," I said. "You know that."

A couple of luxury SUVs pulled up outside the gates as we talked.

"I think that is your sister and her husband," Tunde said. "You should go talk to them. Just wanted to let you know that I can go get those papers back. Grab a few friends from the barracks. We will find him in this Lagos."

My sister had arrived, but her husband was not with her. I watched from inside my car as she, together with two other women, walked into the living room, then reemerged a couple of minutes later. They seemed confused, out of place and unused to feeling that way. They were dressed in formal black attire like they thought it was already a funeral. My sister had a fascinator with a lace side piece hanging over her right eye.

"I am not ready to leave this house, Tunde," I said.

"You will not have to leave, I promise you," Tunde said.

The next morning, we were intertwined in my bed. It was still dark outside when Tunde whispered in my ears.

"I'm not leaving, I'm coming," he said.

Sometimes when we are leaving, we say *I am coming*. It is the influence of Yoruba on our spoken English—instead of goodbye, we say *till next time*, we say we will see each other again.

It is morning and it hits all over again like a fresh blow. I'm thinking about Grandmother and the death she desired. I think she wanted to die slowly, with time to send for the boys, time to hand over her shrine and trinkets and aso-ofi, time to get a priest to say prayers, to give one last admonition.

I think she died from shock—the shock of Father's brutal attack, and then the shock of her own fragility. I think she died sad and afraid.

When Tunde leaves, I pick up a broom and begin cleaning the house. I know daylight will bring with it a new set of visitors needing to be watered, fed, consoled, and listened to.

My daughter's father gets in my car and drives away. He will go to the noncommissioned officers' mess, find two or three sergeants given to drink. He will buy them bottles and bottles of beer. He will describe my father, the suspect—tall, yellow skin, balding. He will tell them what he did—an old woman shaken to her death, her property documents taken away by force. They will promise to find him, it's easy, they insist, they know most of the unscrupulous banks who buy disputed property in this part of Lagos.

Tunde tells me nothing at first. The days go by faster than a dream. We plan a wake. It is well attended. Then the internment. We get a Catholic priest. Then traditional burial rites. Andrew and Peter fly in from Chicago.

Two weeks later, the officers will find Father's house in Abuja. They will arrest him and bring him back to Lagos to answer for his actions. Father follows peacefully. He tells his wife and kids not to worry, he has done nothing wrong.

Somewhere along the Ore Highway, when the military van is stuck in traffic so bad no sirens can help, Father asks to pee in the bushes. He is given permission. A boyish officer walks with him to find a spot. Father hops off the van and

limps down the road, the tar hot like coals on his feet. He
follows a path through the trees, stopping at a little clearing
under shade, away from the gaze of other stranded motor-
ists. The young soldier looks away for a second—there is a
Toyota HiAce bus, and the driver is playing a taped recording of a live comedy show. A young woman in a blue shirt
pokes her head out a window. She is pouring water from a
bottle over her head and face. The water makes a sizzling
sound as it drops to the hot ground.

A short distance away, my father makes a dash for it.
Four or five steps, maybe, before the young soldier notices.
The young soldier calls out to him, but my father ignores
him. He is running toward the center of the forest. The soldier runs after him, repeating the order to stop. The soldier
shoots three quick shots, and two miss. One gets him in the
underarm. It's a nick, really, a tickle. Father does not stop.
The soldier shoots again. Drivers along the road are panick-
ing and he can hear his superiors running up behind him.

This bullet goes right through his back. Father falls forward. He tries to stand again, dragging his upper body a
few inches before falling again. There is a tree stump in the
cleared path, and he does not see it. He trips over it. The
sound his knee makes as it strikes the dry wood is a loud
cracking sound. The young soldier does not know what he
has heard. He thinks he is being shot at, so he shoots again,
two shots to the head.

When Tunde tells me how my father died, I am sitting
in the large living room of my twin sister's home. We have
escaped the chaos of Grandmother's house for a few hours.

Distant relatives we barely remember have camped out, demanding ceremonial displays of justice. It had become unbearable, the unending demands, the constantly flowing suggestions of how to grieve.

My sister screams. She grabs Tunde's collar, latching on to him with childlike tenacity. It is one of his favorite T. M. Lewin shirts, but he looks at her with eyes filled with pity.

"Why? For what?" she screams. "The old house? That old woman who would have died soon anyway?"

I swallow the angry words rising from my belly. I am looking at Tunde and he still isn't angry. Even when she begins dragging him toward the flight of stairs leading to the back entrance.

"Get out of my house." She is weeping and hiccupping now. "I never want to see you here again. Do you hear me? Get out."

She comes so close to pushing him down the stairs, and still he does not resist. I get up and run between them.

"Stop that," I say. "You are hurting him."

"Get out, the two of you, take your bastard daughter, leave my house," she replies.

I do not realize I have smacked her until I hear the sound of my hand across her face.

"Shut up your stupid mouth," I say.

It is Tunde who restrains me. My sister runs down the stairs, calling for her security. Tunde and I go into the guest bedroom. Our daughter is awake but quiet in the crib, staring at her mobile with bright shiny eyes. I pick her up. Tunde picks up the baby bag.

As we go down the stairs, my sister comes back in, and she has three young men with her. They wear blue shirts over black trousers. One of them has a black beret and a policeman's baton in his hand.

"Take a good look at these people," my sister says to her staff. "Anyone who ever lets them in here again will be fired. Not just fired: arrested, sent to prison. Do you all understand me?"

"Yes," they respond, a subdued chorus.

The man with the baton looks at me, then my sister, then back at me. He takes off his beret with the batonless hand, wipes his face with it, then puts it back on.

"Hurry up, you heard Madam, leave," he says to us. He strikes the baton against the steel column of the staircase as he speaks.

"We are leaving already," I say to the security man.

We walk right by my sister. My baby reaches out to touch her nose, but she moves away. The cheek I slapped is bright red and swollen. It looks a lot worse than it really is. It will be much better in a few hours, all she needs is to run cold water over it several times. We have the exact same skin, pretty but tough. We had chicken pox for the first time as adults. The first spots showed up a few days after we turned nineteen. There must have been a thousand spots on my back alone, and we scratched with everything we could find, combs, ladles, garden hoses. Yet not one of those spots left a scar, no, not one.

··

BLACK SUNDAY

ARIYIKE

2015

I AM SITTING by myself in the women's ministry office. It is the Saturday before Mother's Day and the women's choir is practicing in the auditorium. They are incompetent, noisy, and restive. It is going to be a terrible service; they are doubtlessly going to embarrass us all.

I borrowed Tola, the bishop's logistics assistant, a few hours ago, but even he could not help with bringing some order to the chaos. He just sat in the seat on the other side of the table looking at me with judgment-filled eyes and saying over and over, "Just let the regular worship leader lead them. Everyone respects him."

My friend Rosetta, who is leading the women's choir, is a state governor's wife who tithes in the millions and gifts me Balenciaga and Givenchy. She is a mile and a stretch more important to the ministry than all these talentless women combined. Her husband, the state governor, is the reason the church has two private jets. The church is the reason the state governor and his family never again have to fly commercial. This is not the only reason I let Rosetta lead the women's choir. She is good for church membership growth. The younger girls adore her, the older women envy her. When she is present, all the women of this church co-alesce around her like the edges of a wound.

The clank of triangles and drums and voices failing to harmonize sounds like a rowdy party in the distance. The women are succeeding in having fun, I can tell from the laughter traveling through the hallway to my little office in the corner of the building. I can tell Rosetta is being her brightest and most inspirational.

Every so often, after a new family joins our church, the wife finds her way to one of our Anointed Daughters meetings. Rosetta is there, the wife of the state governor serving, cleaning, and holding court. She draws people, makes even the most introverted make an effort to connect. Churches are built around personalities. It's hard to admit, of course, because the goal is to lift Jesus up, but it is true. Rosetta, with her ease and calm, makes people feel like they have known her all their lives. We, Pastor David and I, call Rosetta our little lighthouse.

The television in my office sits on a steel cabinet in a corner. My weekly teaching program is on air and I am watching myself. It is a recap of last year's Mother's Day service. Our network has been playing my old messages throughout the week; yesterday, it was the message I preached on the last Resurrection Sunday. All the reports from last year and the year before that are laid out on my office table. It is a pitiful pile. We are expecting fewer people for Mother's Day this year, even though we spent three times last year's budget in advertising.

There isn't much a church can do when its popularity begins to decline. Nigerian Christians are like little children. The women mostly, you'd find them with the newest, most interesting thing. These days, the most interesting thing is the prophetic, direct messages from God delivered with stunning peculiarity. Pastor David has never been that way; he is not a prophet, he is just a gifted teacher of the Word. Sadly, that counts for little these days.

Now all our programs, regardless of what we let people believe, go toward the strengthening and pampering of our loyal, committed members.

Therefore, I let Rosetta lead the choir. Even though she is tone-deaf and terrible at coordinating.

The door opens, and I am no longer sitting by myself watching myself on TV. My assistant walks in, looking more harried than usual.

"Good afternoon, Pastor Ma," my assistant says.

"Bless you, darling," I say.

"There is a young woman outside I think you should see," she says. She says "young woman" quickly, like it's a bad word, so I know this will be interesting. "Should I tell her to come back some other time, Pastor Ma?" my assistant asks as I hesitate.

"No. I will meet her in the visitors' lounge."

I have a small space next to my office, used for counseling. It's standard practice for all pastors in our ministry to have a semi-open space with doors that cannot lock from the inside to protect our ministers from false accusations and temptations—mostly temptations to tell the truth.

The young girl has angry eyes. She is young, too young for the deep frown lines spread over her forehead like ridges on a yam farm. She has a tiny baby in her hands. At first, I look at her with a smile, but she does not smile back. I understand why she is so angry. It's difficult being a young mother in Lagos. It's a thousand times worse when you are a single mother. We have a welfare program, but we only help married women. We cannot, as a church, support fornicators and adulterers with tithes and offerings. Jesus says not to cast pearls before swine. I have personally, out of my own purse, helped many single mothers. My own twin sister has two children by a man she refuses to marry, even though they carry on like the Couple of the Year, so I'm not prejudiced or unreasonable.

"Good afternoon, Pastor," she says to me.

"Good afternoon, my dear, the Lord bless you, sweetheart, you and your little—" I ask.

"Boy. It's a boy, his name is Pamilerin," she tells me.

"That's a beautiful name, God will cause you to laugh indeed just like his name says, my dear," I say.

"Amen," she answers, and now she relaxes a little. Her frown lines disappear.

I REALIZE, WITH mild shock, that I know who this is. She is one of the music ministers, a worship leader in our

University of Lagos campus church. I haven't seen her in a few months, but no one said anything about a baby. I had assumed she graduated and left the state. I am used to young girls with talent for ministry disappearing from the church. We do not do a good job of retaining females in the ministry. First of all, the leadership of the church does not think females should ascend in ministry from position to position like men do. No, our access is always tied to the men in our lives, the husbands and fathers. Second, Christian practice is very masculine. It's a religion of Father, Son, and Holy Spirit, after all. Our God is a man, His Son is a man. Therefore, all the sent are men. It is just the way things are.

"I am hoping you can help me," she says.

"Of course I will," I say. "How have you been? Are you still at the university?"

"I graduated three months ago," she says.

"Glory to God." My praise is a little louder than necessary, but it's sincere. I am so glad she got her degree regardless. As a young mother, things will be harder for her—that degree is a palliative.

"I know you can speak to Pastor David on my behalf, Ma, so he can talk to his friend. He needs to take care of Pamilerin, time is running out."

"My dear, I will talk to my husband, but I sense you are assuming I know more about this situation than I do," I say, interrupting her. "Who do you need Pastor David to speak to on your behalf?"

"Teddy," she says.

"Teddy?" I shout.

She says his name just like that. Like it is nothing for her, this little slip of a girl. She calls the state governor by his first name like just another one of her playmates.

"It's been almost a year, I thought everyone knew about it," she says.

"Knew about what?" I scream again, but she doesn't flinch. She is used to this, I realize, adults losing their cool around her.

"We met here in church. Pastor David introduced us after last Youth Conference, then Teddy invited me over for a tour of the government house," she says.

The last youth conference was in February. She must mean the conference the year before. We organize big meetings around Valentine's to keep our youth occupied. I know the governor typically speaks at these events. He is such an inspiration, he grew up poor, he is a brilliant banker-turned-politician. He is a king our young people delight to honor.

"So, what does all this have to do with me? Why haven't you gotten in touch with Teddy, as you call him?" I ask her.

She says the last time she heard from him, he gave her half a million naira for an abortion. She says she was going to go through with the abortion but then she heard the voice of the Lord loud and clear as she was sitting in the doctor's office. She says the Lord said, "Alex, you can trust me with him."

She says that's how she knew to expect a son. She says that's why she left Lagos immediately after graduating, why she now lives with her old father in Kwara. He is a retired police officer, she says; he is not rich, but they are comfortable. She has no plans to cause any trouble. She is only here because her son is sick.

"Pamilerin needs heart surgery, he has a hole in his heart, the surgery is very expensive. I have tried to contact Teddy since the week he was born but he has been ignoring all my messages," she says.

"All you little girls who think you know everything, you heard God tell you not to have an abortion. Why did you not hear God and refuse to have sex with my friend's husband? Do you have any idea what parenting is? You thought it was just getting pregnant and pushing it out. Now look at you, your first crisis, you have fallen apart. You think this is a movie? You think this is a storybook? This is real life." I do not recognize the person yelling at this girl. I do not understand this girl, why she is staring me down instead of shaking before me like a leaf in the wind. I want to hug her, but I hate her. All I see as I look at her is someone to hate. I hate what this means for Rosetta and for our church. I hate that she makes me wish she'd had an abortion even though they are illegal in Lagos and the church is very opposed to them.

"I am sorry, I am so sorry." She is crying now. All that confidence has evaporated like boiling water. I forgot for a few seconds how young she is; her initial confidence threw me. She is still barely a teenager, after all, and she is crying like one. Her makeup is melting. She drags a wipe out of her baby bag. She cleans her face with it.

I move as close to her as I can. I clasp her hands in mine. I say many soothing words. When she is composed, she apologizes for crying. She says she is sure I can understand, her son is sick and in pain, her heart is breaking, she is going crazy.

"My dear daughter," I say in the softest voice I can manage, "the Bible says the Lord killeth, the Lord maketh alive. If your child was born to live, he will. Do not be like David, crying in vain for a child of sin."

I KNOW WHAT I am doing, using Scripture for my own ends. It is impossible to spend so much time reading and teaching the Bible and be unskilled in using it as a weapon. Does not the Bible in the book of Hebrews refer to its content as a two-edged sword, cutting and dividing?

She is just a girl. She has no idea that mothering is a lifelong entanglement to families, she does not know that she does not want this lifelong connection to Rosetta or to Teddy.

The girl looks at me with angry red eyes. I can tell I have surprised her. I can tell I have upset her.

"All we need is five million, the operation can be done here in Lagos. We have a doctor in the college teaching hospital, please just help me," she begs.

Now she surprises me with this pleading.

"This is a very personal matter, my dear," I reply. "It is also very sensitive. I cannot get involved. I do not even know if this is the governor's baby. You girls in the university get up to all sorts."

"I came to church to grow, to get better. I trusted all of you. I did not know that it was all a lie." She is angrier now.

She looks like the type of girl who has always been

everybody's favorite, pretty, clever, tall but not tall enough to intimidate men. She seems unaccustomed to suffering. She may have been raised middle class or lower, but she has not known real tragedy. I can tell by the way she looks now, like a balloon filled with water ready to burst.

In the glass door of the counseling room, I look at our reflection. We look like any other counseling session. It is funny how little you can tell by watching bodies move. Beyond the sliding door is my private library. After that is my assistant's cubicle. She shares a space with the youth minister. I get an idea. I suggest the youth minister to her. I tell her I am too closely involved with this thing to give godly counsel. I apologize for my words and actions. I tell her to wait for me to send for the youth pastor.

"Sometimes the godliest thing to do is to wait, my dear," I say.

"He knows," she says interrupting me. "The youth pastor knows, Pastor David knows, everyone knows. Do you think I am the first choir girl Pastor David has handed over to his politician friends? Do you think I am even the first to get pregnant? I am just the stupid girl who decided to keep it."

She must have thought she'd hit a jackpot, didn't she? She must have dreamed of all the child support, the lifestyle of ease and glamour, didn't she? She isn't sorry about what she did, about the pain she caused, she is just sad because her little meal ticket is sick.

I know what it feels like to find a way out and hold on to him. I remember what desperate feels like. I remember the intoxicating combination of fear, anger, and ambition. I can sympathize with her situation except that she's crossed the line with the "God told me to keep my baby" talk. The kind of girl to fuck a married man is the kind of girl who gets a compulsory abortion. This is Lagos, not El Dorado. There is no happily-ever-after for her here.

"You are the head of the women's ministry, you say you are here for me. For us all," she is saying to me. "Yet when Pastor David is using the choir as an escort agency for his friends, you do nothing. You did nothing, you know we went everywhere in the ministry buses, I have even been on the Life Jet."

"You seem ready to blame everyone but yourself, Alex," I reply. "You want me to feel guilt for something my husband does, something he conceals and hides from me, but you will not take responsibility for the part you played. You did not have to say yes to Teddy, you were not raped or kidnapped, little girl. You made this bed. Now lie in it."

She is stunned and silent. She is not ready for the bluntness of my words.

There is an old story Yoruba mothers tell their daughters. It begins with three men, all friends, moaning their misfortunes in marriage. The first believes he is the most unfortunate because his wife is lazy and a bad cook. The second friend says he has it worse, his wife is a day-and-night bed wetter, her condition both chronic and incurable. The third laughs at them both, insisting he would gladly trade places with either of his friends. His fate is the worst of the lot, he says, for he married a woman who lives entirely without shame.

No mother ever tells her daughter what perverse deviance

the third friend's wife performs brazenly to the consternation of her husband. No mother explains to her daughter who these men are, or why they deserve better than the wives they have married. This is the power of the old story: every girl who hears it is shamed for all the things she otherwise feels no shame for. Shame is female, just as merit is male.

"You are right, Pastor Ma, I am so sorry," Alex says. The balloon bursts and it is an avalanche of tears. She is crying and wiping her nose.

She tells me she blames herself. She says all she feels is guilt. Guilt has driven her crazy. She has stopped eating, or even sleeping. She asked God to kill her instead of punishing this little innocent baby for her foolishness. She is overwhelmed.

Even though I am trying to hide it, I feel guilty. I feel lots of guilt. I used to believe that I was helping people here. I used to tell myself I was making a difference and improving lives. These days, I am more accepting of the fact that I became a Christian to help myself. I am a Christian because I believe I am God's most important project. This is the foundation of Christianity, it seems to me; to believe that Jesus died to save my soul is to believe that I am important enough, that I am deserving of the highest kind of love and the sacrifice of an innocent.

This is my personal revolution. All my life, I never dared to think of myself as anything special. I think often of something my twin sister said once, about what happens to you when you grow up as deprived as we did. She said we got our brains locked in survival mode and we will be spending our whole adulthood dealing with that. I think she was right. Even with all this money and influence, I am still as self-serving and needy as I was when I hawked water on busy Lagos streets. But I am a Christian, so this makes it okay, God understands me and gives me His grace.

Alex is crying hard. I watch her cry. She reaches into her baby bag, grabs another wet wipe, cleans her face with it. Her cheeks are wet and shiny. She tells me she is so ashamed of the choices she has made. She realizes the fault is mostly hers. She says she just needs help, she did not create this baby alone.

The compiler of Proverbs, chapter 30, says the way of men with maidens is beyond comprehension. Is it really? It is easy to understand the appeal of youth like Alex's, all that innocence and beauty. The arrogance of power is easily explained as well. If there is any confusion, it lies in why young girls grow into women legitimizing the very systems that shame and vilify our femininity.

When Alex is done, I sit by her. I hold her hand. It is warm and dry. I tell her how sorry I am she is going through this. I tell her all mothers and babies deserve a solid system of support regardless. I apologize for not saying so earlier. I promise that the church will help even if the governor does not. She agrees to come to church for the service tomorrow, acknowledges there is a special opportunity here, its Mother's Day Sunday, we can raise a special offering for her baby's medical bills.

I am surprised that she understands. She smiles a little.

It is possible, after all, that she is more interested in getting care for her son than scandalizing the church.

When she leaves my counseling lounge, I wait a few minutes. I pray to the Lord for help. I am not sure He is listening. I walk to the auditorium; I need to see Rosetta as soon as possible. I will tell her everything I just learned. I will try to prepare her for what is coming. As I walk away from my office, toward the direction of the disconcerting sound of multiple instruments being mishandled, it occurs to me that there is something very odd about Alex's baby, Pamilerin. That baby did not move or whimper the entire time we were in the office. He just slept peacefully in his carrier like he was at home. I think about his unusual stillness for a few seconds with a deep inexplicable dread, but I toss those feelings aside to speak with Rosetta.

My friend Rosetta is as always wearing a long dress with a single-button blazer. She is dressed a little too warmly for the Lagos heat, but her ensemble gives her a cultured put-togetherness. I have always suspected that she wears jackets and blazers all the time to hide her arms. I do not think she has anything to hide.

"You look amazing, my love, have I said that already today?" I hug her as I speak.

"Keke. You are too nice to me. What do you think of us?" she asks, gesturing toward the women.

"Beautiful," I say. "Absolutely beautiful."

Rosetta gathers the women together. It takes a full five minutes but soon they are together like a real choir. Then the choir begins singing a classic Yoruba hymn, "Enikan Be

To Fe Ran Wa." It is a cappella, so the rowdiness is gone. It is pleasant. Their next song, the main song, is Kim Burrell's arrangement of "My Faith Looks Up to Thee." It is a somber song, and I wish they would do away with the drums and triangles, but I say nothing. I know it is more important, for the feeling of community, to give every woman a precise responsibility.

"I need to talk with you, let's go to my office," I whisper to Rosetta as the choir sings.

She cocks her head to the side, with a puzzled, amused look, her eyes rolling like she knows what this is about, and she has already had enough of it.

The choir is singing for fun now. One of the women is playing the role of an exuberant conductor. She stands with her leg bent in a near-perfect K. She is swinging her arms back and forth as the choir sings.

I AM DREADING this conversation with Rosetta. We have talked before about her husband's philandering, and she has always been understandably protective of him. He is a man with his weaknesses like any other, all villages have their idiots, he is a brilliant and kind man who just strays. Now that I think of it, I was not really surprised to hear Alex talk about her relationship with the governor. I was neither surprised nor disappointed about my husband's role in it. What does that say of me as a woman and church leader? What type of men do we let lead God's children?

•

IN CHURCH, WE have many sayings to excuse our poor stewardship. For example, we say God does not call the qualified, he qualifies the called. We also say the church is not a place for perfect people but for perfecting people. We repeat this often enough because we hope our members can decipher the caution encoded: *Be careful around your brethren, they can be injurious.*

Beyond issuing thinly veiled warnings, there is little I can do. As the pastor's wife, I am rarely at the center of anything outside my women's ministry domain. I am invited only after the deals are signed, the guests invited, and the meeting schedule drawn. I am here for the photo opportunity and the celebratory dinner. I have become very good at invisibility, even basking in it, enjoying the protection it affords. There is, however, a dangerous dark side to this silence and the things we hide beneath it. Our Lord has promised to shine his light on every dark thing.

This is how I begin my talk with Rosetta as we sit behind closed doors in my office. I pick up my Bible and begin reading from Luke, chapter 8.

"For all that is secret will eventually be brought into the open, and everything that is concealed will be brought to light and made known to all."

"What I have learned from the Word is that Jesus did not say these words as a threat but as a promise. And it is a good promise. The promise is that God is ridding the dark of its ability to deceive His children. The promise of light is a good promise, do you understand what I am saying?"

Rosetta looks up at me puzzled, like my entering into

spiritual counselor mode is something too strange for her to comprehend.

"My dear Pastor Mrs.," Rosetta says, her tone condescending, "I am listening, but I am not sure I understand you."

I GET TO the point quickly. I tell her Alex's story. I de-emphasize the solicitation to abort and the claim that their meeting in this church was orchestrated by my husband. Instead, I focus on the story's most important parts: the heart-broken, terrified mother and her unnaturally quiet little baby.

"I cannot believe that crazy girl is back in Lagos," Rosetta says. "I cannot believe she got you involved with this nonsense."

Rosetta speaks without any real emotion. I am puzzled by this. She would certainly have reacted with more fear if I had told her she had a housefly sitting on her shoulder. My friend Rosetta is short and lean. She is the kind of woman regularly mistaken for someone much younger. Her body is deceptively fragile. I know from playing tennis with her that she is strong and agile. She tells me her own version of the story. Alex as seductress, a one-night stand that results in a pregnancy.

"Teddy tries to convince her to have an abortion. He pleads, he bribes her. Do you know he bought her a car? You should know that no one told me anything at the beginning," she says.

"How long have you known about her?" I ask, interrupting her.

"Since last Christmas," she says. "So, Teddy has no choice but to arrange the abortion himself. He invites her to the guest house for what she thinks is a birthday dinner. But his assistants take her to a hospital, she is knocked out, the abortion is performed." She is speaking so casually about it. She is showing neither sadness nor remorse.

"Of course, when she comes out of it, she goes crazy," Rosetta says. "God warned her not to kill her baby, she keeps screaming, crying. They have to restrain her. She is sedated and left in the hospital for a few days."

"Is this when you learned about it? After the forced abortion?" I ask.

"Of course not," Rosetta replies with sharpness. She is impatient with me now. "You know these men, they only tell us when the whole thing explodes in their faces. I learned much later, when my friend, editor at *Weekly Trust*, told me Alex contacted the newspaper to say she had birthed the governor's child. The story did not run, of course, because she was clearly crazy with no baby."

"So what did you do then?" I ask.

"I confronted Teddy, and he told me all that had happened. I told him to get the girl some help, and as far as I know, he did."

It is almost unbearable watching the casualness with which she speaks about it all. I wonder how I missed it, this callousness. It is possible it has always been there, but I can only recognize it now because of what is happening, because Alex reminds me of the girl I used to be.

"Don't worry about her, I will tell Teddy that she is

back again. This time I will make sure she gets the help she needs," she says.

I rise from my chair and give her a quick hug.

"Don't worry about that, since we have established it's mental illness. I will get her help, you have done your best, dear. These young girls and their wahala, may God deliver us," I say.

We walk out of the office, toward the underground garages. We are talking about service tomorrow. The dress code is red or gold. We joke about all the tacky outfits we expect to see, we agree that Lagos Christian women try too hard to appear classy. *Someone needs to teach them that style is effortless*, we say.

LATER THAT EVENING at home, I sit in the large nursery Pastor David and I designed the first time I got pregnant. I have been falling asleep in here for months now, and if my husband has noticed I'd rather be here, he says nothing about it. I take off my shoes and sit on the floor. The carpeting is imported, several inches thick. If you accidentally dropped a baby in this room, the only real risk would be carpet burn.

I am praying to God for a sign, for His wisdom in this situation. Do I talk to Pastor David or do I go straight to the governor with this? Who will protect Alex if her governor is angry with her? I want to focus on her recovery, on therapy and treatment. But what about justice? What about all the other girls?

I am not one of those Christians who hears a clear,

distinct voice leading them. What I have experienced over and over is indescribable peace during a chaotic situation or inexplicable insight in the middle of confusion. That is how the Lord leads me. Today, I really wish He would talk plainly to me. I'd give anything for a burning bush, or even a still, small voice.

When I told my departed grandmother that I was going to be Pastor David's wife, she was quiet for a long time.

"Taiwo, ile-oko ile ogun, marriage is a battleground," she said. "Are you sure about this man?"

I was not sure, but I was determined.

"Yes, I am sure," I said.

"The goat and the family whose religion requires a sacrifice of goats cannot be serving the same God, do you understand me?" my grandmother asked.

"Yes, I do," I said. I was lying.

It is easy now, because she is dead, especially because of the manner of her death, to think of my grandmother with fondness, but she was really just a cantankerous, talkative old woman. Nothing was ever good enough for her. Nothing ever made her happy except nagging her grandchildren. She was tolerable only when she was telling us stories.

She told some weird stories. Most of the nightmares I had as a teenager were because of the stories she told of Olokun, goddess of the vast oceans. Olokun was believed to be the most powerful being on earth. It is said that Olokun covered the entire earth with water, trying to prevent Oludumare from creating earth's people. Oludumare had to trick her into giving permission. Grandmother's stories were her way to capture our attention and our imaginations. All those stories, all those proverbs, all they did was ingrain her in our minds. She wanted us to think regularly of her words and her wisdom.

It is three a.m. when Pastor David comes home. I am lying on the carpet, showered and shaven and pretending to be asleep. Everything he likes. He comes into the nursery fifteen minutes after I hear him unlock our front doors. He smells like okra soup and palm oil.

The women who worshipped Olokun used to be the richest, most beautiful women in Grandmother's village in Ondo. Not just Ondo, but all the villages along the Atlantic Ocean had Olokun priestesses. She gave them beauty, wealth, and honor. They were covenant protectors of her waters and life-forms. They did not eat anything from the ocean. They protected her waters from pollution, they did not bury their dead in the sea, they did not allow villagers to eat baby fish.

"Are you ovulating?" Pastor David asks, lying next to me on the carpet.

"No," I say, "I checked."

"Well, is there a difference, really?" Pastor David says. He is leaning into my knees and its hurts.

According to my grandmother, Olokun worship declined because of transatlantic slavery. Women were afraid to worship the ocean because she punished her daughters severely for desecrating her. All the mothers in the villages by the ocean wanted to be free to tell their children, "Run into the ocean if you see the white men coming. If they catch you, jump into the sea." But if you worshipped Olokun, you could not dare do that.

I had many nightmares that I was captive on a slave ship and that people were jumping to my right and left but I would not, I could not. I did not want to offend my mother's goddess.

Pastor David's breath is like steam on my neck. I wipe the invisible vapor. He does not notice. He is carrying on. I repent for all the times I wished Pastor David had a girl-friend. I repent for all the times I wished he came home every day spent, and with no interest in me.

"Pass me that little pillow, Mommy," he says to me. He calls me Mommy in faith. Someday soon, when the Lord wills it, I will get pregnant and carry it to term. I reach out to the cot and pull a little pillow that has HELLO HERO written across in it. He places it under my hips for lift.

It is easy to dismiss the truth contained in stories due to the limits of point of view. How can I accept the stories my grandmother handed down to me? None of my grand-mother's ancestors could tell why captured Yoruba children jumped or didn't jump. Those stories were lost to them as they are to me, trapped on the other side of the ocean, in the stomachs of their stolen children.

I have read about it, and I have several guesses about the captives who did not jump into the ocean. It is more likely that their chains were heavy and shackled to the ship itself. It is also likely that the ships' nets were too tall to jump over.

THIS IS WHAT I did when I was younger—approached her stories with logic, inspected them for improbabilities and inaccuracies. It was important for me to be able to logically dismiss them to stop being so afraid.

It is a common mistake, to hear a story about tragedy and disbelieve it because the telling is off. We think to ourselves, how does the storyteller know this? We are asking the wrong question. The right question is, why is the storyteller telling me this story? Because I was a child, I heard this story about a village full of mothers and the great loss they suffered and assumed it was a story about the pain of a child. Now, as a woman, I know the story is not about lost children. Children move from this plane to the next every day. It is a story about unquantifiable loss. It is a story about a lost goddess. What they lost was a god who looked like them. What they lost was the belief in an omniscient, omnipotent female spirit. Now look at this: all of us are condemned to serving these male gods and their rapacious servants.

PASTOR DAVID HAS passion. Of course, he is a minister, an evangelist. Passion is contagious, endearing. Passion does not replace integrity or courage. Passion is not a substitute for compassion.

"Mommy, did you say something?" Pastor David asks me. I must have mumbled.

"Yes," I say, "I asked if you were finished."

"Soon. I'd be faster if you keep quiet and just let me focus," he says.

It is a little funny how a man who can preach stadiums full of people into a screaming frenzy would be, in his home, as tense as a clenched fist. People tell me they leave our

Sunday services fired up, excited to take on the week. I wish there was someone I could tell that he leaves me hollow, desperate, angry, and raw.

"Have you finished outlining your sermon for tomorrow, Mommy?" Pastor David asks me. He is finished and sitting up next to me.

"A member of the choir came to see me today. Her name is Alex, she needs our help," I say instead.

"What does this have to do with the sermon?" he asks.

"Is her story true?" I ask.

"Are you going to tell me what you have prepared for God's people? Will I have to preach the women's message myself?" he asks.

"I am teaching about light and darkness, Pastor, the words of Jesus. Everything hidden will be manifested, every secret will come to light," I say, even though it is not true. I planned to teach on the faith of Ruth, who is a favorite here at the New Church.

"And what do you expect to happen after this message?" my husband asks.

"The Holy Spirit will correct, convict, cleanse," I say.

"You are just like your father, do you know that?" He gets up off the floor, standing over me like a tree. "When things get rough, you forget you are part of the church. You are looking for a scandal when there is none. You think you can bring me down? This is the church of God. This is going to last forever, do you understand that?"

"The church is only as strong as its weakest link," I say.

"That is stupid nonsense you have gotten from watching

too much TBN. Weakest link? Then the church will be perpetually weak, each day adding new broken people to the fold. The church is the incorruptible bride of the glorified Christ."

He is doing that preacher thing. That *watch me make you look stupid* thing. That *you are out of your league* thing. That *dissecting Scripture is for men* thing.

"She needs our help, Pastor," I say when he is done.

"What she needs is a deliverance minister. That girl is possessed with many sexual demons. They have driven her crazy. She has had too many men to count, she is a fractured shell of a person," he says.

"She also needs an apology, some therapy, something from us," I say.

"You should focus on your own life, your own family. I am halfway out this door and you're barely noticing," he says.

"I'm not blind, Pastor," I say.

"I think you are forgetting you are a nobody. You have nowhere to go, you are a nobody, you have nothing. What will you do if I leave you? Go and live with your sister and her boyfriend? Or in your brothers' college dorm rooms?"

In one of my earliest memories, I am running around with no clothes on. I am two or maybe three years old. I watch myself trip, fall, and I begin to cry. I stop crying as soon as I realize that nothing hurts. I can still hear crying, but it is coming from outside me, the body that fell, the body that is crying is outside me. This is the first time I realize that Bibike and I are different people, with separate bodies.

I go to her. I push her down as she tries to get up. The more she cries, the harder I laugh.

It is possible that my personality has been framed entirely by that moment, by the joy of being separate. It is possible that all my life, I have continued in this vein, intent on proving that I am different, separate from her. This is how I have convinced myself that I am important, that I am not the bonus child. It is possible that this is the reason I needed to work in entertainment, just like I needed to marry into this money and this hypervisibility.

"I am not a nobody and you are not God. You're not the one writing my story," I say to my husband.

"But I am your lord, and you will obey me like Scripture commands," he says.

I say nothing. He grabs me by the nape of my neck, pulling me up on my feet.

"Preach a great sermon tomorrow, Mommy," Pastor says. "Don't stir up trouble. Encourage God's people and look nice."

His grip is stiff around my neck, like a steel necklace.

"Yes, Pastor," I say.

It is a cool Sunday morning. It rained for most of Saturday night. Outside smells both fresh and musty, like a murky village river muddied by erosion. The drive to church is quiet and terrifying. Pastor David and I sit in the back of our Toyota Land Cruiser Prado.

Two men, the driver and Pastor David's assistant, sit in the front of the vehicle. There is gospel music playing.

Whenever we drive into a pothole deep enough to rattle us, Pastor David murmurs something about disrespectful Lagos roads. Whenever we drive past young people hanging out by the streets laughing, smoking, doing whatever, Pastor murmurs something about the perilous end of times.

Alex is waiting inside the lounge of Pastor David's private entrance. Her tiny baby is in one hand, still as stone, In the other hand, she holds a satchel diaper bag. It is white and yellow, pretty like a summer day. There are a few church workers milling around. One man, dressed in the black overalls issued to our camera crew, is pushing a dolly with a large speaker. Another is dragging several feet of cable wrapped around his arm. They are all busy and no one but me seems surprised to see Alex there.

The tightening in my chest is a warning, I know that now.

"Good morning, Pastors," she says to us. "Can I come with you? Pastor Ma?"

"Alex, I have spoken with Pastor about you. He will give you the answers you need," I say.

She looks at me with shock, like I just said the most incredulous thing.

"Pastor sir, I will see you in the service." I say it loud enough for everyone around to hear. "I'm headed to my office."

I do not look back to see if Alex is walking behind me or going with Pastor David. In my office, I search for the outline for my sermon. I will be teaching the story of Ruth and the dignity of her diligent labor. I find it tucked between books on my desk. I read through it, excited and relieved. The service is saved, normalcy is restored, glory to God.

I read the outline again, and I make more notes. "Ruth is one of the mothers of our faith because she learned to listen to the advice of her mother-in-law. Older Christian women have a responsibility of mentorship and guidance toward the younger girls in the church." My sermon is not revolutionary, but it is a start. We can start a spark that will someday become a fire.

The auditorium is filling with worshippers. I can hear the regular worship leader and responses:

There is power in the name of Jesus
To break every chain

I wonder where Rosetta is, where her husband is. It is possible they decided to skip church today. I am not surprised. People are predictably selfish, we are born selfish, even little babies; notice how hard they cry when they need something, screaming and demanding to have their needs met immediately. Selfishness is normal, human.

I wonder what happened to Ruth's sister Orpah.

The phone in my office rings, startling me. My assistant does not work on Sundays. I pick it up. It is Pastor David's assistant, he has heard some high-pitched screaming in the office. He thinks it's Pastor screaming. Yes, Alex is still in there. No, they are not in the counseling room. He cannot go in. He refuses to intrude.

"Can you please come here, Ma, take a look, just to make sure everything is okay?"

Pastor David is on the floor in his office, kicking his legs around. His hands are wrapped around a bleeding penis. His pants are down to his knees. The floor is littered with a bunch of bloody face tissues. He is talking to me, but I do not hear him. My eyes are fixed on Alex. She is standing in the corner with her little doll in her hands, rocking back and forth, her eyes closed like she is trying to soothe herself to sleep.

"Have you also come to take away my baby?" Alex asks. Her eyes are still shut, but her voice is calm. "Are you here to take my baby from me?"

"Call my driver to take me to the hospital, this stupid girl attacked me," Pastor David says.

I am not in a hurry to call for help. I straighten Alex's shirt. I wipe the sides of her mouth with tissue; there is semen, but no blood. I begin tidying up the room. I am also searching for her weapon of choice. I am picking up the stuff strewn all over—church bulletins, Alex's hair tie, A4 paper, a button off Alex's shirt, Scofield's reference Bible, a bloodied staple gun—there it is—several pens.

THE MORNING I married Pastor David, my mother came to me with information she had received from a "reliable" source.

"We were not the only ones who lost everything because of this church," she said.

"I know."

"You know that Pastor David was behind it all? You know that money is how he built this church? Bad money, 419 money?"

"I know."

I did not know. Of course, like any other reasonable person, I had my suspicions, but nothing had ever been confirmed.

"Please, Ariyike mi, oko mi, olowo ori mi, do not marry this man, please, I beg you, there is still time to change your mind."

Mother knelt before me, holding on to my legs like she was the child. She was crying, tears were running down her face to my feet. I stood there for many minutes saying nothing, just listening to her cry.

ALEX STAYS STILL in the corner. She is holding on tight to the little doll, like she expects me to try to take it from her. There's a sprinkle of blood on her hands, on her skirt and shoes.

"He is such a calm little boy, isn't he?" I ask.

"Yes, he is," Alex says to me. "I am so blessed."

The assistant who called me opens the door now, slowly at first, hesitating. He is just checking to see if we are all okay. He screams at the blood, at the pastor writhing on the floor, at the crazy girl in the corner and the calm pastor's wife.

I told my mother that I was marrying Pastor David as part of a well-planned revenge plot. I was going to get the money he stole from my family, and more than that, I was going to get dignity and prestige. Mother did not believe me even though I tried hard to convince her.

"Just give me five years, I'll ruin his entire life," I'd said.

IN MY FAVORITE Yoruba folktale, three children engage in idle boasts. The first one claims he can climb the tallest palm tree in the village. The second one insists he can do better: he can swim across the ocean without getting tired. The third friend boasts of catapulting a pebble all the way up to the heavens, defying the law of gravity. The tortoise, a recurring character in Yoruba stories, overhears their idle boasts and reports them to the king of the land.

The king plans a day of contest. "Now you have the opportunity, do all you have said you can do," he says to the children.

When the contest day arrives, the climber stops halfway and begs to be carried down the tall tree; the swimmer nearly drowns from exhaustion and must be lifted by boat out of the ocean. The boy with the catapult surprises them: his pebble goes up to the heavens and is never seen again. He wins money from the king and the respect and admiration of his village.

As a child, when I learned of the third child's secret, his cunning—he switched the pebble with a tiny bird—I was in awe of it. A meddling king bested by a cunning child, what a triumph.

"JESUS CHRIST! PASTOR, what happened in here? What is all this?" Pastor David's assistant is weeping and shrieking.

The assistant squats next to Pastor David and helps pull his pants up. He is weeping as he does this, asking the same pastor what happened over and over like a song stuck on a loop. Pastor David is telling him to keep quiet and take him to the hospital.

Many more people come in. *Pastor David has fainted*, I hear someone say. Together two or three people surround him like a shield, they lift him up. A different someone screams for the driver to get the Prado. I do not even like that vehicle, but I am irritated that they will get bloodstains all over the back seat and that most of the stains won't come off.

The truth is I never intended to bring down Pastor David. I married him to better my own lot. Just like I admired the third child in that story, I admire this man, somehow. He has done so many things, influenced so many lives. Even if I could, why would I, having tasted this lifestyle, want to destroy it? There is no larger life than this. This is the Kingdom.

Truth be told, it has cost me more than I imagined I was giving up. For example, it's been three years since I last spoke with my twin sister. We were once the closest sisters in all of Lagos. She is an herbalist now, having expanded her beauty supply store. Now she mixes healing potions and ori cleansing lotions for Lagos women. I am a pastor's wife, a television minister. What agreement will light have with darkness? It is for this very reason the Lord Jesus said in the Gospel according to Luke, I have come to turn your families inside out.

•

THERE ARE MANY versions of the kids-making-playful-boasts story. In one, the swimmer drowns in the ocean, his body floats for days on end, the king commands no one to touch it. In another version, the climber dies of heatstroke ascending a tall tree in the noontime. In yet another, the king has both climber and swimmer executed for failing to achieve their goals.

All versions agree, the trickster wins in the end.

ALREADY, I AM exhausted by the months that are coming. I have my eye on Alex, and she is looking up at me with bright, hopeful eyes. She is shivering and afraid. I move closer to her, wrap my arms around her, and hug her over and over.

"IT IS GOING to be okay, I promise," I say to her, lying.

ACKNOWLEDGMENTS

First, a few clarifications. I have taken several liberties with my descriptions of Lagos, Nigeria. All the villages, streets, churches, and neighborhoods depicted here are entirely fictional. These details have only been included to give the novel verisimilitude. I have taken similar liberties with my translation and extrapolation of Yoruba words, proverbs, and myths. Instead of literal translations, I have embraced the more poetic, rhythmic renderings of these ideas.

Writing and publishing a book like this one is impossible without the contributing hard work of so many talented people. My eternal gratitude goes to my editor, Jonathan Lee, and the team at Catapult for being the best advocates for this book.

My very special thanks go to my family; my child, my parents, my siblings. Thank you for being a trusted support system. I love you all so much.

Finally, to the faculty of the Iowa Writers' Workshop, particularly Samantha Chang and Kevin Brockmeier, I am grateful for the guidance and fellowship.

© CAROLE CASSIER

TOLA ROTIMI ABRAHAM
is a writer from Lagos, Nigeria. She
lives in Iowa City and is currently
pursuing a graduate degree in journal-
ism. A graduate of the Iowa Writers'
Workshop, she has taught writing at
the University of Iowa. Her fiction and
nonfiction have appeared in *Catapult*,
The Des Moines Register, *The Nigerian Literary Magazine*, and other
venues. *Black Sunday* is her first novel.

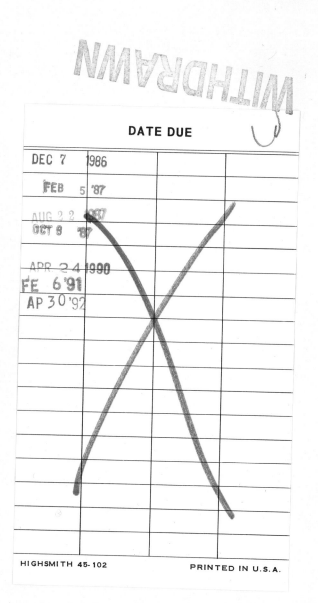

CHAPTER ONE

"I'm going out to the post office," Madge Bingham announced, putting her head round the door of the waiting-room. "I shan't be long. Has Gordon gone?"

She hoped he had, otherwise he might have offered to post the letter for her while he was out on his afternoon house visits, which would have defeated the object of the outing for the letter was only an excuse. There was little chance of Mrs. Locke making a similar offer. She lived in the opposite direction to the village.

But how unnecessarily complex such subterfuges became! Madge thought, waving the letter in Mrs. Locke's direction to show how genuine the trip was; not that Mrs. Locke could see it was only the electricity bill, arrived that morning, which could have waited at least another day.

Mrs. Locke was rearranging her little cubicle, which overlooked the waiting-room, putting away patients' files from morning surgery and placing her notebook and pencil just so on the counter-top. She put her head through the hatch opening.

"Yes, Mrs. Bingham. Doctor left about ten minutes ago. I'm just tidying up before I go. If you won't be in, I'll switch the telephone to the answering machine, shall I?"

It was one of Mrs. Locke's exasperating qualities that, although she had been Gordon's secretary-receptionist for many years and carried out her duties efficiently, she still seemed to think it necessary to defer to Madge's opinion if she happened, as on an occasion such as this, to come into the surgery. It was this touch of servility in her manner which had prevented them from ever becoming on first-name terms.

Seeing her face through the hatch with its pendulous cheeks, freshly powdered because she was going home, and that faintly deferential smile, the features topped off by tightly permed grey hair, Madge had an overwhelming urge to shock her.

She thought, Supposing I said, "I'm not only going to the post office, Mrs. Locke. That's only an excuse. The real reason is I'm hoping to see that man who's just moved into the caravan in Waterend Lane. He looks interesting"?

She had thought so on first meeting him four days earlier in the village shop. It had been the briefest of confrontations as he had been on the point of leaving as she entered. In fact, he had held the door open for her and smiled as she thanked him. And it hadn't been mere civility either. She noticed that he had registered her appearance, taking in her well-cut clothes and her still trim though middle-aged figure with a look of quizzical admiration which she hadn't excited in a man for years; certainly not in Gordon.

As for the man—Alec Lawson, as Mrs. Hunnicutt, who ran the shop, had informed her—she had, in turn, found him attractive. There was something loose and casual about him which she had liked. In his forties, he had one of those creased faces, humorous and different, suggesting an amused, perhaps even a dangerous, disregard for convention.

A free soul, she remembered thinking, her mind hardly on ordering groceries, and felt something flutter in her own breast as if answering an unspoken urging to break out.

But how absurd! she told herself, closing the door on Mrs. Locke and returning down the hall to the private part of the house. I'm forty-eight and happily married. As the doctor's wife, I'm regarded as a pillar of the community. I'm a school governor, a parish councillor and chairwoman of the Ladies' Church Guild. I serve in the Oxfam shop in Studham once a week and help organise the Old Folks' Wednesday socials.

I am also the mother of two children whose photographs smile down at me from the drawing-room mantelpiece.

Lovely children, Mrs. Bingham, and such a credit to you!

And so they are, she thought, opening the drawing-room door and crossing to the fireplace. Claire and Richard, both now at university, Claire reading English, Richard psychology, and neither of them really needing her any longer; not in the same way they used to when they were small.

So I fill my life with other duties—with committees and charitable works, with caring for Gordon who no longer notices me as a person, and with painting very fourth-rate water-colours which my friends pretend to admire.

But, for the first time for years, I am going to make an adventure for myself which involves no one except me, Madge, my sole self. Although not an affair, she thought, looking past the photographs of her children to the mirror above the mantelpiece as she arranged the red-and-cream silk scarf at the neck of her Jaeger coat. I'm too fond of Gordon and besides it isn't what I'm looking for. What I want is contact with someone different, a glimpse through a door into another kind of world which I haven't known since my student days.

All the same, it wasn't that easy to escape.

Locking the back door, she saw Bartlett, the gardener, come limping across the kitchen garden towards her between the rows of newly planted lettuce seedling and beans, signalling to her with one arm as if she were a bus.

"I thought I'd light up a bonfire, Mrs. Bingham. There's a lot of rubbish needs clearing and the wind's right."

He's as bad as Mrs. Locke, Madge thought. Can't he make a decision about lighting his silly fire without asking me first?

"What a good idea!" she said brightly.

"That is, if you'll be around to keep an eye on it," he added. "Only I was going to make a start on the shrubbery in the front. It needs trimming back."

"I was just going out," Madge replied, thinking: Damn his fire! Why should I alter my plans to suit the gardener, for God's sake? Aren't there enough little threads to keep me role-bound without Bartlett trying to bind me down still further? But seeing his long, lugubrious face—poor old Bartlett who'd probably never had an adventure in his life—she heard herself saying, "I shan't be long. I'm only going down to the post office. Why don't you leave the shrubbery until the next time you come and find something to do in the back garden instead? That way, you'll be able to watch the fire yourself."

"Right you are!" Bartlett agreed, pleased that the decision had been made for him. As he moved off to where his jacket was hanging over the handles of the wheelbarrow, she called out after him, "I'll make some tea when I get back."

He acknowledged the offer by raising his hand.

As he left, he was going through his jacket pockets, searching for his matches.

It was only when she was half-way down the road towards the village that she realised she had left the electricity bill on the mantelpiece under Richard's photograph and stopped, wondering whether to turn back and fetch it.

Over the top of the budding hedges, a tall white column of smoke was visible from Bartlett's bonfire, rising quite straight into the still, damp March air and, seeing it, she made up her mind.

I'll go anyway, she decided. I'll simply knock on the door and say, "I'm Madge Bingham, the doctor's wife. I just happened to be passing and I wondered if there's anything either my husband or I can do to help you settle in?" I shall be friendly and welcoming in my best Ladies' Church Guild manner.

I might even ask him to tea one afternoon. Wouldn't that surprise Gordon?

Waterend Lane was a turning off to the left before the main centre of the village, if the two shops, the general store-cum-post office and the butcher's, together with the straggle of houses and cottages between the church at the far end and the Goat on the nearer outskirts could be described in so grandiose a term.

The lane ran behind the Goat, the only public house in the village, skirting its car-park and continuing in a straight line for a short distance before twisting this way and that for about half a mile as it followed the irregular outlines of the surrounding fields. Just before the ford came into sight, the lane swung round in a sharp S-bend and began to dip down to where the stream ran across the hard surface, rising and turning again on the far side to begin the long, slow incline towards Macey's farm, out of sight beyond the brow of the hill.

Madge walked briskly, enjoying the outing. It took a mere ten minutes to cover the distance from the village to the ford, a local beauty spot in summer, and once past the first bend, the public house and the clustered houses were no longer visible. Here the real countryside began. All along the verges the signs of spring were apparent in the clumps of pale primroses and brighter celandines studding the banks and in the new leaves emerging like little vivid green claws, sharp-edged and tightly rolled, which thrust out from the dense mass of winter twigs on the trees and hedges. The air had a buoyancy to it, fresh with the tang of new growth.

The caravan was also out of sight, tucked away on the far side of the ford in a corner of one of Macey's fields. It had been placed there originally to house the Harpers, Macey's former employee and his wife, who the year before had moved to another farm over in Riddleton where they'd been offered a decent, modernised cottage. Since then it had been empty until Alec Lawson's recent occupation of it.

It was reached across a narrow, raised foot-bridge which spanned the ford on the left-hand side, with worn concrete steps leading up to it at both ends and a handrail rubbed smooth by many generations of palms, the water beneath it running quite high and fast after the spring rains; picturesque with its surrounding trees and moist banks but a hazard in Madge's opinion, especially to children who tended to gather there in the summer to paddle. She had raised the matter several times at Parish Council meetings only to have her advice overruled.

On the far side of the ford, a signpost, with a stile beside it, pointed across the fields to a public footpath leading to the church—Waterend Lane, the main village street and the path thus forming the three sides of a triangle.

Crossing the worn planks of the bridge, she continued up the lane for another hundred yards before coming to an opening in the high hawthorn hedge, closed off with a rickety wooden gate. Behind it stood the caravan on its concrete base, surrounded by a derelict patch of garden which dated back to the Harpers' time.

The door of the caravan was set open, so Alec Lawson was at home. In fact, as the gate clicked shut behind her, she saw a head appear at one of the small windows. The next moment, he had come out to stand at the top of the steps, watching her approach with an amused air and a disconcerting lack of surprise as if he had expected her to come.

She began her piece.

"I'm Madge Bingham, the doctor's wife—" But she got no further.

"Come in," he said and, turning his back, reentered the caravan, giving her no choice but to follow.

Its interior dismayed her. It was furnished to the Maceys' taste, she imagined, not his, like a suburban sitting-room in flowered fabric with a black-and-yellow fitted nylon carpet which did not match, all the wood-work varnished a sticky, bright brown. A flap table, covered in speckled plastic, on which stood a portable typewriter and some paper, was set up in front of a cushioned bench seat which she assumed could be let down at night to form a bed.

"I'm sorry," she said. "I see I'm interrupting your work."

"Coffee?" he suggested, ignoring her remark.

"No, I really mustn't stop. I was just passing and I wondered if my husband—"

"The doctor," he put in.

It suddenly occurred to her that he was deliberately trying to put her out of countenance, for quite what reason she wasn't sure but she felt foolish standing there, an unfamiliar and disconcerting experience.

As if aware of it himself, he changed tactics, smiled charmingly and said, indicating the bench seat, "Won't you sit down?"

She perched herself on the end, sitting with her legs turned sideways to avoid the table-top.

"I only wanted to say," she continued, making her tone more brisk and businesslike, "that if there's anything we can do to help you settle in, you only have to ask. There's quite a lot going on in the village, the Men's Club on Monday evenings and the Dramatic Society—"

"I'm only here for a short time," he replied, his head tilted to regard her, his expression still amused.

Seen close to and for a longer time than their first brief meeting, she realised that he was younger than she had imagined—probably no more than in his late thirties—and this realisation together with his reply took her off guard.

"Oh?" she said. "Why is that?"

"I'm opening a bookshop in Studham. As soon as the lease is finalised, I shall be moving in there. So I'm afraid I'm unlikely to make much use of the village activities, delightful though they sound. But it was enormously kind of you to take the trouble to walk all the way down here to tell me about them."

Feeling the colour rise in her face at the irony in his voice, Madge said hurriedly, "I had to go to the post office anyway," and then remembered too late that she hadn't even that excuse for being there.

She got to her feet, feeling oddly humiliated.

"Then I shan't keep you any longer," she replied.

He said nothing, only smiled again as he stood aside to let her move past him towards the door, looking at her with the same quizzical glance with which he had first regarded her in the shop.

Madge could see now that she had been mistaken. It was neither admiring nor appreciative, merely interested in the same entirely objective manner with which she might look up from her sketch-book to survey a part of the scenery she was drawing.

How stupid she'd been!

But although her anger was directed mainly at herself, she was annoyed as well by Alec Lawson's attitude. There was an arrogance about him which was offensive. She was not used to being treated in so derisive a manner.

Well, it had taught her a lesson. She would take care to avoid any contact with him in the future.

Turning out of the gate into the lane, she was surprised to come face to face with Stella Franklin, whom she hadn't seen in the village for almost two years; not since her marriage to some young man from Studham whose surname she had forgotten although it didn't matter. She had known the girl for long enough to call her by her Christian name.

"Hello, Stella," Madge said, thinking how much she had changed since the last time they had met. Although she couldn't be more than twenty-one, she already looked experienced and, not to put too fine a point on it, a little common. But, even as a child, Madge remembered, Stella had been wilful.

"A bit of a handful," as her mother had once expressed it to Madge.

Mrs. Franklin was an unassuming, decent enough woman; too softhearted, perhaps, especially with Stella, the youngest of the three daughters, while Mr. Franklin, when he'd been alive, had been one of those uncomplaining men who would do anything for a quiet life.

As the whole family had been Gordon's patients, Madge knew them well.

In her opinion, the root of the problem with Stella lay in the fact that the girl was more intelligent than either of her parents, which made it difficult for them to know how to handle her.

It had all been wasted, of course. Stella had left school as soon as she could and, after several unrewarding jobs, had got herself pregnant at the age of eighteen by the young man from Studham whom she had

married although she had miscarried the baby a couple of months after
the wedding.

Not long after that, she and her husband, who had been living with
Stella's mother, had moved out of the village to a new council maison-
ette in Studham where Stella was working as a barmaid, or so Mrs.
Franklin had told Madge when they met one day in the shop.

And now here she was back in the village, looking a little defiant,
which made Madge suspect that the marriage was not a success. Stella
had always assumed that bold air of not giving a damn when things
were going badly, a suspicion which seemed confirmed when she
added, "And how are you?" and Stella replied, "Oh, fine, thanks, Mrs.
Bingham," showing too much gum when she smiled and swapping her
satchel handbag casually to her other shoulder.

"And your mother?"

"She's fine, too."

Nothing more was required, Madge felt. Whatever was the reason
for Stella Franklin's sudden return to Wynford, it would no doubt be
common knowledge sooner or later. In the meantime, it was better to
show no curiosity and she walked on after saying goodbye.

It was only when she reached the footbridge over the ford that it
occurred to her to wonder what Stella was doing in Waterend Lane.
Apart from Macey's farm, there was no other house she might be
visiting except, of course, the caravan.

One foot on the planks, she turned to glance back over her shoulder.

Although the gate was out of sight round the bend in the lane, the
hill leading up to the farmhouse was visible and, if the Maceys' place
had been Stella's destination, she would have had time to emerge into
view and be seen walking up the slope towards it. But the road was
empty. Stella, therefore, must have disappeared through the gate which
led into the field.

But what on earth was she doing visiting Alec Lawson? Madge wondered. Unless, of course, they had already met in Studham. And if that
were the case, it might explain Stella's unexpected reappearance in the
village so soon after Alec Lawson's arrival. If they were having an
affair . . .

But it was absurd, Madge decided. Although Stella was quite capable
of chasing after any man, she had imagined Lawson, despite his casual

appearance, to show more discernment, but perhaps she had been wrong in her judgement of him.

As for Stella, she could be playing with fire. In the past, before they had moved to Studham, Madge had seen the husband about the village and he hadn't looked the type who'd take kindly to his wife's infidelity. It was bound to lead to trouble.

What a fool the girl is! Madge thought. It was none of her business, of course, but all the same she couldn't help feeling exasperated at the stupidity of the pair of them.

Stella said, "It's only me. Mind if I come in?"

Alec stopped typing and glanced up. She was standing on the top step, looking in over the open half of the door, smiling and quite clearly expecting a welcome.

Although he had told her to drop in anytime, she had not chosen the best afternoon to call. Not only had he hoped to finish some letters concerning the lease of the shop, work already interrupted by Mrs. Bingham's visit, but he was expecting his wife to arrive with his son to discuss, he assumed, the breakdown of their marriage.

All the same, he felt he could hardly turn Stella away and he replied, "Help yourself," although he began rather ostentatiously to pack the typewriter up, putting on its cover and shoving the letters into the file, which he flapped shut.

She took no notice, a reaction which unexpectedly pleased him. There was a frankness about her which he had liked the first time he had met her a week before in the Swan in Studham where she had been serving behind the bar. He had called in there late one lunchtime on his way back from the solicitor's and, the pub being half empty, they had chatted together while he ate a cheese sandwich and drank a pint of bitter standing at the counter.

He remembered he had asked her her name.

"Stella," she had replied.

"That means a star," he had told her.

She had laughed, her upper lip lifting to show the gums, an openness of expression which he had found attractive.

"I bet my mum doesn't know that," she had said. "I was called after one of my aunties. Where do you live? In Studham?"

"No, although I'm going to move here soon. I'm staying temporarily in Wynford."

He hadn't expected her to know it but she had smiled again, delighted at the coincidence.

"Wynford? I used to live there. My mum still does. You know that row of cottages near the Goat? Well, she lives in the end one. What are you doing in Studham then?"

"I've been to see my solicitor," he had explained. "I'm arranging to lease a shop in the town."

He had been surprised by her reaction.

"A solicitor?" she had asked, her expression suddenly turning serious. "I was thinking of going to see one myself. What would I have to do?"

"Just ring up and ask for an appointment," he had replied.

The reason for her interest had become apparent two days earlier when, calling in at the Goat one evening, he was surprised to see her at the bar, talking to the landlord. With that unaffected warmth of hers, too guileless to be anything but sincere, she had welcomed him like an old friend and, after he had bought her a drink and they had taken their glasses to a quiet corner, she told him she had left her husband.

"So I'm back home with my mum," she had explained. "I'm going to divorce him. Look, you know about solicitors, don't you? Could you put me right? Only I'm a bit scared to go on my own, not knowing what it's all about."

The ingenuousness of the appeal and the similarity in their situations, both of them dealing with broken marriages, had prompted him to say, "You know where I live. Drop by anytime you like and I'll try to help. As a matter of fact, I'm in the process of a divorce myself."

So there she was, unlatching the door to let herself in and saying breezily, "I'm not stopping you from your work, am I?"

"No," he lied, smiling back at her and letting down the flap of the table so that she could sit down more easily on the bench seat. "Come in. Would you like some tea?"

"Yes, please," she said without any hesitation. "Do you want me to make it?"

"I think I can manage," he said drily, going into the tiny kitchen, where he put on the kettle.

He was beginning to enjoy the situation. Stella was looking round the caravan with very much the same curiosity as Mrs. Bingham had done but without her air of surprised concern at its awfulness.

Remembering the doctor's wife, he was prompted to add over his shoulder, "You're my second visitor this afternoon. Mrs. Bingham called on me a little earlier."

"Yes; I passed her in the lane," Stella replied. "What did she want?"

"To satisfy her curiosity, I suspect, although she said she came to welcome me into the village." He still felt vaguely guilty over his reception of her although he tried to brush it to one side as a natural response to Mrs. Bingham's own assumption that he would be suitably grateful for her interest. Partly out of this need for self-justification, he continued, "I'm afraid I rather snubbed her. She was too much the lady of the manor for my liking."

"Oh, she's all right," Stella said offhandedly, "although I see what you mean. She can be a bit bossy at times."

Perfectly at home herself, she had thrown open the fur fabric jacket she was wearing and had crossed her legs in their tight jeans, showing spiky high-heeled shoes, spattered with mud from the lane.

He supposed a lot of men would find her desirable but she was too physical for him; too much breast and hip; too highly coloured with her blond hair, her bright lipstick and iridescent eyelids. The perfume she was wearing was already permeating the caravan, making the back of his nose tickle. He preferred women who were more subtle and low-key.

All the same, it amused him to see her sitting there, knowing what his wife's reaction would be.

"But she's so dreadfully common-looking!"

Joanna would, of course, immediately suspect an affair and be outraged not only at his unfaithfulness but also at his lack of taste.

It was part of his sense of freedom on leaving her that he no longer had to concern himself with her standards. He could choose his friends, his clothes, his way of life, without having them subjected to her judgement of what was or was not good taste, whatever the ridiculous phrase meant. He suspected that Mrs. Bingham shared much the same attitude, which was one of the reasons why he had wanted to put her in her place.

"Been to the solicitor's yet?" he asked, carrying the two mugs of tea through from the kitchen.

"No, not yet. That's why I've come to see you. I didn't like to phone them up 'cos I wasn't sure what to say. I wondered if you'd help me write a letter."

"There's no need," he replied, guessing that she was unused to the telephone. "I'm seeing my solicitor tomorrow. Would you like me to fix up an appointment for you? There's Mr. Sanderson who I deal with—he's rather elderly—or his partner, Mr. Pickering, who's much younger."

"Oh, I'll take the young one," Stella said and laughed. "But would you really do that for me? I'd be ever so grateful."

"Of course; it's no trouble. What time would suit you best?"

"Try to make it an afternoon about four o'clock. I'm starting work at the Goat on Monday behind the bar and I don't want to ask for time off. If it's late afternoon, then I can catch the twenty-past-three bus into Studham after the pub shuts. What should I say when I see him?"

"Just tell him what's happened and why you want a divorce. It's quite straightforward. He'll ask you any questions he thinks necessary. Sugar?" He offered the bowl, hoping to divert her attention away from the subject of her marriage, which she was quite clearly going to recount in detail.

"No, ta; I'm sweet enough already." She smiled briefly. "I suppose it'll be all right. After all, he did knock me about; Ken, I mean. I told him the last time, if he touched me again, I'd leave. But more fool me, I suppose. I should never have married him."

"Why did you?" Despite himself, Alec was curious. The glimpse into another type of marriage interested him.

"I nearly didn't. We'd quarrelled, you see, and I'd broken it off. Then I found I was pregnant so it was on again. Even then I needn't have bothered. I had another offer."

"An offer?" Alec repeated.

She laughed and shrugged.

"Oh, it was daft really. I couldn't have accepted it. Anyway, my mum got onto me about marrying Ken when she found out about the baby. Her nerves were bad, you see, 'cos my dad had just died, so in the end I said yes. If I'd known what was going to happen, I'd've stuck it out. You see, I lost the baby soon afterwards. We were living with my mum then, before we got the maisonette at Studham. It was after we moved that he started knocking me about."

"I'm sorry," Alec said. It seemed an inadequate remark to make, considering the tragic confusion of her life.

She shrugged again, lifting her shoulders as if dismissing both her own situation and his commiseration.

"He was paying me back for having chucked him over, although he'd always had a temper. That's the reason I ditched him in the first place. I thought things'd be different once we were married."

"But they weren't?"

"He seemed to think he owned me. I got fed up with it so I walked out." She started to laugh, throwing back her hair. "I left a pile of his dirty socks on the kitchen table with my wedding ring on top of them. What about you? What made you decide to pack up and leave?"

"Me?" He was still smiling at the image of the socks and the ring. It seemed churlish not to respond although he was careful, not knowing her capacity for discretion, to be noncommittal. "Boredom mainly. Incompatibility. I don't know."

"Been married long?"

"Fifteen years."

"Any kids?"

"Just the one."

She pulled a little face.

"It's always sad, divorce, I mean, when there's kiddies involved."

"He's nearly twelve."

"Oh, well, then it isn't as if he's too young to understand."

"Yes," he said.

The conversation was beginning to wind down. To give Stella her due, she seemed aware of it. Getting to her feet, she swung her bag over her shoulder and pulled the edges of her fur fabric jacket together.

"I ought to be getting along. Ta very much for the tea. You won't forget about fixing up that appointment?"

"I'll remember," he assured her. "I'll let you know the details later."

"Drop by the Goat on Friday evening. I'll be in there I expect and you can tell me then. I'll treat you to a drink at the same time."

"Thanks," he said. "I'll take you up on that."

He watched her leave over the half-door, tit-tupping down the concrete path in her high heels towards the gate, wondering if she might pass Joanna in the lane and what they would make of each other, that is if they troubled to look. He had already guessed Joanna's reaction. Stella's, he thought, would be more warm-hearted and admiring.

CHAPTER TWO

Joanna drew the car into the side of the lane just before the ford and stared at the water which swirled across the road a few feet in front of the wheels.

Alec had told her to take the turning immediately before the Goat public house but had said nothing about this particular hazard.

"Aren't you going to drive across it?" Simon asked.

He had wound down the window on the passenger's side to crane his head out.

"No," Joanna said abruptly.

"Why not?"

"Because it looks too deep and I don't want to stall the car."

"But if you drive very slowly and don't make waves, it should be all right," Simon replied in his grown-up, sensible manner.

"I'm not driving through it!" Joanna retorted, raising her voice.

At times, Simon was so like Alec that she wanted to slap him. Alec had treated her with the same slightly superior rationality, making light of her worries so that they appeared even to her so trivial and of so little consequence that she was forced into unreasonableness in order to defend them.

The damned ford was a typical example. Of course it would probably be quite safe to drive through it. As it was there on a hard-surfaced lane, presumably other cars must use it. No doubt Alec drove through it every day without any difficulty. But as her own driving experience was limited to shopping trips in Chelmsford with only short excursions outside the town, crossing fords was not part of it.

Irrationally—or was it?—she could imagine the car stuck in the middle with water coming up through the floor and the engine irreparably damaged.

And wasn't the whole situation Alec's fault anyway? After all, it was he who had chosen to walk out on them both and then bury himself miles from anywhere without even a telephone.

"If you like, I could go and measure the water with a stick," Simon offered, looking at her with that concerned expression which, at twelve years old, was too adult to be entirely natural or desirable. He was already assuming responsibility for her.

Joanna made up her mind.

"I'm leaving the car here."

"It'll block up the lane," Simon pointed out.

"I don't damn well care!" she exclaimed but all the same, she reversed the car a few yards before bumping it up on to the verge, hearing something scrape along the exhaust pipe as she did so.

Simon winced but kept silent apart from saying in a plaintive voice as he opened the passenger door, "I can't get out this side. There's a ditch."

"Then get out this side!" she said angrily.

He scrambled out, hunching his shoulders as he always did when she raised her voice at him.

Standing together in the lane, they surveyed the car, which was leaning at a drunken angle in the long wet grass, a bramble caught underneath it.

God alone knew how she'd drive it away, Joanna thought. She might even overturn it in the ditch, that is if she could get the damned thing to start. The scraping noise had sounded ominous.

"It's all right, Mummy," Simon assured her although both of them knew it was a crazy place to park. The verge was too high. She'd've done better to attempt the ford.

"Oh, come on," Joanna said wearily, turning to walk away. She felt close to tears with the despair and frustration of it all; not just the car but Alec's desertion after fifteen years of marriage, the worry about paying for the house and Simon's school fees, what she was going to say to her mother.

"How far do we have to go?" Simon asked, hurrying to catch up with her.

"How should I know?" she replied. "I haven't been here before either. It's probably miles."

That was an exaggeration. Alec had written in his letter: 'If you insist on coming to talk things over, although, quite frankly, I don't see the

point, you'll find the caravan on the left about half a mile along Waterend Lane, a turning just before the Goat."

As she had already driven roughly that distance, the caravan couldn't
be more than a couple of hundred yards away.

"I'll ask!" Simon announced, running ahead before she could stop
him towards a woman who was about to cross a narrow, raised foot-
bridge which spanned the left-hand side of the ford, his feet clattering
excitedly on the wooden boards.

Joanna waited in the lane. There was not room enough for them
both to pass on the bridge and besides, she did not want to become
involved with anyone from the place where Alec was now living. The
woman, too, had that bold, overconfident air about her which Joanna
had always found difficult to cope with when she met it in waitresses or
shop-assistants.

She was blond and looked as if she would laugh too loudly and easily.
A satchel handbag was slung casually across one shoulder of a fur fabric
jacket worn over a V-necked blue jumper and a pair of jeans cut so
tight across the hips that the front placket was stretched open to show
the zip.

Her voice in answer to Simon's question could easily be heard across
the few feet of water.

"It's just up there. You can't miss it. There's a gate. Visiting, are
you?"

"Simon!" Joanna called out warningly but too late.

She heard him reply, "We're going to see my father."

"That's nice," the woman replied, her voice indulgent, before walking on across the bridge, giving Joanna a glance and a smile as she
reached the other side.

Joanna ignored her, pretending to see neither, her eyes on Simon
who had run back to lean over the handrail.

"Mind you don't fall!" she called out, hurrying onto the bridge.

"Oh, don't be silly, Mummy," he replied. "Look, I told you it's not
very deep. You could easily have driven through it." Glancing up at
her, he added enthusiastically, "Isn't it super here!"

She looked about her, trying to see the place through his eyes: the
high hedges in small leaf, the brown water sliding under their feet, the
grassy banks scattered with tiny yellow star-shaped flowers, but could

find nothing to say in answer except "It's cold" before turning up her coat collar and walking on.

The caravan was awful. Even Simon seemed subdued at the sight of it. Small, ugly, its tin sides blotched with rust, it squatted in one corner of a field with a pathetic little patch of overgrown garden round it and a plastic washing-line slung between two iron posts.

"Does Daddy really live here?" he asked.

Before Joanna had time to reply, Alec was at the door of the caravan and coming down the steps to ruffle Simon's hair.

"So you found me?" he asked, turning to her last of all.

"Obviously," she replied coldly.

"But Mummy wouldn't drive through the ford," Simon announced. "We left the car on the other side."

"It's perfectly safe, providing you keep in bottom gear and don't take it too fast," Alec said, addressing her over his shoulder as he led the way into the caravan with one of his maddening casual, half-amused, half-impatient glances as if the information was so damned obvious it really didn't need stating.

She guessed then that the omission to mention the ford in his letter had been deliberate. He had wanted her to face it without any warning as some kind of stupid test. Perhaps he had even hoped that the car might have broken down in the middle although she admitted that this was probably unfair. But with Alec, one could never be sure.

She felt her frustration harden into a feeling very like hatred.

"Go out and play, Simon," she said. "I want to talk to Daddy on my own."

He was exploring the caravan with that infuriating curiosity of his which allowed him to leave nothing alone, bouncing on the bench seat, lifting the flap of the table experimentally, pulling aside the curtain to reveal a quite squalid little kitchen fitted with ply cupboards and a tiny cooker, its white enamel top blackened with patches of burnt-on grease.

"But what shall I do?" he demanded, facing her, his mouth gone square, which told her he was close to tears. She understood for the first time the effect all of it was having on him and nearly wept herself.

How dare Alec do this to him? How bloody dare he?

She was pleased to see that Alec himself realised Simon's unhappiness, for his face suddenly went taut.

"There's a stream just over there on the other side of the field," he said in his kind voice, the one he only ever seemed to use now for Simon. "Why don't you go out and have a look at it? I'll come and join you in about a quarter of an hour."

As soon as Simon had gone, clumping down the caravan steps and walking dispiritedly away across the field, his hands in his blazer pockets, Joanna let her anger break.

"Do you realise what this is doing to him?" she demanded furiously.

"I'm sorry," Alec replied. He wouldn't look at her but stood watching Simon through the open doorway.

Her anger seemed to release a new awareness in her so that she was able to study her husband as if he were someone she had just met, noticing with a sense of shock how much he had aged and how neglected he appeared. His hair needed cutting. It was so long at the back that it touched the collar of the open-necked plaid shirt he was wearing. He had on his old trousers, the ones he used to wear at home when he cleaned the car, the torn back pocket, which she had meant to mend but had never got round to doing, still hanging down at one side.

The sight of it seemed to feed her anger and her despair.

"Sorry?" she repeated, aware that her voice had gone shrill. "That's typical of you! So damned glib! You walk out and expect—"

"Look, Joanna," he said swinging round to face her. "If you've come here hoping for a row, then you won't get one. The marriage is over. That's final as far as I'm concerned. All that's left to talk about is what arrangements we can come to. I'm sorry about Simon. I mean that quite genuinely. But I can't go on living with you and trying to keep up the pretence of being happy for his sake. He's young; he'll get over it eventually. I told you in the letter that I wanted a divorce and I'm prepared to make the best settlement I can so that you and Simon won't be too badly off; at least financially. You can have the house and the furniture. All I shall want to take is my books—"

"But how on earth am I expected to keep the house going and pay for Simon's school fees?" she interrupted. It was the greatest of her practical worries. After Alec had left, she had gone through the accounts, which he had always dealt with, totting up the amounts—the insurance, payments to BUPA, the gas, telephone and electricity bills and these didn't include the mortgage or the weekly housekeeping expenses—and had been appalled at the total.

"Then sell the damned place!" he said impatiently. "Get something smaller that you can afford. For God's sake, Joanna, why do you need four bedrooms and a bloody utility room? It's absurd! I told you that when we bought the place but you insisted on having it."

"Absurd! It was you who were absurd, wanting to buy that semiderelict farmhouse in the middle of nowhere, miles from the shops and Simon's prep school . . ."

It was an old quarrel which she thought she had won but which she saw now had been more important to him than she had realised.

He said with a shrugging, weary gesture, "It doesn't matter anymore. That's water under the bridge. We have to face the facts as they are now. If you can't afford to keep the house, then buy something you can or get a job!"

"A job!" It was so outrageous that she laughed.

"Why not?" he demanded. "You're a qualified secretary. You were earning good money before we married."

"But that was fifteen years ago! Things have changed since then. It's all word processors and computers now."

"Then retrain," he told her. "Take a bloody course. You're not incapable and you're the one who's so keen on women's lib."

He turned away in so dismissive a manner that she wanted to hit out at him with her fists. But she was too frightened of him to risk it, not knowing how this new Alec, hard, seedy, utterly unapproachable, would react.

Instead, she said, "You're mad, you know. George Hetherington thinks so, throwing over your job like that. He came to see me the other evening. He said you could have been on the board when Mr. Tolby retires."

That, too, was something of an exaggeration. George Hetherington hadn't actually promised a directorship; he had only said it was likely. As for Alec's madness, he had not expressed that opinion quite so forcibly, merely murmuring vaguely that Alec might be passing through an emotional crisis which some men experienced at certain stages in their lives.

"Probably hormones," he had added in an embarrassed manner.

But none of it had any effect on Alec except to amuse him.

"Really? How typical of old George! But I don't give a damn about his opinion or his directorship. As far as I'm concerned, he can stuff both of them. Can't you understand, Joanna, I've loathed that job for the past five years? Look, now you're here, let's sit down and go over the whole thing sensibly. Sit down!" he repeated sharply, as she hesitated.

As she sat down on the bench seat, she was aware of a perfume lingering on the cushions which was released from the flowered fabric. It was a cheap, musky scent which she remembered catching a trace of from that woman who had passed her in the lane.

Suddenly the whole situation was clear to her. In fact, she was surprised that she hadn't seen it before. The woman had been coming from the caravan. There was nowhere else she could have been; no other house or cottage was in sight. And that fact accounted for her interest in their own visit and the smile and glance she had given to Joanna.

The damned nerve! And here was Alec, so obviously doubly in the wrong now, talking about her selling the house and finding a job when all the time it was he who was to blame by walking out with no real reason and then picking up with that awful, common, blond woman.

". . . I'll get a local solicitor to act for me in Studham where I'm going to be living. That way you can still keep on Blakely, who handled the house. I don't know how long the divorce will take—"

"Divorce?" She began to concentrate on what he was saying. The realisation about the woman had cleared her mind, leaving it quite cold and hard. Ten minutes ago she might have blurted out what she knew in anger. Now, listening to him talking to her in that infuriating reasonable tone of voice, the one she'd heard him use to his secretary on occasions, she knew she must keep that particular piece of information to herself. "On what grounds?"

"For God's sake, Joanna, don't you ever listen to what's said to you? You can use my desertion if you like or the irrevocable breakdown of the marriage."

"And supposing I don't want to?"

"It won't make any difference. If you don't start proceedings, then I shall. The marriage is over. I shan't be coming back. As for Simon's school fees—"

"It doesn't matter," she said stiffly. "I'll manage somehow."

"I'm sorry. I'll try to help out with those if I can. As I said in the letter, I won't make any claims on the house. That's yours outright. It should be worth about eighty thousand pounds, if not more. I'm cashing in my life insurance policy, which will get me started. I'll make the other policy, the endowment, over to you, although you'll have to keep up the payments on it. In addition, there's about two thousand in the building society. I'm sorry it's not more but we seemed to spend most of what I earned. Maintenance for Simon will have to be worked out when I know how much I'll be earning from the shop but it probably won't be much, at least to begin with." Seeing her expression, he broke off to repeat, "I'm sorry, Joanna."

"Yes," she said. There seemed nothing else to add. She got up, brushing her sleeve where it had come into contact with the cheap scent on the cushions.

He got up as well, looking suddenly awkward.

"I'll go and talk to Simon. Do you want to stay here? You could make yourself some tea if you like."

As he indicated the kitchen with its filthy stove, she shook her head.

"No, thank you. Tell Simon I'll be waiting in the car."

She walked to the door, Alec following her. He seemed disconcerted by her new, abrupt manner.

"About access to Simon," he began.

"I'll have to speak to my solicitor about that," she replied, turning away towards the gate.

"Joanna, please don't make any difficulties over Simon!" he called out after her.

Ignoring him, she shut the gate behind her and set off down the lane.

Simon was crouching by the side of the stream, hands on the knees of his grey school-uniform trousers to keep his balance.

Seen like this from the back, he looked small and vulnerable, especially about the nape of his neck, which still had that exposed, fragile nakedness of a much younger child.

Alec said, "Hello, there," and squatted down beside him.

For several seconds they remained in silence, watching the water swirling past, forming miniature eddies and rapids. A twig came into sight, lodged against a stone and then, caught once more in the torrent, hurtled out of sight towards the ford.

Alec had been on the point of saying, "Do you remember playing Pooh sticks when we were on holiday in Cornwall?" But before he could speak, Simon said without turning his head, "Are you really not coming home anymore?"

"No, Simon."

It was better that he learn the truth.

The boy looked up, his eyes troubled.

"Not ever?"

"No."

"But where will you live? Not in that caravan?"

"No. I'm going to move to Studham. I'm buying, or rather leasing, a shop there—a bookshop. You'll be able to come and visit me."

"Will I? But how will I get there?"

"I don't know yet. Perhaps on the bus. There must be a bus. Or perhaps I can come and pick you up from home."

"Mummy says we may have to leave the house. She cried when she told me. If we do, I'll have to give up my bedroom, won't I?"

Alec knew what was going on in his son's mind as clearly as if the thoughts had been printed on his face. Only last year, he had redecorated the boy's bedroom, fitting it up with shelves and a work-top so that he could do his model-making without disorganising the sitting-room. Funnily enough, he minded as much about its potential loss as Simon himself. Messing about with wood and screws in its construction, he had felt genuinely happy for the first time in years. But he was angered, too, by what he saw as Joanna's manipulation of the situation, wondering if the tears had been genuine or contrived.

He said, "I don't know what will happen about the house, Simon. Nothing's been decided yet. But if it's sold, you'll have another bedroom somewhere else."

Harsh though it was, that truth would also have to be faced, but as he spoke, he saw Simon's face close over and he knew that he had already begun to lose his son. He had been a fool not to see the inevitability of it when he had decided to walk out. It was a process which, once started, could never be reversed, like decay. Each time they met from now on, the child would be a little further distanced from him. The thought of it filled him with an overwhelming sadness and a nostalgia for the past he had shared with his son—of games of football on the lawn and of teaching him to swim, his hand cupped under Simon's chin.

Simon stood up. "I think I ought to go back now. Mummy's waiting for me, I expect."

"Yes," Alec replied. "She's gone to the car."

They started back in silence across the field which Alec found too painful to maintain.

"How's school?" he asked, aware that it would have been better to say nothing. His voice was much too bright and interested.

"All right," the boy replied. There was a grudging air about him and they both fell silent again.

But when they parted by the steps of the caravan, neither quite certain how the farewell should be conducted, it was Simon who suddenly seized his father round the waist and buried his face in his shirt before, breaking free, he ran off towards the gate without looking back.

Joanna watched him come clattering across the footbridge towards where she was standing by the car. Returning to it from the caravan, she had at first been reduced to tears at the sight of it, frightened at the thought of having to drive it away. But, waiting for Simon to come back, her tears had dried, although she could still feel the skin under her eyes taut and sore. She was aware now of a new hardness inside her. She was damned if she'd let herself be beaten!

As Simon approached, she got into the driving seat and wound down the window.

"You'll have to help me, Simon," she told him. "I don't want to tip the car over into the ditch."

His face, which had been sullen and closed, took on a more interested expression.

"Do you want me to wave you out?" he asked.

"Please. Watch the wheels on the far side."

As he walked back a few feet to take up his position, she called out, "What did Daddy say?"

"Nothing," he replied, his back towards her.

She started the engine. He would probably tell her later. Knowing him, she guessed he would let it slip out when he was less defensive as a casual remark, spoken before he knew what he was saying.

This realisation, like the one regarding the woman, gave her an unexpected sense of power. It was a new game, the rules of which she was learning faster than she had thought herself capable.

As the car edged forwards and the wheels bumped down onto the road, this feeling of triumph increased.

"Well done, Mummy!" Simon was saying, using one of Alec's expressions as he scrambled into the passenger seat beside her. "You made it!"

She gave him a smile.

Well done indeed!

CHAPTER THREE

Madge heard the front door close as Gordon returned from his house-calls just as the kettle came to the boil. The timing pleased her. It proved that they—the fates, the gods, call them what you like—were on her side after all, although the encounter with Alec Lawson still rankled.

Carrying the tea-tray through to the drawing-room, she found Gordon stooping down towards the fire which she had lit against the damp afternoon, still wearing his overcoat, rubbing his hands and holding them out to the blaze.

He looked flushed and rumpled as he always did after he had made his afternoon visits, a changed image of him which she generally preferred, but today, for some irrational reason, it exasperated her.

A big man, he seemed suddenly too large for the room. She wanted his indoor self, calm, relaxed, unemotional; not this tall, overcoated figure, smelling of the open air and still charged up with the energy of driving from one patient to the other in a large and scattered practice.

"Good to see a fire," he commented, adding almost immediately, "Any messages while I was out?"

"They'll be on the answering machine," she replied.

"Oh, I see. So you were out this afternoon?"

He didn't really expect a full explanation. He never did, which was another of his qualities she found mildly annoying. His lack of curiosity about her life, while well meant, had the effect sometimes of making it seem uninteresting even to herself.

"I went for a walk," she said. She could have left it there but she felt the need to offer some reason, more for her own sake than for his. As it was obviously better not to use the excuse of the electricity bill, still propped up on the mantelpiece, she added, "I wanted some fresh air." After a pause in which she watched Gordon drinking his tea, she continued, "I met Alec Lawson while I was out."

The statement was vague enough to imply nothing more than an accidental encounter in the village.

"Alec Lawson?" Gordon asked. "Do I know the name?"

"I have told you about him," Madge replied. "He's moved into Macey's caravan, the one that's parked in the field near the ford. He was telling me he's opening a bookshop in Studham."

"I shouldn't have thought he'd have much success there," Gordon commented, holding out his cup to be refilled but shaking his head at the proffered ginger cake which Madge had bought in the shop on her way home.

"Why not?" she asked.

She was of the same opinion. After all, there was already one bookshop in Studham, Luckham's, and the town was hardly large enough to support two. But Gordon's sweeping statement annoyed her.

It had the desired effect. He looked at her directly for the first time.

"I don't know, Madge. Perhaps he will. I haven't met the man. He may be the world's best businessman and I'm doing him an injustice."

"He's rather arrogant."

As she said it, Madge felt oddly appeased, as if the whole point of the conversation had now been reached.

But Gordon, who had finished his second cup of tea and was getting to his feet, merely replied, "In that case, he may make a huge success of it. Either way, good luck to him."

"I met someone else while I was out," Madge continued, beginning to pile up the tray with the used china. "Stella Franklin, as she used to be."

That piece of information really interested him as Madge knew it would. Stella's miscarriage following so soon after Mr. Franklin's death had meant that the family had taken up a great deal of Gordon's professional care at the time.

"Stella? What's she doing back in the village? Visiting her mother?"

"I rather doubt that. You know Stella. She had that defiant look about her. I had the feeling she may have left her husband." Madge couldn't resist adding, "Anyway, it seems to be Alec Lawson she's visiting."

"You shouldn't listen to gossip," Gordon told her.

"Sometimes it's very difficult not to, as you very well know yourself," Madge retorted, stung by his attitude, for he had frequently passed on to her little titbits of local news he had picked up on his rounds, usually with an amused air although sometimes with the more serious intention of informing her, in one of her more public roles as school governor or Guild chairwoman, of some cause for her concern.

At the same time, she was pleased that he had assumed that she had been told about Stella and Alec Lawson in the village, not witnessed the evidence of the relationship herself. It saved a lot of explanation.

Gordon was saying, "I thought she'd settle down once she was married. Oh, well. I'll go and see what's on that damned machine."

He held the door open for her as she carried the tray out.

Bartlett had been for his money. As soon as she entered the kitchen, Madge could see that the envelope that she had left on the window-sill above the sink had gone and his empty mug was standing on the draining-board.

Putting the tray down beside it, she went out to the garden to find him but he had already left. The shed door was shut and the bonfire was reduced to a few blackened twigs and a mound of white ash which the wind was blowing away.

Walking back along the path towards the house, she thought with amusement how, even if she had not known him, she might have been able to guess something of Bartlett's character simply by looking at the vegetable garden. It was neat with that slow, painstaking care he showed even when riding his bike, head bowed, as if struggling against a nonexistent wind, one foot pressing down on the pedal, the other fixed because of his lame leg. Perhaps because of this, she had never seen him free-wheel, not even down-hill. He merely slowed down by using his brakes, reducing it to the same rate of solemn progress.

It was because of this lack of imagination and verve that she had never allowed him to touch the flower borders. He would have staked and pruned and trimmed them into submission. Consequently, they burgeoned in a profusion of shrubs and roses and flowers, which she preferred.

Seeing the lines of seedling plants, each one pricked out exactly equidistant from the next, a little wooden peg marking the end of every row, she felt an exasperated compassion for the man.

Poor old Bartlett!

Unmarried, he had lived with his widowed mother until her death, a cantankerous old woman who had been the bane of Gordon's life with her constant complaints; so goodness knows what it had been like for Bartlett sharing the same house with her although he had put up with her with a dour, uncomplaining acceptance. He still occupied the same cottage near the church, unchanged since Mrs. Bartlett's time down to the chipped earthenware sink in the kitchen and the old-fashioned furniture.

Quite apart from his mother when she had been alive, Bartlett had another cross to bear. An accident on a tractor had broken his leg in three places, in consequence of which he had been forced to give up work on Sutton's farm. He'd been insured, of course, and had been awarded a lump sum in compensation as well as a pension which he supplemented by acting as a jobbing gardener to a few people in the village like herself who wanted his services, including the vicar and two or three of the wealthier farmers, whose interest in the land didn't extend to their own vegetable plots.

She wished she liked him better but she found him difficult to talk to. There was a melancholy air about him, understandable when one considered the circumstances of his life although even this didn't make her feel any warmer towards him.

He had a habit, too, of creeping about the place as if afraid of asserting himself which she found exasperating at times. His letting himself into the kitchen to leave his empty mug and collect his money was only one example of this. Anyone else would have called out to let her know he was there. But not Bartlett. He'd probably knocked but not loud enough to be heard because she had been in the drawing-room with Gordon.

She wondered what they'd been talking about and whether Bartlett might have been able to overhear but couldn't remember the conversation apart from her comments on Alec Lawson, which hardly mattered.

And then the silly man had crept off without a word when she had wanted to discuss with him the possibility of moving the strawberry bed to the other side of the garden where it would get more sun or, at least, lopping back some of the overhanging branches which were casting too much shade.

Now it would have to wait until she saw him the following week.

As soon as Stella turned out of Waterend Lane and crossed the road by the Goat, she saw her husband's car parked outside the house and almost went on past it. Then, shrugging, she pushed open the gate and walked up the path and round to the back door.

What else could she do? There was nowhere she could go to wait until he had left apart from the shop and she didn't fancy the thought of going in there and meeting the stares of the other women.

Besides, knowing Ken, he'd go on waiting until she did return. He never gave up easily.

Her mother must have seen her go past the front window because, by the time Stella reached the back door, she was in the kitchen, mouthing through the glass, "Ken's here," and jerking her head in the direction of the living-room.

Stella mouthed back, "I know," at the same time pulling a face to show her distaste.

"He turned up five minutes ago," Mrs. Franklin added in a massive undertone as Stella let herself into the kitchen.

"So what?" she replied in her normal voice.

No one, not even Ken, was going to frighten her into whispering in her own home.

He was standing by the fireplace, wearing his oil-stained overalls, so he must have knocked off work early and come straight from Hubbard's garage.

"What are you doing here?" Stella asked him.

"I want to see you, Stell," he replied.

"You've seen me," she said dismissively, taking off her jacket and hanging it up on the peg behind the front door, which opened directly into the garden. Sitting down on one of the chairs by the fire, she began poking the coals into a blaze, asserting her right to be there and leaving him standing.

She could tell by his expression that he was controlling his temper with difficulty. That taut, white look and the sharp edge to his jaw always meant trouble.

Well, she didn't care. If he started anything, she'd bloody well give him a mouthful in return. And if he laid a finger on her, she'd do what she'd threatened and charge him with assault. So let him put that in his pipe.

All the same, she couldn't help feeling sorry for him. He looked so damned awkward standing there, like some big kid who'd had his bag of sweets taken off him and didn't know whether to cry or lash out with his fists.

She said impatiently, "Oh, for God's sake, sit down now you're here," adding, as he took the chair opposite her, looking pleased as if the invitation were a sign of her capitulation, "You're wasting your time though. I'm not coming back."

He leaned forward and tried to touch her knee which she twitched away out of his reach.

"I'm sorry I hit you, Stell. I didn't mean it. I lost my temper."

"That's no excuse. You're always bloody losing your temper. No one's going to knock me about."

"It won't happen again, promise."

"No, it won't," she said sharply, " 'cos I shan't be there to let it."

"You mean that? You're not coming back?"

He looked so surprised that she nearly burst out laughing.

"What else do you want me to do? Put it in writing for you? You can't say I didn't warn you. 'You touch me again,' I told you, 'and I'll walk out.' Which I did. Which is why I'm here now."

Mrs. Franklin came into the room at this moment, carrying a tray of tea-things which she put down, grim-mouthed, on the table under the window.

Ken turned to her in appeal.

"You talk to her."

"I'm not interfering," Mrs. Franklin replied, rattling the cups onto their saucers. "It's between you and her. All I'll say is this: her father never so much as raised his voice to me in all the forty-five years we was married. And I got my money regular."

"Well, she won't get a penny out of me!" Ken retorted, his own voice getting louder.

"I don't want your bloody money," Stella replied, looking pleased at having provoked him. "I can pay my own way, ta very much."

"Doing what?" Ken asked with a sneer.

"That's enough of that!" Mrs. Franklin cried, the colour high in her face. "If you can't be civil, then you're not welcome in my house."

To emphasise her point, she banged down the jug, sending a little white spurt of milk over the tray, and, marching over to the door, threw it open.

Ken went, pushing his chair back against the wall and slamming the door so violently behind him that the window rattled. A passer-by stopped to stare as, flinging himself into his car, he drove off at speed down the road.

"Bloody maniac!" Stella commented but not without a certain satisfaction in her voice.

Mrs. Franklin sat down hurriedly to hide the trembling in her legs.

"That was Mrs. Armitage outside. It'll be all over the village by tomorrow."

"Who cares?" Stella said carelessly.

"I do," her mother retorted. "It's me who has to live here. Honestly, Stella, I don't know where you get your ideas from. Not from me nor your dad neither. He hated any unpleasantness. You seem to go out of your way to look for it."

"No I don't."

"You do with Ken. You ought to try and butter him up a bit more."

"Butter him up!" Stella repeated the phrase with derisive emphasis.

"Well, you know what I mean," Mrs. Franklin replied, looking flustered. "Give in to him sometimes; make him feel he's the boss. You know how touchy he is and no man likes to be put down, especially by a woman."

"And what about him putting me down?" Stella demanded. " 'Fetch this. Do that. Where's my bloody tea?' I'm not going to be talked to like that by anybody."

"You always did stand up for yourself, even at school," Mrs. Franklin admitted, half admiringly, half in despair. "I remember the fuss there was about that needlework teacher and me having to go up there to see the headmistress."

"If you don't look out for yourself, no one else will," Stella said.

"I don't know where you get it from," Mrs. Franklin repeated helplessly. "And your language, Stella. You really ought to watch that. It's got awful since you've been working in that pub. Your dad wouldn't have liked it." Encouraged by the contrite expression on her daughter's face, she continued, "Perhaps if you'd had the baby, things would've been different."

Stella, who had turned away from the window, paused in the act of lifting the teapot as if about to say something. Then, shrugging, she finished pouring two cups of tea which she carried over to the fire.

"Here," she said, handing one to her mother, "drink that, Mum, and have one of my ciggies to go with it." Bending down to light the cigarette for her, Stella added, "If I'd had the baby, where'd I be now? Even worse off. He'd've probably taken it out on the kid as well. As for me, I'd've had two mouths to feed. I'm better off on my own. Which reminds me; I haven't told you yet. I've got a job."

"What job?" Mrs. Franklin asked, puffing nervously at the cigarette.

"Barmaid over at the Goat. Fred Mitchell asked me if I'd like to work there this lunchtime when I dropped in for a drink. They've been getting a lot more casual trade and they're rushed off their feet. Eva can't cope like she used to. Anyway, I told him yes and I start there on Monday. So I don't need Ken, or anybody else, come to that, to look after me. I can pay my own way and take care of myself."

"I only hope to God you're right," Mrs. Franklin replied.

CHAPTER FOUR

On Friday evening at approximately five past seven, Stella left the house, calling out goodbye to her mother who was listening to "The Archers" on the radio while she did the ironing.

"Shan't be long, Mum. I'm going over to the Goat."

She had gone before Mrs. Franklin could call out in reply.

It had stopped raining and there was a watery moon shining, dodging in and out behind low clouds which threatened further rain. Big puddles still stood in the road, reflecting lighter patches of sky, and Stella picked her way round them as she walked the short distance to the Goat, where the curtains were drawn over the lighted windows and the lamp on the corner of the buildings shed a cone of brilliance onto the car-park, already half full of customers' vehicles.

The interior of the public house was warm and cheerful, a log fire burning at the far end of the bar by the tables with Eva's bits of brass hanging on the wall above it, catching the glow from the flames and reflecting it. The place looked festive and Christmassy.

Smiling, pleased to be there among the crowd and the noise, Stella nodded to several regulars she knew—Ted Macey, Jim and Doreen Saltmarsh, poor old Reg Bartlett sitting morosely by himself in a corner —as she pushed her way towards the counter where Eva, looking flustered, was pulling a pint for a man in a tweed hacking jacket, one of the casuals by the look of him, who was rattling off the rest of his order before she had time to finish getting his first.

Fred, looking hot and bothered himself, his face red and his shirt collar open, came to serve her.

"By God," he said, "I'll be glad when you start here on Monday."

"I'd offer to help you out now," Stella replied, "only I'm expecting to meet someone. Mr. Lawson not in yet?"

"Lawson? Oh, him that's got Macey's caravan. No, I haven't seen him this evening although he was in here at lunchtime. Perhaps he'll drop by later. What'll you have, Stella? The usual?"

"Ta," she said.

She stayed at the counter, drinking her gin and orange and watching the door but, although several more regulars arrived, Alec Lawson wasn't among them. One of the new arrivals, Frank Beamish, joined her at the bar, ordering a pint before turning to speak to her. She had gone out with him in the old days before she met Ken. He was married now with two kids but that didn't stop him from looking her up and down with the same leering smile, so he hadn't changed much.

"What you doing back here, Stella?" he asked, his eyes on the V-neck of her jumper. "Chucked the old man over?"

"Minding my own business, the same as you should be doing," she told him, adding sweetly, "How's Eileen and the kids?"

He took the hint, saying grudgingly, "Oh, all right, I suppose," before moving off to join his friends who were making up a darts four.

Seeing her glass was empty, Fred Mitchell came back to her.

"Want a refill?" he asked. "On the house this time."

"No, thanks," Stella said. She glanced at the clock behind the bar, Fred Mitchell following her eyes. The time was nearly twenty-five past seven. "I'll hang on until Mr. Lawson arrives. I promised to stand him a drink."

"He's usually in here by now, if he's coming. Perhaps he's forgotten," Fred Mitchell suggested.

As he spoke, Reg Bartlett got to his feet and came towards the bar, carrying his empty glass.

Stella crushed out the cigarette she had just lit and drew the edges of her jacket together.

"Perhaps he has," she agreed hurriedly. "I think I'll change my mind and walk up to the caravan to see him. He's got a message for me that's important. I'll drop in again on my way back and give you a hand behind the bar."

"See you later then," Mitchell called out as she turned away and began edging through the crowd towards the door, which swung shut behind her.

"Damn!" Gordon said, coming back into the drawing-room from having answered the telephone. He was struggling to put on his overcoat while holding his medical bag and a small white paper sack in which prescriptions were put.

"Who was it?" Madge asked.

"Mrs. Baxter. Her son's had another of his asthma attacks. I'd better get over there straightaway. I was saying 'damn' about this though." Putting down his bag, he held up the paper sack. "Ted Macey's prescription. He said he'd call for it on his way back from Studham later this morning. I've just found it in the dispensary. My fault entirely. Mrs. Locke did tell me he hadn't collected it. I meant to drop it off at his house while I was out on my afternoon rounds."

"Is it important?" Madge asked.

"He evidently doesn't think so; otherwise he'd've made an effort to pick it up himself. But you know Ted. He never takes that ulcer of his seriously until it starts playing him up. He probably felt better and thought he wouldn't be bothered."

"Then I don't see why you should," Madge said firmly. She felt Gordon was too soft with some of his patients.

"Oh, I don't know," he replied in the vague, harassed manner he always adopted when she was critical. "I suppose I could call there this evening on my way back from the Baxters'."

"But it'll take you miles out of your way," Madge pointed out. As he hesitated, torn between his sense of duty and the inconvenience of carrying it out, she made up his mind for him: "Give it to me. I'll take it."

"But why should you be put out?" Gordon asked.

"I could say the same for you," she replied. "But it'll be less of a nuisance for me. It'll only take me ten minutes to drive over to the Maceys'. Besides, I want to see Pam. I've been hoping to catch her in the village but I've missed her all week. I want her to help out with the teas at the Old Folks' socials on Wednesday afternoons. She said she would but, of course, that's as far as it's gone even though her own mother never misses a meeting. If I see her at home, I'll be able to pin her down to a definite date, especially if I've done the family a favour by delivering Ted's prescription." Going into the hall to fetch her coat, she continued, raising her voice so that Gordon could hear her through the open door, "Those Maceys! They contribute nothing to the village. I don't think Pam's ever offered me a thing for the Oxfam shop. As for

Ted, it wouldn't surprise me in the least if he isn't down at the Goat at this very minute."

"He'll be a fool if he is," Gordon replied as she came back into the room, her coat on, a scarf tucked inside its collar. "I've told him quite specifically that he must cut out any alcohol."

"You're wasting your time," Madge replied briskly, holding out her hand for the prescription. Putting it away in her handbag, she checked that she had her car-keys and her diary. "There!" she said, snapping the bag shut. "I'm ready. If you are as well, Gordon, we might as well leave together. Then I can lock up the house behind us both."

Ken Reeve banged on the front door of Mrs. Franklin's house. He knew someone was in. The lights were on and he could hear the telly, the volume of which was suddenly turned down.

"Stella!" he shouted. If she thought she was going to lie low, pretending she wasn't at home, then she had another think coming.

Mrs. Franklin opened the door a mere two inches and peered round the crack.

"She's not here, Ken," she said, "so it's no use you banging and shouting."

"Then where is she?" Ken demanded.

Mrs. Franklin hesitated. If she said she didn't know, the chances were that he'd sit outside the house in his car, which she could see parked at the gate, waiting for Stella to come home, and then start a row in the road in full view of the neighbours. It was better, perhaps, that they met in the Goat, where at least Fred Mitchell would chuck Ken out if he got too loud-mouthed, not that he probably would in front of the other customers. It seemed the lesser of two evils.

"She's gone over to the pub," Mrs. Franklin said, opening the door wider to call after him as he went striding off down the path. "And don't start any arguments over there, Ken. Mr. Mitchell won't stand for it."

He ignored her and set off across the road towards the Goat, not even bothering to get back in the car, which she had hoped he would do and clear off back to Studham.

She shut the door reluctantly.

There was nothing else she could do. Stella could stand up for herself but, all the same, Mrs. Franklin was concerned.

If only Stella had married someone decent, she thought, and settled down like the other two girls, who had never given her a day's worry. Sometimes she had the feeling that Stella attracted trouble to herself, almost as if she needed some drama going on to add a bit of excitement to her life.

As Fred Mitchell saw the door open and Ken Reeve come in, he moved down the bar so that he could serve him. That way, he could make it quite clear to him that he wasn't going to tolerate any nonsense before it started. And if Reeve wouldn't take the hint, then he'd ban the bugger. As he'd told Stella when they'd first fixed up for her to work behind the bar, he wasn't having Ken using his pub as a place to sort out his marital problems. It'd been bad enough before they were married, and he remembered one evening in particular when Ken had bawled her out in front of the other customers and she'd run outside in tears. It was because of that occasion that Stella had chucked him over but, like a fool, had married him after all when she found out the baby was on the way.

Women! he thought disgustedly. They never bloody learn.

Even so, he wasn't quite quick enough. Eva got to him first.

"Pint of bitter," Ken Reeve told her.

No bloody please, of course, Fred Mitchell noticed. The man looked edgy, too, tapping the corner of the pound note he was holding on the counter as Eva drew his beer and looking all round the bar to check who was there, noticing, of course, that Stella wasn't.

When Eva handed him his glass, he spoke again, but so mildly and reasonably that she was fooled.

"Stella not in tonight? Only her mum told me I'd find her in here."

And before Fred could stop her, Eva, the silly bitch, had said, "No; she left about ten minutes ago. She's gone to see Mr. Lawson up at the caravan."

"Get some of those glasses cleared," Fred Mitchell told her abruptly, at which, Eva, giving him a look, lifted the counter flap and began to make the rounds of the tables, collecting up the empties.

Fred took her place at the beer pumps, ostensibly emptying the trays under them and tipping the dregs into the sink but at the same time keeping a watch on the back of Ken Reeve's head. He had turned away as if interested in the darts players at the other end of the bar. But Mitchell wasn't fooled.

Reeve was knocking back the beer as fast as he could swallow it and then, without so much as a glance in Mitchell's direction, left his empty glass on the counter and walked towards the door, hands in pockets and trying to look so damned casual and unhurried that Mitchell almost followed him outside to warn him quietly against causing any trouble.

But before he could make a move, he saw Reg Bartlett get up and also head for the door so he decided against it. Having a quiet word with Ken on his own was one thing; doing it in front of a witness when all Reeve had done so far was to drink a pint of beer was another.

Besides, Eva chose that moment to come back, fingers of both hands thrust down into the dirty glasses, which she dumped in the sink, and began running water furiously over them and he took the opportunity to say to her in a low voice, "What the hell did you want to tell Ken Reeve where Stella's gone? Couldn't you see he's looking for trouble?"

Her sudden, startled, guilty look appeased him.

"Oh, God!" she said, putting a wet hand up to her mouth. "I just didn't think."

"Just watch it next time," he told her before sauntering out to the back store-room to bring in another crate of mixers.

Putting Eva in her place was almost as good as warning off Stella's husband.

Joanna parked the car in the yard behind the Goat and switched off the lights and the engine. Ahead of her, the back windows of the public house showed up as oblongs of brightness in its white-painted clapboard façade. A lamp, high up on the corner of the building, further illuminated the car-park, shining down on the roofs of the other vehicles already drawn up and on the puddles gleaming inkily in the asphalt. In the silence, the faint sound of voices and laughter came from the pub's interior. It comforted her.

"You'll be all right," she assured Simon. "Wait for me here. I shan't be long."

"Why can't I come with you?" Simon demanded. He was sunk low in the passenger's seat, sulking at having missed his favourite programme on the television but secretly excited by the change of routine, the sudden, unexpected evening excursion and the drive through the dark countryside. It was a let-down that it had ended here in a car-park with nothing to do except look at the other cars or a distant view of trees outlined against patches of clouds.

"Because I want to talk to Daddy on my own," Joanna told him.

It was a lie, a realisation which added to the mixture of tension and excitement which the journey had roused in her. The situation had taken on a conspiratorial quality which was pleasurable as well as dangerous and in which her own boldness in coming to a decision both elated and alarmed her.

Speaking to her solicitor that afternoon, she had expressed her suspicions regarding Alec and the woman she had seen in the lane and Blakely, a lawyer of the old school who still regarded adultery as the prime cause for divorce, had suggested to her that, if Alec's infidelity could be proved, the proceedings might be more straightforward.

"And possibly more advantageous to you, Mrs. Lawson," he had added, "although, of course, the final decision must be yours."

The idea had appealed to her. She felt that, by walking out on her, Alec had somehow put her subtly in the wrong, although quite where her fault lay in the breakdown of the marriage, she wasn't herself sure. But if it could be proved that Alec was having an affair with that woman, then the blame would rest entirely on his shoulders.

Proving it was the only difficulty. Mr. Blakely had offered her the name and telephone number of a private inquiry agent should she need his services but the expense had deterred her. Frightened by the thought of the bills coming in, she had already cancelled her sunbed treatment for the following week and gone round the house turning off any unnecessary lights.

The idea of driving out to Wynford and doing her own investigation had only occurred to her that evening and she had put on her coat and bustled Simon out to the car before she had time to change her mind, excited by the thought of taking positive action in a situation which, since Alec's departure, had dwindled down to a mere waiting on events.

Now, having arrived at the village, she wasn't sure what to do next. Quite clearly she couldn't go on sitting in the car-park of the Goat.

She gathered up her handbag and headscarf.

"Stay in the car and don't talk to anybody," she told Simon. "I shan't be long."

"How long?" he asked plaintively.

She glanced at her watch. It was just before ten to eight.

"I should be back in about half an hour."

"But that's ages."

Joanna got out of the car, bending down to look at him through the open door. He had on his hard-done-by look, quietly mutinous, the expression he assumed when he knew he wasn't going to get his own way. She hardened her heart, suddenly struck by the thought that bringing him up on her own wasn't going to be easy, especially as he grew older. Until that moment, she had seen herself and Simon sharing in adversity, both rejected by Alec, equally wronged. The idea that his loyalties were divided and that he might regard her as partly to blame for Alec's desertion came as a shock to her.

"Please, Simon, don't be difficult," she said.

He looked up at her over the lapels of his blazer, which had ridden up round his ears, but he wouldn't answer. After a moment, she shut the door on him and walked towards the car-park entrance, resisting the urge to pause and look back.

He'll be all right, she assured herself. No harm could come to him in so public and well-lit a place.

It was herself she was more concerned about. She had not thought to bring a torch with her and the lane did not appear to have any lamps, a realisation which only occurred to her as she set off along it. But as the lights from the public house illuminated the first stretch, she wasn't too worried on this account.

Besides, she told herself, the caravan couldn't be far. It had taken her only a few minutes to drive there.

She had no clear idea what she would do when she got to it. Listen outside for voices? It seemed an underhand way to behave, like being a spy, and she preferred not to consider it too clearly. She would finally decide what to do when she was actually there.

For the moment, it was enough that she was taking action rather than sitting about at home.

Encouraged by this thought and by her new-found boldness, Joanna began to walk quickly away from the Goat along Waterend Lane.

CHAPTER FIVE

Alec said, opening the caravan door, "Oh, it's you. Come in."

He tried to sound welcoming but the sight of Stella standing on the steps didn't exactly please him. He had been to an auction that afternoon at Bedleigh, where he had bought two lots of books, and he had planned to spend the evening sorting them out, pricing those he could resell. Stella's arrival, especially as the floor of the caravan was taken up with the boxes and their contents, was ill-timed.

"Forgive the mess," he added, not really meaning it, as he moved a pile of books off the cushioned seat to make room for her.

"I won't stop," she replied, sitting down all the same and crossing her legs as if she intended settling in for a talk. "Only I expected to see you down at the Goat this evening. Remember?"

"Oh, God!" This time he was genuinely contrite. "I'd forgotten. At least, I thought we'd arranged it for tomorrow evening, Saturday."

"It doesn't matter. I'll buy you that drink I promised you tomorrow then," she said, smiling, not at all put out, it seemed.

Joanna would have minded, Alec thought. She would have taken it as proof that he didn't care enough about her to remember the appointment.

"Let me give you a drink to make up for it. No, please," he insisted when she began to protest. "You've had to walk all this way to find me."

"Ten minutes up the lane!" she said derisively as if it really were nothing and to her it probably wasn't. It was only townees, or ex-townees like himself, who found a ten-minute walk along a dark country road at all out of the ordinary. As for himself, he usually drove down to the village.

He realised also as he strode over the piles of books to get to the kitchen why she was there and, as he found glasses and unscrewed the cap of the gin bottle, he called out round the edge of the dividing curtain, "I've booked an appointment for you at the solicitor's with Mr. Pickering for next Thursday. It was the only afternoon he was free at four o'clock. Will that suit you?"

He meant the gin and tonic he handed her as well as the appointment and she said, "Oh, thanks! That's lovely," meaning both.

"You know where to find the office?" he asked. "It's in Market Street on the left-hand side, just past the shoe shop."

"I'll find it," she assured him. "I'm ever so grateful." She paused to sip at her drink before adding, "Ken's been round to my mum's, asking me to go back to him. He isn't going to like it, me divorcing him."

"Then mention that to the solicitor when you see him on Thursday," Alec advised her. "If there's any trouble, Pickering can arrange a court order to stop your husband molesting you."

"Yes. Well." She didn't seem too sure of that and Alex almost offered to go with her to the solicitor's and then changed his mind. After all, he hardly knew her and it wasn't any of his business.

She changed the subject anyway, asking, as she bent down to examine the titles of the books which were nearest to her on the floor, "Are you going to sell these in your shop?" When he nodded, she read the words on the cover of the top one with an experimental air, as if testing them out. " 'Science in the Service of Industry.' Will people want to buy that?"

"They probably won't rush the doors to get their hands on it," he agreed, amused by her common sense and the absurdity of his own image.

She laughed with him, then added, "Well, I shouldn't want to read it. I like a book with a bit of love in it. If you can't promise me something with wedding bells at the end, I shan't bother."

"Wedding bells?" he asked with a derisive lift to his eyebrows. "Even after your experience with Ken?"

She took it in good part, smiling back at him.

"You know us women. We never give up hope of finding a tall, dark stranger and being happy ever after. Why a bookshop though? It isn't what you used to do for a living, is it?"

It was shrewd of her and he asked curiously, "Why do you say that?"

"I could tell when you came into the Swan that dinnertime and told me about the lease. You looked so pleased and excited."

"Did I?" He was surprised by her perception although he assumed that working behind a bar had given her a good knowledge of human nature. "Yes, I suppose I was. I used to work for a computer firm but I got bored with it." It was only an approximation of the truth but it would have to do. He had no intention of describing to her in detail the sense of frustration the job had roused in him, the feeling of being trapped so that there were days when he had wanted to smash the windows and let real light and air into his overheated, artificially lit office.

"But why a bookshop?" she persisted.

"Why not?" he said dismissively. "I like books. Over the years, I've collected up quite a lot. It seemed logical to try my hand at selling them for a change. So when the lease on the shop in Studham fell vacant, I thought I'd have a go."

He meant to treat the subject lightly, anxious not to let her see his enthusiasm a second time but, as he spoke, he felt his excitement rise and he wanted absurdly to share it with her.

"It's a former seed-merchant's in Brook Street, just off the town centre," he continued, "so it's in a good position. It needs a lot doing to it, which was why the lease was going cheap. I'll do most of the renovation myself to save on the costs although I'll enjoy it." Leaning across to the corner of the table, he opened the file and drew out a sheet of paper, explaining as he handed it to her, "These are just the rough plans. I shall have to draw up proper ones to scale once I've done the measuring. But they'll give you some idea of what I had in mind. There'll be pine shelves round the walls but the centre will be left free. I thought I'd get hold of an old table to stand there with some of the more interesting books laid out on display. I want it to look, you see, more like someone's library than a shop, with lots of plants about the place and a few lamps. Am I boring you?"

"No, of course not!" Stella protested. "I think it sounds super. I tell you what: when you open, I'll buy you one of them cheese plants—you know the sort, with holes in their leaves?—as a present and I'll be your first customer. When do you move in?"

"I signed the lease this morning," Alec said. He had deliberately kept this piece of news until the last, hugging it to himself, although he was pleased he had someone to share it with. He had mentioned it to no one else except the landlord of the Goat when he called in there for a celebratory drink on his way back from the solicitor's. Breaking through her exclamations of delight, which he found oddly embarrassing, he added, "But I shan't be able to open for another month. There's a lot to be done to the place; not just the shop but the rooms over it. So I'll stay on here until it's more or less ready."

"I'm ever so pleased," Stella repeated. She seemed to mean it genuinely. Putting down her empty glass, she glanced at her watch. "Thanks for the drink. I think I ought to be going. I've been here for ages and I'm keeping you from working."

"Why, what's the time?" he asked.

"Nearly eight o'clock. I told Fred Mitchell I'd drop by the Goat on my way back. They were ever so busy when I was in there earlier so I said I'd help him out behind the bar."

"I'll see you to the gate," Alec said, getting to his feet.

After the lighted interior of the caravan, the night seemed very dark. As they walked down the path, Alec was aware of the closeness of the trees in which the wind was keeping up a low persistent roar like heavy gunfire heard at a distance. The same tumult was visible in the sky, across which low banks of clouds were driven, constantly forming and re-forming. A few drops of rain fell, one hitting his cheek.

They paused at the gate, which he opened for her.

"So I'll see you at the Goat tomorrow evening?" Stella asked.

Alec hesitated. Although he liked her, he was beginning to regret having confided in her. It had been a mistake. He didn't want to encourage too close a relationship with her which could cause problems. Absurd though the idea was as far as he was concerned, he could imagine a time when Stella might start to consider him as a possible lover. Despite her air of independence, he guessed she was probably the type of woman who was not happy without a man in her life.

As he hesitated, he saw the headlights of a car come tipping over the brow of the hill from the direction of Macey's farm and, anxious not to be seen with her and become the subject of gossip in the village, he said hurriedly, "I'm not sure. I may be out tomorrow evening. Perhaps I'll see you another time." While not exactly rejecting her, the remark was vague enough to be noncommittal. As she turned to go, he added, putting out his hand, "Be careful on the verge. It's slippery."

His haste to get rid of her was wasted anyway for, as he spoke, the car drew almost level with them.

Stella was saying, "I'm all right." All the same, she stumbled, then laughed as she said, "Oh, hell!" before walking away, the sound of her high heels clipping smartly on the hard surface of the lane.

The car had gone by that time, disappearing round the corner towards the ford.

Stella, too, was out of sight within seconds, the high hedges cutting off any view of her retreating figure.

Alec returned to the caravan, aware as he entered of the lingering, musky odour of her scent, mingled with the smell of old books and leather bindings. He left the door open behind him to clear the air, the light from the interior shining out and glittering on the raindrops, which were falling more frequently now. He could hear them, too, pinging on the tin roof of the caravan.

It was only then that it occurred to him that he ought to have offered her a lift back to the village, but he shrugged and let it pass. By the time he had walked to where the car was parked in the far corner of the field, opened the five-barred gate and driven down the lane, she'd be almost at the Goat anyway. Besides, to go chasing after her might give her the wrong idea.

All the same, he felt a little guilty at his negligence. Had she been Joanna or one of her friends, the courtesy would have been automatic. Because she was only Stella, he hadn't felt the need, but the thought left him with the uncomfortable feeling that, despite his rejection of middle-class attitudes, there was a part of him which preserved, however subconsciously, that snobbery which he had so despised in his wife.

Madge parked the car in Macey's yard and, getting out, picked her way towards the house, thankful she was wearing her old shoes. The yard was a mess of mud and puddles.

The house wasn't much better, she noticed, as Pam Macey showed her through the hall into the sitting-room, littered with clothes and newspapers, Ted's boots lying drunkenly by the fireplace.

And yet it could have been a beautiful room. Low-ceilinged and well-proportioned, it cried out for simple white walls and a few choice pieces of antique furniture, not the jazzy wallpaper and modern three-piece suite which the Maceys had chosen, although, remembering the interior of the caravan, Madge was not surprised at its ugliness.

" 'Scuse the mess," Pam was saying, turning off the television set which was booming away in one corner and hastily grabbing up some of the scattered belongings. She was a small, harassed-looking woman with untidy, greying hair and an air of constant hurry and anxiety.

"I've brought Ted's prescription," Madge announced. "He forgot to pick it up from the surgery today and my husband thought he might need it."

Getting it out of her handbag, she took the opportunity to find her diary at the same time.

"That's ever so kind of you," Pam said. "Ted's out at the moment."

Madge let the remark pass without comment, although it seemed to confirm her suspicion that he was probably at the Goat. In that case, he'd almost certainly need the pills before the night was over.

"Can I make you some tea?" Pam offered.

"I won't stop now," Madge replied, "although while I'm here I'd like to arrange a Wednesday afternoon when you could help with the teas at the Old Folks' social." Pencil poised over the open diary, she looked at Pam and smiled encouragingly. "Shall we say the twenty-fourth? I've only got Mrs. Franklin down for that afternoon and she can't possibly manage on her own."

The moral blackmail worked as it usually did. Her social conscience stirred and lacking the courage to say no, Pam said reluctantly, "Oh, all right. I'll give a hand."

"Good. I'll phone you on the morning of the social to confirm it," Madge said.

And to remind her, she added to herself. Judging by the physical disorder in the room, she wouldn't be at all surprised if Pam's attitude to dates and appointments were equally disorganised.

While she was on the subject, it seemed worthwhile to run over the arrangements so that there would be no confusion when the time came.

". . . And you'll find clean tea-towels in the drawer by the sink," she concluded. "I'd be grateful if you left everything tidy before you go because there have been complaints in the past about the kitchen not being quite as clean as it should be which isn't very nice for other people. If you have any problems, ask Mrs. Franklin. She knows where everything's kept." As if it were a continuation of the same conversation, she added, "By the way, I saw Stella, Mrs. Franklin's daughter, the other day. It's so stupid of me but I can't remember her married name."

"Reeve," Pam said promptly. "Her husband's Ken Reeve from Studham; works in Hubbard's garage opposite Tenby's. I know because Ted used to go there to get his van serviced only there was some row about an oil leak not being fixed properly so he goes over to Latchingham now. She's left him," she added with apparent inconsequentiality.

"Stella, you mean?" Madge asked. Despite herself, she was interested. "But surely they've only been married about two years?"

"So her mum told me. I was talking to her in the shop the other day and she said Stella turned up on the bus last Friday with a suitcase and said she wasn't going back."

It was incredible, Madge thought, putting away her diary and shutting her handbag, how even someone like Pam Macey, living nearly a mile from the village, managed to hear the gossip almost as soon as it began circulating.

As Pam showed her to the door, Madge couldn't resist adding, "How's your tenant getting on? I hear he's opening a bookshop in Studham."

"Oh, he's all right." Pam sounded indifferent as if Alec Lawson wasn't of much interest to her. "I don't see a lot of him. He's out a good deal, going round the sales, buying up books. Ted's storing them for him in one of the sheds."

"So he'll be selling second-hand books?" Madge asked, pleased to have this point cleared up. Perhaps Studham could support two bookshops after all. The other one, Luckham's, stocked mainly paperbacks. If you wanted anything else, it always took weeks before the order arrived.

Crossing the yard and getting into the car, she waved to Pam, who half raised her hand in reply as if embarrassed at making the gesture. The next moment, she had gone back into the house and shut the door.

Madge turned into the lane. As she did so, the first drops of rain fell, starring the windscreen; not enough to make it worthwhile turning on the wipers. She drove slowly, conscious of the muddy surface and the ford at the bottom of the hill where she would have to drop down into bottom gear.

Ahead of her, on the right, she caught a glimpse of oblongs of yellowish light, partly obscured by the hedges, which were the windows of the caravan.

The next moment, the headlights picked out two figures standing by the gate. She had passed them almost as soon as she registered their presence and recognised them. One was Alec Lawson. The other was Stella Franklin. At least, Madge was almost certain it was her. The light shone on the blond hair of a woman who was carrying a satchel handbag over one shoulder. Madge saw it swing as the figure turned away.

It was only after she had passed them and she braked as she came to the dip in the road just before the ford that the significance of their postures struck her.

They had been quarrelling. Of that she was quite sure. Alec Lawson had been leaning forward, one hand raised, and Stella hadn't just been turning away. She had been on the point of losing her balance as if avoiding a blow.

So it would seem, Madge thought, that she was right after all. Alec Lawson and Stella had been having an affair although it seemed likely, from what she had just witnessed, that the relationship was already breaking up. Which didn't surprise her in the least.

Joanna walked quickly until she reached the S-bend in the lane. She realised that the ford could not be far away for she remembered having to change down to take the double corner when she had driven to the caravan with Simon two days earlier.

Besides, she had already been walking for what seemed like hours, although she knew that was an exaggeration. It couldn't be more than about ten minutes. All the same, the caravan was much further from the public house than she had imagined.

She was in real darkness now. Even the scattered lights of the village were invisible behind the high hedges and the trees which had crowded closer as the lane narrowed. She could see their branches threshing about against the sky. Everywhere there was movement and noise—the low moaning sound of the wind in the telephone wires, the creaking of branches, subdued rustlings in the hedges which could have been the stirring of dead grasses or the scuttlings of some unknown and unseen creatures.

Her resolution began to falter. She had been mad to come, she thought. Even if that woman was with Alec in the caravan, a divorce court wouldn't necessarily accept this as evidence of adultery. She would need better proof than that.

As she hesitated, it began to rain. She felt a few drops on her face. With them, the tumult in the trees seemed to intensify. The wind snatched at her silk scarf, whipping it about her head until it cracked like a sail and tearing open the skirts of her coat.

At the same moment, the headlights of a car appeared somewhere ahead of her, swooping down over the brow of a hill.

They should have reassured her. Instead, gripped by the thought of the unknown driver behind the lights, of the terror of rape at the roadside under the booming trees, Joanna turned and ran, thankful for the wind, which, now behind her, thrust her along in front of it as if a huge hand were pushing against her back, urging her forward towards the lights of the village.

"Time, *if* you please!" Fred Mitchell shouted.

It was a mere ritual. People were already making for the door while Eva was darting about, collecting up the glasses as soon as the last customers emptied them, dumping them down on the counter, from where Fred whisked them out of sight into the sink.

Ted Macey drained his glass and handed it to Eva as she dashed past.

"Ta," she said distractedly, her mind already on the ashtrays and wiping down the tables.

It was time to go before she returned with a damp cloth.

Ted Macey got to his feet, wincing as he did so. He had been aware of a dull ache in his guts all evening. Now, the effort of standing seemed to set it off and he felt the pain stab viciously.

Bloody ulcer, he thought. It's really giving me gyp tonight.

He knew he shouldn't have come out drinking. The doctor had warned him to cut out the beer but a couple of pints hadn't seemed too much at the time. Besides, if he didn't come down to the Goat of an evening, what the hell else was there to do? He wasn't going to sit at home with Pam, watching some stupid programme on the telly.

As he walked to the door, he remembered he hadn't any tablets left either. He'd meant to call in at the surgery on his way back from Studham to collect his prescription and then had forgotten in his hurry to get home and finish spraying the top field.

* ·

Hell!

"Good night, Ted!" Fred Mitchell was shouting.

He merely grunted in reply, not even bothering to turn his head.

"He's in a mood tonight," Eva commented, pausing in the act of wiping down the table where he had been sitting.

"Yeah," Fred agreed, shrugging as he swilled glasses. He was put out that Stella hadn't dropped by on her way back from seeing Lawson. Another pair of hands behind the bar would have been useful, especially when it came to clearing-up time. He assumed she'd changed her mind or stayed on at Lawson's longer than she'd intended.

It crossed his mind to wonder what exactly was the relationship between Lawson and Stella. They weren't having an affair, he thought; at least, not yet. All the same, it was a bit of an odd friendship, him obviously educated and Stella— Well, Stella was all right but not Lawson's type, he would have thought. Not that it was any of his business.

Yawning hugely, he upturned the last glass to drain and switched off the lights in the bar.

Outside, Ted Macey paused under the porch to turn up his collar against the rain, which was now falling steadily, before trudging round the corner of the building to the car-park, empty now except for his van.

Climbing carefully in behind the wheel, one hand on his stomach where the pain seemed to be concentrated, he started the engine and turned into Waterend Lane.

He drove slowly, peering ahead through the windscreen wipers to look out for and avoid the pot-holes, unevenly patched with tarmac.

After the S-bend, which he took in second gear, he didn't bother to pick up speed. The ford was just ahead of him and it wasn't worth changing up.

Seconds later, he saw the lights of the van glittering on the water.

And on something else.

He thought at first it was a sack of rubbish thrown into the ford.

"Bloody gyppoes!" he said out loud to himself. They were always dumping their junk anywhere.

Well, whatever it was, he'd have to shift it. It was blocking up the ford.

Grimacing, he got out of the van and approached the edge.

It was only then, when the water was lapping the toes of his shoes, that he was able to make out a tangle of wet blond hair, looking very pale against the dark stream, and a pair of legs spread-eagled in the graceless attitude of death.

CHAPTER SIX

Detective Chief Inspector Rudd of Chelmsford C.I.D. crouched at the edge of the ford, hands on knees to keep his balance, the collar of his mackintosh turned up against the rain.

It was a hell of a night to be called out on an investigation and a hell of a place for a death to have taken place. Lit by the headlamps of the police cars drawn up along the verge, the hedges and the surface of the stream glittered blackly, made darker still by the hundreds of raindrops gathered on the twigs and by the tiny, broken eddies in the water which caught the light and refracted it, causing the shadows behind this surface brightness to seem still more dense.

Behind him he could hear voices and the tramp of feet as men set up the arc lamps and manhandled a van out of the way which had been found blocking the lane a few feet from the ford, its battery flat. A car door slammed. Someone swore.

If he were aware of these distractions, Rudd showed no sign. Crouched immobile, like a small boy watching intently for minnows, he studied the body, which was lying face downwards in the water, turning his head to one side to get a better view of the features seen only in profile.

She was young; he could see that much. Blond hair was spread out, half submerged, lifting and falling a little as the ford ran past and over it, already tangled up with the debris, pieces of twig and grass, that a stream in full spring spate brings down with it. The hip-length fur fabric jacket she was wearing was sodden with water. Below it, legs clad in jeans were lying open and both arms were extended at roughly shoulder level. She looked as if she had been suspended in the act of falling, like one of those parachutists caught on film in the seconds before the canopy opens, stretched out on the air.

He sharpened his attention to the lower part of the body, picking up a detail which he had only partly registered and which he now confirmed. The heel of the right shoe was missing, broken off at the point where it met the sole. The other shoe with its spike heel was intact, the base of it worn down.

Not exactly suitable footwear for a country lane on a wet night, he thought distractedly.

"See that?" he said to Boyce.

The detective sergeant, who had been standing at Rudd's side, lowered his bulk cautiously into a squatting position and peered along the line of the chief inspector's finger. To Rudd's relief, he didn't make the obvious comment but, lifting his head, looked up at the wooden footbridge which ran along the left-hand side of the ford, before glancing down again at the sprawled figure. Even before he spoke, it was possible to guess what he was thinking. Rudd himself had just come to a similar conclusion.

"She could have caught her heel in the planking and lost her balance."

If she wasn't pushed, Rudd added silently.

He shouldn't even have thought it. Nothing had so far been discovered to suggest that the girl hadn't met her death accidentally, as Boyce had suggested.

And yet, there was a taint of violence about the scene which Rudd couldn't rationalise but which he could sense almost as if it had been an odour in the air.

He straightened up, hearing his knees crack as he did so.

"Get Bannister to make a search of that foot-bridge, Tom. I want a word with the local bobby."

As if on cue, the arc lamps were suddenly switched on, flooding the scene with a strong, white light and, momentarily blinded, Rudd stumbled to the edge of the lane, calling for Hadley, whom he couldn't now distinguish among the huddle of uniformed and plainclothes men who were waiting about for instructions.

Hadley stepped forward. He was a tall, fresh-faced young constable, keen to get on but lacking some basic quality which would probably bar his promotion. Rudd hadn't yet been able to define it although he suspected it was imagination. Hadley was solid, dependable, responsible; that was all.

It was evident in his answer to the chief inspector's first question, "Who is she?"

"Stella Reeve, sir."

Just the one fact which told him, Rudd thought sourly, damn all.

"Go on," he said.

Hadley seemed at a loss.

"I don't know what else you want to know, sir."

"The lot, man," Rudd told him. "Come on. You live in the place. You must know something about her. What's the gossip?"

"Gossip?" Hadley sounded surprised. "You mean what people have been saying about her?"

"Exactly. How long have you been stationed here?"

"Three years, sir."

"Then you must have heard something. So out with it."

"Well, sir, she was married about two years ago to a chap called Ken Reeve; a bit of a tearaway from Studham. I don't know how they met but anyway there was a quarrel and the wedding was called off. Then she found she was pregnant so it was on again—a registry-office do in Studham. After that, they moved in with Stella's mother, Mrs. Franklin, for a couple of months while they were waiting for a council place in Studham. Ken Reeve works there in a garage, Hubbard's. But shortly before they moved, she lost the baby. There was a lot of talk at the time, although it was Mrs. Franklin most people felt sorry for. You see, her husband had died only six months before all this happened and they felt if anyone needed sympathy it was her. Things couldn't have worked out between Stella and her husband, though, because she turned up in the village about a week ago and moved back in with her mother."

"Quarrelled with her husband?" Rudd suggested.

"Could be," Hadley agreed. "Like I said, he's a bit of a tearaway; tends to throw his weight about, especially when he's had a few jars."

"And Stella Reeve? What's she like?" Rudd asked, indicating the body, now brilliantly lit by the arc lamps which had bleached out her hair and darkened the colour of her clothes so that she looked like a black-and-white flash photograph permanently fixed at the moment of exposure, the water dramatically highlighted, chopped into ebony-and-silver stars and ribbons of shifting light and shadow.

Hadley hesitated as if choosing what to say.

"Worked as a barmaid at the Swan in Studham," he replied at last, "but don't get me wrong. Some people couldn't see further than what she looked like—blond hair and tight jeans; you know the sort of thing. But there was more to Stella Reeve than that."

"Such as?" Rudd suggested as Hadley seemed at a loss for words.

"Difficult to explain, sir. She was open; she'd say what she meant but she was never unpleasant with it, at least not with me. She was good-hearted, too, provided you went half way to meet her . . ." He broke off, paused and then tried again. "Let me put it this way, sir. Being the local bobby, I find people tend to treat me as if I'm different. Know what I mean? If I drop in at the Goat for a drink when I'm off duty or call in at the shop, people stop talking for a moment and then make an effort to include me. Stella wasn't like that. She always spoke to me as *me*, if you get my meaning. I liked that."

"I know exactly what you mean," Rudd replied. He meant it sincerely, too; not as a mere conversational gambit. Such frankness was rare. He himself had encountered it only occasionally, most importantly in Marion Greave, a woman doctor who had acted as locum when Pardoe, the police surgeon, had been on leave. She, too, possessed that gift of seeing people as individuals, which was one of the reasons why he had fallen in love with her, however ridiculous it had seemed at the time for a middle-aged policeman like himself to behave. Short, stocky, with the bluff features of a farmer, he hadn't thought of himself in the role of lover for years. Nor had he been willing to commit himself. A bachelor, cared for by his widowed sister, he had been content with his life, which had assumed a comfortable routine he was not willing to disrupt. Selfish, perhaps; but his uncertainty had also been compounded of a sense of his own inadequacy in any deep or lasting relationship and he wasn't prepared to settle for less. The irony was that, when he had finally found the courage to declare his feelings, Marion had rejected him for precisely the same reasons.

They still saw each other occasionally—as friends, although, on his part, he still felt that uncomfortable but now familiar lurch of his heart whenever he met her. He had learnt to live with it, accepting it with a patient and even good-humoured stoicism of which, two years ago when he had first fallen in love with her, he wouldn't have imagined he was capable.

Listening to Hadley's description of Stella Reeve and turning to look at the body lying face down in the dazzling black-and-silver water, he felt drawn to the dead woman in a manner in which, as a professional policeman, he had no right to respond. Objectivity was everything in an investigation. All the same, he was touched by the sight of the wet, blond hair, the cheap fur fabric jacket, the ridiculously unsuitable high-heeled shoes.

As if to emphasise the connection with Marion, Pardoe chose that moment to arrive, parking his car behind the other vehicles drawn up along the lane and stumping bad-temperedly towards them, bowed against the rain, clutching his medical bag and a pair of wellington boots.

His first remark, however, removed any sentimental aura which the scene might have held for the chief inspector. Small, sandy, irascible, Pardoe was not the type to waste time, especially late on a wet Friday night when he might have been home in bed. Nodding briefly to Rudd to acknowledge his presence, he turned to McCullum, who had been photographing the body and its surroundings.

"Finished with it?" he snapped, and as the tall, laconic Scotsman nodded and began picking up his equipment, ready to withdraw, Pardoe changed into his wellingtons, one hand on the shoulder of a young uniformed constable to steady himself, before wading into the water, remarking to no one in particular, "God, what a place to choose!"

"Who found her?" Rudd asked Hadley, getting back to his own part of the investigation.

"Ted Macey, sir. That was his van parked in front of the ford. It seems he was in the Goat until closing time and found the body on his way home. He lives on a farm about a quarter of a mile further up the lane, just over the brow of the hill. He phoned me from home."

"So he used the bridge?" Rudd asked.

"Well, yes, sir, I suppose he must have done. There's no other way of getting across the ford on foot unless you wade through it, and the water's all of fourteen inches deep."

"Damn!" Rudd said softly. If, as seemed likely, the dead girl had been crossing the bridge just before she met her death, valuable evidence might have been destroyed, a point which Hadley seemed aware of, for he said, "Sorry, sir," in a subdued voice, as if it were all his fault.

But not quite everything had been lost for, as Pardoe walked into the water and bent down over the body, Bannister called out from the foot-bridge that he had found something.

Indicating that he would join him shortly, Rudd turned back to Hadley.

"Is that the lot?" he asked.

"Not quite, sir. Perhaps I ought to add that I had a few words with Mr. Lawson while I was waiting for you to arrive. It seems he heard my car and noticed my headlamps and Ted's in the lane; Macey had forgotten to turn his off. So Lawson came down to the other side of the ford to see what was up. No," he put in quickly as the chief inspector seemed about to interrupt, "I told him not to get too close. But he said Stella Reeve had called on him this evening, leaving about eight o'clock and that he'd walked with her as far as his gate. He lives in a caravan about a hundred yards up the lane. He said that, as she left, a car passed them coming down the hill from Macey's farm but he doesn't know who was driving it. It couldn't have been Macey, sir. According to him, he left home about ten to seven to go down to the Goat and anyway, he drives a van, not a car."

"Lawson?" Rudd asked.

"Hasn't been in the village all that long," Hadley explained. "It seems he's setting up some shop or other in Studham and he's been renting Macey's caravan until he can take over the premises. I don't know much more about him."

Rudd nodded to Hadley, acknowledging the information and dismissing him at the same time before walking over to the foot-bridge, where Bannister was waiting for him.

The object which had excited the detective constable's attention was the heel broken off the dead woman's shoe. It was wedged in a gap between the planks, the tiny nails which had fastened it to the sole still in place.

Rudd squatted down over it. Judging by its position, it appeared that the girl had been walking across the bridge in the direction of the village when the heel had become caught.

What had happened afterwards was pure speculation, of course, but it was feasible, Rudd thought, getting to his feet and peering down over the handrail, that this was what had caused her to lose her balance and fall. From the slightly elevated position, for the bridge was about four feet above the ford, he could see her body lying almost directly below the place where the heel had been found, Pardoe still bent over her.

He called out to Boyce, who was setting up a search of the immediate area.

"Sergeant, I'd like you and McCullum up here. Get Wylie as well."
When the three men had joined him on the foot-bridge, he continued,
"I want a few shots of the heel and some general views from up here as
well. Wylie, you go over the handrail for prints and anything else you
can find. The wood's worn smooth so you may be lucky in picking up
something. After that, I want the whole of this area searched." Drawing Boyce to one side, he added in a lower voice, "I'll leave you in
charge here, Tom. I'm going to have a word with Macey, the man who
found the body, and also with a chap called Lawson. According to
Hadley, Lawson told him that Stella Reeve called on him earlier this
evening. I'll make the interviews short at this stage. If Pardoe's finished, I'll see to getting the body moved before I go."

"Right," Boyce replied before moving off to supervise the men.

Rudd clumped his way back along the bridge to the edge of the ford,
watching as Pardoe, with the help of two uniformed constables, turned
the body over onto its back, the doctor remarking over his shoulder to
the chief inspector, "See that?" with an air of satisfaction.

Rudd didn't bother to reply. The bruise on the girl's forehead was
too obvious to remark on. It stood out on the skin, bleached white by
the bright lights, as a livid stain, matching the red lipstick and the blue
eye-shadow on the closed lids like another, bizarre form of make-up.

Pardoe waded forward the few feet to join him.

"I'll need to have her on the slab to make a proper examination but
it looks obvious to me what happened. She fell off that bridge into the
water, struck her forehead on the hard surface and was knocked unconscious. Lying as she was face downwards, she'd've drowned."

As an explanation, it was perfectly feasible.

"No other marks on her apart from that bruise?" Rudd asked.

"Not that I can see," Pardoe replied. He looked sideways at the chief
inspector. "If you mean was she pushed, I can't answer that question;
not for the moment anyway. As for how long she's been in the water,
I'd say two or three hours at least. But that's only a guess at this stage.
You can move her when you're ready."

Her.

It was strange, Rudd thought, as Pardoe walked away to his car, that
the doctor had referred to the dead woman in this way and not by the

more impersonal "it" which he had used when he had first arrived. In death, Stella Reeve was still very feminine. Even the two constables who were lifting her body from the water and carrying her to the stretcher at the side of the lane seemed to treat her body more tenderly than usual, although that could have been his imagination.

The water ran from her clothes and hair, strands of which had washed across her face as they lifted her up, partly obscuring the bruise on her forehead. She might have been merely asleep or unconscious.

It was not a beautiful face. Studying it in the few seconds it lay there before the ambulance men closed the body bag and carried the stretcher away, Rudd could see a coarseness in the features. The mouth was a little too wide for real beauty, the angle of the jaw too heavy. But she had probably been attractive in life. All the face needed was animation.

He followed the stretcher as far as his own car, where he changed into the wellingtons he always kept in the boot. By the time he had put them on, the ambulance had left, its tail-lights disappearing down the road in the direction of the village.

Torch in hand, another piece of basic equipment he never travelled without, he walked back towards the brightly illuminated scene, curiously isolated and self-contained in the surrounding darkness, about which the figures of the men were moving as if taking part in some ritual, and, having had a last word with Boyce on the bridge, Rudd set off into the darkness which lay on the other side.

He could have taken the car. Now that the body had been moved, there was no reason why he shouldn't have driven through the ford. But, despite the rain, he preferred to walk. He was wet through anyway and, on foot, he could get a better idea of the layout of the place.

Once past the ford, the lane began to rise in a long incline, at the same time turning to the right so that by the time he noticed the lights of the caravan on his left, the ford was obscured by hedges although the arc lights indicated its position. Immediately in front of the caravan, the hedge was broke by a small, white-painted gate, the verge leading to it trampled into mud.

Rudd walked on. Lawson was evidently still up and could be interviewed later.

The lane continued to rise and, as he reached the top, Rudd paused to look back. The hill was steeper than he had thought. From the brow, he had a view across dark fields towards the village where a few lights still twinkled through the rain. He'd need to look at the place in daylight, he decided, and preferably with a large scale map, in order to get an idea of the details of the area.

The patch of brightness round the ford was still clearly visible, the lights shining upwards to illuminate the trees. He could even pick out the figures moving round it.

Lights were also visible behind him on the left. Macey, too, was up, it seemed.

The farmhouse stood a little way back from the road behind a yard surrounded by a huddle of outbuildings and low-roofed barns. Seen in the darkness and the rain, it had a crouched, neglected air about it. Water pattered down from a broken gutter above the front door, which was opened to him by a thin-faced, middle-aged man wearing a collarless shirt and an old V-necked sweater.

"You the police?" he demanded and when Rudd announced his name and produced his identification, the man replied, "And about bloody time, too. I've been sitting up, waiting for you to come."

Without any further comment, he started to lead the way down the dimly lit hall, clearly expecting the chief inspector to follow him and, with a shrug, Rudd walked behind him into the sitting-room.

"Mr. Macey?" he asked as he entered. It was the first opportunity the man had given him to establish his identity.

Macey nodded. He had taken up a position standing in front of an open fire which had smouldered away to mere ash. As he did not invite Rudd to sit down and as every chair was cluttered up with newspapers and clothes, the chief inspector also remained standing just inside the room. Macey evidently expected the interview to be over and done with in as short a time as possible.

The first part was, in fact, completed in a few minutes as Macey's statement regarding his own movements was straightforward.

He'd left the house about ten to seven, spent the evening in the Goat and discovered the body lying in the ford on his way back after closing time. No, he hadn't touched it, he added. He'd taken a look and then walked up to the house, where he'd phoned Hadley, the village copper.

"You'll find your van's been moved to a gateway further down the lane," Rudd put in. "The battery's flat, by the way. You left the lights on."

"Oh, bloody hell!" Macey said gloomily. This piece of information seemed to confirm his feeling that events weren't going his way that evening.

"You recognised her?" Rudd asked, ignoring Macey's comment.

"Course I did. It was Stella Franklin."

"Franklin?"

"Well, Reeve then. She married Ken Reeve from Studham but she's been known as Stella Franklin round here for years. She was in the Goat earlier this evening so I recognised her coat as soon as I saw it."

"What time was she in there?" Rudd asked. This was new information as far as he was concerned.

"I dunno. About ten past seven, I suppose. She got there not long after me. She didn't stay much above a quarter of an hour, long enough for a drink and a chat with Fred Mitchell—the landlord," Macey added quickly as Rudd seemed about to query Mitchell's identity. "According to him, she was due to start work behind the bar on Monday. Well, she won't now."

It was said with morose satisfaction as if Macey found his own problems diminished by the thought of someone else's.

"No," Rudd agreed. He paused momentarily before moving on to the next part of his inquiry. "A car was seen driving down the lane at roughly eight o'clock this evening. It could have come from this place. Do you know if there were any callers here this evening about that time?"

"Car?" Macey seemed nonplussed for a moment and then his face cleared. "Oh, yes. That'd be Mrs. Bingham, the doctor's wife. She dropped off a prescription for me I forgot to collect from the surgery."

"So she'd've spoken to Mrs. Macey as you were at the Goat?" Rudd asked.

All he had intended was to clear this point up but Macey seemed to think the chief inspector wanted confirmation for, pushing past him, he went out into the hall and shouted up the stairs, "Pam! Get down here! The police want to talk to you." Returning into the room, he added, "She'll tell you."

Mrs. Macey appeared a few minutes later, a dressing-gown clutched about her and her hair hastily combed. She looked tired and apprehensive, glancing nervously first at her husband and then at Rudd.

"It's all right, Mrs. Macey," Rudd assured her. "I only want to check the time Mrs. Bingham left here."

"It was just before eight o'clock," Mrs. Macey replied.

"You're sure?"

"Yes, because there was a serial I wanted to watch on the telly. As soon as she'd gone, I switched it on and the adverts were just finishing."

"So you didn't miss it," Rudd said cheerfully. "I understand she came to leave a prescription?"

"That's right. And to fix up for me to help out with the Old Folks' teas. It's no good you looking like that," she added, turning to her husband with an unexpected flash of spirit before looking at Rudd in appeal. "I couldn't refuse, could I? My mum goes every Wednesday. It's the least I could do. Besides, she wouldn't take no for an answer."

"Well, don't expect me to drive you down there," Macey commented.

"Don't you bother yourself," Mrs. Macey retorted. "I'll walk down to the village, the same as I always do."

"What time did Mrs. Bingham arrive?" Rudd asked the question more to interrupt what appeared to be the airing of a long-standing grievance between husband and wife than to establish the fact, although, if the case turned out to be a murder investigation, he might very well need to know the exact movements of any possible witnesses or suspects.

In the event, Mrs. Macey's answer wasn't helpful.

"I'm not sure. About half past seven, I think."

"Thank you, Mrs. Macey," Rudd replied.

"Can I go back to bed now?" She directed the appeal at both men and didn't finally leave the room until Rudd's nod was confirmed by a look from her husband.

"Is that the lot?" Macey demanded after she had gone.

"Just one other point," Rudd said. He tried to appear casual. Having been brought up himself in a village, he knew the capacity of local people to gossip about outsiders who were not part of the established community and he did not want to cause any problems for Lawson, whoever he was, by appearing too interested in him. But in the light of what Hadley had told him and as Macey appeared to be the man's landlord, the question would have to be asked. "I believe you rent a caravan to a Mr. Lawson."

As he had feared, Macey bristled up at once.

"Lawson? What's he got to do with it?"

"Nothing as far as I know, except the caravan's close to the ford," Rudd said blandly. It was better, he decided, to say nothing about Stella Reeve having visited Lawson that evening. Apart from not wishing to arouse Macey's suspicions further, Rudd had not yet confirmed this fact with Lawson himself.

"How did she die?" Macey countered. He had swung round to look directly at the chief inspector. "Was it an accident or murder?"

"I can't answer that," Rudd said in his official voice. "The investigation isn't finished yet."

"But you're making an investigation?"

"Yes, as in any case of sudden death." Rudd could almost read the thought on Macey's face: no smoke without fire. Well, even if it made things difficult for Lawson, he still had to press on with the inquiry. "About Mr. Lawson—"

"He moved into the caravan about a fortnight ago; saw it advertised in the local paper. He wanted somewhere temporary to live while he's sorting out about a shop he's going to lease in Studham, selling second-hand books, or so he told me. I've been storing some of them for him in one of the sheds. What you want to know about him for?"

"Thank you Mr. Macey," Rudd said pleasantly, brushing aside the question. "That's the lot for the time being. You won't object to making an official statement some time later, will you? I'll see myself out."

All the same, Macey followed him to the front door, watching as Rudd crossed the yard and set off down the lane towards the village.

CHAPTER SEVEN

Lawson was still up; probably waiting, like Macey, for the police to arrive to question him.

Rudd trod carefully across the muddy verge towards the gate, beyond which a concrete path, its surface cracked and broken, was almost as much as a hazard, although the light, shining out through the thin, flowered curtains drawn across the caravan windows, made it possible for him to see to pick his way.

Lawson opened the door immediately to his knock, waving him inside impatiently as Rudd hesitated on the step.

"Come in!"

"I'm a bit wet and muddy," Rudd confessed.

"That doesn't matter," Lawson said abruptly. "The place is in a mess anyway."

It was, too, although it was at least warm and dry. Books were piled everywhere and he had to step over them to get inside.

"Part of the stock," Lawson explained. "I've been sorting them out. Tea? Or would you prefer something stronger?"

"Tea would be fine," Rudd replied, loosening his wet raincoat and perching himself on the end of a long cushioned seat which Lawson had indicated with a wave of his hand.

"On duty, I suppose?" Lawson commented with an ironic inflection in his voice and, without waiting for a reply, disappeared into a curtained-off kitchen area where he began setting out two mugs on a tiny work surface.

"I'm Detective Chief Inspector Rudd, Chelmsford C.I.D., by the way," Rudd added, addressing Lawson's back.

Without bothering to turn round, Lawson replied, "And I'm Alec Lawson. Now we've got the introductions out of the way, I assume we'll get down to business."

"That's what I'm here for," Rudd replied equably.

He had met Lawson's type before. Educated, confident, still relatively young, for Lawson was only in his mid-thirties, he possessed an impatient and irreverent attitude to authority which could be offensive.

So be it, Rudd thought, planting his muddy wellingtons firmly side by side on the black-and-yellow carpet. He was here to do a job and he'd bloody well carry it out to the best of his ability whatever Lawson's response.

Lawson came back, carrying two mugs, one of which he handed to the chief inspector. Rudd took it gratefully, cradling his hands round its warm sides.

"I'm sorry about Stella," Lawson said unexpectedly. He had retreated with his own mug to an upright chair on the other side of the caravan and his thin, dark face looked suddenly older. "I liked her. She was what I suppose would be called 'a good sort.' "

Even so, he couldn't resist putting a wry emphasis on the last words as if deriding the compliment.

"You knew her?" Rudd asked.

"Not all that well. I met her first about ten days ago. She was working as a barmaid in the Swan in Studham. I called in there one lunchtime and we got talking. I'd been to see my solicitor about the lease of a shop and she seemed interested. I knew she came originally from this village but I was surprised all the same when I saw her in the Goat one evening a few days ago."

"Do you know why she came back here?"

"Yes, as a matter of fact I do. I suppose you'll want to hear the gossip?"

Again the sarcasm was evident in his voice.

"I need to find out about her," Rudd replied. "I can't carry out an investigation without asking questions, Mr. Lawson."

"Point taken," Alec Lawson conceded. "But I need to know something first myself. Was it an accident or not?"

"If you mean was she murdered, I'm not in a position yet to say," Rudd countered. If Lawson was so keen on a confrontation for whatever motive, then let him face the unpleasant word "murder" directly. "So far we're treating it as a suspicious death. Even so, I still have to ask questions in order to establish exactly how she died."

Lawson considered this comment in silence for a few moments and then appeared to come to a decision.

"All right. Stella told me that she'd left her husband and was thinking of divorcing him. She wanted my help in getting in touch with a solicitor. We got talking about it and it seems I'd arranged to meet her at the Goat this evening."

" 'Seems'?" Rudd broke in, picking up the equivocation.

For the first time, Lawson looked defensive and less sure of himself.

"To be honest, I'd forgotten. It was one of those casual arrangements; nothing definite. She called here on Wednesday afternoon to ask my advice and I promised I'd arrange an appointment for her one afternoon next week with the same firm I deal with. When she left, she said something about treating me to a drink at the Goat on Friday—tonight, that is."

"But you weren't there?"

"No, I wasn't. I'd been to a sale this afternoon and got involved in sorting out the stuff I'd bought. Then Stella turned up. It seems she called in at the Goat and, not finding me there, had walked up from the pub. She was anxious to know if I'd fixed the appointment for her. Which I had."

"What time did she arrive?"

"God knows. I told you, I was busy. I didn't take much notice. I know she left just before eight because she looked at her watch and mentioned it."

"And then?" Rudd asked.

"As I said, she left. I went with her as far as the gate." He paused before adding more emotionally, "I wish to God I'd offered her a lift! It occurred to me afterwards. But it meant getting the car out and she seemed quite happy to walk. It wasn't raining all that much either. Just a few occasional spots."

"Yes, I see," Rudd said noncommittally.

All the same, he felt he knew Lawson a little better. He was not a callous man; just averagely selfish and prone, like most people, to put his own interests first. But it also occurred to him that Lawson had treated Stella Reeve with less consideration than he might have done another woman friend simply because she was a barmaid and less educated than himself and that he was aware of it.

Lawson certainly looked uncomfortable as if this were indeed the case.

"Are you married, sir?" Rudd asked. The question wasn't as inconsequential as it appeared. He was curious to know the man's marital status.

The query caught Lawson off guard.

"Yes, but I'm separated from my wife," he replied before adding, "I don't see what that's got to do with Stella's death."

"Not a lot, Mr. Lawson," Rudd admitted blandly.

"If you think I was having an affair with her, then you're quite wrong," Lawson continued.

"The idea hadn't occurred to me," Rudd replied. Interesting though, he thought, that Lawson should mention it. It suggested that the idea had crossed *his* mind in his brief relationship with the dead woman even though he might not have acted on it. "To get back to this evening," he went on. "You saw her off at the gate. In what direction was she walking?"

"Towards the village."

"Did you see her cross the ford?"

"No. There's a slight bend in the lane and the hedge is too high. Besides, it was dark."

"And what did you do after she'd gone?"

"I came back here and got on with sorting the books."

"I believe you mentioned to P.C. Hadley that you saw a car about the time Mrs. Reeve left?"

"Oh, yes, that's right. I'd forgotten about it. It was coming down the hill and passed us just as Stella was on the point of leaving. I don't know who was driving it."

Rudd let it pass. It was none of Lawson's business to be told that the driver was probably the doctor's wife, especially as he hadn't yet checked this with Mrs. Bingham herself.

He continued, "And you remained here in the caravan for the rest of the evening?"

"Yes, until I went into the lane to speak to Hadley. I took some rubbish out to the dustbin and noticed lights by the ford. I thought there might have been an accident. There were two sets of headlamps, you see. So, wondering if I ought to help, I walked down there. Hadley told me what had happened. When I found out it was Stella, I mentioned she'd called on me earlier this evening. Then I cleared off back here. There was nothing I could do and Hadley didn't seem to want me trampling about the place."

Good for Hadley, Rudd thought, closing his notebook and finishing his tea, which had gone cold during the interview.

"Is that all?" Lawson asked as Rudd put down his mug and rose, buttoning his raincoat.

"For the time being, Mr. Lawson. Thank you for your help. I may need to ask you to make an official statement at some later time."

"Of course." Lawson sounded distracted as he, too, got to his feet. "I'd like to say something else, Chief Inspector, before you go."

"Yes?" Rudd paused at the door.

Even then Lawson seemed reluctant to come to the point.

"I don't usually like passing on gossip but perhaps you ought to know, just in case, that Stella had left her husband because he'd been violent to her a couple of times."

"She told you that?" Rudd inquired, intrigued by the form in which the remark had been made. Just in case of what? That Stella had been murdered? If that were so, was Lawson suggesting that the husband might be a likely suspect? It was an interesting speculation.

"You've met him?" he asked Lawson.

"No, but from what Stella told me, he wasn't the best of husbands."

Not the best of husbands. Another curious phrase. Was that how Lawson saw himself? The man was obviously very much on the defensive.

"And?" Rudd prompted.

Lawson hadn't quite finished. Almost imperceptibly, he had drawn a breath as if about to continue.

"She mentioned something else while she was here on Wednesday afternoon. I don't know if it's important. Anyway, she told me that she and Ken quarrelled before they were married and she broke it off. Then she found she was pregnant and married him after all, largely to please her mother. At least, that's the impression I got. But that's beside the point. The point is that she said she needn't have married him. She had another offer from someone else."

"An offer?" Rudd said sharply. "You mean another man wanted to marry her?"

"She didn't explain but, whatever the offer was, she didn't seem to take it very seriously."

"Can you remember her exact words?"

Lawson frowned in concentration.

"I'm sorry, I don't think I can. It was said almost as an aside, something along the lines of, 'I needn't have married him. I had another offer.' Then she went on to say, 'It was stupid,' although I think the exact word she used was 'daft.' I'm merely passing it on for what it's worth. It may mean nothing at all."

Rudd made no comment, apart from repeating, "Thank you, Mr. Lawson," before nodding farewell and letting himself out of the caravan.

He paused by the gate to check Lawson's statement that he hadn't been able to see Stella Reeve cross the ford. In this, at least, Lawson was correct. The slight bend in the lane, apart from the hedge, even with its sparse spring foliage, cut off any view of either the ford or the foot-bridge. Within seconds of leaving the gate, Stella Reeve would have been out of sight.

As for the offer, Rudd put that piece of information at the back of his mind for future consideration. Along with Alec Lawson's other statement, that Reeve had been violent towards his wife, it would need checking on, of course, but, for the moment, he had more urgent demands on his time, such as the search of the area where Stella Reeve's body had been found.

Boyce stepped forward as soon as Rudd emerged from the darkness and crossed the bridge into the circle of light.

"So you're back, sir!" he announced, as if the chief inspector needed informing of this fact.

"You've found something." Rudd's remark was a statement rather than a question. Having worked with Boyce on many investigations, he knew that eager look by now.

"Two things. First this."

Leading the way back on to the foot-bridge, he pointed to a section of the wooden handrail. The surface was dark with rain but the tiny tuft of brown fibres was clearly visible, caught in a rough patch where the wood was splintered.

"Off her coat?" Rudd suggested.

"That's what I thought," Boyce agreed. "And it's in line with where the heel was found."

He indicated a chalked circle on the planking. As Rudd stepped back to get a measure of the two pieces of evidence, Boyce continued, "She was lying immediately below so it looks as if she could have got her heel stuck, lost her balance trying to get it free and pitched head first over the rail, catching her coat as she did so."

"Then she was facing the ford." Rudd offered the idea almost to himself.

"With her torso twisted round and her hands gripping the rail?" Boyce suggested. "When the heel snapped off, she'd've gone forwards."

Standing there, Rudd tried the movement for himself, oblivious to the glances of a couple of uniformed men, yellow jackets gleaming in the rain, who were searching the ditch on the other side of the lane and who stopped in their task to watch.

"Possible," Rudd grunted. The movement wasn't an easy one. The waist and upper part of his body were unnaturally turned but, by holding onto the rail, he was able to maintain the position. At the same time, he wriggled his right foot backwards and forwards as if the heel of his shoe were caught and he were trying to free it.

Boyce stood back, surveying the chief inspector critically and, when Rudd stood four-square again, he said, "Definitely possible," in a tone of voice which brooked no denial.

Rudd made no comment. At this early stage in the investigation, he wasn't prepared to be dogmatic about any theory.

It crossed his mind to wonder why the hell she hadn't slipped her foot out of the shoe and used her hands to wrench the heel free.

The answer, he told himself, was probably because it was beginning to rain. She wouldn't have wanted to put her bare foot down on the wet planking. Hence her attempt to free the shoe while the foot was still in it. The rest appeared to follow logically: the sudden snapping of the heel, the fall forwards, the loss of consciousness as she struck her head and the subsequent death by drowning in a mere fourteen inches of water.

An accident, in other words.

But the chief inspector wasn't willing to be dogmatic about that either.

"What about that other bit of evidence you mentioned?" he asked Boyce.

"It's her bag. One of the men searching the ford found it about a foot from where she had been lying."

The handbag, a satchel type with a long strap which could be carried over one shoulder, was laid out for his inspection on the verge, the metal clasp still fastened. Rudd merely stopped to look at it briefly before straightening up again. Its contents could be examined in detail later.

"Get Wylie to pack it up," he told Boyce, "and tell him not to get his prints on it. I want those fibres bagged up as well. They've been photographed?"

"Yes, sir. McCullum's taken some shots of them." As he spoke, Boyce was taking a critical look round the scene. "I reckon we've more or less finished here. The ford's been searched as well as the immediate area. I've got some men to go through the ditches on the far side of the lane." The sergeant was forced to raise his voice as Rudd suddenly set off in that direction, Boyce loping to keep up with him, anxious that the chief inspector had noticed some inadequacy in the men's activity which he should have seen for himself and put right.

But it wasn't the two constables, who were slashing at the long wet grass with sticks, which had caught the chief inspector's attention.

Ignoring them, he had mounted the stile where a green-painted finger-post pointed across the adjacent field. White lettering on it announced: "Public Footpath to the Church."

A faint track led from the stile across the meadow before disappearing into the darkness.

"Just getting my bearings, Tom," Rudd explained, clambering down. He put into words the idea which had occurred to him as he had paused at the top of the hill to look back at the darkened village. "We'll have to get a large-scale map of the area, just in case."

As he said it, he realised with a sense of exasperation that he had used the same phrase as Lawson and was further exasperated when Boyce picked it up.

"In case of what? That it wasn't an accident?"

Rudd humped his shoulders, a gesture which indicated he'd rather not explain himself and Boyce, taking the hint, had the good sense to keep his mouth shut for once.

All the same, he couldn't resist looking up and down the lane before glancing up at the finger-post to show the chief inspector that he had followed the drift of his thoughts.

If it wasn't an accident, these glances implied, then there were two routes which a possible murderer could have taken: along the lane itself or across the field by the footpath.

Rudd was moving away.

"We'll get this lot packed up then," he said, taking up a position in the middle of the scene.

Boyce visibly cheered up at the prospect of returning to headquarters, to hot tea and the chance to get out of his wet clothes, only to have his hopes dashed when the chief inspector added, "We'll have a word with the dead girl's mother on our way back through the village. Find Hadley and get the address."

They were met at the front door of the house, the last in a row of brick-built cottages only a short distance from the Goat, by the W.P.C., whom Rudd had despatched earlier to break the news of Stella Reeve's death to her mother as soon as Hadley had confirmed the identification.

There was no hall, the front door opening directly into the living-room, and the W.P.C. came out on to the doorstep to confer with them briefly.

"The doctor's been and has left her a sedative to take when she goes to bed. And a neighbour's with her. She's agreed to stay the night," she told them in a low voice before, pushing open the front door, she preceded Rudd and Boyce into the room, announcing in too bright a tone, "Detective Chief Inspector Rudd is here, Mrs. Franklin."

The little living-room was hot and bright and so packed with objects and patterns that, after the starkness of the night outside, Rudd was overwhelmed for a moment. Flowered curtains, flowered wallpaper, cretonne covers on a pair of low armchairs drawn up the fireplace, potted plants and ornaments in profusion, winking brasses and a collection of framed photographs on the sideboard bewildered the eye. There were too many people as well. In addition to himself, Boyce and the W.P.C., two women were sitting in the fireside chairs, one plump and clearly not Mrs. Franklin, judging by the look of bright-eyed curiosity she directed at the chief inspector and his sergeant as they entered the room. This must be the neighbour, shocked by the news, no doubt, but enjoying the excitement of it all at the same time.

The other chair was occupied by a small woman who, as if diminished by grief, had shrunk back against the patterned fabric of the cushions, her hands in her lap, immobilised, it seemed, by the news of her daughter's death. She had a faded prettiness about her. Her soft grey hair might once have been fair and, underneath the fallen flesh, a delicate bone structure was still apparent, more refined than her daughter's for it lacked that fullness and heaviness about the mouth and jaw.

Rudd said, "I'm sorry, Mrs. Franklin."

He felt doubly ill at ease; emotionally, because he had never learned to cope with other people's grief; physically, because in the crowded room it was impossible to approach her without stumbling into the furniture.

Boyce had the good sense to hang back in the relatively uncluttered space by the door.

The neighbour also showed some sensibility.

"I'll make some tea," she announced, heaving herself up. "I'm sure we could all do with a cup."

Rudd sat down in the vacated chair, feeling its seat warm from her ample backside.

"I won't keep you too long, Mrs. Franklin," he said. "At this stage, all I want to know is the time your daughter went out this evening and if you have any idea where she was going."

They were sitting so close together that their knees were almost touching across the hearth, where a coal fire burned fiercely, adding to Rudd's discomfort.

"I want to know what happened," Mrs. Franklin replied. "*She* won't tell me much."

She indicated with a jerk of her head the W.P.C. who had taken up the stand-easy position in front of the sideboard.

"That's because we're not sure ourselves," Rudd said in defence of the woman, although he made a mental note not to use her again on a similar duty. She evidently lacked the right touch. "We think she lost her balance and fell off the foot-bridge into the ford but we can't be certain until we've made further inquiries. That's why I need to know what your daughter was doing this evening."

"Yes, I see that." Mrs. Franklin seemed to accept him, leaning forward to establish closer contact with him as she might have done the vicar, the doctor or, he liked to think, a friend. "She left here about five past seven. I didn't see her go. I was ironing in the kitchen." Again, she nodded her head to indicate the door through which the neighbour had gone and behind which could be heard the subdued rattle of china. "She just called out goodbye and then I heard the front door shut."

"You're sure of the time?"

"I was listening to 'The Archers' on the radio. It'd been on for only a minute when she left."

"And do you know where she was going?"

"Yes; over to the Goat to have a word with Fred Mitchell. She was starting work there on Monday. When she didn't come back at closing time, I thought at first she was with Ken."

"Ken? Her husband, you mean?"

"That's right. He'd called here, you see, soon after she left, wanting to see her. I told him she'd gone to the Goat. Knowing him, I didn't want him hanging about outside the house, waiting for her. I thought if he met her over at the Goat and made a row, Fred Mitchell'd sort him out. She left him, you see; walked out about a week ago. He was round here on Wednesday, asking her to go back, but she wasn't having any. She'd made up her mind to pack him in."

"Why was that?" Rudd asked. Although he already knew Lawson's version, he wanted to hear hers.

It was the same.

"Ken knocked her about a few times and Stella wasn't going to put up with it. She believed in standing up for herself. I don't say it happened often but Ken can be short-tempered, especially when he's had a bit too much to drink. Anyway, she turned up here with her things, talking about getting a divorce."

"I see," Rudd said quietly and left it there. It wasn't the time, he felt, to question her further about Stella's marriage. That could come later at a second interview when Mrs. Franklin had recovered from the first shock of her daughter's death. He would also, on this later occasion, try to find out if she knew anything about the offer which Lawson had mentioned. At the moment, he was more concerned with establishing the husband's movements earlier in the evening, Mrs. Franklin's statement that Ken Reeve had been looking for his wife having opened up a new and unexpected line of inquiry.

"At what time did Ken—Mr. Reeve—arrive?"

"About half an hour after Stella left. Perhaps a bit less."

"So that would be roughly between half past seven and twenty-five to eight?"

"I suppose so. I didn't look at the clock. He'd parked his car outside and walked over to the Goat. It was still there at nine o'clock. I know that 'cos I watched the serial on the telly and I had a look out of the window just after it finished."

Thank God for the television serial, Rudd thought. Two individual timings had been established fairly accurately that evening because of its popularity.

"But you don't know what time he left?"

"No. There's quite a few cars going up and down the village, especially at closing time. I had another look at quarter to eleven but Ken's car had gone. I was ready for bed by then and thinking that Stella ought to be home soon."

She began to cry for the first time, quietly, shamefacedly, the tears running down her face.

"Tea!" announced the plump neighbour, bustling in with the tray. At her arrival, Mrs. Franklin dabbed at her eyes with a crumpled handkerchief she had been holding in her lap and accepted a cup, trying to smile her thanks.

It put an end to the interview although, swilling his own tea down hastily, Rudd put one last question.

"So you don't know if your daughter and her husband met at the Goat?"

"No; you'll have to ask Fred Mitchell that," Mrs. Franklin replied.

CHAPTER EIGHT

Rudd asked Mitchell the following morning, in company with Boyce.

It had stopped raining, thank God, for they were on their way to the ford to supervise the rephotographing and a further search of the area in daylight and Rudd didn't relish the thought of another hour or so spent soaked to the skin.

Watery sunlight brightened up the countryside, revealing trees and hedgerows in new spiky growth and daffodils in green bud in front gardens. On such a morning, it was possible to believe that spring had actually arrived.

Thus revealed, Wynford looked pleasant enough. It was a long village, strung out along the main street, punctuated by the Goat public house at one end and the church at the other, each building forming, as it were, a bracket round its development for beyond them fields and farmland took over.

The Goat was not yet open for business although the rear door was set back with a brick and a man in shirt sleeves was carrying crates of empties out of a store-room to pile up in the yard.

He was a middle-aged man with wide, tufty sideboards of sandy-coloured hair and a brushed-up moustache which gave his face the whiskery, amiable appearance of a character from a children's animal story—Mr. Badger, perhaps, dressed in check shirt and grey Terylene trousers. But his eyes had the hard, watchful look of a man who has seen it all, while the powerful forearms suggested considerable physical strength. It was no surprise that Mrs. Franklin had relied on Fred Mitchell to sort out her son-in-law, as she had put it. He looked capable of dealing with a whole bar full of trouble-makers if need be.

After Rudd had introduced himself and Boyce, Mitchell led them into a small, private sitting-room behind the public bar, where he came straight to the point.

"I've got a pub to open, Chief Inspector, so what do you want to know?"

"What time Stella Reeve arrived here yesterday evening," Rudd replied.

"Just after five past seven at a rough guess. She had a gin and orange and then she went."

"So she wasn't here all that long?"

"Not much above fifteen minutes. It was just before twenty-five past when she left. I know that because I happened to glance at the time."

"Have you any idea where she went?"

"Yes; she was going to call on Mr. Lawson, or so she said. She seemed disappointed not to find him here. She mentioned there was something she wanted to discuss with him."

Her appointment with the solicitor, Rudd thought, although he said nothing.

"And I believe," he continued, his voice carefully casual, "that her husband, Mr. Reeve, also called in here last night?"

"That's right. He arrived about ten minutes after Stella left. He didn't stop long either. He had a pint and then he cleared off."

"He came in here looking for her?" Rudd asked in the same throw-away manner.

Fred Mitchell wasn't fooled.

"Yes, he did. And looking for trouble, too. I nearly followed him outside to warn him off but another customer went out at the same time and I didn't want to show him up in front of someone else. It's a bit of a tricky business running a pub, Chief Inspector, rather like you lot controlling a crowd. You try to keep it pleasant and not go out of your way to stir things up but if anyone looks as if they're going to cause trouble then you've got to step in and stop it, preferably before it starts; nip it in the bud. You get my meaning? Well, Ken Reeve hadn't done anything I could object to but he had a look on his face which made me think he was spoiling for a row."

"Between himself and Stella?"

"That's right. And then when Eva—that's the wife—let slip that Stella'd gone up to Lawson's caravan, it crossed my mind that Ken might go after her. He didn't though, did he? I mean, according to the rumours going round the village, she fell off the foot-bridge. There was no funny business?"

The last remark was in the form of an appeal which Rudd responded to pleasantly without committing himself.

"So it would seem, Mr. Mitchell. Even so, inquiries have to be made. I believe Mr. Macey was also in the pub last night. What time did he arrive?"

"Ted? Not long before Stella turned up; say about seven o'clock. He left at closing time. Here, you don't think Ted had anything to do with it?"

"Only as a potential witness, Mr. Mitchell. He found the body," Rudd pointed out, at which Mitchell nodded, satisfied with this explanation, before remarking, his face behind the sandy whiskers suddenly gloomy, "It's a hell of a thing to happen. I liked Stella. She was a good looker, too, and it's always an advantage to have an attractive face behind the bar. And friendly with it; the sort who enjoyed a bit of a chat and a laugh although she wouldn't stand for any old acid from anyone, no matter who. God knows who I'll find to take her place. I was counting on her starting here on Monday."

"I'm sorry," Rudd said in general commiseration as he rose to leave, adding as he went into the passage leading to the back door, "By the way, if we need it, would you be able to give me a list of all the customers who were in the bar last night when Stella Reeve was in there?"

"All of them?" Fred Mitchell sounded outraged although he softened this initial reaction by remarking more reasonably, "I suppose I could. Most of them were regulars anyway."

"I'll let you know if I'll need it," Rudd said before walking away with Boyce across the car-park to where their vehicle was parked.

In the few minutes it took to drive to the ford along Waterend Lane, there wasn't much time for Boyce to comment on the interview, although he remarked, "I suppose you'll want that list in case it turns out to be murder after all."

Rudd merely grunted in reply. He was trying to keep an open mind on Stella Reeve's death and was reluctant to discuss with Boyce the flicker of doubt which had crossed his mind the night before as he had stood looking down at her body. Besides, he was more interested in studying the scene in daylight.

After running relatively straight for a short distance, the lane began to twist and narrow down between high hedges for about half a mile

before swinging round in a wide S-bend where it tilted down towards
the ford, thirty yards ahead. On the other side, it started to rise again in
the long slope which led towards Macey's farm.

Boyce drew the car on to the verge and Rudd got out, strolling with
his hands in his pockets towards the ford.

McCullum, the police photographer, and some of the other men
were already there, a smaller group than yesterday, their cars drawn up
along the edge of the lane.

When Rudd had set them up the task of resuming the search, he
stood to one side, making his own assessment of the surroundings,
which he had seen only in the artificial illumination of the arc lamps
the night before.

In daylight, the place looked less sinister and dramatic. The water,
no longer theatrically black and silver, was tinted brown by the soil
washed down into it from the surrounding fields by the spring rains.

It was a picturesque scene, or would have been in high summer with
the trees and hedges in full leaf. On such a March morning of thin,
chilly sunlight, it had a cold, austere beauty, only partly softened by the
small, yellow stars of the celandines growing on the banks and by the
new, tender grass pushing up through last year's dead growth. The
bones of winter were still too visible. Even in the fields, flushed green
with sprouting corn, it was possible to see under the top mantle the
ribbed furrows, streaked silver with the standing water which had collected in the hollows.

Rudd mounted the stile by the signpost as he had done the night
before and looked out across the meadow in the direction of the village.
He could now trace the line of the footpath across the grass towards
the church, the tower of which stood out against the surrounding trees,
still bare of foliage, it seemed, at that distance, although on the nearer
trees and hedges the new leaves were everywhere apparent.

Climbing down, he crossed the foot-bridge, pausing to look down
over the handrail before walking on towards Lawson's caravan, noting
again the bend in the lane and stopping at the gate to check that, from
this position, the ford and bridge were now out of sight.

Lawson was probably at home. At least, glancing across, Rudd could
see a car, a Volvo estate, parked in the field a little distance away where
a five-barred gate gave access. A window in the caravan was also open.
But the chief inspector made no attempt to approach any nearer and,

turning away, walked back towards the ford where he sought out Stapleton, the tall, slow-moving uniformed inspector.

"I'm leaving you in charge here, George. There's a couple of people I want to interview. But I should be back before you've finished."

"Very good, sir," Stapleton replied.

Beckoning to Boyce to follow, Rudd returned to the car.

"Where now?" the sergeant asked, getting in behind the wheel.

"Studham," Rudd told him. "I want to have a chat with Ken Reeve, Stella's husband. On the way, though, we'll drop in on Mrs. Bingham."

The doctor's house was on the outskirts of the village, a large Edwardian detached residence, solid and comfortable, set back from the road behind a wide, well-kept garden of lawn, shrubbery and rose beds. A modern-looking, one-storey addition on one side with a separate entrance housed, he assumed, the surgery and waiting-room.

Rudd rang the bell at the front door, which was opened to him by an attractive, well-dressed woman in her forties—Mrs. Bingham herself, as she acknowledged in answer to his first question. When Rudd had introduced himself and Boyce, she showed them into a drawing-room at the back of the house, overlooking another broad sweep of garden, where she invited him to sit down.

Rudd looked about him covertly as he lowered himself into an armchair. It was an appealing room, furnished with a mixture of comfortable, cushioned chairs and a pair of matching sofas, covered in crisp cream-and-blue-flowered linen, combined with a few choice antiques, paintings and silver; a suitable setting for Mrs. Bingham, for she was a good-looking woman although a little too dominating for his taste, Rudd thought, summing her up silently. She had a positive tilt to her head and fine dark eyes which regarded him with a challenging directness. Here was someone used to authority and undoubtedly intelligent although, underneath the carefully maintained image of the doctor's wife, he sensed an energy and restlessness which he detected in the movements of her hands and a rapid, rather impatient manner of speaking.

"I'm afraid I can't tell you a great deal, Chief Inspector," she replied when Rudd had explained the reason for the visit. "I called at the Maceys' to leave a prescription which Ted Macey had forgotten or hadn't been bothered to collect from the surgery. I also wanted to arrange for Pam Macey to help with the old people's teas one Wednesday afternoon. I'm not sure what time I arrived, although I left, I suppose, about eight o'clock."

"Then I believe you must have passed the caravan on your way home just as Mrs. Reeve and Mr. Lawson were saying goodbye. At least Mr. Lawson spoke of seeing a car go by as they were standing at the gate. The timing would appear to coincide."

As he spoke, he saw that Boyce, seated on the opposite side of the fireplace, had begun quietly to take notes of the conversation. Mrs. Bingham, too, was aware of it for she glanced briefly in his direction before replying.

"Yes, that would have been me," she agreed. "As a matter of fact, I noticed them, but only briefly, in the headlights."

"Yes?" Rudd prompted.

There was something in her manner which persuaded him that this was not all she could tell him. The signs were almost imperceptible: a faint hesitation, the slightest possible upward intonation at the end of the sentence as if she had been about to add another remark.

She looked across at him and then averted her eyes.

"That's all. I only saw them for a few seconds."

"But long enough, I think, Mrs. Bingham, for you to have gained an impression. What was it?"

"It's too vague to be of any use to you, Chief Inspector. And besides, it was an accident, wasn't it?"

"So it would appear," Rudd said. "But our inquiries aren't yet complete. I need to have as much evidence as I can before any such conclusions can be reached."

He was aware that he was using his official, formal voice but Mrs. Bingham was hardly the type of woman with whom he could settle down for a quiet chat, knee to knee, as he had done the night before with Mrs. Franklin.

"I see." There was a pause in which she seemed to consider his comment. Then she continued. "I thought they were quarrelling. At least, that's the impression I had. As I said, I saw them only briefly and I could be wrong."

"But you don't think you are?" Rudd persisted. When she didn't reply, he took her silence for assent, adding, "What gave you that impression?"

"Mr. Lawson had his hand raised. Stella Franklin was turning away rather abruptly, as if she were trying to keep her balance. It seemed to me they were arguing."

"Mr. Lawson was about to strike her? Is that what you're saying?" Rudd asked sharply.

The question seemed to distress her. She got up from the chair in which she had been sitting and went to stand by the fireplace, on the shelf above which was a collection of silver-framed photographs—of her children, Rudd guessed, at various stages of their development from babies to young adults.

"Yes, that was my impression, Chief Inspector," she replied, her face averted. "It was only after I passed them that I realised who they were and what was happening."

"You didn't stop?"

"No, I thought it was none of my business so I drove on."

"Where to?"

She looked annoyed.

"Here, of course."

Where else? she seemed to imply.

"You knew Stella Reeve?" Rudd asked, shifting the subject slightly.

"Of course. We've lived in the village for twenty years. The Franklins are my husband's patients and, in a place like Wynford, you know everybody if only by sight."

"And Mr. Lawson?"

"I've only met him once or twice. But I certainly recognised him as the man I saw yesterday evening with Stella."

There seemed nothing more to ask. Rudd thanked her and rose to his feet, following her, with Boyce in tow, to the front door, where she let them out of the house.

"What did you make of that?" the sergeant asked as they got into the car and turned out of the driveway into the road.

"I don't know, Tom," Rudd replied. He genuinely didn't. The interview had left him feeling uncomfortable, largely, he suspected, because of Mrs. Bingham's attitude. Seated in her drawing-room, he had felt very much the outsider, not one of the community, asking questions which she seemed to regard as faintly impertinent.

Much of the problem arose from the case itself. If it had been a straightforward murder, he could have carried out his inquiries with complete authority, but, as it had not yet proved that Stella Reeve had met her death other than accidentally, he was aware of having to proceed more carefully and of unseen barriers going up; not just in the case of Mrs. Bingham either. During the interviews with the Maceys and with Mitchell, he had had the feeling that, deep down, they wanted Stella's death to be treated as accidental and had resented, however covertly, any suggestion on his part that it might be otherwise.

Boyce was saying, voicing aloud his dilemma, "If it turns out to be murder, Mrs. Bingham's evidence about Lawson could be useful. Will you interview him again?"

Which wasn't what Rudd wanted to be asked at that moment; certainly not so directly. He was aware that his own reticence about discussing the case with Boyce didn't help the situation although he could not rationalise this reluctance. If only he were seeing Marion Greave in the near future, he thought. She would understand better than Boyce, disloyal though such a comparison might be towards the sergeant. But no such arrangements had been made and he did not like to ring her up to suggest a meeting. To do so might be pushing his luck a little too far. Since her rejection of him as a lover, he had become self-conscious about getting in touch with her even as a friend. The barriers had gone up there, too, leaving him again on the outside.

He said, "Let's wait until we get some confirmation on that one, Tom."

"Perhaps Pardoe will come up with something," Boyce suggested with a helpful air.

Rudd merely replied, "Turn left at the crossroads for Studham."

The town had begun life as a small market centre for the surrounding farms and villages and still preserved the original narrow streets, choked now with modern traffic, although the outskirts were spreading out beyond the original perimeter into new housing estates and small industrial developments.

Hubbard's garage was in a side street behind a cramped forecourt allowing barely room for a motorist to draw off the road to reach the petrol pumps. The building itself was of brick-and-corrugated iron construction, a pair of wooden doors set open to reveal the interior, minimally equipped with an inspection pit and a ramp. The place looked badly run. A work-bench was littered with tools while bits of cars, wheels, inner tubes, pieces of bodywork, were piled up along the walls. At the far end, a small office had been knocked together out of lath

and boarding where, under a dangling light bulb, Mr. Hubbard was
drinking tea at a desk covered with papers, discarded sparking-plugs
and dirty ashtrays.

Ken Reeve, he informed them, was out in the yard and he waved a
negligent hand towards a door at the back.

The yard showed as much disorganisation as the workshop with cars
in various stages of repair or dismantling drawn up haphazardly, although in a relatively clear area in the centre a van was standing with
its bonnet up, a young man in overalls bending down over the engine.

He wasn't aware of their approach until Rudd spoke to him.

"Mr. Reeve?"

He straightened up and turned to face them.

Seeing him, Rudd could understand both Mrs. Franklin's and
Mitchell's remarks which had suggested that Ken Reeve was a potential
trouble-maker. It was evident in his expression as he looked them over.
He wasn't bad-looking in an obvious swaggering and macho manner
with black wavy hair and strong features, but the look on his face was
immediately belligerent.

"You're the police," he said with an accusing air.

"Detective Chief Inspector Rudd and Detective Sergeant Boyce,"
Rudd replied more equably than he felt. He recognised the type at
once. Reeve, who liked to think of himself as a hard man, would consider it demeaning to be cooperative even though he knew they were
there to inquire into his wife's death. He'd been informed of that fact
earlier by the Studham police, who'd been sent round to his address
soon after the official investigation started. But the need to maintain
this image of himself would prevent him from showing any grief he
might feel. Or guilt, come to that, Rudd realised.

"I'm sorry about your wife," Rudd said, testing out this theory. "It
must have come as a shock."

"Yeah," Reeve replied. He seemed about to add more but, changing
his mind, kept silent.

"I'm afraid," Rudd continued in the same pleasant tone, "that we
have to ask you a few questions concerning your movements last night.
I believe you were in Wynford?"

"That's right," Reeve replied with a truculent air, as much as to say,
So what?

"What exactly were you doing there?" It was Boyce who asked the question, moving forward to interpose his bulk.

Reeve, seemingly unimpressed, looked him up and down before replying.

"I called on Stella's mum."

"At what time?"

"How the hell should I know?" As Boyce waited, massively silent, Reeve added, "I suppose about half past seven."

"And what happened?"

"The old bat wouldn't let me in; spoke to me on the doorstep."

"She told you where your wife had gone?"

Rudd took up the questioning this time.

Reeve glanced from one to the other of them and then laid down the spanner he had been holding on the wing of the van. The action seemed to signal some kind of truce, to Rudd's relief, for when he answered he spoke more reasonably.

"Yeah, that's right. She said Stella had gone over to the Goat. So I went over there myself, only Stella had left about ten minutes earlier, or so the woman behind the bar told me. I had a pint and then cleared off."

"Where to?" Boyce asked.

"Back to the car," Reeve replied. "I'd left it parked outside Stella's mum's house. I thought I'd sit in it and wait for Stella to turn up. When she didn't, I went home."

"But I think you knew where your wife had gone," Rudd pointed out. "Mrs. Mitchell, the landlord's wife, told you."

Reeve shrugged indifferently.

"She might have done. I didn't take much notice. She said something about a caravan but I wasn't going to go traipsing about the place looking for it. So, like I said, I waited in the car."

"Until when?" Rudd asked.

He had a rough idea of the time from Mrs. Franklin's statement. It would be interesting to see just how far Reeve told the truth.

"I don't know," Reeve replied. "An hour, I suppose. It could be more. I listened to the car radio and smoked a few ciggies. Then I got fed up with it and drove home."

"Did you leave the car at any time?" Boyce asked.

"No, I bloody didn't!" Reeve raised his voice. "It had started to rain.

And what the hell's all this about anyway? I was told she'd probably had an accident. The way you're bloody questioning me, anyone'd think I'd killed her."

"Questions have to be asked, Mr. Reeve," Rudd said quietly, aware that with each interview he'd so far made, the same query had been raised and wishing to hell the case were more straightforward. "When was the last time you saw your wife, by the way?"

Again, he knew what the answer ought to be from his interview with Mrs. Franklin and he waited, keeping his expression bland, for Reeve's reply.

"About ten days ago before she cleared off," Reeve began and then paused. "No; hang on a minute. I called round her mum's a few days ago."

"You'd forgotten?" Rudd hinted.

Reeve gave him a strange look, half defiant, half shamefaced. He clearly preferred not to remember what had happened on that last occasion but whether deliberately or because he had genuinely forgotten in an attempt to protect his own self-esteem, Rudd couldn't tell.

"I wasn't there much more than a quarter of an hour," he said, avoiding Rudd's eyes. "I wanted Stella to come back."

"But she wouldn't?" Rudd asked.

Reeve turned aside and, picking up the spanner, flourished it in the direction of the van.

"Look, I've got work to do," he said. "I can't waste half the morning answering your fool questions. If that's all you want to know, then push off and let me get on."

"I won't keep you much longer," Rudd replied. "I shall need you to make a formal identification of the body. Would this afternoon at three o'clock suit you?"

He had postponed the timing of this formality in order to be present when Reeve identified his wife, curious to witness the man's reaction.

Reeve's immediate response was also interesting.

"Do I have to?" he asked.

"If you don't, it means asking Mrs. Franklin, which I'd rather not do. She's still in a state of shock."

"All right then," Reeve conceded reluctantly.

"Thank you, Mr. Reeve," Rudd said courteously. "I'll see you then this afternoon at Divisional Headquarters in Chelmsford. Ask for me at the desk," and nodding to Boyce to follow, he picked his way back across the yard towards the garage.

"That's all you're going to ask him?" Boyce demanded as they emerged on to the forecourt. "Nothing about the divorce? Not a word about him knocking his wife about?"

"That can come later, Tom," Rudd replied, climbing into the passenger seat of the car. "I want to keep a few cards up my sleeve."

"In case it turns out to be murder?" Boyce finished the sentence for him, again voicing out loud the thought which Rudd would have preferred kept silent. "Well, if it is, Reeve's capable of shoving anyone off a bridge, by my reckoning."

It was too soon to come to such a conclusion and Rudd was exasperated enough to reply, "If it is murder, then Reeve's not the only one who could have a motive. Don't forget Mrs. Bingham's statement about Lawson. According to her, he and Stella Reeve were quarrelling only a few minutes before she must have died."

Which hardly helped in keeping an open mind on the case, Rudd thought, regretting the remark as soon as he made it. But at least it had the effect of diverting Boyce's attention from the husband.

"Yes, you're right there," he agreed, looking thoughtful before adding more briskly, "Where to now? Back to Wynford to see how the search is going?"

CHAPTER NINE

The arrival of a uniformed constable at the caravan had alerted Alec Lawson to the presence of the police in the lane that morning. They were, the man explained, continuing the search in daylight and they'd be grateful if no traffic used the road into the village until the task was completed, probably in a couple of hours. He had then left on foot in the direction of Macey's farm, presumably to repeat the request.

As far as Alec Lawson was concerned, the restriction wasn't a nuisance. He had no plans to leave the caravan until later that morning anyway, having made up his mind to finish sorting through the books before putting them into boxes and taking them up to the farm, where they would be stored in one of Macey's outbuildings until he could transfer them to the shop.

The arrangement was far from ideal. The shed, for which he paid an additional five pounds a week on top of the rent for the caravan, was weatherproof but damp and the books could not be left there for too long without running the risk of them becoming mildewed.

Now that he had the keys to the shop and the place was legally his, he could have taken the boxes there but he wanted to wait a few days in order to get the interior into some kind of fit state, a few shelves put up and the floor cleared before he started moving in stock. As it was, he estimated that at least a fortnight's work had to be done before he could open for business.

Once the police had gone and the lane was again open to traffic, he intended driving into Studham that afternoon and making a start by ordering the materials he would need and getting an estimate for the fascia board to be repainted; nothing elaborate, of course; he hadn't the capital to waste on anything expensive. All he had envisaged was the name "Lawson's" and the words "Second-hand Books" in white lettering on a black background.

But only half his mind was on his long-term plans. Kneeling on the floor and opening the books in turn to examine their contents briefly before pencilling a price inside the cover, he thought of Stella.

Her death had distressed him more than he had been willing to admit to Rudd or even, at the time, to himself. Although he had hardly known her, he found himself mourning her death as if she had been an old friend.

Stella, the bright star, he thought and then smiled wryly at the image. But the comparison wasn't without some validity. She had possessed a certain luminous quality of her own although the concept of the star was perhaps too pure and virginal to be entirely apt.

And, if he were honest with himself, would he have continued the relationship? Probably not. Once he had moved away from Wynford, he doubted if he would have taken the trouble to see her again although she might have dropped in at the shop occasionally when she happened to be in Studham. That was all.

All the same, he regretted not having accompanied her as far as the ford or gone to the bother of getting the car out and driving her home. It had been thoughtless of him; selfish even. Since walking out on Joanna and Simon, he had been aware of a hardening in his attitude to other people, a tendency he'd have to watch, he decided. There must be a middle way between being too soft and total self-interest.

At eleven o'clock, just as he was thinking of making himself coffee, he heard the sound of cars backing and turning in the lane. The police seemed to be leaving and, curious to see their departure, he walked as far as the corner, where it was possible to look down the slight incline towards the ford.

Rudd was aware of Lawson's presence but ignored it. He and Boyce had arrived only twenty minutes earlier to find the search almost completed. Three policemen in waders had moved from the ford itself further down the stream in the direction of the footpath leading to the village. Here, at the point where the path branched off from the bank and struck out across the field, they had halted before returning for further orders.

Stapleton looked at Rudd.

"Is it worth going on?"

Rudd humped his shoulders.

So far they had discovered nothing more from either the stream or the ditches than the usual sodden litter which accumulates at the side of any road, however little used. The whole operation seemed to have been a waste of time, especially since the inquiry was not yet officially designated a full-scale murder investigation. Once that fact had been established, or not, as the case might be, he'd know better whether to commit more time and men to it. In the event, they had covered the immediate vicinity. To extend the search seemed unnecessary.

"We'll pack it in for now," he told Stapleton.

As the men began to move off, the cars and vans heading for the village, Rudd noticed that Alec Lawson had strolled into view round the bend in the lane and was standing watching them.

He appeared casual and unhurried, as if he had merely sauntered down from the caravan to see how the search was progressing, unconcerned whether anyone noticed him or not.

Rudd deliberately turned his back on him and caught up with Boyce, who had moved away towards the car.

"Pick me up in the village," he told the sergeant. "I'm going to walk back by the footpath."

"Any particular reason?" Boyce asked nosily.

"Just to check how long it would take. Besides, I want to stretch my legs. I'll meet you outside the Goat."

"Okay by me," Boyce replied, getting into the car and seeming relieved that the chief inspector hadn't wanted his company.

Lawson was still there, Rudd noticed as he mounted the stile, although he had moved to the side of the lane and was now standing up against the hedge, where his presence was less obvious. Ignoring him, Rudd checked his watch before climbing down on the other side and setting off along the footpath. But, as he left the bank to follow the path across the fields, he couldn't resist looking back. Lawson hadn't moved.

The walk invigorated him. He spent too much time, he decided, sitting behind a desk or in a car. It was good to be out in the fresh air again.

The meadow sloped gently downwards, allowing him a panoramic view of the village, which straggled along the line of the road. On his right was the white-painted clapboard gable end of the Goat and, further off still and just visible above the trees in the garden, the red-tiled roof of Mrs. Bingham's house. To his left, the church tower jogged into nearer view as he approached until finally the path turned off into a narrow alley running between the churchyard wall on one side and the high boundary hedge of the vicarage garden on the other. At the end of it, he emerged into the village street.

Rudd looked at his watch again. The walk had taken him nine minutes but that was in daylight and downhill. Anyone using the path at night and in the opposite direction would take longer; how much longer would have to be checked on if necessary.

If necessary. He grimaced impatiently. Surely he didn't need to use that euphemism to himself? If his instinct was right and the case turned out to be murder, he corrected himself.

The walk from the church to the Goat took another three minutes. On the way, he glanced about him, taking in the details of the village, which so far he'd only glimpsed briefly from the car earlier that morning: the parish hall; the war memorial, standing on a little patch of grass; the shop with a wholesaler's van parked outside; the three-gabled primary school with its asphalt playground and children's paintings Sellotaped to the classroom windows; a self-contained place very much like the village where he had spent his own childhood and in which, even with today's increased mobility, the majority of its inhabitants would spend their lives.

It was a community in which the people knew each other, better, in some cases, than members of those families who were physically separated from one another and met on only rare occasions. As a way of life, it had its disadvantages. Gossip was rife, as no doubt Stella Reeve had discovered. But, at the same time, it offered protection from the outside world and, like a family, would close ranks at the first sign of danger.

He was an outsider, he realised. So, too, was Alec Lawson and, to a lesser extent, Ken Reeve. None of them really belonged to the place as the Maceys did or the Franklins. But what about Stella herself? She had been born and brought up in the village but had married someone outside it and had left, returning only recently, a mere seven days before her death, in fact. Was she, too, considered as an outsider who had posed some threat to the little community she had abandoned?

It was possible. And if that theory were right, it might account for the anxiety on the part of some of those he had interviewed—Fred Mitchell, Ted Macey and Mrs. Bingham—for her death to be considered an accident. Not that he suspected them of covering up evidence of murder; that was too extreme. No, the process was more subtle than that. But they were closing ranks against the idea of murder, shutting it out, because if they admitted to themselves that murder was a possibility, then they had to admit to something else: that someone from the village could be the killer. The reaction was probably instinctive. Rudd doubted if anyone had worked it out rationally. It was a collective response to danger. Better for it to be an accident than to face the alternative.

And as the thought crossed his mind, Rudd was suddenly aware of the reason behind his reluctance to discuss the case with Boyce. It was not simply because he had nothing else to support his belief that Stella Reeve had probably been murdered except his own intuition, although that was bad enough. Boyce had never been sympathetic to mere supposition and quite rightly, too. It was evidence that mattered.

What also bothered him was the thought that his instinct might be wrong. For the first time in his professional life, he doubted that sixth sense on which he had so often relied. For, if he were wrong and Stella Reeve had after all died accidentally, he could, by continuing the inquiry, be uncovering old wounds which, in a small place like Wynford, could go on festering for years.

That was the crux of his dilemma, he realised. His own loyalties were divided. Part of his instinct worked on a professional level; it was the reaction of a policeman who, after years of being in the business, learns to pick up certain scents as a Labrador, trained for the gun, will search out game. But, like the dog, he, too, possessed other, less directed impulses which in his case had their origins much further back in time than his years as a policeman; to his childhood, in fact, spent in a village like Wynford and to that much earlier training which had never been expressed in so many words, merely in a shake of the head or a folding of the lips but which, nevertheless, had made it quite clear that there were certain subjects which should never be discussed, certainly not with strangers.

As a child, he had never questioned this unspoken tenet or indeed attempted to put it into words himself. It was only now, as he reached the end of the village street and drew level with Mrs. Franklin's cottage, that he realised he had unconsciously been sharing in the primitive and collective response of the herd under threat to group together against the danger.

The curtains in Mrs. Franklin's cottage were drawn; so, too, were those of her immediate neighbours, he noticed; a sign of mourning, of course, but a symbol of something more, he felt—of that closing of the ranks and the shutting out of strangers to which that part of himself, still loyal to the old pattern of village allegiance, wanted to respond.

But how the hell did he express this dilemma to Boyce, for whom such loyalties would be incomprehensible? And, more importantly still, how was he to reconcile them with his professional duties?

The answer, of course, was he couldn't. The old instincts were still there but had to be resisted. Like Stella Reeve, he had turned his back on his community, but for him there was no return. As a professional policeman, his commitments lay elsewhere, and as he walked past the gate of Mrs. Franklin's house, he checked his watch again, shooting back his cuff with more determination than was strictly needed for such a trivial act.

It had taken him one and a half minutes to walk from the church to the cottage; a further one and a half minutes to reach the Goat, three minutes in all, so, when these timings were added together, it gave him a total of twelve minutes to cover the distance from the ford to the public house.

The other route, on foot, from the Goat to the ford along Waterend Lane, would have to be checked another time.

Boyce was sitting in the car parked behind the pub, arms spread out over the steering-wheel, reading the *Daily Mirror*, which he folded up and pitched on to the back seat as Rudd climbed in behind him.

"Satisfied?" he asked.

"For the time being," Rudd replied noncommittedly. Catching the sergeant's glance turned expectantly towards the Goat, he added, "No, not here, Tom. We'll stop at another pub on the way back to headquarters. We're bound to find one in the next village."

"All right with me," Boyce replied, starting the engine. "I just thought you'd like to soak up a bit of the local atmosphere."

He grinned as he said it, amused by his own disingenuousness, knowing full well that he'd made the suggestion entirely for his own benefit.

Rudd smiled back although he did not explain that, as far as he was concerned, the last thing he wanted was to become too involved with

the place until the exact manner in which Stella Reeve had met her
death had been established. Far better not to stir up the water too
much at this stage in the investigation.

Which was hardly an apt turn of phrase under the circumstances, he
added to himself.

Alec Lawson watched Rudd climb over the stile and set off along the
footpath. The action surprised him at first. What the hell was he doing? The other policemen had all taken to their cars and driven off
down the lane towards the village. One explanation was that the chief
inspector fancied a country walk but this was not entirely satisfactory.
Lawson doubted if Rudd did anything for the obvious reason. Despite
the man's apparently bland manner and bluff, open features, Lawson
wasn't fooled. During the short interview which had taken place the
previous evening, he had been aware of a quiet, watchful intelligence
about the man, suggesting that he had been absorbing a great deal
more than either his expression or his attitude had indicated.

So, on the basis that Rudd's decision to walk back to the village
across the fields had some ulterior motive behind it, Lawson moved to
the side of the lane where his own presence was less obvious and from
where he could watch, with less chance of being observed himself, as
the short, stocky figure of the chief inspector went stumping off along
the footpath.

He was timing the walk. As Rudd mounted the stile, Lawson noticed
him turn his wrist to look at his watch. And if that were the purpose
behind his actions, then there was only one possible inference which
could be drawn from it: Rudd had reason to believe that someone had
used that route to reach the ford and, given this assumption, Stella's
death might not have been an accident after all. Would Rudd have
gone to the trouble of checking the distance and the timing unless
there was some doubt in his mind?

Which left the possibility of murder.

Until the thought crossed his mind, Alec Lawson had been merely
amused by the idea of watching the chief inspector, unobserved himself as he imagined. It was a case of the biter being bitten, a reversal of
roles which had a pleasurably ironic twist to it.

But even as the idea occurred to him, Rudd reached the point at
which the footpath diverted from the bank of the stream to strike off

across the meadow, where he paused momentarily to glance back over his shoulder. It was done so casually that, had Alec Lawson not been watching the man closely, he might have missed it.

But that quick movement of the head in his direction made one fact uncomfortably clear to him: Rudd was aware of his presence and, in turn, was keeping him under observation.

I should have known better, Lawson thought, turning away himself and walking back along the lane towards the caravan. Never underestimate the opposition.

Although quite what he meant by thinking of Rudd as the enemy was not quite clear even to himself.

All the same, the episode disturbed him and, as he resumed the task of sorting and pricing the books, he found his thoughts turning again and again to the question of Stella's death.

Supposing it were murder? As the last person to see her alive before she met her death, wouldn't he be placed in a difficult position? The police would be bound to treat his statement with suspicion.

Come to that, what exactly was going on in Rudd's mind? Had he reason to suppose someone had come across the fields and met her at the ford? If this were so and Stella had indeed been murdered, it could have been either a spur-of-the-moment killing following an accidental meeting or a premeditated crime. In the latter case, the only assumption which could be logically drawn from that was that the killer had known she had been visiting him at the caravan and had lain in wait for her.

Lawson put down the book he had been examining and stared straight ahead.

Why the hell hadn't he offered to drive her home?

Until that moment, he had dismissed his omission as mere thoughtlessness. Now, faced with the possibility that, by offering her a lift, he might have saved her life, he realised that he could not shrug off his responsibility quite so lightly, especially when he remembered her body lying face downwards in the stream.

She had looked so damned pathetic, her blond hair bedraggled, the cheap fur fabric coat, which had smelt of the scent she wore, dark and sodden with water.

He tried to thrust the image and his own thoughts to one side but they refused to be banished.

The real reason behind his omission was, of course, that he had wanted to punish Joanna through Stella. Let her bloody well cope on her own. I'm no longer responsible for her.

Hadn't that been at the back of his mind?

If he were totally honest with himself, the answer had to be yes, which left him facing the unpleasant fact that he had been not only thoughtless but callous and arrogant as well. It was not a very worthy truth to come to terms with.

He finished sorting the books, although any pleasure in the task or of opening up his own business had lost its brightness and sense of anticipation. It was all spoilt.

The job done, he made himself lunch, heating up a tin of soup on the miniature stove before carrying the boxes out to the car.

As he turned into the farmyard, Macey came out of the front door of the house to meet him. His presence there and his expression, not at all welcoming, warned Alec even before Macey opened his mouth.

"You planning on storing more boxes in that shed?" he asked.

"That was the idea," Alec replied.

"Well, it don't suit me no more," Macey retorted.

"Why not?" Alec tried to make his voice sound pleasant.

"Because I need it myself."

"I see." Alec paused before pointing out, "I have paid rent on the shed, Mr. Macey, which doesn't run out until Monday."

Macey didn't reply immediately. Instead, he felt in his pocket and, producing a roll of dirty pound notes, thumbed through it before handing it over.

"You'll find twenty quid there," he said. "That'll cover the two days' rent on the caravan and the shed up to Monday that I'll owe you, plus a tenner for any trouble you'll be put to."

"You want me out?" Alec demanded. It seemed a superfluous question to ask, especially as Macey had clearly had the money ready on him, but he wanted to make the man admit the fact.

Macey wouldn't meet his eyes or answer directly.

"I've changed my mind about letting them," he said.

"And you want me to leave at once?" Alec pressed the point home.

"If you can't make it today because it's too short notice, then I'll give you till tomorrow."

"Supposing I've nowhere else to go?"

"But you have, haven't you?" Macey countered in a jeering manner. "Fred Mitchell said you'd told him you'd collected the keys to that shop of yours in Studham yesterday."

Alec Lawson smiled as if amused at having to concede the point. Macey was quite right. The day before he had called in at the Goat at lunchtime on his way back from seeing the solicitor and, pleased that the lease had been signed, had confided this fact to Fred Mitchell. He had even, he remembered, got the keys to the shop out of his pocket to show the landlord and had treated both of them to a whisky on the strength of his new ownership.

Well, that would teach him not to discuss his business with others in the future.

He had, moreover, no intention of pleading his case with Macey or of explaining that, while he might be in possession of the keys to the shop, the place was hardly habitable. The electricity hadn't been switched on yet and he had no furniture to put in the place, not even a bed.

Shrugging as if Macey's decision did not affect him in the least, he said indifferently, "It suits me, Mr. Macey. I'll clear out this afternoon." He couldn't resist adding as Macey turned away, "Why the sudden hurry to get rid of me?"

He guessed the reason but was determined to hear it from Macey's own mouth.

In the event, Macey refused to give him that satisfaction. Walking back to the house, he pretended not to hear as he slammed the front door shut.

Inside the house, Pam Macey met him in the hall, her face anxious. "You've told him?" she asked. "Is he going?"

Macey made no reply but, pushing past her, went into the sitting-room where he stood at the window watching as Lawson, having opened the shed door, was beginning to carry the boxes out to his car. Pam, who had followed her husband into the room, came to stand behind him.

"He'll see you, Ted," she protested.

"I don't give a bugger if he does," he retorted. "He's leaving, that's all I care."

"Are you sure it'll be all right?" she asked. "Only he's got a solicitor, hasn't he? He could make trouble if he wants to."

The thought didn't seem to worry her husband.

"Then let him try. If he starts anything, I'll get a solicitor of my own and tell him straight out why I don't want Lawson on my property."

"But you haven't got any proof," his wife objected. "The police seem to think it was an accident."

"Proof!" Macey swung round to face her and she shrank back. "She was with him yesterday evening just before she died, or so Mitchell told me. What more proof do you want? The bloody police don't know what they're at! They should have run him in this morning; stuck him behind bars. I know what I'd bloody do to him, given half a chance."

"I'll make some tea," Pam said uneasily, moving away from the window.

"You didn't see her lying there!" Macey shouted after her as she left the room. "Animals like him ought to be strung up!" A sudden pain made him clutch his stomach. Half bent over, he followed her to the door. "And fetch those bloody pills of mine while you're at it!" he added, wincing as he raised his voice.

Alec Lawson drove into the small yard behind the shop, where he parked, remaining behind the wheel for a few minutes as he contemplated the back of the premises.

He had looked forward to this occasion eagerly ever since he had first decided to take up the lease. Now everything was changed. Even the place looked different. The bars on the ground-floor windows and the rubbish littering the yard gave it the grim, dilapidated air of some abandoned institution.

At the sight of it, he felt his anger, which had sustained him during the confrontation with Macey and his return to the caravan to pack up his possessions, evaporate, leaving an overwhelming sense of depression.

The adventure had gone sour.

To make matters worse, it had started raining again.

You'll bloody well have to make the best of it, he told himself, climbing out of the car and crossing the yard to the back door, which he unlocked.

The smell of the place came to meet him, a mingled odour of damp plaster and old food turned rancid.

Leaving the door open to let in the air, he made a tour of the interior, tramping up the uncarpetted stairs to the upper rooms, which the previous occupants had used as their living accommodation, and noticing details which he had not seen before when he had gone round with the estate agent or which he had discounted as unimportant.

Floorboards creaked underfoot. A sash window rattled where a broken cord hung down. The bath was stained brown under the cold tap.

The shop itself was no better. As he stood in the doorway surveying it, he wondered what the hell had persuaded him he could do anything with it. The dream he had had of pine shelves full of books, of plants and a few choice volumes displayed artistically, now seemed ridiculous.

It would take weeks of work to strip out the old fitments and repaint the discoloured walls before he could open for business.

Kicking at the pile of circulars which had collected under the letter-box in the front door, he went back to the car and began to move in his belongings; first the boxes of books, which he piled up in the back room behind the shop; then his personal possessions. These he carried upstairs to the room overlooking the yard, which he had decided he would use as a temporary bed-sitter until he could afford to redecorate and furnish the other rooms. It was equipped with a cupboard in which he hung his clothes. Lastly, he moved in the camping gear which he had bought at Poulson's on the way there, stopping in the town centre before driving to the shop.

With the bed unfolded and the canvas chair set up by its side, the little spirit stove placed in the hearth and the gas lamp standing on an empty crate he had found in the yard, the room began to take on a makeshift homeliness.

But, God, what would Joanna think of it!

He imagined her standing in the doorway, wearing that light grey coat of hers with the silver fox collar and raising her eyebrows in horrified disbelief.

Suddenly he began to laugh.

The whole situation was so absurd that laughter was the only possible reaction. Any other was unthinkable.

He'd celebrate, he decided, by buying himself a fish-and-chip supper and a tin of lager.

Checking the money in his pocket, he found he had three pounds and sixty-seven pence left after his purchases, all that he possessed until the banks opened on Monday.

And he'd bloody well buy a plant, too. The market hadn't yet closed and he'd probably be able to pick up something from one of the stalls selling garden produce for a few bob.

Still laughing, he clattered down the stairs.

CHAPTER TEN

Madge was annoyed. She had expected Bartlett to arrive as usual for work on Wednesday afternoon and had spent part of the morning inspecting the kitchen garden and marking out a new site for the strawberry bed.

The far end would be best, she decided, where the ground lay in full sun for most of the day; not that Bartlett would be pleased. It was the plot he used as a nursery to raise wallflower seedlings for the herbaceous borders. But she was determined to have her own way. After all, it was her garden and Bartlett grew far too many wallflowers anyway. Every spring she was forced to give away bundles of plants to anyone who'd accept them, grateful to be rid of them.

In view of her own plans and Bartlett's normal reliability, his unexpected nonappearance was both surprising and exasperating.

She expressed her annoyance to Gordon over tea, the only time of the day when she had the opportunity to discuss her interests with him. By the time evening came, he was too exhausted to listen properly.

"He simply didn't turn up," she explained. "You'd think he would have sent a message. He's not ill, is he?"

"Not to my knowledge," Gordon replied. "At least he's not called at the surgery or asked for a visit. No one said anything to me either when I was in the village this afternoon. I dropped in on Mrs. Franklin, by the way."

"How is she?" Madge asked, adding as she raised the pot, "More tea?"

"Please." He held out his cup for her to fill. "A little better but still shocked. That woman's aged ten years in the last few days. I feel desperately sorry for her."

"But what can you do?" Madge asked. "What can anybody do? One feels so helpless. I'd call myself but I don't think she'd welcome a visit. Besides, the vicar told me that her next-door neighbour, Mrs. Rattney, has been staying with her practically day and night and, quite frankly, Gordon, I'm not too eager to run across her again, remembering all the fuss there was last month over the church jumble sale. As if I'd accuse her of pocketing some of the money! I simply said that wasn't it disappointing that her stall hadn't done as well as last year. That's all. But that's beside the point. Honestly, I really feel that you ought to persuade Mrs. Franklin to go and stay with one of her daughters. I'm sure Helen would willingly have her. They've got that nice modern bungalow over at Latchingham and being with the grandchildren would take her mind off the whole ghastly business. Can't you speak to her?"

"I think she prefers to stay here until the inquiry's over," Gordon replied.

"Which will be when?" Madge demanded. "I can't imagine what the police think they're doing, although, judging by that chief inspector who's in charge of the case, I'm not surprised it's taking them so long. It was obviously an accident. In fact, I understand she'd been drinking at the Goat before she called on Alec Lawson. It's possible she'd had too much and that's why she fell."

"If she did, it'll come out at the inquest," Gordon pointed out. "There's bound to be a post-mortem and that'll show how much alcohol was in the stomach."

"Oh, Gordon, don't!" Madge protested, putting a hand on the front of her tweed skirt. "For some reason, just the thought of it makes me go quite cold."

"Sorry. I didn't realise it would upset you. You usually take such things in your stride."

"Accidents, yes, when there's something practical one can do to help. I've never minded that. But the idea of some pathologist quite dispassionately— Oh, it doesn't bear thinking about! I don't know how anyone could seriously choose such a profession."

"It has to be done," Gordon put in mildly, "although I don't mind admitting it wouldn't be my choice of a career. I prefer to work with the living rather than the dead. You'll be all right at the inquest?" he added, looking into her face with quick anxiety.

Madge shook back her hair. For some reason, his concern made her feel impatient as if he were suggesting she couldn't cope.

"Of course I shall. I imagine it'll be quite straightforward, especially if Broderick's the coroner. He usually is, isn't he? The last time I met him, at that Conservative do at Lyston Hall, he didn't strike me as being particularly formidable. Rather the opposite, I thought. Besides, I shan't have much to contribute, shall I? If I'm called at all, it will simply be because I happened to see Stella with Alec Lawson on my way back from the Maceys', which will hardly be useful except for establishing the timing."

"But that's not all you saw," Gordon reminded her. "You may be asked about the rest of it—Lawson raising his hand and Stella seeming to stumble."

"Shall I?" Madge seemed distressed at the idea. At times she regretted having told Gordon about this part of her interview with Rudd, although she could hardly have kept it from him. She was still angry with herself for having been tricked, as she felt, into making the admission in the first place by the chief inspector, who hadn't seemed capable of such subtlety nor perception. But, as Gordon had pointed out, it had been her duty to speak. To do otherwise would be to withhold evidence. "But surely, if it's an accident, Broderick won't be interested in details like that?"

"He may ask you about it and I think you ought to be prepared in case he does. After all, we don't know what the verdict will be."

"But it's absurd!" Madge protested. "That bridge is notoriously dangerous. If you remember, I raised the whole question with the parish council only last year and if that fool of a man Sutton hadn't insisted on the money being spent on new equipment for the Youth Club, it could have been put right. The steps need repairing as well as the actual planking itself and another rail ought to be placed below the top one to act as an extra safeguard. It's a miracle no child has fallen into the ford. They often play there in the summer."

"Yes. Well," Gordon said, not committing himself. It was an old source of discussion between them and one which, while he agreed with her basic argument, Madge hadn't at the time handled all that well in his opinion, although he had refrained from pointing this out to her. She should have got the vicar and the P.T.A. on her side before tackling Sutton, who was a stubborn man when crossed in committee and didn't like to be defeated, especially by a woman. He ought to have talked to her about it at greater length, he felt. He had let her down. And not just over that particular subject but over many others. It was his fault entirely, of course, although there never seemed enough time.

Since the children had grown up and left home to go to university, he had sensed a restlessness and dissatisfaction about her. Of course, being Madge, she kept herself busy and never complained but he had the feeling that much of the village activity in which she involved herself was a mere stopgap for something else which was missing from her life which he ought to fill but which somehow in the busy years since their courtship and the early years of marriage he had lost the knack of supplying.

To make it up a little to her now, he said, "You were right, of course, about the bridge. Perhaps something will be done about it."

"When it's too late," Madge replied with some bitterness.

"Exactly," he agreed. "But we've strayed rather from the main issue, Madge. The point is, if you're questioned at the inquest about Lawson, what will you say?"

"The truth, of course," she said sharply. "I shall tell them exactly what I saw. I'm not for a moment suggesting that Alec Lawson had anything to do with Stella Franklin's death and I shall make that quite clear, although I can't imagine Broderick will raise the matter anyway. As I said before, I'm convinced it was an accident. But that doesn't alter the fact that I saw Lawson quarrelling with her."

"It could be awkward for him if the verdict isn't accidental death," Gordon remarked.

"But what else could it possibly be?"

"I don't know, Madge. Murder? I know it's unlikely but it depends on what other evidence the police have. Or there could be an open verdict. Either way, it could make life difficult for Lawson, even if he isn't named. You know Macey's asked him to leave the caravan? More or less chucked him out as far as I can gather."

"Who told you that?"

"Oh, I don't know," Gordon replied vaguely. "I heard it in the village this afternoon. It seems Macey was suspicious of the part Lawson might have played in Stella's death and told him to go. It's absurd, of course, but there you are. Once the mud gets churned up, some of it's bound to stick, even on the innocent."

"God!" Madge said furiously and began rattling the tea-things onto the tray as if finding some solace in the crash of china. "People round here are impossible! I sometimes hate their—" She broke off. Gordon had never encouraged her to show emotion. A controlled man himself, he was embarrassed by such outbursts. She began again, more calmly. "Although I didn't much like him, I'm sorry this has happened. I wouldn't have wished it on him for the world. I'd rather hoped he was our kind of person."

"What do you mean by that?" Gordon asked. He had half risen from his chair but sat down again, looking across at her.

Madge laughed and shrugged as she continued loading the tray.

"Oh, I don't know," she replied. "Someone interested in books, I suppose, and art and things like that. But it doesn't matter now. Didn't you say earlier that you had a letter to write to the specialist in Chelmsford about the Baxter boy? If you'd like to get it done, Gordon, I'll post it for you in the village. I was thinking of walking down there anyway to call on Bartlett, so I could put it in the box for you. Someone ought to find out what's the matter in case he's ill. Besides, I want to know if he's coming tomorrow or not. I had planned on driving into Studham to change my library books but I'd rather wait in and see him, that is if he comes. I must discuss the garden with him. What a nuisance it all is! I had tomorrow all arranged."

Bartlett was at home. He was sitting in the kitchen with the back door open as Madge arrived, gazing morosely down the garden at the long vegetable plot where strips of old blue fertilizer bags, fixed to the top of tall canes to act as bird-scarers, fluttered over the neatly ridged earth.

He didn't look particularly ill to Madge, merely sullen, lifting his head unwillingly to look at her as she walked round the side of the cottage.

"I've come to see how you are," she announced.

"I'm all right," Bartlett mumbled, returning his gaze to the garden.

"Only you didn't come this afternoon," Madge continued. She had been expecting an apology and, when Bartlett still didn't respond, she felt a further explanation was needed. "To do the garden."

"No," he agreed.

"Aren't you feeling very well?" Madge asked. He had made no attempt to get up from the kitchen chair, which was placed just inside the doorway, or to invite her into the house and she was forced to remain standing outside on the patch of concrete by the step, looking up at him. Seen from this angle, his face looked longer than ever, the jaw sagging slackly, dragging down the corners of his mouth so that the features had the exaggerated appearance of a grotesque mask depicting melancholy.

Perhaps he was ill after all, Madge thought.

"If it's your leg that's bothering you," she added quickly, before Bartlett had time to reply to her question, "I could ask my husband to call or I could drive you up to the surgery myself. I'm perfectly willing to do so."

The offer seemed to mollify Bartlett a little. He got up from the chair and carried it back to its place by the deal table which, covered with a flowered plastic cloth, took up most of the centre of the room. A jerk of his head invited her to enter. Madge mounted the step and stood just inside the door, resisting the temptation to look too closely about her at the signs of Bartlett's disorganised bachelor existence.

A grey woollen vest hung on a string over the mottled boiler, its arms dangling down while, on the table, a loaf of bread sat among crumbs on a worn round board, the wood cut about with countless knife marks. Beside it were two slices of ham in a piece of greasy wrapping paper and a jar of pickles, with its lid off, showing a dried brown crust round the rim.

"I see I'm interrupting your tea," she added, feeling the need to say something as Bartlett remained silent.

"I'd finished," he replied.

"Would you like my husband to call?" Madge asked again. She had noticed that, as Bartlett had carried in the chair, he had moved more stiffly than usual, one hip pushed forward as if he were attempting to take the weight off his damaged leg.

"I ain't been sleeping too well lately," Bartlett said with apparent inconsequentiality, although the remark seemed to be intended as an oblique explanation of his present physical state as well as his nonappearance that afternoon.

"If you're in pain—" Madge began.

"It ain't my leg," Bartlett said. He remained standing on the other side of the table, still holding on to the back of the chair. "It's the shock."

"Shock?" Madge didn't understand.

"Of that girl dying."

"Stella Franklin, you mean?"

Her first reaction was one of surprise. Why on earth should Bartlett care about Stella Franklin? Of course, he knew her as everyone else in the village did. One couldn't live in a place like Wynford without getting to know each individual by name at least. But Bartlett had never struck her as the type who would take much interest in his neighbours nor in local gossip like some she could think of. He had always seemed an uncommunicative man who had held himself aloof from personal contacts. She could conceive of no reason why the girl's death had affected him so deeply, as it obviously had, unless the very idea of someone dying had reminded him of his own mother's death, which, Madge remembered, had occurred about the same time last year. Madge had visited her in her last illness on several occasions, bringing flowers and women's magazines and grapes, the usual contributions which the healthy offer to the sick, like sacrifices made to some pagan goddess of vitality to ensure one's own continuing physical well-being, Madge had thought at the time; not that the comparison had been exactly apt in old Mrs. Bartlett's case. Madge recollected a beaky nose sticking out over the bedclothes, thin white hair spreading out on the pillow and a sour-sweet smell of urine and old, unwashed flesh.

All Bartlett had said when she finally died was, "She's well out of it."

Madge had the impression that the relief he expressed was as much for his own sake as hers.

"Stella's death was a shock to all of us," she remarked. She hoped Bartlett would leave it there but, now he was embarked on the subject, he seemed unable to let it go.

"I saw her last Friday night, not long before she must have died," he continued. "She was in the Goat. Then she left and *he* came in."

"Who?" Madge asked.

Bartlett couldn't possibly mean Alec Lawson, she thought. As far as she knew, Lawson had been in the caravan all evening. At least that was the interpretation local rumour put on the events. Stella Franklin had walked up to the caravan to find him because he hadn't been in the Goat as she had expected.

"Him. Her husband," Bartlett explained.

"Oh, I see," Madge replied. There was not much else she could say as she still couldn't remember Stella's husband's name or much else about him except he came from Studham, where he worked in a garage and was, judging from the rare occasions when she had seen him in the village after the wedding when he and Stella were still living with Mrs.

Franklin, a dark-haired young man with a glowering expression and a disturbing air of suppressed violence about him. "Didn't he knock Stella about and that's why she left him?"

"She should never have married him!" Bartlett shouted in an unexpected outburst of emotion.

"Yes, of course," Madge agreed.

But how extraordinary! she added to herself. Why in heaven's name should Bartlett feel so involved with Stella Franklin's life? Or death, come to that? Unless he was going through some emotional crisis to do with his age. He was—what?—in his fifties, she supposed, at the time of life when such disturbances were said to occur, and even Bartlett, who never gave any indication of having any interests apart from work or any real feelings except for a plodding, dogged acceptance of what could only be a dull and routine existence, must nevertheless be susceptible to hormonal changes. She remembered Gordon telling her about a farmer at Latchingham, also in his fifties, who had shot his wife and two sons before hanging himself in the barn. Gordon had attributed that fourfold tragedy to the man's age.

The memory of it made her uneasy, as did Bartlett's face, pushed forward towards her, the eyes staring and the mouth open, blobs of spittle gathered at the corners of his lips, and his hands grasping the back of the chair with such force that she could see the knuckles showing yellowish white under the skin.

She had been about to add that Stella had been forced to marry the young man from Studham, whatever his name was. After all, she'd been pregnant by him, hadn't she? But, at the sight of Bartlett's face and gripping hands, she changed her mind.

Instead, she said, "If you're not sleeping very well, Mr. Bartlett, I'm sure my husband could prescribe something for you."

To her relief, the spasm of anger passed and his face fell back again into its normal, melancholy folds.

"I don't want no tablets," he muttered, turning away so that she could only see his profile. "I don't hold with dosing myself up."

"But you should take something to help you relax, if only a nightcap."

Opening her handbag, Madge took out her purse and extracted a five-pound note, which she held out to him.

"Won't you treat yourself to a bottle of whisky or brandy? I'm sure it would do you good last thing at night. Go on, take it," she urged as Bartlett shook his head and turned even further from her and the proffered note.

"I ain't short of money," he retorted and his head went up, showing the same beaky profile as his mother spurning the copies of *Woman's Own* and the black hot-house grapes, an ironic expression glittering under her wrinkled lids.

"Very well," Madge said briskly. If that was his attitude, she had no intention of pleading with him. She put the purse away and snapped the bag shut, at the same time making up her mind to speak to Gordon about the man. Clearly Bartlett was under some stress although for quite what reason she couldn't imagine. It couldn't just be caused by the girl's death. No doubt Gordon would be able to contrive a visit without it appearing too obvious when he was calling on other patients in the village.

"I'll leave you then, Mr. Bartlett," she concluded. "I hope you'll feel better soon. When you do, I expect I'll be seeing you back at work."

She gave a slight interrogative lift to the last remark, inviting Bartlett's reply but instead of saying as she had expected that he'd be round the following afternoon or early the next week, he made no comment and Madge was forced to let herself out of the cottage with no definite idea of when he would return.

It was a nuisance. She was hoping to get the new strawberry bed prepared and planted before the main work on the vegetable garden began. In a few days' time it would be April, when there would be so many other jobs to be done outside, and she couldn't possibly cope with them on her own. It was no good expecting Gordon to help either. He was far too busy as it was.

Damn Bartlett! she thought. He'd always been so reliable in the past. If he let her down, who could she find to replace him? There was no one else in the village who was willing to be employed as a jobbing gardener despite the fact that several young men she could think of were out of work, such as Mrs. Wilson's son, who spent all day lounging about at home when he wasn't scrounging money from his mother to go into Studham to a disco. Not that she would dream of asking him anyway. She doubted if he'd recognise a strawberry plant if he saw one.

Walking back along the village street, she was overwhelmed with the feeling that everything was changing and for the worse. Wynford wasn't the same as it had been when she and Gordon first came to live there. The children had been small then, Richard only a baby. Life had seemed so very full and rich with promise. And easier, too. There had been no problem getting help with the housework. Mrs. Stone—dead now—clean, respectful, eager to earn a little extra, had come in every morning while her husband, also dead now, had seen to the garden, working on it every Saturday afternoon for ten shillings, despite the fact that he had a full-time job as a farm labourer all the rest of the week. Shops had delivered. Tradesmen went out of their way to be obliging.

People were more content, too. There was none of this desperation to acquire material things. Teenagers were happy if they went to Studham on the bus once a week to the cinema. The fare then had been one and tenpence. Now the cinema was closed and turned into a bingo hall with a disco twice a week and a wine bar. God knows what the fare was these days. Over a pound, she believed.

Madge reached the end of the street and paused outside Mrs. Franklin's house. As the doctor's wife, she ought to go in, she supposed. Gordon obviously expected her to pay a visit but what on earth would she say? The conventional expressions of sympathy seemed quite inadequate.

As she hesitated, the front door to the next house opened and Mrs. Rattney came out, carrying something in a pudding basin covered with a white cloth, and eased herself sideways through the gap in the hedge between the two gardens. The sight of her, that formidable backside and fat, foolish face with its little turtle mouth clamped shut, decided her and as the woman let herself into Mrs. Franklin's cottage, calling out "Coo-ee!" as she did so, Madge walked on, pretending she hadn't seen her.

She had no intention of confronting Mrs. Rattney; at least not yet. There would be a more suitable opportunity at some later date at one of the Ladies' Church Guild meetings when it was Mrs. Rattney's turn to supply the refreshments and Madge, by praising her scones, could make her peace with the woman.

But how stupid it all is! Madge thought suddenly. And what a waste!

Although a waste of what, she herself wasn't quite sure.

CHAPTER ELEVEN

It was early the following week before Rudd received Pardoe's report. Until it arrived, there was little he could do except write up his own reports and wait for Pardoe to submit his.

Meanwhile, forensic examination of the dead woman's clothing had come up with nothing positive to help the investigation. Her handbag had also proved negative, for tests had shown that only Stella Reeve's fingerprints were found on it, while it had contained nothing more than might have been expected—a box of matches, a half-empty packet of cigarettes, a lipstick, comb and powder compact together with a purse containing a couple of pound notes and some loose change —no vital evidence, in other words.

No useful fingerprints had been found on the handrail either, only blurred smudges which it was impossible to identify.

The only positive test was on the fibres caught on the rail. These had come from Stella Reeve's coat, not that this was any help in establishing whether or not she had been murdered. In fact, if anything, it tended to support the theory of accidental death.

The body was formally identified by Ken Reeve on Saturday afternoon after Rudd's return from Wynford, an arrangement he had made in order to be present to witness Reeve's reaction.

In the event, he was disappointed. It was a brief, sombre occasion, Reeve merely glancing down at the face before turning away.

"That's her," he said.

He seemed subdued, less challenging and macho in a suit and a white shirt, his thick black hair combed flat.

And that was that.

He said nothing more, not even looking in Rudd's direction as he was led away to sign the necessary statement.

Rudd lingered to take a last glimpse of Stella Reeve's face before the trolley containing her body was rolled back into its refrigerated compartment. The hair had dried and, under the strip lighting, looked coarse. He noticed for the first time the dark roots and the artificial kink in the ends from a perm which was growing out and which the submersion in the water had turned frizzy. Without make-up, the features looked less well-defined, while the mouth had fallen slightly open, revealing the prominent teeth and accentuating the heavy line of the jaw.

Death had not been kind to Stella Reeve as it was to some.

Seeing her, Rudd felt an overwhelming sense of waste. She had been robbed, not just of life, but of some special vitality which had been uniquely hers, like a light suddenly quenched.

"How did Reeve take it?" Boyce asked when Rudd returned to the office.

"He didn't confess if that's what you're hoping to hear," Rudd snapped.

He felt in low spirits, a reaction which a visit to the mortuary always roused in him, although in this case it was worse than usual.

Boyce shrugged it off. Having worked with Rudd over many years, he knew the chief inspector too well by now to be affected by his moods. The inquiry itself didn't help, of course. Until the exact circumstances of the death had been established, a question mark hung over the investigation which was inhibiting to everyone concerned but especially to Rudd, who was in charge of it.

"Perhaps Pardoe will come up with his report soon," he said with a helpful air.

Ignoring him, Rudd went to stand hump-shouldered at the window, where he stared morosely out at the rain.

The report came three days later. Pardoe brought it himself, bustling into the office in his usual hurried manner as if the visit had interrupted much more important and pressing matters.

"As I thought when I made the preliminary examination, the cause of death was drowning," he announced briskly. "And the time was approximately three to four hours before I examined the body, that is between eight and nine o'clock that night. My theory that she was knocked unconscious by the fall seems to be borne out by the evidence, by the way. Forensic has identified some small pieces of gravel and debris in the wound tissue on the forehead which correspond to the sample your men collected up from the bed of the stream where the body was found."

"Any other marks on her?" Rudd asked, trying to disguise his eagerness.

"I was coming to that," Pardoe retorted, annoyed at the interruption. "There's bruising on the right forearm. I can't be too precise about it because the thickness of the coat she was wearing absorbed a lot of the pressure. But from the position of the marks, it looks as if someone grasped her fairly tightly just above the elbow, and not long before she died, either. The bruises were fresh. What you make of it is your own affair."

And with that, he handed over his report and left the room.

"Wait a minute," Rudd said quickly as Boyce seemed about to speak. "Don't let's jump to any conclusions. Those bruises don't necessarily mean she was murdered. They could have happened earlier in the evening."

"At Lawson's, you mean?" Boyce replied. "That's true. Mrs. Bingham said she thought Lawson and Stella Reeve were quarrelling as she drove past. You'll check with him, of course?"

"Yes; get your coat; we'll go over to Wynford straight away."

As he put on his own coat, Rudd didn't add that, as far as he was concerned, Pardoe's report had confirmed the impression which he had received when he had first viewed the body—that taint of violence which had seemed to hang over the scene. Whether or not it amounted to murder had still, as he had pointed out to Boyce, to be proved. But at least it justified a further inquiry into the exact circumstances surrounding Stella Reeve's death. It confirmed something else as well. There was now no question where his own loyalties lay. He was fully committed to his professional allegiances.

Lawson wasn't in the caravan, which they found locked and, when Rudd mounted the steps to peer through the glass panel in the door, stripped as well of all the man's possessions.

"It looks as if he's gone," he announced.

Inquiries of Mrs. Macey at the farm elicited the information that he'd moved to the shop in Studham.

"Sudden, wasn't it?" Rudd asked.

Obviously ill at ease, Mrs. Macey had nothing more to say to them except to smile nervously before closing the front door.

The reason for her embarrassment was explained later when, having driven into Studham and found the shop, they put the question to Lawson, who replied, "I got chucked out by Macey."

"Why?" Rudd demanded.

Lawson shrugged and tried to look amused.

"He didn't give a reason but I can guess. I was the last person to see Stella alive. As some mystery seems to surround her death, rumour has it she might have been murdered and I seem to be the most likely candidate for the role of killer."

"I see," Rudd said blankly.

"I notice you don't deny the possibility," Lawson commented.

"Our inquiries aren't yet complete," Rudd replied. In view of the reason for his visit, he felt uncomfortable and unexpectedly sorry for the man. Lawson looked exhausted and dispirited, quite unlike his usual cocky, rather self-assured manner.

Looking about him, Rudd realised it wasn't hard to understand the reason for the change. The shop interior was in confusion. Chunks of plaster had fallen from the walls where the old fitments had been removed and were littering the floorboards, some of which had been torn up. Lawson himself was covered in dirt, his clothes and hands filthy, his hair full of plaster dust.

Some comment seemed called for and he remarked, "You've got a job on your hands by the look of it. Are you tackling it yourself?"

Alec Lawson's mouth twisted with some of his former irony.

"In the absence of money to pay a builder, yes, Chief Inspector, I am. Don't tell me I've bitten off more than I can chew, which is the comment most people make when they see it. I'm well aware of it myself. We'll go upstairs to talk, shall we? I assume that's the reason why you're here. At least the floor up there is whole."

They tramped up a narrow, uncarpeted staircase to a back room, minimally furnished with a camp-bed, a canvas chair and a crate.

"Sit down," Lawson told them.

He had recovered sufficiently to be genuinely amused at the situation, smiling broadly as Rudd claimed the canvas chair while Boyce lowered himself reluctantly onto the crate. He himself remained standing, one elbow propped on the mantelpiece.

"Well?" he asked.

"I wanted to check on the statement you made on Friday evening,"

Rudd replied. "You said Mrs. Reeve was with you for about half an hour. Was there any quarrel or disagreement in which you grasped her by the arm?"

Lawson looked at him directly. He seemed about to lose his temper and then changed his mind.

"No," he said evenly although Rudd noticed the muscles tighten along his jaw. "There was no quarrel and I didn't touch her."

"Or later when you said goodbye to her at the gate?"

This time Lawson merely repeated the single negative, "No."

"You didn't raise your hand as if to strike her?"

Lawson paused before replying.

"Someone saw us?" he suggested at last and as Rudd appeared about to open his mouth to protest, he continued, "It's the only obvious explanation, isn't it? You wouldn't have come here asking that sort of question unless you have evidence. So there was a witness." He made the remark musingly, half to himself. "The driver of the car, of course! The one that passed as Stella and I were standing at the gate. Who was it?"

"I'm not prepared to divulge the witness's name," Rudd said in his best officialese.

"Just answer the question, Mr. Lawson," Boyce put in, adding his own weight to the situation, pen poised over his notebook.

Lawson looked from one to the other of them.

"It would be funny if it weren't so damned serious," he commented. "You know, I can see exactly how your mind's working. What are you trying to prove? Murder? Does that count higher in the crime ratings than accidental death? I don't know what the hell your witness saw in the few seconds it took for the car to pass us, in the dark, too, with only the headlamps to see by, but it wasn't a quarrel or a fight, I can assure you."

"Your hand was raised, according to our witness," Rudd persisted. He tried to keep his voice noncommittal but was aware of a growing dislike for the man. Lawson quite clearly had a chip on his shoulder; quite why, he wasn't sure. But for whatever reason, Lawson's bitterness seemed to find expression in attacking any form of authority as if, by doing so, he was trying to justify his own rejection of what it stood for.

For his own part, Rudd realised that he had to make a conscious effort to control his antipathy in order to remain objective.

"Did I raise my hand?" Lawson was saying with pretended lightness. "I suppose I must have done, as your witness saw me. Oh, yes." He began laughing. "I remember now. How absurd! The verge was muddy. I believe I did lift my hand to point this out to Stella. She was wearing ridiculous high-heeled shoes and I thought she might slip."

There was a contemptuous note in his voice as he spoke of the shoes, dismissive not just of Stella but of all women and, hearing it, Rudd thought he understood the man a little better. The arrogance was largely defensive. For some reason, perhaps because of the break-up of his marriage, Lawson felt threatened by his own guilt and needed to strike out at others in order to protect his own self-esteem.

Which would make a good motive for murder, Rudd thought, if Stella Reeve, by something she had said or done, had damaged Lawson's pride.

"I see," he said blandly, his expression giving away nothing of what he was thinking. "I'd like you to make an official statement, Mr. Lawson. Would tomorrow afternoon at Divisional Headquarters at half past two suit you?"

"It won't, but I suppose I'll be expected to put in an appearance. Is that all?" Lawson asked as Rudd rose to go.

"One other point," the chief inspector added almost as an afterthought. "At the first interview, you said Stella Reeve had spoken of an offer she'd had. I'd like you to give the matter a little more thought before tomorrow so that we can include it in your statement."

"What offer?" Boyce asked when they emerged from the shop and got into the car.

"Didn't I mention it?" Rudd sounded distracted, glancing back as the car drew away from the kerb at the shop front with its dirty windows and shabby paint. He was thinking that Lawson would have a hell of a job putting the place into any sort of shape before he could open for business. He felt almost sorry for the man. "According to him, it was something Stella Reeve said in passing. She needn't have married Reeve, she told Lawson. She had another offer. That was all."

"So?" Boyce asked.

"So it occurred to me that someone else might have been interested in her and could have resented her marrying Reeve."

"You think it could be a motive for murder?"

"If it's murder," Rudd pointed out.

They were coming up the roundabout on the outskirts of Studham.

"Where to?" Boyce asked.

"Wynford," Rudd said, making up his mind. "I think we'll have another talk with Mrs. Franklin, Stella Reeve's mother."

"Any particular reason?"

"About the offer, among other things. She may be able to tell us if Stella had any other boy-friends before she married Reeve. I'd like to have a look at her belongings as well. You never know, she might have brought something with her when she left her husband that'll be a help in the inquiry."

Mrs. Franklin knew nothing of the offer.

"Stella never said anything to me about it," she said in answer to Rudd's question.

They were sitting together in the living-room, Mrs. Franklin looking pale and a little dazed. Rudd wondered if she had been prescribed tranquillisers. A small bottle of pills was standing on the mantelpiece but he couldn't see the label.

"But she had other boy-friends before she met Ken?" Rudd asked. It seemed natural to use Christian names when referring to the individuals involved in the case, almost as if he were a member of the family. And indeed he felt perfectly at ease. Many of the objects around him, the potted plants on the window-sill, the picture calendar hanging on a hook by the fireplace, the crocheted chairbacks, reminded him of his own childhood home.

"Oh, yes; Stella went out with quite a few. They're all married now, though."

"Could you let me have their names all the same?" Rudd asked.

Boyce jotted them down as she went through the list. There were about five of them.

"Stella was never short of a boy-friend," Mrs. Franklin added in explanation, "although it was generally her who chucked them over. Then she met Ken."

"Where did they meet?"

"At a disco in Studham. Stella was working in the town then, in Baxter's on the cooked-meats counter. That was before she went in for barwork. Ken had a car and he used to come over here to pick her up."

"But I believe they quarrelled?" Rudd put the question casually.

Mrs. Franklin seemed to accept without resentment the fact that he had picked up some of the local gossip.

"That's right. Stella said he wanted to be too much the boss. She wouldn't stand for anyone ordering her about so she threw him over."

"They got married though," Rudd hinted. He knew the reason, having learned it from Hadley, the local bobby, as well as Lawson, but he wanted to hear her version of the events.

"That was my doing," Mrs. Franklin confessed. "Stella found she was expecting and it was me who pushed her into marrying him. I knew people were talking and who else would have wanted her, with another man's baby on the way? So they got married. Later, I wished to God I hadn't got onto her about it. That was after they'd moved in with me and I could see the marriage wouldn't last although I hoped once they'd got their own place over at Studham they'd make a go of things."

"But they didn't," Rudd said. He had learned that much from Mrs. Franklin herself at the first interview.

"No," she agreed quietly.

"You told me, Mrs. Franklin, that when Stella came home she brought some of her belongings with her. Would you mind if my sergeant and I had a look through them?"

She accepted the request without question, perhaps in the belief that this was normal procedure in a sudden death.

"She had the back room, the one where she used to sleep before she married Ken," Mrs. Franklin explained, leading the way up a flight of steep stairs which ran from a narrow inner hallway between the kitchen and the living-room. It opened on to a tiny landing with two doors.

The bedroom was small with a sloping ceiling and was almost entirely filled by a double bed with oak head and footboards.

"I'll leave you to it," Mrs. Franklin added as she ushered them into the room.

When she had gone, Boyce squeezed himself past the end of the bed towards a wardrobe which was wedged in on the far side under the slope of the ceiling and, opening the door, began searching through the contents.

After a few minutes, he announced, "Nothing much here except clothes and shoes."

Rudd was having no better luck with the dressing-table which stood under the window. The top two drawers were crammed with jumpers and underwear, pushed in haphazardly, although the contents of the bottom drawer, evidently her best clothes, were more carefully arranged.

Tucked under a nylon blouse with sequin embroidery, he found what he had been hoping for: a box with a picture of black kittens on the lid which had once held chocolates.

It contained, as he discovered when he carried it over to the bed to examine it, a collection of cheap jewellery, underneath which were several cards—twenty-first-birthday greetings mostly, inscribed with the senders' names. But one was different. It was a Valentine card with a traditional red heart on the front, surrounded by a garland of flowers. Inside, the verse read:

> The flowers are for you, my dear,
> The heart is just like mine.
> Remember I am always here
> And long to be your Valentine.

There was no name.

Boyce, who had shut the wardrobe door, came across to peer over the chief inspector's shoulder.

"Could be from the husband," he pointed out.

"Somehow I don't think so," Rudd replied. "He didn't strike me as the type who'd send his wife an anonymous Valentine card, not with a verse like that on it. Have you got something we can put it into, Tom? I'd like to have it fingerprinted."

Boyce took a clear plastic envelope from his wallet and Rudd, having slipped the card inside it, carried it downstairs where he showed it to Mrs. Franklin.

"Have you any idea who might have sent it to your daughter?" he asked.

Mrs. Franklin shook her head.

"It was in a box with some twenty-first-birthday cards," Rudd added. Her face cleared.

"It was Stella's twenty-first at the end of January. An envelope came here a few days later, at the beginning of February with 'Please Forward' written across the front. I posted it on to her, thinking it was another birthday card. It could have been that one, I suppose. I remember thinking at the time: If it's for her birthday, she'll get it too late."

"You didn't recognise the handwriting on the envelope?"

"No. The name and address were printed in capitals."

"I see." Rudd's expression was blank. "You don't mind if we take it with us?"

"Not if you need it. Has it something to do with Stella's death?"

"I don't know, Mrs. Franklin," Rudd confessed. "We still haven't finished our inquiries."

Outside, Boyce said unexpectedly, "Something's up. I can tell by the look on your face."

His tone was almost accusatory.

They were standing in the road by the front gate to Mrs. Franklin's cottage, where Rudd had paused to look up and down the street as if uncertain which way to go. He grinned at Boyce a little ruefully.

"Let's get in the car, Tom," he replied. "I don't want to stand out here talking about the case. Drive up to the church."

"Well?" Boyce asked as he drew up at the churchyard gate.

"All right," Rudd agreed. "There is something the matter and that Valentine card clinches it. What do we do with it, Tom? Have it fingerprinted? And what then? Fingerprint every man in the village who knew Stella Reeve and might have sent it to her? Where the hell do we draw the line? I didn't want to discuss it with you before because I wasn't sure myself. And I still haven't made up my mind. Stella Reeve could have died accidentally although the case smells to me of murder. No, don't ask me why," he put in quickly as the sergeant seemed about to open his mouth. "I admit I have no real reason for thinking that. I hoped Pardoe's report would clear the matter up but it hasn't. Those bruises on her arm could be unconnected with her death. We're not even sure how she got them. I know Mrs. Bingham's statement about seeing Stella Reeve and Alec Lawson quarrelling would suggest him but he denies this and his explanation seems plausible enough. The point he raised, too, about the car passing too quickly for the driver to have had more than a fleeting glimpse is a valid one."

"So you're suggesting we cross him off the list?" Boyce asked.

Rudd felt exasperation rise. It was this same literal-mindedness on the sergeant's part which had been one of the reasons behind his reluctance to take Boyce into his confidence in the first place and he wished to God he hadn't been drawn into the discussion. Boyce lacked subtlety. As far as he was concerned, facts were all that mattered. Speculation was dangerous. In that respect, he shared Pardoe's approach to evidence.

And he was right, too, up to a point. But Rudd could not help regretting that Marion Greave hadn't been involved on the inquiry. She would have understood his doubt over the case and his need to discuss it as an intellectual exercise without committing either of them to rigid conclusions as Boyce was doing. She might, or so he liked to think, have also appreciated his dilemma over his sense of divided loyalties, which still disturbed him, although, with his conscious mind at least, the choice had been made.

He wondered if he should phone her and then dismissed the idea. It smacked too much of a mere excuse to contact her again and he was anxious not to appear too eager.

It was better perhaps to remain aloof from her and try to explain himself to Boyce, who was at least on the inquiry with him and ought to be fully involved, although he could hardly admit that his reluctance to do so was entirely due to the sergeant's own limitations.

Trying to keep his voice even, he replied, "That's the whole point, Tom. There isn't a list. Or rather there shouldn't be if Stella Reeve died accidentally. But if she didn't, can we prove it was murder? I don't think we can on the evidence we've so far collected even though I'm still convinced it wasn't an accident. Besides, there's something else that's bothering me." He paused and for once Boyce had the good sense to keep silent. "In a place like this we could stir up a lot of mud which could stick. Take Lawson as an example. Macey soon got rid of him. And that could be only a beginning. If it's a case of murder, we have no choice in the matter. But supposing it isn't?"

It was only an approximation of his real feelings, the nearest he could get to expressing himself out loud. As he finished, he glanced sideways at Boyce, who was sitting with his arms folded. Seen like that, his heavy shoulders squared, he looked too positive and challenging, hardly in the frame of mind to listen sympathetically to Rudd's tentative explanation.

His answer surprised Rudd.

"I don't see we have any choice," he replied. "You've smelt a wrong'un so we go on with the inquiry."

Rudd nearly laughed out loud with relief and genuine amusement. After all his own uncertainty and mental anguishing over the dilemma, it was Boyce who had cut through to the heart of the matter with a few laconic sentences, typical of the man and yet expressing his complete faith in the chief inspector's judgment.

He realised something else as well: that Marion Greave would have given him exactly the same advice only expressed more cogently. He could almost hear her saying it: "Trust your own instinct, Jack. There's no alternative."

And it was the only possible answer. He saw that now.

"Right!" he said with new vigour. "So we carry on. We'll get that card checked for prints and see if we can find out who sent it. We'll also check Lawson's statement this afternoon. In fact, we'll go over all the evidence again, Tom."

"Okay by me," Boyce replied in the same offhand manner. "Where to now? Back to headquarters?"

CHAPTER TWELVE

Alec Lawson came out of Divisional Headquarters and paused on the steps to button up his coat before walking to his car.

It was still raining, a fine misty drizzle, and the air felt cold and damp after the centrally heated warmth of Rudd's office.

During the interview, while his statement had been taken down and read over to him, he had managed to preserve an aloof, amused air as if he were indulging the chief inspector and his sergeant in some ridiculous game they had chosen to play, but the truth was that, despite himself, he had been impressed by Rudd's quiet authority and his imperturbability, which nothing seemed to shake.

At the end of the interview, after the statement had been signed, Rudd had merely gathered up his papers, nodded pleasantly to Lawson and left the room with the sergeant, sending in a uniformed constable to conduct him downstairs.

Walking back to the entrance, Lawson had been aware of an atmosphere of activity and busy commitment about the place. Telephones rang in offices. Typewriters clattered. Passing an open door, he caught a glimpse of three men bent over a desk, examining a large sheet of paper spread out over its top.

He was reminded of Tierson's, where he used to work and, for a moment, he regretted having lost that sense of belonging and participation which, in the good days before his disillusionment had set in, he had enjoyed.

It was absurd, of course. This was Rudd's little kingdom, not his. All the same, he half envied the chief inspector his familiarity with these corridors and rooms, the fact that the girl he passed, carrying a pile of folders, would no doubt recognise him and smile as she said hello.

For his own part, he got nothing; not so much as a glance. He was the outsider who had no place here.

As he emerged into the rain, this sense of alienation deepened as he realised that he had nowhere to go except back to the shop in Studham, to the cheerless upstairs room and the shop itself, stripped down to the plaster.

It wasn't until he had driven away from Divisional Headquarters into the one-way system that it occurred to him as he approached the traffic lights that, if he turned right, he could go home.

No, not home, he corrected himself. He no longer had the right to call it that. It was merely the house where he used to live.

The urge to revisit it was quite irrational, although he told himself that, since he was so near, it would be stupid not to call and make arrangements for collecting his books.

Simon would be at school, and for that he was grateful. He didn't want to meet the boy in such familiar surroundings. Joanna, too, might be out. If she was, he'd let himself in and leave a note for her.

But she was at home. As he turned into Claremont Drive, he could see her Renault parked on the hardstand in front of the garage.

At the sight of it, he almost turned back. It had been a mistake to come, he realised. The house and its setting reminded him too painfully of the weeks of anguish which had preceded his decision to leave.

It stood in a small, exclusive development of what the planners called "executive residences"—detached, four-bedroomed houses with white-painted cladding on the upper storeys; vaguely Swedish in conception, although the brass carriage lamps at the front doors and the landscaped gardens were entirely English, neo-Georgian with a dash of Capability Brown.

It was their pretentiousness which he had rebelled against and the realisation that they represented a life-style which he had found increasingly antipathetic. They epitomised for him a safe, smug, middle-class conformity which dictated the make of car you drove and the brand of sherry you served before dinner; the upmarket image which Joanna had seized on so eagerly. She had wanted nothing more than to be an executive wife with an account at Harrods and a son at St. Mark's prep school.

What the hell did any of it matter?

And yet the anger which had sustained him no longer seemed to matter either. He felt he had moved on to another plane and all he experienced now was a curiosity to observe once again what he had so violently rejected.

He rang the bell like any other visitor, although he still had his own keys to the house in his pocket.

Joanna answered the door. For a few moments, he saw her with a stranger's eyes: an attractive, dark-haired woman, no longer young but carrying about her the unmistakable gloss of class. Then he noticed, with more familiar eyes, that she looked tired and unexpectedly harder, as if something inside her had stiffened. Her hostility towards him was apparent.

"Oh, it's you," she said coldly. "I suppose you'd better come in."

"I called to make arrangements about picking up the books," he replied awkwardly, addressing her back as she preceded him down the hall to the drawing-room.

"They're packed," she said. "You can take them with you."

The room, too, was familiar and yet different. The shelves which filled both fireplace alcoves were empty, apart from a few books he recognised as hers. Piled up on the floor near them were supermarket cartons, printed with the names of the different products which they had once contained, neatly fastened down with parcel tape and labelled according to their contents: Biography, History, Fiction.

Seeing them, he felt oddly humble and grateful.

"You shouldn't have gone to all that trouble," he said.

"I wanted them out of the way," she replied. "The house is on the market."

"So soon?"

"Wasn't that what you wanted?" she retorted. "I thought that was the idea. If there's anything else you want, you'd better take it while you're here."

"There's nothing else," he said, trying not to look about him at the furniture, the big chesterfield covered in buttoned velvet, the wing armchair which had always been his. He was aware suddenly of how comfortable and attractive the room was. Anyone who visited the house had always admired Joanna's taste. Hesitating, he added, "Except perhaps the horse."

It was a bronze figurine he had picked up cheap in a junk-shop, one of his few contributions to the furnishings. It stood on the stripped pine mantelpiece, rearing up to flourish its front hooves. He had bought it because it seemed to symbolise freedom and an unwillingness to submit.

"I'll pack it up," Joanna said.

When he returned from having carried the books out to the car, she had it ready for him, wrapped in several layers of newspaper.

"Give Simon my love," he said as he took it. "How is he?"

"He's well," she replied.

They might have been talking about some distant relative in whom both of them had only a peripheral interest.

"Perhaps I could call another time when he's home and take him out," he suggested.

"If you wish. But I'd be grateful if you telephoned first to let me know you're coming. It could be inconvenient if you just turned up."

"Yes, I see that," he agreed quickly. He felt some apology was needed for his unexpected arrival there that afternoon. Absurdly, too, he wanted to confide in her the reason in order to gain—what? Her sympathy? He wasn't sure. "I had to come to Chelmsford to make a statement to the police so I thought I'd call on the way back."

"The police?" she said sharply.

Now that he had her interest, he wanted perversely to treat the matter dismissively.

"A girl was found dead in the ford on Friday night. Funnily enough, you might have seen her on the Wednesday when you came with Simon. You probably passed her in the lane. She was young, blonde, a bit buxom."

He could tell from Joanna's expression that she recognised the description, although all she said was, "Why did the police want a statement from you?"

"Because she called to see me on the Friday shortly before she died. It was almost certainly an accident, although the police seem to view my relationship with her with some suspicion. They appear to think we were having an affair." He paused before adding, "We weren't."

This time he aroused no reaction in her except withdrawal.

"If there's nothing else you want," she said.

He tucked the paper-wrapped horse under his arm.

"No, thank you. Next time I'll phone before I come."

She accompanied him to the front door as if she were showing a stranger out but shut it as soon as he crossed the threshold.

So that was that, he thought.

Joanna returned to the drawing-room. Alec's arrival had disturbed her more than she was willing to admit, although, up to the time of his explanation for his sudden visit, she congratulated herself on having handled the situation well.

His admission about his statement to the police had shaken that self-assurance. It brought back the memory of that terrifying walk along the lane and her reason for making it.

Alec's denial that he had been having an affair with the girl seemed genuine. He rarely lied, she realised; a quality in him which she had not fully appreciated before, although the reason for it was not so much a regard for the truth as an impatience with deceit, especially the socially conventional kind. It could at times be a form of cruelty, a stripping away of any covering of pretence.

In this particular instance, however, she felt he had used the truth in self-defence. He felt vulnerable and the realisation of this made her feel strangely protective towards him, the first time she had ever experienced such a reaction. It was always she who had turned to him for comfort and support.

Her suspicion of him and the girl now seemed mean-spirited and unworthy, more especially since the girl was dead.

It was absurd, of course, for the police to think that Alec was in any way involved, although her own action in trying to spy on him the night the girl died seemed to place her, in her own eyes, on their side. However badly Alec had treated her, she felt that she nevertheless owed him some loyalty.

But what could she tell the police that would help him? She had seen nobody on that walk, only the headlights of a car in the distance. Could that be significant? Not knowing exactly when the girl had died made it impossible for her to judge.

On the other hand, even if what she had to tell them wasn't useful to Alec, she could at least make it clear to the police that she believed he was speaking the truth when he said his relationship with the dead woman had been innocent. She could also explain that Alec had never once, during their fifteen years of marriage, shown any signs of violence.

I'll go and see them, she decided and went immediately into the hall to fetch her coat from the downstairs cloakroom, pleased with her own decisiveness. Since Alec's desertion, she had learned quite a few useful lessons in coping on her own.

Checking she had her keys with her, she let herself out of the house.

Her arrival surprised Rudd, who had been discussing the Stella Reeve case with Boyce.

The first intimation he had of it was when the constable on desk duty telephoned through with the information that a Mrs. Lawson was downstairs and wished to speak to someone about the death of a young woman in Wynford. Rudd immediately instructed him that she was to be brought up to his office.

The name Lawson had given him an idea of her relationship with Alec Lawson but, all the same, he was taken aback when the WPC ushered her into the room. She was not at all what he had been expecting.

Lawson was careless about his clothes and appearance. Mrs. Lawson was smartly dressed and carefully made up, although under the surface pose he detected a certain nervousness as she sat down opposite him.

She began speaking at once, as soon as he had introduced himself and Boyce.

"I really know very little about what has happened," she said. "Alec called on me about half an hour ago and said he'd been asked to make a statement about the death of a girl in Wynford on Friday evening. I don't know her, although I think I may have seen her."

"When was this?" Rudd asked.

"On the previous Wednesday afternoon. I believe I passed her in the lane. Alec said she called on him. She was blond, wasn't she? Quite young? I don't know anything else about her, not even her name."

"Her name was Stella Reeve," Rudd explained. Intrigued to discover just how much she knew and the reason for her visit, he was reluctant to give away too much information. "Can you describe the woman you saw in more detail?"

Mrs. Lawson hesitated.

"She was dressed in jeans and a fur jacket; not real fur. As we were coming up to the footbridge, she was walking across it."

"We?" Rudd prompted.

"Simon, my son, was with me."

"And you were calling on your husband?"

Mrs. Lawson's chin went up in a defensive manner.

"I don't know if Alec has told you about us. We are separated. I went to see him to discuss a possible divorce."

"I see." Rudd remained bland. "So it was while you were on your way to the caravan that you passed this woman? Did you speak?"

"I didn't. Simon asked her if she knew where the caravan was and she told him it wasn't far."

"So you didn't speak to her yourself?"

It was Boyce who asked the question. Mrs. Lawson turned to look at him with a slight frown, as if resenting his interference. Probably out of snobbery, Rudd guessed. Boyce's rank of sergeant didn't count for as much in her estimation as his own. As far as she was concerned, he was a mere hanger-on.

This superior attitude was confirmed by her reply.

"No, I didn't. I had no wish to become involved with anyone from the village where Alec was now living. Besides, she was a little"—she made a vague, deprecatory gesture with one hand before continuing—"over-friendly, I thought."

Common, she really meant, Rudd suspected, although Mrs. Lawson was too careful of her own image to use the word openly.

His own expression courteous, he resumed the questioning.

"Did you know she'd called on your husband that afternoon?"

Her reply came too quickly.

"I had no idea. Alec didn't say anything to me at the time."

But she'd guessed. Rudd was convinced of that, although quite how she knew he could only surmise. Possibly something in her husband's manner had given her a clue; that, together with Stella Reeve's knowledge of where the caravan was to be found, would have been enough. Mrs. Lawson was no fool, and it wouldn't have taken much intelligence to put two and two together.

He was curious also to discover exactly why she had turned up at headquarters that afternoon. So far she had said nothing to explain her purpose. It was time she was brought to the point.

He began with deliberate vagueness, letting the sentence remain unfinished in order to allow her to complete it in her own way.

"About what happened last Friday evening, Mrs. Lawson . . ."

She seized on it eagerly.

"I was there!"

"*There!*"

Boyce was too quick off the mark and was rewarded with another of Mrs. Lawson's quick little frowns.

"I mean, I was in the village that evening."

"I think," Rudd broke in smoothly, "that you'd better tell us exactly what happened in your own words, Mrs. Lawson."

And giving Boyce a small warning glance not to interrupt, he settled back comfortably in his chair to listen.

The explanation came so pat that he suspected she had rehearsed it on the way.

"I decided on the spur of the moment on Friday evening to see Alec again. The discussion we'd had on Wednesday afternoon hadn't been very satisfactory and, as I'd been to see my solicitor in the meantime, I'd found there were one or two points which I wanted to clear up."

Lie number one, Rudd thought, although his expression betrayed nothing more than official interest, polite but non-committal.

"I took Simon with me but left him in the car which I parked behind the Goat." Even she seemed aware that this part of her story hardly stood up to close examination, for she added, giving Rudd a quick smile to invite his sympathy, "I'm not a very good driver, you see, Chief Inspector. I was nervous of taking the car through the ford in the dark and then having to turn it in the lane. On Wednesday, I'd nearly driven it into a ditch. So I decided to walk."

Lie number two, Rudd decided, at the same time nodding pleasantly as if in perfect agreement with this explanation.

"I got as far as the S-bend and then decided to turn back. It was darker than I'd expected and it was just beginning to rain. The whole idea suddenly seemed rather stupid."

"What time was this?" Rudd asked.

"I suppose about eight o'clock."

If the answer meant anything to him, there was no suggestion of it in either his voice or manner.

"I see. So you turned back before you reached the ford?"

"Yes, as I said, at the corner. I realised the ford wasn't far off, but it was too dark to see it."

"Did you meet anyone on the way?"

"No, no one."

"Or hear anything such as footsteps which might suggest someone else was out and about at the same time?"

"No. All I saw were the headlights of a car coming down the hill towards me. It was one of the reasons why I decided not to go on." She smiled again, trying to win his approval. "It may sound silly but I was rather frightened at being out alone in the dark with a car, driven by God knows who, likely to pass me at any moment."

"Understandable," Rudd murmured sympathetically. "And it was at this moment you turned back?"

"Yes. I thought I'd write to Alec instead or get my solicitor to contact him. I realised the whole idea of going to see him had been irrational and rather melodramatic."

In this, at least, she was speaking the truth. There was genuine embarrassment in her manner, which Rudd could understand. Humiliated and distressed, no doubt, by her husband's desertion, she had felt the need to make some emotional gesture, but not quite, he thought, in the manner in which she had described it.

She was adding, "I don't know if any of this has helped you in investigating that girl's death but I felt I had to come forward and explain that I was in Wynford that evening in case it was of any use to you. I also wanted to say that I don't for a moment believe Alec had anything to do with it. We've been married for fifteen years, Chief Inspector, and, although I'm divorcing him, I'd like to make it clear that he's never shown any violence to either me or our son. The marriage broke up for quite different reasons."

It was said not without a certain dignity, which Rudd responded to with a small nod of his head, acknowledging if not his official acceptance of her statement, then at least his recognition of her loyalty to her husband.

"Thank you, Mrs. Lawson," he said. "I'm grateful for what you've told me. All information is useful. In fact, I may ask you to make an official statement at some later date. There's just one further point I'd like cleared up. I assume you walked straight back along the lane to the Goat?"

"Yes, Chief Inspector, although 'run' would be a better word."

"Did you pass anyone on the way?"

"No, I met no one, much to my relief, I might add. As soon as I got back to the car, I drove straight home."

Rudd rose to his feet and, after thanking her again, signalled to Boyce to escort her downstairs.

"Well, there's a turn-up for the books," the sergeant commented as soon as he re-entered the room. "Who'd've thought Mrs. Lawson was in Waterend Lane on the night Stella Reeve died?"

"She was lying, Tom," Rudd replied. He was standing, staring down at the large-scale map of the area which one of the DCs had been sent out to buy that morning and which, while Boyce was out of the room, Rudd had spread out on the desk. Boyce went across to join him.

"Lying? You mean she wasn't there?"

"No, she was there all right. I meant she was lying about the reason. My guess is she wanted to catch her husband on the hop. That's why she left the car at the pub and walked. She didn't want to warn him of her arrival."

"But what was the idea?" Boyce asked. At times his naïvety could be astonishing.

"Looking for evidence for a divorce?" Rudd suggested. "I think she suspected Lawson of having an affair with Stella Reeve and she hoped to catch them at it. It was her way of getting a bit of her own back on him for walking out on her. But the point is this: how far was she lying? She said she turned back here, at the S-bend." Rudd jabbed a finger at the map. "We only have her word for that. Supposing she didn't? If she'd walked on, she'd've met Stella Reeve on or near the footbridge. The timing would have been right. Lawson said the girl left the gate of the caravan and started to walk down the lane seconds after the car Mrs. Bingham was driving passed them. Mrs. Bingham's statement corroborates that. Now, according to Mrs. Lawson, she saw the head-lights of a car coming down the hill towards her as she reached the S-bend, which is about thirty yards from the ford. That would place her within—what? a half minute's walking distance from it. In other words, she'd've arrived at the footbridge at roughly the same time as Stella Reeve, who was approaching it from the other direction. If that's what happened, then Mrs. Lawson would have been there when Stella Reeve met her death."

"You think she could have murdered the girl?" Boyce demanded.

"I'm not saying she did," Rudd replied, feeling some of his former exasperation return. "I'm merely putting the idea forward as a possibility. The bruises on Stella Reeve's arm suggest someone grasped her quite forcibly not long before she died, perhaps in a quarrel. On her own admission, Mrs. Lawson already knew her by sight. She'd passed her in the lane only two days earlier. If, as I believe likely, she suspected her husband and the girl were having an affair, she'd have motive, especially if she thought the girl had come from another evening making love to her husband. She admitted in her statement that she was frightened and overwrought. It wouldn't take much to make her lose complete control. She might not even have intended to kill Stella Reeve deliberately. You remember the set-up, Tom? The evidence tends to show that Stella caught her heel in the planking of the bridge as she crossed over it. Supposing at the moment she was trying to free it, Mrs. Lawson came up . . ."

"Hang on a moment," Boyce protested. "How did either of them know who the other one was? It was eight o'clock at night and pitch dark."

"All right." Rudd conceded the point. "Mrs. Lawson could have recognised Stella Reeve's voice. She said the girl spoke to her son on Wednesday afternoon when they passed in the lane. As for Stella Reeve not knowing who Mrs. Lawson was, that hardly matters, although Mrs. Lawson could have let slip some remark about Stella visiting her husband, Alec. The point is, Tom, a quarrel could have broken out in which Mrs. Lawson grabbed the girl by the arm and pushed her off the footbridge. Or there's another explanation which is just as plausible— that Stella Reeve lost her balance when Mrs. Lawson grabbed her. But whatever version is the true one, if Mrs. Lawson *was* on that bridge on Friday evening, the outcome amounts to the same—she walked away and left the girl to drown in fourteen inches of water and did nothing to save her."

"Except one's murder and the other's manslaughter," Boyce pointed out. "There's only one thing wrong with it as a theory, though. If Mrs. Lawson was involved in Stella Reeve's death, why the hell did she come forward and make a statement? No one knew she was in Waterend Lane on Friday evening. If she'd've kept her mouth shut, we would've been none the wiser."

"Perhaps she thought she'd been seen. She said she left the car at the Goat, so it's possible a customer from the pub saw her. Or the driver of the car, Mrs. Bingham. There could be another reason which would apply if she's not guilty: she wanted to protect her husband or, at least, divert our attention from him. And if that's the case, it raises some interesting questions. Does she suspect he could be guilty and, if so, has she any evidence of her own to make her think that?"

"But aren't they getting divorced?" Boyce asked. "I'd've thought the last thing she'd do is to stick up for him."

"I don't know, Tom," Rudd admitted. "Women do things sometimes for the oddest reasons."

As he said it, he was ashamed of the chauvinism in the remark, more so when he saw Boyce smile in agreement. What would Marion Greave have thought of it?

"Anyway," he added briskly to cover up the slip, "there isn't just Mrs. Lawson to consider. There's still Lawson himself, not to mention Reeve or whoever sent that Valentine. You took it along to be fingerprinted?"

"Yes, although it's a hell of a long shot, isn't it? Besides, what are we going to do if Wylie comes up with a set of prints which aren't Stella Reeve's? Check on every male in Wynford, like you suggested?"

Boyce seemed plunged into gloom at the possibility.

"Not necessarily, but we might make a start on the regulars who were in the Goat on Friday night and eliminate them first. I'll get that list off Mitchell tomorrow. At the same time, we could find out if anyone saw Mrs. Lawson leave her car behind the pub. Get the file out, will you, Tom? It's on top of the cabinet. I just want to go over again exactly what Mitchell said when we interviewed him."

Boyce fetched the file and laid it down on the desk, watching over Rudd's shoulder with a casual air as if he considered the chief inspector's meticulousness unnecessarily pernickety.

He was quite unprepared for Rudd's reaction.

"My God, look at that!" he exclaimed, holding out the typewritten report for the sergeant to read, one finger pointing to a line a couple of inches from the bottom. "How the hell did I miss it?"

Joanna sat in her car outside headquarters for several minutes before driving away, trying to persuade herself that the interview had gone well.

But it was no use. The truth was, it had been a disaster. Rudd had known she had been lying about her reason for being in Wynford on that Friday evening. Underneath his polite blandness, she had detected a scepticism. He hadn't been fooled.

God, what a mistake she'd made! She'd done nothing to help Alec; perhaps had even made it worse for him and, what was more, had involved herself.

Well, it was too late now. There was no turning back. All she could do was hope that nothing would come of it and the girl's death would turn out to have been an accident after all.

If it wasn't . . . But that didn't bear thinking about.

Starting the car, she drove slowly out of the car-park into the one-way system which led home.

CHAPTER THIRTEEN

Mitchell said, "Oh, God, you don't want that list now, do you, Chief Inspector? It's the day the brewery delivers and I'm expecting the lorry any moment."

Rudd and Boyce had found him in the store-room of the Goat, where he was stacking up crates, trying to clear a space for the new assignment.

"No, not the list," Rudd replied. "At least not at this stage. There's just a couple of questions I want to ask you. Firstly, did anyone park a car behind the pub on the Friday Stella Reeve died and then walk away from it? There was a boy left sitting in the car while it was parked."

Mitchell shook his head.

"Sorry, I can't help you there. I was busy in the bar that night from the time we opened till we closed so I've no idea what cars were parked out the back."

"Did any of your customers mention seeing it?"

"Not to me they didn't. Mind you, that's not to say none of them noticed it. You'd have to ask them yourself."

"It may come to that," Rudd agreed. "In that case, the list would be useful, Mr. Mitchell. I'll let you know if I need it. The second thing I want from you is a name. You said when I interviewed you the first time that you were going to follow Ken Reeve outside to warn him off but changed your mind because another customer left at the same time as Reeve or shortly after. Who was it?"

He said it casually, although it was this part of Mitchell's statement which had excited his interest and to which he had drawn the sergeant's attention. As he waited for Mitchell's answer, he avoided Boyce's eyes. The identity of the man could be important to the inquiry.

Mitchell looked from the chief inspector to the sergeant, who had taken up a position in the passageway just outside the store-room, not only blocking out the light but preventing him from leaving. He put down the crate he had been in the act of moving, his expression wary.

"What is this?" he demanded. "I thought Stella's death was an accident."

"The name, sir."

It was Boyce who spoke, looming in the doorway and almost filling it with his bulk.

Mitchell looked at him, sizing him up, and then shrugged.

"All right. I suppose I'll have to tell you. I don't want to stand in the way of any inquiries you're making. It was Reg Bartlett. I'll say this, though. If you think Reg had anything to do with what happened to Stella, you're barking up the wrong tree. He wouldn't hurt a fly, although—"

"Yes?" Rudd prompted as Mitchell hesitated.

"It's nothing much," Mitchell continued, "but I've just remembered something. On that Friday evening, Reg came up to the bar for a refill as Stella was standing there chatting to me. Only a moment before she'd said she'd wait in case Lawson turned up. Then suddenly she changed her mind and decided to walk up to the caravan to find him."

"As if she were trying to avoid Bartlett?" Rudd suggested.

Mitchell looked unhappy.

"It could be," he admitted.

"Tell me a bit about him," Rudd asked casually as if his interest were only marginal. "What does he do for a living, for instance?"

"He used to work for George Sutton, a local farmer, till he had an accident about two years ago and had to give it up. He does a bit of gardening now to earn himself a few bob, although he's got a pension."

"And he knew Stella Reeve?"

"Of course." Mitchell seemed surprised that Rudd should ask the question. "Both of them have lived in the village all their lives. Reg must have known Stella since she was born. But look, Chief Inspector—"

"And where does he live?" Rudd broke in.

"There's a pair of cottages on the left-hand side, just before you get to the church. Reg lives in the last one."

He seemed about to add another protest but Rudd thanked him briskly and walked away, Boyce following.

Bartlett was at home. A bike was propped up against the wall near the back door when Boyce and Rudd tramped down the path past a front garden full of daffodils just coming into flower to the rear of the cottage. Here, a long vegetable plot, neatly dug and planted, extended down to the boundary hedge which separated it from the adjoining field; the same field, Rudd noted, across which the footpath ran from the church to the ford in Waterend Lane.

Bartlett must have heard them coming, for he was on the back doorstep to meet them.

He was in his fifties, older than Rudd had expected; a loose-limbed, gangling man with a long, melancholy face, who was dressed in old working trousers and a waistcoat, worn over a collarless shirt open at the neck.

"What you want?" he demanded.

"Mr. Bartlett?" Rudd said cheerfully. "I'm Detective Chief Inspector Rudd and this is my detective sergeant, Boyce. Do you mind if we come in? We're making inquiries into the death of Stella Reeve and there's a few questions we'd like to ask you."

Bartlett made no direct reply but merely jerked his head, inviting them inside. Walking with a pronounced limp, he went ahead of them into a small front room, full of old-fashioned furniture which was too large for it. Heavy curtains cut out most of the light. In the gloom, the large-patterned, floral wallpaper took on a sepia colour making the whole effect sombre and claustrophobic. Even the air seemed thick and stale as if it had been shut away inside there for years.

"Sit down," Bartlett told them grudgingly.

They sat on either side of the fireplace on armchairs covered with worn velvet, Bartlett perching himself awkwardly on a straight-backed chair with a horsehair seat near the window. Of the three of them, he looked the most ill at ease.

"Well?" he asked.

During the short drive from the Goat to Bartlett's cottage, Rudd had worked out a stratagem with Boyce. If Bartlett seemed amenable to questioning, the interview would proceed slowly. If any problems seemed likely, then, at a signal from the chief inspector, Boyce would start straight in with the heavy guns.

Summing up Bartlett briefly and realising that the chatty, low-key approach was not likely to succeed, Rudd gave the sergeant a look and a nod at which Boyce produced the clear plastic envelope containing the Valentine card from the folder he was carrying.

"Do you recognise that, Mr. Bartlett?" he asked.

Bartlett took it from him. It had been handed to him with the blank, reverse side uppermost, another ploy previously agreed on, so that the man had to turn the envelope over in order to see the front of the card.

Rudd watched Bartlett's face closely as he stared down at the coloured picture of the heart and the garland of flowers but could read nothing in it except a look of sad bewilderment.

"Where did you get this from?" he asked.

"Never mind that," Rudd told him. "Did you send it to Stella Reeve?" As the man was silent, he continued in a sterner voice, "Look, Mr. Bartlett, if you did, I'd advise you to admit it. It'll save us a lot of trouble. You see, whoever sent it left his fingerprints on it and, if need be, we can take you into headquarters and have your prints checked on. I'm sure you wouldn't want that. It's the sort of thing that gets talked of in a place like Wynford. So, if it was you, you'd do better to tell us now while it involves just the three of us."

Bartlett muttered something but in so low a voice that Rudd couldn't hear the words.

"What did you say?" he asked sharply.

Bartlett lifted his head and looked at him, his expression closed.

"I said I sent it," he repeated. "What else do you want me to say? There was no harm in posting it to her."

"What exactly was your relationship with her?"

The man appeared not to understand.

"Relationship?" he asked dully.

"Were you in love with her?"

"Love?" Again Bartlett repeated the word, this time as if testing it out. Then he shook his head. "No, but I was fond of her."

"Did you make her a proposal?" It was Boyce who spoke this time and Bartlett turned his head slowly to look at the sergeant. "Of marriage," Boyce added as the man didn't respond.

"No," he said at last. "Marriage? Her and me? It never crossed my mind."

"But you made her an offer?" Rudd resumed the questioning as Boyce seemed taken aback by the denial. "An offer of what?"

Bartlett's head swung back in the chief inspector's direction. It took so long for his reactions to register that it was like prodding some great farm animal, Rudd thought.

"To help her out with money," he said. "I'd got some compensation, see, from the accident and I wanted her to have it. That was before she married Ken Reeve. I knew she wouldn't be happy with him. I'd seen them together in the Goat and I could tell by the way he treated her. It wasn't right. She knew it, too, 'cos she threw him over. Then the talk was that she was going to marry him after all . . ."

He broke off and looked down at his feet, planted side by side in their working boots on the worn carpet.

"Because she was expecting his child," Rudd put in to help the man out. Clearly Bartlett was unwilling to admit this fact out loud.

He looked up at the chief inspector, his expression oddly grateful for this assistance.

"I knew her mother wanted her to marry him. I'd heard the gossip about it. That's when I decided to say something to her."

"To Stella, you mean?" Rudd wanted this point quite clear.

"That's right. I saw her going into the Goat one evening. There was no one about so I spoke to her."

"And offered her your compensation money? What for?"

"What for?" Bartlett seemed surprised that Rudd hadn't understood. "So she wouldn't have to marry him, that's why."

Rudd left it there. It was pointless, he decided, to press Bartlett for an explanation of exactly how he had intended the money to be used. Probably he had no clear idea himself whether he had wanted Stella, had she accepted it, to spend it on an abortion or to support herself and the child. Bartlett's mind did not work on such clear-cut lines. To him, it was enough simply to offer the money.

"But she wouldn't take it?" Rudd asked.

"No," Bartlett replied. "That's why I sent the card. It was to let her know that I hadn't forgotten her and the money was still there if she needed it. I knew she'd realise it was from me. I was fond of her, see. I'd seen her grow up and I didn't want her marrying *him*."

"I understand," Rudd said. He did, too, although, judging by Boyce's expression, the sergeant hadn't fully grasped the situation. Bartlett had loved her, although he was probably speaking the truth when he said marriage had never entered his mind. What he had felt for Stella Reeve had been the inarticulate longing of a lonely, older man for a young girl who was far beyond his sphere of expectation. So he had offered her all that he had, his compensation money, but she had refused even that. Rudd could see the pathos in the situation. At the same time, it proved that Stella had possessed some special quality when she had been alive which so many people had found appealing— Mitchell, Lawson, even Hadley. And now Bartlett. Again he felt that sense of waste which he had experienced when he had looked down at her body in the mortuary. A light had been put out.

As for Stella herself, she must have been touched by Bartlett's gesture even though she had laughed about it to Lawson. She had at least kept his card.

"Now, Mr. Bartlett," he continued, "I'd like to move on to more recent events. You were in the Goat on that Friday evening, I believe? You saw Stella come in? But she didn't stay long?"

Bartlett, who had merely nodded his head at the first two questions, expanded a little on the third by saying, "About quarter of an hour. Then she left."

"You knew where she was going?" Rudd asked and when Bartlett didn't reply immediately, he went on, "Come on, Mr. Bartlett, you knew, didn't you? She told Fred Mitchell she was going to the caravan to see Lawson and you overheard."

It was a shot in the dark but it had to be right. All the same, Bartlett's reply surprised him.

"I knew she'd been seeing Mr. Lawson before that. I heard it from Mrs. Bingham on the Wednesday."

"From Mrs. Bingham?" Rudd asked sharply. "She told you?"

Something like a smile passed over Bartlett's face.

"No, she didn't tell me. I heard. I'd been doing her garden, see, that afternoon. She went out, down to the post office she said, and when she came back she brought me out a mug of tea. When I was ready to finish work, I took the mug back to the kitchen. I knocked on the back door but she couldn't have heard me. But I heard her. I let myself in to leave the mug and pick up my wages from the window-sill." He paused as if waiting for some sign from the chief inspector that he had followed the account up to that point and when Rudd nodded, Bartlett resumed. "She was in the sitting-room, talking to her husband. She said she'd seen Mr. Lawson and then she said about Stella being back in the village, only it wasn't her mother she was visiting, it was him."

"How did Mrs. Bingham know?" Rudd asked.

Bartlett lifted his shoulders.

"I dunno. But that's what she said and that's how I knew about Stella being friendly with Mr. Lawson before that Friday night."

"And that's all she said?" Rudd asked as the man seemed to have finished his account.

"That's right," Bartlett agreed.

Rudd glanced at Boyce, who raised his eyebrows, expressing the same idea that Rudd had in his own mind: so what? The story, such as it was, had proved little except Bartlett's previous knowledge of the friendship between Stella Reeve and Alec Lawson, a point which the chief inspector picked up when he resumed the questioning.

"So on the Friday evening you knew where Stella was going when she left the pub?" Bartlett, who had reverted to his more inarticulate method of replying, merely nodded in agreement. "And then a little later her husband, Ken Reeve, came in. I believe he didn't stay long?"

"Not much above five minutes," Bartlett replied.

"And when he left, you followed him outside. Why, Mr. Bartlett?"

"To see what he was up to. I thought he might be looking for Stella."

"Did you speak to him?" Boyce asked.

"No. I just followed him."

"Where did he go?"

"Back to his car, which was parked outside Stella's house. He stood beside it to light a cigarette and then he got in."

"And what about you, Mr. Bartlett?"

"Me? I was standing outside the Goat watching him."

Boyce had difficulty suppressing his impatience at the man's obtuseness.

"I mean afterwards. You didn't stand there watching him all evening, did you?"

"Course not!" Bartlett sounded unexpectedly derisive. "I waited for a few minutes till he got settled in and then I came back here."

"To the house, you mean?"

"That's right."

"You didn't go up to the caravan?" Rudd asked.

Bartlett turned to look at him with that slow, swinging movement of the head. He seemed to miss the point of the question for he replied,

"No, I didn't. There was no need. I could see Ken Reeve wasn't likely to go looking for her so I reckoned it'd be all right." He began to add something more. "She was—" but broke off and stared down at his boots again, his expression morose.

"Yes?" Rudd prompted.

Bartlett looked up and met his eyes.

"Perhaps if I'd gone after her I might have saved her. But I didn't like to push myself forward. She was a bit—I don't know how to put it —funny with me after I'd offered her the money; not as friendly as she'd once been."

"Perhaps she was embarrassed at having to turn it down," Rudd suggested to help the man out, although he suspected that this was only partly the reason. Stella hadn't wanted to encourage whatever unspoken sexual longings Bartlett had felt for her.

"Could be," Bartlett agreed. "I don't know. But I'll miss her just the same. It ain't right that someone as young as her should die."

"Yes," Rudd said. At least in that they were in agreement. There seemed nothing more to add and he got to his feet. "Thank you, Mr. Bartlett. We may need a written statement from you later. I'll let you know."

Outside, Boyce could hardly wait to ask the question which he had obviously had in his mind throughout the interview.

"What the hell did you make of that?"

"I don't know, Tom," Rudd replied. He genuinely didn't and would have preferred to keep silent until he had time to consider it at greater length.

He walked on past the car which was parked outside Bartlett's gate towards the church, which was only a short distance away, Boyce hurrying to catch up with him.

In the narrow entrance to the footpath, where it ran between the churchyard wall and the hedge of the rectory garden, he stopped to look up at the signpost which read in white lettering on the green paint: Public Footpath to the Ford.

Boyce put his thoughts into words.

"You think Bartlett could have gone to the ford after all?"

Rudd humped his shoulders.

"It's possible," he agreed.

"By the footpath?" Boyce persisted.

Rudd merely nodded this time.

"What about the timing?" Boyce asked. "If he followed Reeve out of the pub, would he have had time to get to the ford before Stella Reeve?"

Despite himself, Rudd looked interested.

"We'll have to work it out, Tom. It took me nine minutes to walk it from here the other day in the opposite direction but that was downhill and in daylight. Bartlett's got a game leg as well so it would have taken him even longer."

"He could have gone on his bike," Boyce pointed out.

"Oh, hell!" Rudd said. "Yes, he could have done. That'll mess up the timing even more."

"Come to that, Bartlett could have been speaking the truth," the sergeant put in. "Ken Reeve could just have easily met Stella at the ford and shoved her off that bridge. I know Bartlett said he saw him get in his car, which would seem to corroborate Reeve's statement, but there was nothing to stop him from getting out of it again and walking along the lane towards the caravan."

"But Mrs. Lawson was walking along it at roughly the time Stella Reeve died. She'd've seen him."

"Would she? It was dark, remember. Reeve could have been just behind her. If he kept to the verge, she wouldn't have heard him and, when she turned back, he had only to keep close up to the hedge and the chances were she wouldn't have seen him either. Come to that, he could have used this footpath. He'd lived in the village for a few months with Stella's mother before they moved to Studham so he'd've got to know the area fairly well. He must have known about the path. Here, where are you off to now?" Boyce broke off to ask as Rudd had done a smart about-turn and was heading back to the car.

"Headquarters, Tom," he said over his shoulder. "We'll need to look up the statements and get the timings worked out. We'll also need that large scale map."

There was a message waiting for him when they returned to the office. It was lying on top of his in-tray and, as Rudd glanced down at it, the name "Dr. Greave" seemed to stand out from the other words as if it had been written in larger letters.

Boyce, thank God, was on the other side of the room, fetching the map and the file on the case and Rudd was able to read it through quickly before the sergeant came back.

In the event, the message was brief and businesslike, hardly designed to raise romantic illusions. It simply read: "Dr. Greave telephoned at 11:25 a.m. and said that, if you were free at 8 p.m. tomorrow evening, she would like to see you."

That was all.

All the same, as he stuffed the piece of paper into his pocket, Rudd felt a lifting of his spirits. She wanted to see him! Absurdly, he felt as excited as an adolescent about to embark on his first date.

"Here we are," Boyce was saying, crossing to the desk and spreading out the map. "I've got the reports as well so let's see what we make of them."

They didn't make a great deal. After an hour and a half in which they pored over both in turn, they had reduced the information to a few facts, which Rudd jotted down. In all, they hardly filled one side of a page.

STELLA REEVE—victim. Died by drowning at approx. 8:03 p.m.

Possible Suspects:

1. ALEC LAWSON.   Within a hundred yards of victim at time of death. Had possibly been quarrelling with her shortly before. May have been having an affair with her. MOTIVE—jealousy, fear, revenge?

2. MRS. BINGHAM.   Passed Lawson and victim in car at approx. 8:02. Knew victim. MOTIVE—none known.

3. MRS. LAWSON.   Lawson's wife. In lane within thirty yards of victim at approx. 8:02. Timing verified by Mrs. Bingham's statement. May have suspected husband was having an affair with victim. MOTIVE—jealousy?

4. REG BARTLETT.   Left Goat at approx. 7:40 p.m. Waited to observe Ken Reeve for a few minutes. Could have left for ford at approx. 7:42, either

along lane or by footpath, on foot or by bike. Timings and distances to be checked. Was fond of victim. Knew of her relationship with Lawson. MOTIVE—jealousy?

5. KEN REEVE. Victim's husband. Separated. Known to want victim to return to him. Left Goat at approx. 7:40. Seen in car by Bartlett at approx. 7:42. Car still in village at 9 p.m.—seen by victim's mother. Could have walked to ford by lane or by footpath. Timings to be checked. MOTIVE—jealousy, revenge?

"It's too wide-open, Tom," Rudd pointed out, straightening up from the desk and grimacing as the muscles in his back protested. There was something else unsatisfactory about the report which he couldn't quite put his finger on but which was connected with the suggested motives, all of them involving jealousy, which was acceptable in theory and yet he felt in some inexplicable way was inadequate. As there seemed no point in trying to express this further doubt to Boyce, he continued, "We'll have to establish the timings much more accurately. For example, we must find out exactly how long it might have taken Bartlett to walk or cycle to the ford along the footpath. Then there's Ken Reeve. If we assume he was sitting in the car at 7:42, could he have got to the same place in time to kill his wife? We don't even know how long it would have taken him to walk from the gate of Mrs. Franklin's house where he was parked along the lane to the ford."

"What do you suggest?" Boyce asked.

"Going over the area on foot with a stop-watch?" Rudd put the idea forward without much enthusiasm, an attitude which the sergeant seemed to share.

"You mean tramp round it ourselves?"

"That's the general idea, Tom. I know it could be a waste of time if the case turns out to be accidental death after all, but until it does, we're doubly in the dark."

"All right," Boyce conceded unwillingly.

"Look at it as an intellectual exercise, like doing a crossword puzzle," Rudd told him, amused despite himself at the gloomy expression on the sergeant's face as he retorted, "I hate crossword puzzles but I suppose the timings will have to be checked. When were you thinking of doing it?"

"Tomorrow morning?" Rudd suggested. "That way, we can get it over and done with and spend the afternoon revising the provisional timetable we've drawn up. By the way," he added with studied careless-ness, putting his hand in his pocket to finger the folded sheet of paper with Marion Greave's message on it, "I'm hoping to knock off reason-ably early tomorrow. I've got an appointment."

"To do with the case?" Boyce asked nosily.

"Could be," Rudd replied. It wasn't exactly a lie. He might very well discuss the inquiry with Marion. It crossed his mind to wonder why she wanted to see him and then dismissed the thought as useless specula-tion. He'd find out soon enough when he met her the following eve-ning.

Tomorrow evening! A mere thirty-six hours or so away. Not long and yet it seemed like an eternity.

Anxious to get rid of the sergeant before he asked any more awkward questions, he continued, "Right, Tom! If you'd like to push off now, I'll get on with writing up my notes on the Bartlett interview. In the meantime, perhaps you'd expand these into a proper report."

Knowing himself dismissed, Boyce took the proffered sheet of paper on which the timings were written down and went towards the door, where he paused to look back.

But the chief inspector already had his head bent over his desk, seemingly absorbed in the new task and, reluctant to interrupt him, Boyce walked away although he couldn't resist shutting the door be-hind him with more ostentation than was strictly necessary.

CHAPTER FOURTEEN

"Nearly home now," Alec Lawson said with pretended cheerfulness as if the prospect held out Dickensian delights of log fires, hot punch and welcoming company.

Beside him in the passenger seat, Simon was silent.

As an outing, the afternoon had not been a success.

Alec had telephoned Joanna the previous day, suggesting a meeting with Simon, whom he had not seen since the Wednesday afternoon when Joanna had brought him to the caravan. He had meant to arrange to take his son out on the following Saturday for the whole day but Joanna, cold and distant on the telephone, had vetoed that idea. Other arrangements, she didn't specify what, had already been made for the week-end. He could, however, she said, meet Simon from school if he wished but the boy had to be home by seven o'clock at the latest as he had homework to do before he went to bed. It was like, Alec had thought, trying to make an appointment with some important stranger through an aloof and difficult receptionist. All the same, he had acquiesced.

Simon had been embarrassed at meeting him at the school gate, scuttling into the car before his friends could see him and sinking low in the seat.

As there was nothing suitable on at the cinema, they had gone instead to the park, where they had walked about largely in silence; at least Alec had made conversation and Simon had answered in monosyllables. Even the ducks hadn't cooperated. Discovering they were not going to be fed, for Alec had not thought to bring any bread with him, they had waddled back into the water and swum silently away.

Tea had been only marginally better. In a last effort to introduce some joy into the occasion, Alec had ordered a double hamburger and a banana-cream surprise for his son; not the type of tea he imagined Joanna would approve of. She had once followed a course of evening classes on diet, largely for her own benefit as she had been conscious at the time of putting on weight, but all of them had been subjected to a regimen of low-fat, high-fibre food in which he imagined, watching Simon munch his way steadily through the meal, chips and synthetic cream were not included.

But at least Simon's silence was more acceptable. With his mouth full and his eyes intent on his plate, his lack of conversation had not seemed so alienating.

It had been half past six when Alec paid the bill. Time to go.

The house, he noticed, as he turned into Claremont Drive, now had a for-sale sign outside it. It reared up out of the clumps of azaleas like a protest banner, much too obvious and challenging, as if advertising, in its strong black lettering, his desertion of his family for everyone to see.

He stared up at it as he turned the car into the entrance to the house. Of course, it was only what he should have expected. He had, after all, told Joanna to put the house on the market. Once the divorce went through, there was no reason why she and Simon should continue to occupy four bedrooms and two reception-rooms, not to mention a utility-room and a downstairs cloakroom.

And yet he was overcome with sudden guilt at the process of disintegration for which he was responsible. It would all be dispersed: the wing chair and the china, the little Victorian dressing-table mirror he had bought as a birthday present for Joanna in happier times, Simon's books and toys and precious models which he had helped the boy to glue and fit together so painstakingly.

For some absurd reason, he imagined them living as he did, crammed into some substandard accommodation with rattling windows and a damp kitchen which smelt of rot and sour food.

Simon was saying, turning in his seat to look up at him as he drew up in front of the house, "Are you coming in, Daddy?"

"No," Alec replied, "but I'll see you to the door."

All the same, after he had rung the bell, he waited, although, if he had really not intended entering, he should have walked away as soon as he saw Joanna's figure, looking oddly distorted through the reeded glass, coming towards them along the hall.

She looked surprised and then disdainful on seeing him standing with Simon on the doorstep. Ignoring him, she spoke to Simon first, asking, as he stepped into the hall, "Did you have a good time?" her voice too bright and at the same time faintly commiserating as if she knew the outing had been a disaster.

Alec followed him into the house, one hand on the boy's shoulder and almost treading on his heels in his eagerness to get inside before she shut the door on him.

"I want to talk to you, Joanna," he said.

He had to admire the way in which she coped with the situation, but then Joanna had never been lacking in social poise. It was one of the qualities which had first attracted him to her. Without showing the slightest hesitation, she said to Simon, "Go upstairs and start your homework, darling," before turning and leading the way into the sitting-room, where she closed the door behind them.

"Sherry?" she asked as if he were a guest who, while not exactly welcome, had to be shown some sign of hospitality for the sake of mere politeness.

"Yes, please," he replied.

Standing just inside the door, he watched as she crossed to the side-table on which the sherry decanter and glasses were placed. He was aware of an unfamiliar and disconcerting assurance about her. She even walked differently, as if something inside her had tightened, stiffening her backbone and giving a more positive tilt to the angle of her head. She had had her hair cut, too, in a new, shorter style. Seen from the back, she looked almost boyish in jeans and a loose, red sweater.

"Well?" she asked, handing him his glass and looking into his eyes with a challenging air in which he seemed to detect amusement.

In fact, her attitude towards him was very largely a pose. Since the interview with Rudd, her feelings had changed. She had been frightened by the chief inspector's response to her and this had put her on the defensive. It was far better, she had decided, to keep aloof both from Alec and the situation regarding the dead girl. As it was, she had no intention of telling Alec that she had been to see Rudd. She saw it now as foolishness on her part which had done neither of them any good and she regretted her impulsiveness. She would involve herself no further. After all, they were now quite separate people, responsible only for themselves, as Alec had made very clear to her when they had talked together that Wednesday afternoon in the caravan.

Aware of the change in her, Alec didn't know what he was doing there or what it was he had wanted to say.

"I just wondered how everything was going," he said awkwardly.

"Going?" She raised her eyebrows. "If you mean the house, it's going splendidly. I already have someone interested in buying it. If you mean the divorce, that's all in hand, too, or so my solicitor tells me."

"I'm sorry," he said, looking down into his glass.

"About what?" she asked sharply.

"About everything; you, Simon, the marriage—"

"Isn't that water under the bridge, as you put it?"

"I am still concerned about you," he said.

She was silent for a moment before replying, "I can understand your feelings, Alec, but you can't have it both ways. You lost the right to be concerned when you walked out. What you really mean is you like the idea of being a warm, caring husband and father without having to accept the real responsibility of the roles."

"That's not fair, Joanna!" he protested, although as she spoke he remembered Stella Reeve walking away from the gate alone into the darkness because it hadn't occurred to him to offer her a lift.

"Fair?" she repeated. "No, it probably isn't, but a lot of things aren't exactly fair. Your desertion wasn't fair. My having to bring up Simon on my own isn't fair either. If I said that all of this appears to be what you want, I suppose I could also be accused of being unjust. If so, I'm sorry but that's how I see it."

"I didn't want it to happen this way!" he exclaimed.

"Then in what way was it supposed to happen?" she demanded. "For God's sake, it's your doing, not mine. What *do* you want, Alec?"

"I don't know," he said. And suddenly he didn't. It had all seemed so glittering before—the prospect of freedom, of owning the bookshop, of being his own master at last. But it had been, as Joanna had pointed out, only an idea after all. The reality had turned out to be very different, sad, tarnished, reduced to a for-sale notice in a front garden, a silent walk through a park with his son, splintered floorboards piled up in a back yard.

"I don't know," he repeated. "If only . . ."

"If only what?" she asked.

"I honestly don't know that either, Joanna," he confessed. "I just wondered if perhaps we might somehow start again. Not in the old way but as if we were just beginning—"

He stopped, unable to articulate what he wanted to say because he wasn't sure himself.

She turned away to put her glass down on the mantelshelf so that he could only see her face in profile. It looked suddenly tired and old. She was silent for so long that he wondered if she were weeping and he said her name in quick anxiety.

"Joanna?"

"I'm sorry, Alec," she said at last, still not looking at him. "I think it's too late. I've changed but not enough for you, only for myself. You see,"—and as she said the words she turned to look at him—"unlike you, I do know what I want and you're not part of it anymore. I've learned to do without you. You spoke of your concern for us and that was considerate of you. But the truth is, I'm not concerned about you anymore. If I didn't see you again, it wouldn't really matter. Does that sound unkind? I'm sorry if it does. You see, I'm picking up the pieces you so carelessly scattered and I'm putting them together again. I've got a job with a good salary which I'm starting after Easter. I've found rather a nice house which I'll be able to afford. My father's lending me the money for Simon's education. It's all coming together into a new pattern."

"In which I haven't any place," Alec said, finishing the sentence for her.

"I'm sorry," she repeated.

He walked across the room to put his empty glass down on the side-table.

"But I'll be able to see Simon?" he asked, his back to her.

"Of course," she replied. "Whenever you want."

"Thank you," he said. "I'll see myself out."

"Hell!" said Rudd. He was standing, stop-watch in hand, on the step of the stile. "This isn't going to work."

"Why not?" Boyce demanded. He had been sheltering in the lee of the hedge near the ford, having walked up Waterend Lane from the direction of the Goat, timing himself with his own stop-watch. As the distance was shorter than Rudd's own timed walk from the public house to the same destination along the footpath, the sergeant had been waiting for the chief inspector's arrival for several minutes and, in consequence, he looked pinched with the cold.

Spring, promised earlier in the week in the sudden burst of sunshine, had retreated and, if it weren't for the leaves on the bushes and the celandines sprinkling the banks, it might have been February again. An overcast sky hung low over sullen-looking fields and a chill little wind, with the breath of winter still about it, was blowing down the lane, ruffling the brown water of the ford into tiny, white-capped waves.

"It took me eight minutes and thirty-five seconds to walk from the car-park of the Goat," Boyce continued in an aggrieved voice as if Rudd's comment on the failure of the experiment reflected on his own part in it. "I timed it exactly."

"That's not the problem, Tom," Rudd explained, climbing down from the stile. "Although the individual timings are important, it's not that I'm complaining about. It's something else. It struck me as I was walking across the footpath. I happened to catch sight of you passing that gateway further down the lane and it was then it occurred to me."

"What did?" Boyce demanded, only partly mollified.

"That it's the way the timings coincide that really matters. We've got, what? Four people who could have been approaching the ford just before Stella Reeve died—Lawson, his wife, Reeve and Bartlett; five, if we count Mrs. Bingham in her car. And that doesn't take into account Stella Reeve herself. I know we could work it out on paper but that's not going to give us a proper idea of how the timings mesh together. I want to actually *see* it happening."

"What do you mean?" Boyce asked, shifting from one foot to the other to get the blood moving.

"A reconstruction," Rudd said.

"Oh, God!" the sergeant muttered under his breath.

"It shouldn't take too much organisation," Rudd continued, ignoring Boyce's interpolation. "We'd have to block the lane off at both ends to make sure no other traffic used it, so we'd need a couple of men posted on that duty, plus two W.P.C.s to take the parts of Stella Reeve and Mrs. Lawson. Lawson's timing isn't a problem. As we know he'd've had plenty of opportunity to follow Stella Reeve to the foot-bridge, we shan't need to cover his movements. But we'll have to have a couple of P.C.s to be Reeve and Bartlett and to come across the fields by the path, one on foot, one on a bike."

"Won't you want a third in case Reeve came by the lane?" Boyce asked.

"Not now you've timed it and we've established it takes roughly nine minutes. We've already worked out that Bartlett last saw Reeve sitting in his car outside Mrs. Franklin's cottage at approximately seven forty-two on that Friday evening, so, assuming Stella Reeve died a couple of minutes after eight, he'd've had over a quarter of an hour to walk to the ford along Waterend Lane which is more than enough time. It's the other route, across the fields, that bothers me. Because it's uphill it took me nearly eighteen minutes to cover the distance from the Goat to the foot-bridge—six minutes longer than it takes in the other direction—which is cutting the time down to a very close thing for both Reeve and Bartlett if they came along the path. It's that timing which I'll want checked."

"What about Mrs. Bingham's?" Boyce put in, looking interested despite himself. "You'll want someone in a car to cover hers."

"Right!" Rudd agreed. He seemed pleased at the sergeant's apparent willingness to cooperate.

"So when were you thinking of setting it up? Tomorrow night?"

"No. I'd prefer it to be done in daylight. I know that won't be the right conditions but I want to see what happens."

"How are you going to manage that?" Boyce asked.

Rudd grinned at him as he remounted the stile.

"If I stand up here, I'll have a good view in both directions, as far down as the S-bend, where Mrs. Lawson says she turned back, as well as up the lane towards the gate of the caravan. The footpath's no problem. Anyone coming in that direction will be easily seen. You know, Tom," he added, climbing down, "I think we'll ask the witnesses we know were in the area, Lawson and his wife as well as Mrs. Bingham, to come along and watch the reconstruction. It could jog their memories. There could be something they saw or heard which they've forgotten to tell us about."

"Could be," Boyce said without much enthusiasm. "On the other hand, it could turn out to be a complete waste of time and manpower. Still . . ."

He didn't complete the sentence although the implication behind the last word was apparent to both of them; still that was Rudd's decision and, ultimately, his responsibility.

Ignoring the remark, Rudd started to walk away.

"Come on," he said over his shoulder. "Let's get back to the car.

We've got a lot of sorting out to do this afternoon and I don't want to work late tonight."

"Oh, of course, your appointment," Boyce remarked, catching up with him. He gave the chief inspector a sideways look, full of curiosity, which Rudd pretended not to see. It had never been easy to deceive the sergeant.

Dorothy, his sister, was less suspicious. When Rudd arrived home soon after half past six that evening, announcing that he had to go out again to interview a possible witness in the case he was working on, she expressed nothing more than commiseration on his behalf that his free time should be taken up with official duties.

So it was that at eight o'clock precisely, showered, shaved and wearing a clean shirt, that Rudd feeling elated but also a little guilty at lying to his sister, presented himself at Marion Greave's house, a detached Victorian villa at the end of a quiet, tree-lined cul-de-sac in the Springfield area of the town.

He had not seen her for several weeks. Both of them were busy, professional people and their relationship, if that's what it was, had never been committed on the part of either of them to regular meetings, although the decision was hers rather than his.

All the same, as she answered the door to him, she showed that warmth of welcome which made him feel that perhaps she did care for him more than he dared believe at his lowest moments.

"I'm so pleased to see you again, Jack!"

He smiled but said nothing, following her down the hall to the large, book-lined sitting-room at the back of the house, where the lamps were switched on and bowls of hyacinths scented the air.

Coffee was ready on a low table.

"You wanted to see me, Marion?" he said as he sat down opposite her, watching as she poured the coffee and familiarising himself again with her features.

He had been right in thinking that she was not beautiful. Not even the love he felt for her could persuade him otherwise. For him, her attractiveness lay entirely in her inner self-containment, a still centre of being, so quiet and composed that it was easy for the casual observer to dismiss her without a second glance. It was only after he himself had worked with her on a case that he had realised that her face with its smooth, high planes above the cheek-bones and the little humorous puckers underneath the eyes had a beauty of its own not apparent to most people.

She passed him his cup of coffee and then sat back in her chair, her short dark hair, tucked behind her ears, as glossy as a blackbird's wing in the lamplight.

"My news can wait until later," she said. "Tell me about your case first."

He told her, knowing she would be interested but largely for his own sake because he was able to explain to her more easily than he could to Boyce the doubts he had felt throughout the investigation.

"So you're convinced the girl didn't die accidentally, although there's no evidence apart from the bruises on her arm."

She had, of course, uncovered the root of his dilemma at once.

"The taint of violence," he said, although it wasn't just the bruises he was referring to; it was also the atmosphere which had been present at the scene of Stella Reeve's death and which was too subjective to put into words. She understood that, too.

"But sufficiently strong to make you want to carry out the inquiry as if it were murder," she continued. "You don't have any choice, do you, Jack? You must trust your instincts."

The advice was, as he had expected, much the same as Boyce had given him and yet it was good to hear her say it. It swept away any last lingering doubts he might have had.

"Yes, I have to go on," he agreed, "if not for my sake, then for Stella Reeve's. When I saw her lying in the mortuary, I thought—"

He broke off, unable to articulate his feelings even to her.

"What? You must try to put it into words, Jack. What did you think when you saw her?"

"What a damned waste!" he said, smiling at her ruefully.

"A waste of what? Her life?"

"No, not just that. I feel that every time I get called out on a case which involves a death. With Stella Reeve it was different. She had an interesting face; not particularly beautiful, although it would have been attractive in life. Talking to people about her, too—Hadley, the local P.C., the girl's mother, Lawson as well—I got a strong impression of her personality. She was very likeable, friendly but positive, prepared to stand up for herself although she'd taken a few knocks in her time but, in spite of it all, she was still on the side of life." Like you, he added silently, addressing Marion Greave as she sat opposite him across the low table. "That's why her death seemed particularly—oh, I don't know—inapt, unkind . . ."

"And deliberate?" Marion suggested. "Because of what she was?"

He stared at her, astonished. She had expressed an idea which even he had not been fully aware of, although he realised it had been lingering at the back of his mind when, on drawing up the timetable with Boyce, he had been struck by the apparent inadequacy of the motives.

"Exactly! Someone wanted Stella Reeve dead because she had the courage to be herself—a bit common, I suspect, and not very subtle in her relationships with other people but honest and therefore vulnerable. Does that make sense?" He paused to look across at Marion, searching for her agreement, and, when she nodded, encouraging him to go on, he continued, "I feel that someone killed her not just out of jealousy, although that seems to be the most obvious motive. But underneath there was a less apparent and more subtle reason which probably even her killer doesn't fully recognise: an envy or a resentment of that special quality which Stella possessed."

"Her name means a star," Marion said.

"Of course!" Rudd was silent for a moment before adding, half to himself, "The giver of light!"

It seemed to crystallise his feelings.

"So," he continued, rousing himself, "I've set up a reconstruction for tomorrow morning. God knows if it will prove anything, but at least I'll have a clearer idea of the movements of the various suspects on the night Stella died. Boyce thinks it'll be a waste of time and manpower but I'll know I've done everything I can towards solving the case. There's no other line of inquiry I can follow up. If nothing comes of it, we'll have to drop the investigation and it'll probably be written off as an accidental death at the inquest."

"The coroner may bring in an open verdict," Marion pointed out.

Rudd shrugged but didn't seem very convinced.

"On just the evidence of the bruises on her arm? I doubt it." He smiled, trying to appear unconcerned. "But I've talked for long enough about my own affairs. What about you? You wanted to see me about something in particular?"

Even before she spoke, he knew it was going to be bad news and he felt a hollow sensation in his chest as if all the breath had suddenly been sucked out of him.

She was too honest not to come straight to the point.

"I've been offered the post of pathologist at Leeds General Hospital, so I'll be selling the practice and moving there."

"When?" he asked. The word seemed to come involuntarily and, after he said it, he ran his tongue over his lips. They felt dry and stiff.

"In June." When he didn't speak, she continued, "I'm sorry I didn't tell you about it before, Jack. I only heard I'd been accepted on Monday. It seemed pointless to speculate before I had definite news."

"Yes, of course I see that," Rudd replied. Under the circumstances, what else could he say? All the same, he would have been grateful for some warning which would have prepared him for the shock. But was it really any of his business? She had her own life to lead and he had no claim on any of it. And in not telling him until now she had acted as she always did, not out of heartlessness but out of that untouchable sense of self-containment and independence which had made her reject him as a lover—clean, sharp, as bright as a diamond or the blade of a knife.

Realising this didn't make it any easier. He felt the edge cut deep, although he struggled to conceal the wound.

"Congratulations! It's what you've always wanted," he said. "After all, you trained to be a pathologist, not a G.P. I'm pleased you've got the post." He hesitated before adding, "I suppose we'll still be able to meet from time to time? It isn't as if Leeds is the other side of the world."

"Yes, of course we must keep in touch."

He smiled and nodded, grateful at least for that, although he knew, and suspected that she did, too, that their relationship would never be quite the same again and that, of the two of them, it was he who had lost the most.

So what was left? Not a great deal, Rudd thought bleakly. Perhaps an occasional telephone call and an exchange of letters or cards at Christmas. He didn't hold out much hope for anything more.

"I must go," he said, trying to act normally as he rose to his feet. "I've got this reconstruction organised for tomorrow morning and I still have to write up the final instructions for those who'll be taking part."

She made no attempt to keep him, realising that he wanted to be alone, although on the doorstep, when he turned to offer his congratulations again before they parted, she said, holding out her hand, "I'm sorry, Jack."

They had never touched before except to shake hands when Pardoe had first introduced them and on that occasion the contact had been a mere social gesture. Now their hands met to express something more complex which neither of them wanted to put into words but which, on Rudd's part at least, expressed regret, gratitude and the depth of affection which no other woman, he suspected, would ever again rouse in him.

The next moment, by mutual consent, their hands parted.

"One thing before you go," Marion added as he began to walk away. "That envy you were speaking of. Remember? Your victim was a woman. I think you'll find in that case it's more likely to be another woman who felt it, although I could be wrong."

"Thanks. I'll bear it in mind," he said. As he drove away, catching a glimpse of her in his driving-mirror in the act of closing the front door, he wondered what had prompted the remark. Some special experience of her own? Or a reaction she had noticed in someone close to her? He didn't know and he doubted now if he would ever ask her. The process of separation had already begun. It was better that way.

Driving home, he turned his thoughts to the investigation. For what else was left? The world hadn't come to an end, after all; only some warm, secret place inside himself had shrivelled and died, but not any part that Boyce or his sister or any of his colleagues would ever be permitted to see.

A woman, Marion had suggested, and, despite it all, he still trusted her judgement.

Mrs. Lawson perhaps? She seemed the most likely candidate.

CHAPTER FIFTEEN

From his elevated position on the step of the style, Rudd glanced across at Mrs. Lawson. She was standing a few yards away from him where he had instructed Boyce to place her, on the side of the ford nearest to the village, within sight of the stream and the foot-bridge in one direction and the S-bend in the other.

She seemed ill at ease, he thought, and quite unsuitably dressed for the occasion in court shoes and a pale grey cloth coat, too light-weight for such a chilly morning, with a wide silver-fox collar which she had turned up against the wind. He could see the pastel fur shiver as the breeze ran across it, ruffling the fine, silky surface. Cocooned in its texture, her face looked drawn and tense.

A little further along the verge, Mrs. Bingham, in a more sensible tweed skirt and calf-high leather boots, was moving restlessly from foot to foot as if impatient at the delay, her hands thrust deep into the pockets of a sheepskin jacket.

The cars belonging to the two women were drawn up on the other side of the lane where they would not obscure the view.

Neither woman spoke to one another, the distance between them being too great for conversation, another deliberate stratagem on Rudd's part. He wanted his witnesses visible to him but incommunicado except, when the time came, to himself.

Alec Lawson's position had been chosen with the same care, this time on the other side of the stream nearest to the caravan and on the verge facing the foot-bridge where the lane began to turn before starting the long climb up to Macey's farm. The caravan and the stretch of lane leading up to it were therefore out of sight of him and the others, Lawson's car, drawn up behind him, acting as a further shield to any activity which might be taking place near the gate to the caravan.

Lawson looked strained, Rudd thought, turning briefly in his direction to check his position. He had evidently come straight from working on the shop without bothering to shave or change his clothes and the dark stubble on his chin gave him a hollow, starved look.

He had reacted strongly when his wife first appeared, starting forward as if eager to talk to her, but Boyce had bustled him into his place without giving either of them a chance to speak to one another. Since that initial shock, Lawson had looked across at her several times as if appealing to her for some response but she had ignored him, turning up the deep collar of her coat and averting her face. The gesture and their physical separation, with the stream running between them like some Rubicon, seemed to express a deep alienation which Rudd, in his turn, found symbolic of his own mood.

As a professional policeman, he was alert and acutely aware of the reactions of those about him but, on a deeper and more personal level, he functioned as if in a coma, all feelings deadened, the conscious world a mere transparency.

"We're ready, sir."

It was Boyce, moving across to speak to him, timing schedule in hand, the microphone of his radio telephone attached to the lapel of his coat. He seemed suddenly aware of the chief inspector's distraction for he added with quick concern, "Are you all right?"

Rudd made an effort to rouse himself, straightening his shoulders.

"Yes, Tom, I'm fine, thanks."

"Well, you don't look it."

There was nothing Rudd wanted less at that moment than the sergeant's solicitude. It seemed to bore into him like a probe, piercing the deadened nerve ends and teasing them back to life. For a moment, as he gazed down into Boyce's face, he remembered Marion Greave's expression of concern as she had sat opposite him in the lamp-lit room the previous evening, a memory which he had managed to thrust into some small, hidden corner of his mind but which now came peeping out at him.

"I said I'm all right," he snapped.

Boyce's expression turned from one of commiseration to the closed formality of the subordinate.

"Sorry, sir," he said and, turning his back, took up his position at the foot of the stile.

It would have been easy enough for Rudd to apologise in his turn. Glancing at his watch, he saw he had two minutes to spare before the reconstruction was due to begin, time in which to touch Boyce on the shoulder and offer some excuse. But the effort seemed too much to make.

Instead he looked about him as if unaware of the sergeant, who was standing immediately in front of him, his shoulders squared and his spine rigid, expressing even in this back view of himself his sense of injured pride.

Madge Bingham witnessed this brief exchange between the chief inspector and his sergeant and, although its full significance was lost on her, took it to mean that the reconstruction was about to begin.

It was about time.

The whole affair struck her as absurd. What on earth did Rudd hope to prove by this ridiculous charade? The girl had died accidentally. That much was obvious and no other evidence to the contrary could possibly be discovered at this late stage in the investigation.

A few feet away from her, Mrs. Lawson shivered and drew the collar of her coat closer about her face. Madge glanced at her quickly.

God knows what she was doing there. As far as Madge was aware, only she herself and Alec Lawson had been anywhere near Waterend Lane when the accident happened. She could only suppose that Lawson's wife had been somewhere in the area on her way to visit him at roughly the time Stella Franklin died and that Rudd had called her in to check on her movements. There was no other explanation.

On the other side of the ford, Lawson, too, glanced across at Joanna and wondered why the hell she was present at the reconstruction. He had not been in contact with her since his disastrous attempt at a reconciliation, although several times he had been tempted to phone her.

Her unexpected arrival on the scene that morning had totally bewildered him and, like Madge Bingham, he could only conclude that Joanna had been in or near Wynford on that Friday evening and the purpose of her visit had been to see him.

But why, for God's sake?

He wanted to believe that her intention had been to persuade him to come back to her and Simon. At least that interpretation would have given him some hope for the future. But he wasn't sure. Her refusal to look at him or even acknowledge his presence seemed to rule out that possibility. She was aloof, like a stranger. And also, he realised, afraid.

Her tension communicated itself even across the several yards of space which separated them.

Aware of this, he was afraid on her account.

Joanna stood rigid, keeping her face deliberately turned from her husband. It was the only way she was able to keep herself under any pretence of control. Alec's physical presence had disturbed her more than she dared show. He looked so ill, she thought; a mere shadow of his former self as if in the few days since she had last seen him the strength had gone out of him. Seeing him, she felt her resolve, built up so painstakingly day by day, begin to weaken. She had persuaded herself that she could cope without him and, had she not become involved in the girl's death, she might have found the courage to carry on alone.

Now she felt that confidence drain away. The return to the scene of that terrifying walk in the dark had aroused the same irrational sense of fear which she had experienced then.

What did Rudd know? What did he hope to prove?

She had seen nothing, heard nothing, that night, only the wind booming in the trees. She heard the sound again as the branches stirred overhead and she shuddered with a mixture of fear and physical discomfort as she clutched her coat collar tighter to her throat, aware of Rudd's eyes turned towards her with that look of cool, sceptical appraisal with which he had regarded her when she had gone to see him in his office.

Too late, she thought. Too late for everything; for denial that she had been anywhere near the ford on the night the girl died; for her and Alec. It had all gone beyond the point where she might have chosen another, safer path.

For the reconstruction was beginning. The sergeant was checking his watch before glancing back over his shoulder to address the chief inspector.

"We're ready, sir," Boyce was announcing.

"Then get the men moving," Rudd replied.

As he spoke, he glanced at his own watch and his copy of the time schedule, which he had fastened to a clipboard. It was 10:40 A.M.—the approximate minutes to the hour when he estimated that Bartlett and Reeve had left the Goat on that Friday evening. The two constables, Marsh and Johnson, who were to take their parts, would be setting off at any second from the door of the public house to walk through the village to the church.

He heard Boyce pass on the instruction through his radio microphone and looked back across the meadow towards the footpath, although he did not expect either man to appear for another five minutes, the time it would take them to cover the distance from the Goat to the far end of the village street, including the two minutes he estimated Bartlett had spent watching Reeve as he stood by his parked car.

Until they appeared, it was a question of waiting and he humped his shoulders, alternatively glancing at the second hand on his watch as it swept round the dial and then across at the church tower, where the two men would shortly come into sight in the gap between the trees.

Ten-fifty A.M.

Boyce was again murmuring into his radio microphone, this time to W.P.C. Drake, who was reenacting Mrs. Lawson's role and was waiting in the car-park of the Goat to walk to the ford along Waterend Lane as she had done on that Friday night.

He exchanged a nod with the sergeant, who passed on the order.

"Right! You can start now."

It had been Rudd's intention to concentrate on the timings and to ignore the witnesses until the plainclothes men and women appeared in sight. It was then that their reactions would be worth observing. But he could not resist looking round quickly at the three of them, at Lawson, over to his right, shabby and unshaven, and, to his left, Mrs. Bingham, upright and trim, aware that events were about to happen and glancing this way and that with a quick, intelligent interest. And then, past her, to Mrs. Lawson, who, anticipating the next stage in the reconstruction, had turned her head to watch the bend in the lane, where, at any minute, the figure of the policewoman who was taking her part would come into view.

He wondered what was going on in their minds, especially Mrs. Lawson's. Before assigning them their positions, Boyce had instructed each in turn to observe the reconstruction carefully and then to report at the end of it if anything they saw or heard differed from their memories of the events which had happened on the night that Stella Reeve died.

It was a long shot but one which he hoped to God was worth playing. Otherwise, he would have to admit defeat and close the investigation, letting Stella Reeve's death pass unpunished into the catalogue of unsolved crimes.

Not if he could help it, he thought grimly, turning his glance lastly at the stream, its water running fast and flashing brightly in the sudden sun and shadow of that windy morning. Someone was responsible and, even if the reconstruction proved nothing, as far as he was concerned, the file on Stella Reeve would never be closed.

But the action was speeding up at last and needed his immediate attention. Boyce was looking round at him for further orders. It was ten fifty-six, time for the car to set off from Macey's yard; time, too, to alert the last participant in the events.

He gave the instructions with an increasing sense of exhilaration. The play had begun in earnest for, as if across a huge stage, the actors were now beginning to converge on this one small arena where the final enactment was to take place.

A quick glance over his shoulder confirmed the arrival into sight of Marsh and Johnson on the footpath which led from the church, Marsh still on foot, Johnson now riding the bike which he had picked up at the gate of Bartlett's cottage. Rudd saw him dismount half-way up the slope and start to push it. The two men were only yards apart.

So far so good. The timing seemed to be working.

As they approached, the car also came into view, the sunlight flashing briefly on its windscreen as it began the long descent from Macey's farm towards the ford, as Mrs. Bingham's had done on that Friday night.

When it reached a point midway down the hill, almost opposite the caravan, which was out of sight behind the hedge, the figure of W.P.C. Drake suddenly appeared at the other end of the lane where the S-bend straightened out before the road dipped down towards the ford.

She stood in the middle of the lane for several seconds, only thirty yards away from them, conspicuous if only by the solitariness of her position under the trees, the wind blowing the scarf she was wearing about her head.

Mrs. Lawson registered her presence. Rudd saw her start visibly as if she had been confronted by her own ghost. Mrs. Bingham had also noticed her sudden appearance and was straining forward to get a better view, puzzled, no doubt, at her arrival. After all, like Lawson, she knew nothing of Mrs. Lawson's involvement in the events of that

Friday evening. Rudd could not see her face clearly, only part of her profile outlined against the dark mass of the hedge, her chin raised and the whole set of her head watchful and intent.

The next moment, the figure turned and began walking rapidly away in the direction from which it had come towards the village, disappearing from sight beyond the curve in the lane.

At the same time, the other figure appeared.

She was a young W.P.C. whom Rudd had chosen for her similarity to the dead girl. They were of the same height and build and possessed certain features in common, particularly a fullness about the mouth and chin.

Now, dressed in jeans and a fur fabric jacket of the same colour as the one Stella Reeve had been wearing, a satchel handbag slung over one shoulder and a blond wig covering her own short brown hair, she stepped from the place where she had been kept hidden behind the caravan out of sight of the witnesses and came walking into view.

Rudd had intended her appearance to be sudden and dramatic. Lawson's car, parked strategically against the verge, effectively blocked off any sighting of her until the last moment so that it seemed as if she had been conjured up out of the air. But even he had not bargained for the reaction of the witnesses.

As she walked past Lawson towards the ford, her high heels clipping smartly on the hard surface of the lane, the blond hair bouncing on the shoulders of her jacket, the man put out a hand as if to touch her and convince himself that she was real.

Mrs. Bingham, too, took a step forward in startled recognition.

Mrs. Lawson was the last to register the girl's presence. She still had her head turned away in the direction of the S-bend, round which W.P.C. Drake had, a few moments earlier, disappeared from sight, as if her interest were centred solely on the reenactment of her own movements.

The sudden shudder which passed through the others, almost audible in the strength of the reaction, drew her attention back to the ford and to the scene which was taking place there.

The car, which had passed the young W.P.C. as she set off to walk from the gate of the caravan towards the foot-bridge, was now edging its way slowly across the ford in bottom gear, sending long, slow ripples lapping out to touch the banks and to slap up against the wooden supports.

But no one seemed interested in it as, having reached the other side of the stream, it picked up speed and disappeared up the lane towards the village in the same direction as W.P.C. Drake.

Nor was any attention paid to the two plainclothes policemen, Marsh and Johnson, who had by this time reached the stile by the footpath and were standing just behind the chief inspector, spectators themselves now, although Rudd had noted down the time of their arrival.

Everyone was watching Stella; even Rudd thought of the young policewoman by that name as if, in assuming her appearance and actions, she had taken on the dead woman's identity and, by some mysterious process of metamorphosis, had become the victim herself.

She was only seconds from the moment at which she had died, mounting the worn concrete steps to the foot-bridge before stepping forward onto the bridge itself.

There was no other sound or movement, Rudd noticed. Everyone stood silent and immobile. Even the wind seemed to drop so that the trees were motionless as, in the great silence, Stella's footsteps rang out on the planking with a hollow insistence, clearly audible above the sound of running water as the stream slid under the bridge.

In the centre, she stopped abruptly and, bending down, began pulling at her shoe as if the heel had become caught in a gap between the planking before, straightening up, she turned to grasp the rail, twisting the upper part of her body and leaning forward so that her reflection appeared suddenly on the surface of the water beneath her, blond hair glinting, the oval of her face disintegrating into patches of paler colour as the ripples caught it and swept it away.

"Oh, God, no! Don't let her fall!"

It was Mrs. Lawson who had cried out. She had run into the centre of the lane and stood facing the ford, her arms held out in protest.

As if on a signal, the scene began to break up.

Lawson, who until that moment had stood transfixed, also started forward, shouting out, "Joanna, stay where you are!" before setting off at a charge for the bridge.

"Bloody idiot!" Rudd heard Boyce bellow and he, too, ran forward a few paces in warning as Lawson pushed roughly past the young W.P.C., who, alerted of the danger, clung to the rail.

The same thought was going through the chief inspector's mind as he scrambled down off the stile.

Bloody idiot, indeed!

The answer was so damned obvious that he couldn't think why he hadn't seen it before.

"Boyce!" he shouted furiously.

But it was too late.

The sergeant's sudden movement had served as a further catalyst to the others, although he could hardly blame the man. If he hadn't acted, the girl might have lost her balance and fallen face downwards into the stream as Stella Reeve had done and that was too dangerously close to reality.

All the same, the damage had been done.

As Boyce, looking shame-faced, turned back towards him and the W.P.C. straightened up and walked a little shakily to the end of the bridge, Rudd saw Lawson, who had run past him, seize his wife by the shoulders and draw her onto the verge, where he stood, his arms round her and his head lowered protectively against hers.

Mrs. Bingham, too, had moved out of her position. Until the moment when Boyce had called out and started forward, she had remained where she had been placed, a few yards from the stile, her hands still plunged into the pockets of her sheepskin jacket.

Now, as Boyce walked back, his expression contrite, she seemed to hesitate and then, making up her mind, crossed the lane towards her car and, getting in, started the engine.

"Sorry about that," Boyce was saying, raising his voice above the sound of Mrs. Bingham's car as it made a neat three-point turn and headed off towards the village. "I thought the girl was going to fall. God knows what Lawson thought he was playing at. Still, no harm's done." He broke off to repeat in a tone of exasperated amusement, "Bloody idiot! Just look at him now!"

Rudd followed his gaze to where Lawson and his wife were still standing in one another's arms at the side of the lane and felt a brief jolt of emotion pass through him, although quite what his feelings were he wasn't sure.

Envy? That certainly played a part. He was aware also of a sense of loss which was like a physical pain under his ribs. But he was conscious mostly of a mixture of anger and exhilaration—anger that the reconstruction had ended in this confusion; excitement that he had, after all, been proved right. Stella Reeve's death was no accident.

He shouted briefly, "Get yourselves organised!," to Marsh and Johnson, who, together with the young W.P.C., were milling about near the end of the bridge, talking too loudly and, as they fell silent, he pulled Boyce to one side out of earshot, jabbing at the timing schedule with his forefinger to emphasise his point.

Boyce listened, his face impassive although, as Rudd finished his explanation, he looked across at the Lawsons, who were still standing on the verge some distance away, unaware of anyone else's presence except their own. They had broken free from one another's arms, although Lawson was now holding his wife by the elbows as, head bent, he talked to her quickly and urgently. She appeared to be crying.

"Which of us is going to break it up?" Boyce asked. From his expression, it was clear he preferred it not to be him. Almost as an afterthought, he added, as if aware for the first time of her absence, "And where the hell's Mrs. Bingham?"

"Left a few minutes ago," Rudd said succinctly. He tucked the timing schedule under his arm. "Okay then, Tom? You agree it couldn't have happened any other way?"

As Boyce nodded in confirmation, Rudd touched him lightly on the arm before turning away. As a gesture, it could have meant anything or nothing—an indication to the sergeant to remain where he was, a recognition of Boyce's agreement with the facts as presented to him, a mere wish-me-luck token. But, as far as Rudd was concerned, it was the gesture he should have made before the reconstruction began when he had spurned the sergeant's sympathy and which he offered now as his own form of reconciliation.

The Lawsons were still too concerned with themselves to be aware of Rudd until he was only a few feet away from them.

He heard Mrs. Lawson say, "I don't know, Alec, I honestly don't know," and Lawson's reply, his voice rough and urgent, "For God's sake, Joanna, we can make it work, I promise you." He broke off suddenly, conscious of Rudd's presence. "What the hell do you want?"

"To speak to your wife," Rudd replied. He deliberately used his official voice, flat and unemotional but all the same he saw the look of alarm on her face. Lawson had taken her by the arm, showing every sign of remaining with her. "On her own, Mr. Lawson," Rudd added, this time with the full weight of his professional rank, and was human enough to feel a sense of satisfaction as Lawson, after hesitating for a second, stepped back in deference to that authority.

CHAPTER SIXTEEN

Boyce was saying, "So it wasn't a waste of time, after all."

It was meant, Rudd realised, as an apology on the sergeant's part for having doubted the chief inspector's decision to hold the reconstruction.

They were on their way by car to the outskirts of the village to make the arrest, another police car containing a uniformed woman sergeant and a W.P.C. following behind them.

"I'm not so sure about that, Tom," Rudd confessed. "If I'd been quicker off the mark in the first place, there'd have been no need to hold it. I could kick myself for not noticing the discrepancy in Mrs. Lawson's statement at the time she made it. It stood out a mile."

Boyce kept prudently silent. After all, he, too, had failed to pick up the omission in her evidence. He was aware also of a moroseness about the chief inspector's mood which, while he wasn't sure what had caused it, he felt had nothing to do with the case.

In this, he was right. Once the elation at establishing the identity of the guilty person had passed, Rudd had descended rapidly into the trough of despair on the other side. The excitement was over. All that remained was the formality of the arrest, a duty which he had never looked forward to with much pleasure. And after that—what?

Nothing very much that he could see, apart from the usual routine of professional duties, which was little consolation. He was suddenly sick of crime. He wanted to be assured that other human qualities such as love and tenderness and compassion were as important and as widely practised as greed, revenge and violence. But once Marion had gone, would he be able to sustain such a belief? It seemed impossible.

Looking ahead, he could see no reason for optimism. The future stretched out in front of him like a barren landscape across which he would have to toil with no promise of any celestial city at the end of it.

"Here we are," Boyce announced, stating the obvious as usual as he turned into the driveway of the Binghams' house.

Dr. Bingham met them at the door. It was the first time Rudd had seen him and he found himself facing a tall, rumpled, middle-aged man, wearing an expression of dignified grief, sick with worry but trying not to show it. However much one's own distress, it was bad form to inflict it on others.

"Come in," he said. "We've been expecting you. My wife's through here."

Avoiding his eyes, Rudd stepped past him into the hall, standing to one side as the doctor went ahead into the large, comfortable drawing-room at the back of the house.

Mrs. Bingham, who was sitting in an armchair drawn up to the fire, got to her feet as they entered, her husband crossing the room to take up his position beside her, Rudd, Boyce and the two women police officers remaining just inside the door and placed according to rank, the chief inspector a little in front of the others.

The piece of ritual which followed might have been rehearsed. As Dr. Bingham took his wife's hand, Boyce, with a glance at Rudd, moved forward a pace and began to announce the formal words of the official caution.

"Mrs. Bingham, you are not obliged to say anything unless you wish to do so but whatever you say will be taken down in writing and may be given in evidence."

As he listened, Rudd fixed his gaze on the neutral space between himself and the Binghams although, just before Boyce finished, he took a surreptitious glance at Mrs. Bingham's face to reassure himself that she would not break down and could not help admiring her self-control.

She was frightened but she wasn't going to admit it in front of others. Head up, lips pressed together, she didn't once take her eyes off Boyce's face.

Rudd was touched, too, by her husband's concern. As they stood there hand in hand, he comforted himself with the thought that, whatever happened to Mrs. Bingham, she would not have to endure the punishment alone. Bingham would remain loyal to her and Rudd found himself half envying her that assurance of unchanging love.

As Boyce finished and stepped back, leaving Rudd to take over, a small rustle and stir of movement ran through the group as at the end of any ceremony.

It was Dr. Bingham who suggested, "Shall we sit down, Chief Inspector? I know my wife would like to explain what happened."

They took their places, Dr. Bingham on the arm of his wife's chair, Rudd and Boyce side by side on one of the chintz-covered sofas, the two women police officers on the other.

Rudd began in his formal voice.

"Although you are not obliged to say anything, Mrs. Bingham, I should like to go over the evidence with you. If you prefer, however, we could do this at headquarters, where a written statement will have to be drawn up later. But I take it that you wish to make a verbal account first?"

"Yes, I do," she replied.

"Very well." Rudd glanced down at his notes before continuing. "We have reason to believe, Mrs. Bingham, that you were present when Mrs. Reeve died. The reconstruction which took place earlier this morning would seem to confirm this. Mrs. Lawson has made a statement in which she says—"

"So she was there on that Friday evening?" Madge Bingham broke in. "I thought she must have been somewhere in the area when she arrived at the reconstruction but I had no idea she was in Waterend Lane until that woman suddenly appeared at the bend in the lane. I realised then that she must be taking Mrs. Lawson's part. That's why I left as soon as it was all over. I knew you'd discover the truth."

"Mrs. Lawson was on her way to visit her husband," Rudd explained, grateful for the opportunity her interruption gave him to drop some of his official manner, although he was careful to keep his voice guarded and impersonal. This account of Mrs. Lawson's presence in Waterend Lane would have to do. He had no intention of explaining her real motive, which anyway he only suspected. At the same time, he could not help silently applauding Mrs. Bingham's intelligence. It hadn't taken her long to grasp the significance of the evidence against her. "She saw the headlights of a car coming down the hill towards her as she reached the S-bend in the lane; your car, Mrs. Bingham. As soon as she saw the lights, Mrs. Lawson turned and began walking back towards the village, but the point is"—and here he gave Boyce a small, sideways glance to confirm the admission he'd made earlier that he should have noticed this fact much earlier in the case—"no car passed her on the way back. I spoke to her after the reconstruction and confirmed this with her. The only possible conclusion that we can draw is that you stopped somewhere along the lane before you reached the bend—I believe at the ford."

Rudd paused, inviting her to comment, and, thinking that she was going to remain silent, was about to continue when he saw Dr. Bingham put a hand on her shoulder, encouraging her to speak.

"As I told you in my statement when you first came here," she said, "I passed Stella and Mr. Lawson at the gate of the caravan and I thought they were quarrelling. That was a genuine impression, Chief Inspector. I had no wish to make it appear that Mr. Lawson was in any way involved in Stella's death."

Rudd let it pass, merely nodding to her to continue, although he had his doubts about the statement. Mrs. Bingham had seen what she wanted to see which was another matter altogether. Even quite impartial eyewitnesses are notoriously prone to put their own interpretation on events, without intending to twist the facts, and Mrs. Bingham had, he suspected, her own reasons for convincing herself that Stella Reeve and Lawson had been quarrelling.

"It had begun raining," Mrs. Bingham went on, "and as soon as I passed them, it occurred to me to offer Stella a lift home."

That, too, was passed over without comment although Rudd guessed that this wasn't her only reason for stopping. Curiosity to find out exactly what had been going on between Stella Reeve and Lawson had also been a motive.

Her statement raised another issue which he blamed himself for not having considered before. Of course she would have offered Stella a lift. In a village, it went without saying that, if you passed someone you knew, you stopped the car as an accepted courtesy. You didn't ignore the person and drive on.

"So you pulled up?" Rudd asked. "Where exactly?"

"On the far side of the ford. I left the engine running while I waited."

"Which was how long?" Boyce put in.

She glanced at him with a slightly impatient look, similar to that which Rudd remembered Mrs. Lawson giving the sergeant during her interview, as if Boyce's inferiority of rank made him less of a human being. Boyce, thank God, was not thin-skinned enough to notice.

"At most, two minutes. Then I saw her coming across the foot-bridge. I opened the car door and called out, 'Do you want a lift?' She said she did and thanked me."

"And then?" Rudd prompted as Mrs. Bingham hesitated. He knew why, too. She had come to that difficult part of her account where she would have to admit the truth of her subsequent actions. To give her her due, she was courageous enough to face it. Rudd saw her chin go up.

"It was one of those ridiculous situations, Chief Inspector. As she walked across the bridge, she caught her heel between the planks. I had the passenger door open ready for her to get in. When she called out that her heel was stuck, I got out of the car to help her. She was trying to wriggle the shoe free while she was still wearing it. I said, 'Don't be silly, Stella. Why don't you take your foot out? It'll be easier.' She didn't reply but went on trying to free it. I admit I was annoyed. I'd stopped to offer her a lift when I needn't have bothered. It was beginning to rain more heavily by this time, too. I didn't see why I should have to stand there getting wet while I waited for her. But she'd never been willing to take advice even when it was well meant, had she, Gordon?" She turned to her husband in quick appeal but he did not respond apart from making a slight, deprecatory gesture with one hand which seemed to Rudd to convey a warning as well, although Mrs. Bingham appeared to be unaware of its full significance.

Rudd kept his own expression neutral. It was important, he realised, that he express no sense of moral judgement. Having reached this stage in her account, Madge Bingham's overriding need was one of self-justification. If he criticised that by showing even the slightest flicker of disapproval, she would not admit to the full truth.

She seemed disappointed at her husband's apparent lack of response for she turned instead to Rudd, speaking more rapidly now, her eyes fixed on his. He was aware of the force of her personality and that quality of self-righteousness which kept it charged as if a current were constantly passing through it, driving her forward.

"I told her to hurry up. I said, 'If you're not ready in one minute exactly, Stella, I shall leave you here.' " Although her eyes did not leave Rudd's face, she hesitated for a moment and he saw her gaze shift focus slightly to a point midway between them and he knew she had come to that part of her statement which even she found difficult to defend. "I suppose, strictly speaking, it was none of my business, Chief Inspector. But I had seen her quarrelling, as I thought, with Alec Lawson and I knew she was the type of girl to get herself into all kinds of trouble without thinking what she was doing. I mean, she was expecting a baby before she was eighteen and had to get married. And it wasn't just herself who suffered. Her mother was worried to death about her and Gordon was run off his feet at the time caring for them all. I could see that, if she were having an affair with Alec Lawson, it would only lead to more problems. But, of course, I should have known she wouldn't take kindly to advice."

Rudd, who had decided to say nothing during her account, refrained from pointing out that Lawson and Stella had not been lovers. It was Dr. Bingham who broke in.

"What did you say to her, Madge?"

He had sat silent during the first part of his wife's statement, gazing down at the floor, his expression pained and oddly humiliated as if he found the revelations embarrassing. Now he raised his head to look at her.

She reacted at once as if still annoyed at his earlier lack of sympathy.

"What I thought she needed to be told, of course. I said, 'I think you're very unwise to get involved with Mr. Lawson, Stella. In a small place like Wynford, people are bound to gossip.' Which was perfectly true. If I'd noticed them together, others were certain to do so sooner or later.

"I'd left the car headlights on so I was able to see her quite clearly. She had straightened up and twisted round to grasp hold of the rail as she tried to pull the shoe free. I suppose what I said angered her. I can only excuse her reply on that account although I'm not used to being talked to in that manner, Chief Inspector." She again addressed him directly and Rudd saw the colour had risen in her face. "She said, 'Just because you're the bloody doctor's wife, it doesn't give you the right to interfere. What's the matter? Do you fancy him yourself?' It was quite inexcusable! As far as Alec Lawson was concerned, I'd done nothing more than try to welcome him into the village. But I could hardly expect someone like Stella Franklin to appreciate that."

"I see," Rudd said in the same, noncommittal voice.

But he saw more than the simple, unemotional statement implied. In reporting Stella's reply, Madge Bingham had mimicked the girl's voice, emphasising not only the local accent which she must have used but the irreverent and mocking tone in which the words had been spoken. It explained a great deal about Mrs. Bingham's attitude of social superiority towards Stella as well as her sense of her own esteem which, in speaking those words, the girl, who had learned to stand up for herself in a harsher world than Mrs. Bingham's, had dared to attack.

As for Lawson, in questioning him after the reconstruction, Rudd had learned for the first time of Mrs. Bingham's visit to the caravan and his rejection of her overtures of friendship out of pique at what he, too, called her sense of superiority. "As if," as he had explained, "being the doctor's wife gave her a special recommendation."

And yet it was because of such trivial-seeming circumstances that Stella's death had occurred.

"I mean, they had nothing in common," Madge Bingham continued. "She wasn't the type, I should have thought, to appeal to a man like that, obviously educated and interested in books."

More your type, Mrs. Bingham?

Although Rudd did not ask the question out loud, she must have been aware of the unspoken thought, which perhaps she had enough sensitivity to see in his face or even to ask herself, for she avoided his eyes.

"I had started to walk back along the bridge towards the car. It was my intention to drive off and leave her there. As I did so, the heel of her shoe snapped off and she lost her balance. I tried to save her. I turned back and caught her by the arm but there wasn't time to take a proper grip and, besides, she was too heavy for me. She fell face downwards into the stream and must have hit her head because she didn't move. I called her name and ran down the steps at the end of the bridge. I was going to pull her out and then . . ."

"And then, Mrs. Bingham?" Rudd repeated gently as she hesitated.

She lifted her chin and met his eyes again.

"I went over to the car and drove home."

"And left her there? For God's sake, why, Madge? I still don't understand."

Dr. Bingham asked the question, his voice expressing the pain and bewilderment which so far had shown only in his face.

"I don't know," she said flatly. "At the time, it didn't seem wrong. I remember thinking: Even if I hadn't stopped to offer her a lift, she'd've fallen. It would have been an accident and no one's fault except her own."

"Her fault?" Rudd asked.

Although it had been his intention to say nothing, the words came involuntarily.

"Because she had no business being there in the first place," Mrs. Bingham said sharply. "And because, being the sort of girl she was, it seemed inevitable. But I told you, I really don't know why."

Rudd got to his feet. He had heard enough. If Mrs. Bingham did not fully understand her own motives, he felt he had a glimmer of perception. She had left the girl to die as a punishment, not just because of what she had said or done but simply because she was Stella, too bright and individual a star in the little firmament of Wynford in which Madge Bingham was accustomed to shine supreme.

Put out the light and then put out the light.

He left the woman police sergeant to explain to Mrs. Bingham the arrangements for taking her to headquarters and went with Boyce into the hall.

Dr. Bingham caught up with them at the front door.

"What will happen now, Chief Inspector?" he asked.

"Your wife will be charged, sir."

"With murder?"

"No; with manslaughter."

"I see." The man stood in silence for a moment before adding, his pleasant face rigid with the effort of controlling his emotions, "I'm sorry."

It seemed a ludicrously inadequate comment to make under the circumstances but Rudd had noticed before the inability of people under stress to find the words to express their feelings.

Sorry for what, in God's name? he wondered.

For everything, he supposed. For Stella's death; for his wife's involvement with it; perhaps even for himself.

At the same time, it crossed his mind that Mrs. Bingham herself had not so far uttered even the most banal apology for her part in the tragedy.

"What will you do, Dr. Bingham?" he asked. It was not mere curiosity. He was genuinely concerned for this large, crumpled, kindly man.

"I shall stand by her, of course," Dr. Bingham replied. "Afterwards, when it's all over, I shall sell up the practice here and move somewhere else; make a fresh start for us both." He held out his hand. "Goodbye, Chief Inspector. I'd better get back to her. She's going to need all my support."

As they got into the car, Boyce asked, "What do you reckon she'll get on a manslaughter charge?"

"I don't know, Tom. It'll depend on the court," Rudd replied. "It could be two years, I suppose."

Boyce started the engine.

"Two bloody years for leaving someone to drown? It doesn't seem enough."

"No," Rudd agreed.

But only half his mind was on Mrs. Bingham's future. His own had begun to reoccupy his thoughts, jogged into fresh awareness by Dr. Bingham's parting comment. The parallel between his decision and Marion's was painfully obvious.

"Where to?" Boyce was asking as the car approached the end of the drive. "Back to headquarters?"

Rudd came to a sudden decision.

"No, not straight away. I want to stop off in Studham for a few minutes to see Alec Lawson."

"What the hell for?"

"To tidy up a few loose ends, that's all."

He was grateful that Boyce didn't press the point and that, when they drew up outside the shop, he accepted the chief inspector's order, "Wait here!" without any argument. It wouldn't have been easy to explain that the only loose end he hoped to tie off concerned himself, not Lawson.

Lawson was less easy to fool.

"I've dropped by to let you know we've made an arrest," Rudd said when the man let him in. "I assume you can guess who it is."

"Yes, I can," Lawson replied and waited.

He seemed aware that this wasn't the only reason for Rudd's visit for he was watching the chief inspector with a speculative, inquiring air, encouraging him to continue.

To cover up his awkwardness, Rudd looked about him. Some progress had been made with the interior. The missing floorboards had been replaced with new timber, looking very pale against the old wood and smelling sweetly of pine. The ceiling, too, had been painted white and several light flexes dangled down.

"So you'll be staying on here after all?" he asked.

He thought Lawson would not understand the purpose behind the question for, in his anxiety to appear casual, he had put it too obliquely. But Lawson seemed to catch the drift for he replied, "If you mean, will my wife and I get together again, I don't honestly know, Chief Inspector. I assume that's what you're getting at. You must have seen what seemed like a reconciliation this morning."

"It's none of my business," Rudd began, hoping that Lawson would not take the remark at face value.

To his relief, the man seemed eager to talk.

"I've made a cock-up all round, haven't I? First my marriage and then the relationship, such as it was, with Stella. Even though it was totally innocent, I feel partly to blame for the whole tragic business. If I hadn't met her that day in Studham, if I'd been a little less arrogant towards Mrs. Bingham, if I hadn't bloody well been in Wynford in the first place, none of it would have happened. Well, I began the God-awful mess when I walked out on Joanna so it's up to me to clear that part of it up at least; pick up the pieces and try to fit them together again. I'm willing but Joanna won't commit herself at this stage and I don't blame her. I wouldn't if I were in her place. So, as far as the future's concerned, only time will tell."

It was hardly worth waiting for and yet, as Rudd held out his hand, he felt oddly appeased.

Only time would tell.

There was nothing else he could do except wait, like Lawson, for events to happen. The end hadn't been tied off after all, but contrary to his expectations, he found it a source of hope rather than disappointment.

"So?" Boyce asked as he climbed back into the passenger seat.

"Nothing much, Tom. I just thought I'd let him know what happened."

"Well, I suppose we owed it to him," Boyce agreed reluctantly. "After all, he was one of our suspects and that got him chucked out of the caravan."

Rudd let it pass. If that was the interpretation which the sergeant put on the visit, then it was better he left it there.

"Back to headquarters?" Boyce added.

"Yes," Rudd said.

There was nowhere else to go and it was, after all, his world. He knew no other. Like Lawson, he would have to pick up the pieces of his life as best he could. Whether Marion, his own particular bright star, would ever again form part of the pattern, he did not know. Only time would tell.

"Treat you to a beer tonight?" Boyce was asking. "Sort of celebration now that the case is over."

Rudd was about to refuse and then changed his mind. Why not? he thought. Life had to go on.

"Yes, I'd like that, Tom," he replied, adding after a pause, "Thanks."

It was meant to convey more than just the mere surface meaning of the word. Whether Boyce realised this, Rudd wasn't sure but, as they slowed down at the roundabout on the outskirts of Studham before taking the right-hand fork for Chelmsford, the sergeant turned to grin at him before concentrating his attention again on the road ahead.

ABOUT THE AUTHOR

June Thomson was brought up in an Essex village very much like the setting of her novels. She was educated at London University. A teacher by profession, she has spent her spare time writing the twelve Inspector Rudd novels which have brought her a wide following in both England and the United States. Her most recent novels are *A Dying Fall*, *Sound Evidence* and *Portrait of Lilith*.